Minus One

Mark Kolody

ISBN: 978-1-7381156-2-4 ebook
ISBN: 978-1-7381156-3-1 print

For my wife and son.

1

Mathis

"Your stalker's back, Mathis."

Tariq casually pointed through the floor-to-ceiling windows of Hikari International's thirty-fourth-floor cafeteria. A cloaked figure dressed all in white perched gargoyle-like on a nearby rooftop in Toronto's downtown core. The chill, early winter wind whipped taut the loose outer fabric of their clothing. The slight figure's face was concealed by mirrored goggles, a stylized white respirator, and the cowl-like hood of an overcoat.

Logan shook his head, adjusted his oversized, retro-style UkiyoAR glasses, and chewed absently on his third cookie. "He's just jealous, buddy. Tariq assumes every girl should be interested in him."

"I have a relationship score inside the top three percentile. Do you blame them?" Tariq flashed a mischievous grin of immaculate teeth. "She's definitely stalking Mathis, though. That's what, every day for the past week?"

Mathis didn't appreciate the disconcerting attention of the stranger or his co-workers' pleasure in speculating. He resisted the urge to look, having already spent hours combing over Hikari International's corporate surveillance recordings only to be frustrated with a translucent, blurred image flickering intermittently. Utilizing high-grade jammers and digital countermeasures made sense to cover serious crimes, but to trespass? He couldn't reconcile the tech stack with the misdemeanour.

Mathis forced himself to glance aside dismissively. "We don't know if they're even a woman. You can't make out any details behind the mask and clothes."

Logan wiped his hand on his pant leg and touched the solid-state button on his UkiyoAR glasses, gesturing with his outstretched fingers to zoom, enhance, and sharpen. "She's in full view today, and the wind's snapping her coat like a flagpole. Probably weighs less than forty-five kilos under all her clothing." He pursed his lips. "Maybe a boy?"

Tariq put on his designer UkiyoARs and followed suit with a series of hand gestures. "Those boots are Kenzo, and the coat is probably a Junko Koshino. The half mask and respirator combo are custom. I can't get a match on any database with my optics filter, but they look like something The Viridi-Anne would design if they did facial accessories."

Mathis feigned indifference. "You say that like it's supposed to mean something."

"It means your little Minus One terrorist isn't after your salary, my good man. And they're definitely a *she*—you can tell by the hips. Aren't you even a little curious?"

Mathis was well past curiosity and into the frustrating realm of powerlessness, no closer to a resolution despite his efforts. "We shouldn't even joke about Minus One when we're on corporate property. Technically, Hikari owns and can audit everything we say while we're on site."

Logan combed his fingers through his unkempt hair and folded his arms over his belly. "You worry too much, Mathis. I doubt Hikari will waste processing ticks to set algorithms against our lunch conversations."

Mathis shook his head. "I've heard HR will terminate any employee who's part of the rent strike or attends rallies."

Logan leaned back in his chair, eyes betraying guilty self-interest. "No shit?"

"None. Evy gave me the heads-up. The head office in Osaka doesn't want any bad press about employees participating in civil disobedience."

"But... but that can't be legal, right?"

Mathis put a hand on Logan's thick shoulder, immediately regretting it for the tactile sensation of unwashed clothes. "You need to reread your employment contract."

Tariq fretted. "Sucks. Those protest Netstreams get the most engagement on my socials, and it's easy to meet girls when it seems like you care."

Logan leaned forward, excited. "Hold up. Now you're dating terrorists?"

"No way! With those masks, you don't know what you're getting into. I even stay away from the ones in all-white, pretending they're the real deal." Tariq winked. "If it comes up, let Evy know I was doing it for... well... you'll know how best to phrase it. You always do."

Mathis shook his head in disbelief. He couldn't picture Tariq in his expensive wardrobe successfully mixing amongst the tens of thousands of near-destitute, working poor and disenfranchised youth locking up the downtown core in protests. "Seriously?" He sighed audibly at Tariq's wide grin. "Guys, please tell me you're not skipping rent payments."

"I like where I live," Tariq scoffed.

"I'll get caught up. Promise." Logan slapped his thick hands on the table in forced excitement. "But let's segue on disobedience. It'd be pretty awesome if your stalker is one of those proper anarchists."

"Anarchist or terrorist?" Tariq shrugged. "Either way, you should be grateful for the attention, Mathis. You're tracking an even lower relationship ranking than our asexual colleague."

"He's got a point, buddy." Logan abused his share privileges and projected content to the group's Net-connected accessories. Noticing Mathis wasn't wearing UkiyoARs, he started reading aloud. "Despondent would be an oversimplification. He didn't even offer the courtesy of setting up an auto-responder, says OutgoingCurious. Smart, aloof, and utterly unapproachable. I left the table halfway through our meal to see if he'd notice, and he didn't, says 29Spiritual. It's too bad he's cute, single, and has a good job. I mistook his remoteness for courtesy. Big mistake, says Sarahol."

Mathis tried to control the irritation and embarrassment in his tone, but the litany of indictment remained legible in his near-invisible Net contacts. "Do you have that bookmarked?"

Logan shrugged. "There's half a dozen more along those lines. Care to hear the distinctions you've earned?"

Tariq laughed. "Oh, snap! You shared his dating summary with the international team!"

"No, I didn't. Oh, wait. Uhm, delete last post."

Mathis closed his eyes and took a deep breath, trying to smother the blindsiding humiliation. Kazuo Ogawa, Hikari International's global Chief Technical Officer, was on the thread. "Just stop."

Logan fiddled in front of his glasses. "It's gone. Like it never happened, boss-man."

"And no more talk of my stalker, either. There's no reason for anyone to be interested in me. As soon as she realizes that, I'm sure she'll disappear."

"Wouldn't it be easier to talk to her so she can lose interest right away?" Logan giggled.

Tariq laughed again.

"You know, if it were a man up there, creeping along like some sketchy parkour vigilante, you'd have already organized an office pool on whether I'd live out the week and prepped your CVs for my job." Mathis tried to sound playful, but his words were tainted with frustration.

"Yeah, we're nowhere near your industry percentile rank, but thanks for the insincere vote of confidence." Logan took an oversized bite of his cookie, glanced accusingly at the portion remaining in his fingers, and stuffed it in his mouth. Talking while chewing, he continued, "There's no chance Hikari would risk losing their golden boy, either. They'd send ninjas from the head office in Japan to save you. You could probably even be a member of Minus One, and HR would bend the rules for you. Don't you want to get to the bottom of it before the opportunity goes away?"

Mathis shook his head. "Zero interest. I just want it to stop."

"What do you have going on that's anywhere near as interesting?" Tariq asked.

Unconsciously, Mathis lowered his voice to an ardent whisper. "Preparing for the wetware trials? We're at the cusp of exponentially increasing our fundamental capacities as a species. I'm pretty sure that qualifies as both interesting and important."

Tariq rolled his eyes. "Save the pitch for the investors, golden boy. It's time to man up."

Logan nodded earnestly. "I'm with Tariq on this one."

A five-minute alert fired on Mathis' thought-connected, prototype Net contacts. He had an investor meeting with Evy Carter, the Director of Technical Operations, and some American suit. The alert's perspective still needed legibility adjustments. Irritated, he injected the refinement task into his personal build schedule for off-hours development.

"Fine. If she follows me home tonight, I'll deal with her." Mathis didn't believe his own words. He was already exhausted from the stress of being followed, and had never trusted himself in a non-professional confrontation. "Tariq, purge your social accounts of action shots and protest girls. Logan, I don't want to have to replace my lead dev because you're too cheap to pay your damn rent, okay? Don't be greedy. I know what you make." He gestured to the partially filled glasses of thick, nutrient-rich, nootropic liquid that Hikari's cafeteria provided for employees. "Drink your lunch. Our twenty minutes are up, and I have to go meet Evy at the Pod now."

Logan perked up, anxious at the concept of a meeting being held in a secure room designed to inhibit digital transmissions. "What's going on? She's not supposed to audit our progress until Monday, right? Tell her I'm planning on working the weekend and evenings to get caught up, and I'm about to solve—"

Mathis wasn't in the mood to endure another set of excuses. "It's another dog and pony show for some prospective investor from the States."

Tariq leaned back in his chair, arms folded behind his head, exuding confidence, "In that case, tell her she's been looking pretty fine since her divorce. You can let her know I said it, too."

The idea of Tariq and Evy Carter together made Mathis laugh out loud. Stranger things had happened, but not by much. He shook his head. "Get back to work, gents."

He left the table and executed a quick Net search on the American investor as he walked to the elevator bay at the far end of the cafeteria. He was still getting used to reading the data overlays as the text adjusted to his vision's depth of field while in motion. He paused to filter the results through an uncredited, open-source profiling algorithm allegedly modelled on Carnivore, the secretive intellectual property of the federal security apparatus.

Having distilled volumes of online data into an easily digestible character manifest, there was little to distinguish the investor, Aiden Frost, from any other corporate type. His personal online accounts showed him as the father to two tween-aged children, husband to a loving wife, and yet another avid golfer. Self-identifying with such an extravagant activity when streets were clogged with desperate protests against economic inequality seemed especially tone-deaf to Mathis.

He was American, though.

Professional accounts situated Frost working in vendor relations with a tech startup out of Omaha, Nebraska. Mathis combed the man's interests, searching for something to give them common ground to talk about, but came up empty.

All the Net content was either saccharine or stereotypically modelled around a person trying to appear successful to the outside world. Meeting Frost in Hikari's Pod felt incongruent, and Mathis chalked it up to an underwhelming individual being needlessly overprotective.

By the time the elevator deposited him on the fifty-first floor, he'd decided the whole thing was a waste of time and resolved to keep the meeting to less than half an hour. The more Mathis considered it, the less it made sense to pull him into the pitch. Evy was more than capable of handling that calibre of investor.

Evy Carter was waiting for him outside the Pod, shifting her weight nervously. Her reflection in the near-glass surface of polished white marble showcased her anxious state. Mathis had never seen her apprehensive, no matter the size of the deal she'd been tasked to broker. Uncharacteristically, she'd elected to wear a conservative navy-blue skirt suit with tie and jacket rather than the borderline haute couture she preferred. Even her makeup and accessories were muted today.

Mathis unconsciously adopted some of her unsettled energy.

Her face visibly relaxed at his approach but remained etched with unease. "You're late. He's been waiting for ten minutes already." She cast an anxious glance down the hallway before appearing to smother the action in another gesture.

"I'm still technically on my lunch, Evy, and the meeting isn't scheduled to start until two," he amiably protested, still perplexed by her demeanour. "And you could've gone in without me."

"I've already concluded my portion. This is all about you now." She assessed his attire critically. "I thought I told you to dress nice for today. Would it have killed you to have run an iron over your shirt?"

"That would entail me owning an iron." He grinned through the uncharacteristically awkward vibe between the two. Historically, Evy had been easy to get along with—for him, at least. They weren't friends by any means but they were friendly, and she'd afforded him allowances provided he kept his end of the covenant by delivering innovation on schedule. Jeans, an untucked collared shirt, and a loosened tie were about as professional as he'd ever dressed. "At least it's not a t-shirt day."

She narrowed her eyes at him, and harshly whispered, "Don't screw this up, Mathis. I'm serious. Everything's already been green-lit from the head office in Osaka."

"When have I ever messed up an investor meeting?"

She pressed with urgency, "I need you to go in there, listen patiently, and agree to everything you hear. Tell me you understand." She shot another nervous glance down the hallway.

Mathis tried to figure out what she was scanning for but couldn't detect anything out of place. An adoptive, low-grade panic started taking hold. "What if he starts talking crazy?"

"Especially when he starts talking crazy. Don't rock the boat. As much as this is about you, it's not just you. We're all on board. Remember that, okay?"

She put her palm to the biometric scanner, and the Pod doors opened with the gentle hiss of hydraulics.

The man inside the Pod was nothing like his online accounts. Instead of a rack-purchased suit, corporate-safe tie, and fake toothy smile, Aiden Frost wore a form-fitting, black, high-collared jacket, grey military-style utility pants, and dark leather gloves. He had two days' worth of grey stubble on his face, and his short-cropped hair was untended. The skin of his face was stretched taut against his sharp cheekbones and chin. The man's blue eyes were interrogative, and the smile on his face appeared as insincere as it was menacing. His feet were slung casually on the corner of the cheap folding chair facing opposite him. He wore short, sturdy boots with hardened treads.

The typical furniture in the room had been cleared out.

Mathis' ears rang dully as the door closed behind him, and all ambient sound was devoured by the aggressive geometric obtrusions lining the walls or suspended from the ceiling. His heart's gentle, rhythmic beat was audible, and his breathing was distractingly loud. The Net connection on his contact lenses cut out and automatically rerouted his vision feed to a local storage device.

Frost nudged a folding chair towards Mathis and sat upright. "Take a seat, Grenier."

Immediately uncomfortable, Mathis did as he was asked after positioning the chair closer to the door, maximizing the distance between them. The lack of a table or other obstruction between the two increased his discomfort. Mathis swallowed reflexively. The man opposite him was wildly incongruent within a corporate environment, but somehow, he appeared at ease in the Hikari Pod. The UkiyoAR digital overlays, usually hovering inconspicuously adjacent to individuals, were unnervingly but understandably blank—there was no subscription-based facial recognition lookup possible with the Pod's connectivity suppression.

"Mr. Frost?" Mathis hoped the man didn't detect the hint of a squeak in his voice.

"You're going to remove those fancy contacts you're wearing, and I'll need your localized data storage."

Mathis didn't expect his near-invisible lenses to get called out. "I'm not recording."

Frost leaned back in his chair, one side of his mouth curling upwards in a smirk. "One of us is going to take those lenses out of your eyes."

The threat was delivered impossibly casual, but struck Mathis as entirely credible. He grudgingly removed the contacts and carefully placed them in their protective case.

Frost extended his left arm with his palm open, snapping once. "The storage."

"There are mission-critical files on it which haven't been merged with our version control servers," he protested. Mathis correctly interpreted Frost's hard stare and reluctantly placed a microdrive the size of a child's fingertip in the man's hand.

Frost pulled a small bottle with an inverted eye dropper cap from his inner coat pocket. Unhurried, he squeezed two drops on the drive—the sharp scent of corrosive acid immediately filled the room, triggering the HVAC and air sanitizers to fire into action. His hand didn't tremble throughout the process. When the drive stopped smouldering, he tossed it to Mathis.

"If there's anything else, now would be the time to mention it."

"There's nothing else," Mathis stated through clenched teeth. He could reconstitute the drive contents, but the willful destruction of data was a deliberate affront. He wanted to walk out of the Pod, but Evy's uncharacteristic plea kept him in place.

Frost leaned forward, his gaze deconstructing Mathis. "There are two narratives I'm prepared to offer. The longer one won't allow for questions. Either way, you've got exactly five minutes. I suggest you not waste time being pissy."

"Short, then."

"From now on, I'll be directing the wetware initiative."

Mathis scoffed at the crass assertion. "No way. I brought a decade of preliminary work in human-machine convergence to Hikari for the promise of funding without losing program control."

"I'm constantly amazed at how stupid academics can be. If I say that's how it is, that's exactly how it is. There's a timetable in your forecasts to conclude the human trials, secure regulatory approval, and launch the product for consumer release. Those dates need to be accelerated. I'll provide bodies for your trials—as many as you can handle with no concerns around ethics boards or governmental interference. I'll sew up regulatory so tight the rubber stamp will be waiting before the trial data is even complete. In return, you'll implement a backdoor into the consumer product line for me."

"You're no investor."

"To the contrary, I'm all in."

Mathis was repulsed by the concept of any group or government having real-time access to distill or subvert the thoughts of the global citizenry. "You want to turn anyone with wetware into a Manchurian Candidate? Not a chance. It's completely unethical."

Frost shook his head in disapproval. "The correct response is, *what's in it for me*? You see, I take care of my friends, and my pockets are deep. My reach is even deeper. What's in it for you is the same thing you risk losing. The success, prosperity, and freedom of everyone you care for. Three and half minutes left."

"This is extortion." Mathis got to his feet.

"Sit down and listen. This is about winning long-term, viable security in a world already grossly destabilized by environmental refugees, resource conflicts, and ideologically driven terrorism. You can either wait for China to finish ripping off your work and mass-produce wetware with their backdoors in place, or you can work with the good guys and be part of the winning team. And speaking of teams, your developers will be replaced with my guys."

Still standing, he involuntarily took a half step back, bumping the chair askew. "Not a chance."

"Logan Mahler farms out half his workload to a Chinese AI code generator the CCP directly controls, and Tariq Mustafa's family has ties to the Muslim Brotherhood. The rest of your crew aren't skilled enough to be irreplaceable. You've got two minutes left. And sit the fuck down."

Mathis struggled against a creeping panic, his breathing shallow. He tried to maintain eye contact while reaching back to correct the chair's angle, fumbling awkwardly until it at last faced Frost. The handful of seconds felt like an eternity. "All of this needs me. I won't do it."

"You're convenient to the timeline, but enough exists between the different branches of your version control system that I could parachute in a handpicked team to bridge the gaps in the current technical architecture. It'd cost time, however, and that's not something I'm willing to risk. I'm heavily incentivized to ensure a slip won't happen."

Mathis felt a rivulet of sweat roll down the side of his face. His hands were cold and clammy. He wiped them reflexively on his pant legs and tried to mask the gesture in an overcorrection of his posture. "This isn't legal."

"I could give a shit what you think is legal. It's happening," Frost scornfully pronounced. "You've got the chance to be a hero in this or a footnote who's been wrongfully extradited to a windowless cell, wondering where your parents disappeared to and agonizing over the swath of misfortune that's beset everyone you know. Despite what the dossier says, I hoped you'd be receptive to logic, but you're insufferably predictable. You'll soon grasp there's no way out other than to cooperate. You'll use your big brain to weigh the consequences of potential actions to everything you value and come to appreciate you've got no options. I don't waste time on losing propositions. Or losers. Thirty seconds remaining. Speed round. It's time for you to start negotiating."

"My team stays."

"Fine. I'll be replacing bodies when they fuck up. Next?"

"No spying on me outside work. I won't be able to function if I'm paranoid."

"Deliver, and there'll be no need to get invasive."

"You'll subsidize the cost of the commercial wetware for developing nations."

"Think smaller. Time's almost up."

He'd given up everything and gained nothing in the process. The conversation was rigged to play out as a negative sum game. Mathis' mind was scrambling, but the thoughts were fragmented by panic and lacked coherence. He desperately needed to make the deficit less dangerous for the world but was coming up empty.

"The right to interpret your goals," he blurted out.

"Sounds antagonistic."

"You're not a systems architect. You'll ask for things that'll destabilize the platform. I've dedicated the last ten years of my life to this vision, and I'm committed to it, even if it means shaking hands with the devil. No offense."

Aiden Frost stood up and extended his hand. His skin was callused, and his grip was stronger than Mathis expected. Awkwardly, Mathis shook it.

"It's been a pleasure doing business with you, Grenier."

2

Rei

It was an agonizingly familiar walk to the Osaka Minami Central police station and with each step, Rei tried to shake the burden of shame her father was impervious to. As she made her way down the block and a half from the south exit of the Sakai-suji train station, Rei selectively scanned the dense throng of commuters for facial recognition hits on a Dark Net profiling service. She was looking for anyone linked to the Mori yakuza clan, anxious and hoping she could isolate them before they pattern-matched her movement gait.

She wove through salarymen, career women, and small clusters of youths dressed in all-white with their faces concealed by UkiyoAR goggles and rebreathers. Rei still managed to draw people's attention since her full-face mask was coupled with an outfit designed to seduce a corporate executive. Her pace quickened.

The automatic doors at the police station entrance didn't open to her proximity. Her devices routed data packets through a server in the Philippines, and the articulating patterns of eInk on her mask were designed to defy facial recognition. She was a non-participant in legal society in terms of modern automation and systems. A government building refusing to admit met her expectation.

She stepped closer and gently rapped on the frosted glass doors with her gloved hand. A moment later, the doors opened, and she walked inside, stopping to return the bow of the familiar, older officer behind the intake desk. His uniform was impeccable, and even from a distance, the glint of his brightly polished buttons and crisp ironing lines of his clothes were noticeable. Rei glanced at the security cameras, torn between her habitual need to remain anonymous and etiquette.

Officer Matsumoto gestured for her to wait and nodded after some quick hand movements. She retracted the full-face mask with the press of a solid-state button, and it folded itself into a thick hair band atop her head. Rei was confident the officer had temporarily suspended the recording and recognition software. Without the modified rebreather, she took in the stale, recycled air of the police station and unconsciously made a sour face. Her expression then softened at Officer Matsumoto's genuine warmth.

"Miss Yoshida. It's a sincere pleasure to see you again. I wish the auspices were better, however."

Matsumoto had comforted her and Miyu countless times as children when officers had led her father away. He'd never made her feel her father was the criminal he was.

"Thank you, Matsumoto-*san*. How's your wife?"

He squinted, forcing a thin-lipped smile. "Aiko is enduring well, thank you. It's good of you to remember."

She made a mental note to send a tasteful floral arrangement to the hospice. Rei carefully adopted a pleasant expression, trying to shed the weight of her concern from her voice. "What's my father done this time, Matsumoto-*san*?"

"I'm afraid it's all a terrible misunderstanding for which I hold myself partially responsible. You see, we get new recruits from the academy who... " He pressed his lips tightly together. "They can get overzealous and ignore the council of more seasoned veterans of the force."

"May I speak to this officer? Perhaps I can help smooth things over. Dad isn't much for words and may have exacerbated the situation."

"The young man is taking some time off after the *misunderstanding*."

She forced a wary smile, familiar with her father's ways. "Broken ribs?"

"Ah, yes." He glanced around nervously. "Him and his partner, both."

"If I were to send cards, could I entrust you to deliver them?" Rei was confident Matsumoto recognized the euphemism and was capable of smoothing things over as he'd always done.

"You may find it unnecessary. The other young officers, well... They took the opportunity to teach your father a lesson." Matsumoto looked down and away, shaking his head.

"I can assure you my father's impervious to lessons." She smiled pleasantly but her shoulders stiffened, expecting the worst. Some of the most savage beatings her father had ever taken were at the hands of police behind closed doors, and Rei had no desire to nurse him back to health for the next several weeks. Again.

"Would you be good enough to get him for me? That is, if he's alright to walk."

Matsumoto, thin-lipped, bowed sharply and disappeared down a corridor. Rei scolded herself for not having gone to the pharmacy for medical supplies earlier. She further chastised herself for caring, and found herself trembling in a blend of anger and anxiousness.

Several minutes later, her father's large form came striding out in front of Matsumoto, seemingly without a care in the world. One eye was swollen shut with a jagged gash on the forehead, his lip was split, and dried blood could be seen from a scalp wound hidden under his short, matted locks. With his cauliflower ears, broad crooked nose and wealth of scar tissue on his brow, he looked like the fighter he once was. She recalled all the times he'd come home from a match when she was a kid—thoroughly beaten but equally upbeat.

Her father smiled broadly, opened his arms wide, and embraced Rei. She wished he could be like an ordinary Japanese father and forgo the physical intimacies, especially in public. Her body went rigid in his bear-like grip, but his force was overwhelming. She felt tiny in his grasp. Childlike. She wiggled her elbows in and pushed away with the force of her whole body. He allowed it, infuriatingly tussling her hair and slinging a heavy arm over her shoulders. She shrugged out from under it, angled and bowed to the officer.

"You have my thanks, Matsumoto-*san*. If I could ask you to gauge the level of *misunderstanding* with the officers recovering at the hospital, I'd be most appreciative. And please pass along our very best wishes to your wife."

"I'm sure she'll be pleased to receive them, Miss Yoshida."

Tatsuo grinned wide and winked. "See you around, Ken!"

Matsumoto nodded cautiously. "Take care, Tatsuo."

Rei pushed an oversized respirator into her father's hands. "Wear it."

Her mask slipped over her face silently as she pulled the hooded cowl forward and led her father outside to where the driverless car service would arrive in a few minutes.

"I'll help you convert yen into cryptocurrency for the payoff. I'll need at least two million yen for each."

"I don't have it."

Rei's lips snarled behind her mask. "How can you not have any money?"

"Miyu." Tatsuo shrugged.

Rei couldn't swallow her frustration any longer. "Dad, you're not on the hook to finance her princess lifestyle."

"She said Toronto's expensive."

"Of course it's expensive! She knew that before she went. You're incapable of denying her anything."

"Just let it go, okay? She's your sister."

Rei closed her eyes, blocked out her father's conciliatory tone, and let out a deep breath. "I'll handle the bribes, but this is the last time. Do you understand?"

Tatsuo nodded and grunted in acknowledgement. A moment later, he added, "Hey, you look nice."

"I had to cancel a private appointment with the Hikari CTO thanks to you. It took me months to engineer the opportunity thanks to you."

"There'll be another chance."

"You're not getting it. Shinoda-*sama* is already thin on patience, and the clan will run out of funds if I don't pull this off soon."

"Ichirou will be fine."

Her eyes narrowed. "He's the head of the clan, Dad. You can't call him that anymore."

Tatsuo scoffed, crossing his arms in front of his chest. "I've known him since we were kids."

"It's not like that anymore. It hasn't been for a long time." Rei shook her head slowly. "You need to get out of the country."

"The Moris can get fucked."

"Dad, you put Shinoda-*sama* and the rest of us in a terrible position. What were you thinking with an unsanctioned firebombing of their headquarters?"

"They needed a reminder about territory."

She clenched her fists, incredulous. "You've given Akira Mori every reason to push his father into a clan war we have no chance of surviving."

Tatsuo fixed his gaze elsewhere, silently signalling there was no more conversation to be had on the subject. A minute passed before the car service pulled up and he gestured to the wheelchair access sign. "Why'd you get a cripple car?"

"Because I didn't know if you'd come out of the station on a stretcher!"

Rei eyes welled with tears of pent-up frustration, and she was thankful the mask spared her the indignity of having him see her cry. She understood he believed he was indomitable, but his chin was shot—a strike he'd walk through at the start of his fighting career would drop him now. She'd listened to enough doctors try to explain traumatic brain injuries to him, but he'd ignored her counsel to give up recreational sparring and avoid street fights. However well-intentioned, she was trying to convince him to become someone he wasn't when she suspected it was all he could do to hold onto what was left of him. One day, he'd die alone in some depressing holding cell or dirty alleyway, surrounded and beaten to death, with no one to protect him from the killing blow he would've both invited and welcomed.

Tatsuo grabbed her with his powerful arms, pulled her close and rubbed her back. He cradled the back of her head, tucking her forehead into his broad chest until she stopped resisting him.

"I can't keep doing this, Dad." She despised the quiver in her voice, and how weak she felt.

"I know. You're a good girl, but don't worry about me. I'm okay." He took off the respirator and kissed the top of her head. "We'll always be okay."

3
Miyu

A GUST OF WIND caught Miyu off guard—she lurched dangerously, desperate to secure her footing on the ledge overlooking the entrance of Hikari International's Toronto office. Incongruent movements could draw rare attention from a populace who never looked up anymore, but she trusted the potent combination of broad-spectrum jammers and digital countermeasures her Minus One colleague, Teo Hagen, had kitted her out with.

Another incoming conference request from her sister tripped alerts in Miyu's hard-jacked optics. Rei had always been relentless. Miyu cursed, wishing she could ignore the notifications, but ever since her botched surgery, her digital vision was always on.

Once expressive and full of life, her eyes were now large, cold, convex ovals of brushed metal firmly affixed into the bone of her eye sockets. Her skin had grown over the outer edges in several places, and swollen, callused areas remained from when she'd fought off the series of infections, creating a disturbing visual fusion of flesh and metal. Several lesions were swollen with pus and threatened to rupture anytime. Below the surface, her eyes were irrecoverably ruined, and she'd lost most of the sensation in her face.

She retreated from the edge of the overhang, slipped into the office building through the service room window, and grudgingly accepted the request to an encrypted channel. A translucent image of her sister filled her vision, and Miyu irritatedly gestured to minimize her to the bottom right corner. Rei, always calculated and perfect, wore dark red lipstick, and her hair was styled into a sharp bob with long bangs. Her exaggeratedly dark eye makeup reminded Miyu of the contrivances of a film noir actress—determined, scheming, a trap concealed within an object of desire.

"Turn off the damn avatar, Miyu. And what exactly do you mean by the money's for something important?"

Miyu suspected the AI-based social service she filtered communications with must've been too vague to satisfy her sister. She swallowed Rei's righteousness.

"You're up early, Rei."

"I went through Dad's accounts, and you've been siphoning him dry. He's living like a pauper, renting a miserable storage room above an *okonomiyaki* restaurant. It stinks of cabbage and oil. He doesn't even have space for a rice cooker!"

She felt a pang of homesickness at the thought of the Kansai region junk food. "How is he?"

"Maybe if you thanked him for all the money you've been swindling, you'd know."

Miyu cringed. "So... you're not going to tell me?"

"He's had the shit kicked out of him by the police again and has to get out of the country."

Miyu fondly recalled all the times her father had come home bloodied up, and she and Rei had nursed him back to health. He'd always been especially thankful when he was hurt, and she adored when the three of them could spend family time together.

"Oh."

"He's good enough to fly. He'll arrive in Toronto late tomorrow, provided he doesn't get stuck at immigration. I'll make sure all his documents are in order and send him along with clean bandages and pain meds. I've sent his itinerary to you."

Panicking, she shook her head vigorously—the action translating perfectly to her avatar. "I can't take him, Rei. I'm not even supposed to be talking to you."

"What the hell's that supposed to mean?"

She flinched involuntarily. "It doesn't matter. I can't take care of Dad."

Rei took a deep breath, and narrowed her eyes. "Do you realize how hard it is to get a regular civilian on a transpacific flight? Do you know what sorts of bribes I had to pay and favors I cashed? While you've been bleeding him dry, I've been bailing him out of trouble for the last three years by myself. I'm done, Miyu. It's your turn now."

Rei's righteous tone cut into her. Miyu made a mental inventory of all the ways the situation could backfire. Her father was a square peg seeking a round hole in the wrong puzzle.

"No, not here." Miyu instinctively shook her head again. "It's impossible."

"Akira Mori has already put a bounty on his head and Shinoda-*sama* can't protect him without starting a clan war."

"Wait, I thought you said it was the police."

"Ask him about it yourself. I'm late for a meeting and don't have time for your excuses. He's your responsibility until things get smoothed over with the Mori clan."

"How long is that going to take?"

"As long as it does."

"I'll need money." She bit her lip, recoiling at the expected fury of her sister's reply.

Rei held her breath and let it out over several heartbeats. "Fine. If you want the cash to flow, I'll expect receipts for everything you spend."

Her irritation flared at being treated even more like a child. "You can't possibly expect me to—"

"I'm not a sucker like Dad. My money, my rules. And the next time we connect, don't run your output through a fucking avatar. Are you some junkie now that you have to hide yourself?"

"I'm not a junkie," she lied, silently seething at being accurately judged by her sister.

"Should I bother asking about Hikari?"

"Nope." It was satisfying to deny Rei the information she was so desperate for.

"Have you even tried, Miyu? I've been the only one protecting Dad while you're off having your little princess adventure overseas. This is to help him, not me. Got it?"

She swallowed Rei's barbed words. "Yeah."

"Get your shit together by tomorrow, Miyu. And don't be late to pick up Dad."

The image of her sister winking out of her net-enhanced vision left Miyu with the same irritated sensation as all their infrequent interactions since Rei had assumed the mantle of the family matriarch. Doubly so since her sister had tried to set Miyu to task.

Rei couldn't have chosen a worse possible day to have thrown the grenade of their father's responsibility into her life. Miyu had publicly vowed never to see him again, and even Rei's intermittent calls could have her sanctioned. Calamitous thoughts suffocated her.

Miyu tried to push the catastrophic images from her mind to focus on her assigned task—Mathis. If he held true to form, he'd be leaving Hikari International from the north exit to avoid the active King Street protests on the building's south side.

She amplified her audio inputs, listening for activity on the other side of the door. When Miyu suspected it was clear, she slipped into the bleak grey corridors, past the elevator bay, and hurried to the staircase. She paired a proximity-based bypass tool to the door sensor, tripping the lock mechanism as though she'd held a physical passkey.

She took the stairs two at a time, racing down the flights, her footfalls echoing throughout the stairwell. The burst of movement after holding herself motionless for most of the afternoon was a welcome change. The location broadcast from the tiny, sub-dermal implant showed Mathis moving within the office tower on her optics. The cowl of her coat snapped back at her speed, allowing a rush of cool air over her forehead and shaved scalp.

She tugged the deep cowl back in place at the base of the foyer stairwell and slipped into the bustle of human traffic with her head lowered, assuming the anonymity of the herd.

Few people took note of her. She was just another person masked, goggled, and enshrouded in all white. A few months ago, she would've been a curiosity, but Minus One's uniform had been co-opted by protesters and Net influencers alike. She despised her extravagant clothes and accessories, constantly fearing punishment for not being mindful of her burden of privilege.

As she spilled out onto Adelaide Street with the salaried workers, she scanned the crowd for Mathis. He was holding two coffee containers in a half tray in one hand, standing at the edge of the curb on the other side of the street. He was craning his neck, scanning nearby ledges and rooftops. His light fall coat wasn't sufficient for the crisp weather of the early winter evening, and unlike everyone else coming out from the office towers after their twelve-hour workdays, he didn't wear UkiyoAR glasses. Instead, he was squinting, moving his gaze anxiously from one elevated perch to the next.

She stepped to the curb, facing him, separated by four treacherous lanes of swiftly moving, one-way traffic. Eventually, his eyes fell on her, and he smiled. His shoulders relaxed, and he awkwardly raised the two coffees before gesturing for her to wait. He seemed to be trying to time the traffic, but she shook her head and held out one hand. Mathis was far too precious to lose to something as banal as a traffic accident. His death couldn't be left to chance. When it happened, it had to mean something.

Miyu gestured towards Cloud Gardens, a small park tucked in amongst the forest of downtown office towers with numerous escape routes and vandalized surveillance equipment. She wasn't sure he understood, but merged with the east-west stream of bodies and started walking, letting him follow from the other side of the street. She was confident he'd figure out how to keep track of her from the concealing press of pedestrians as she disappeared into the foot traffic. It was impossible to see him directly, but her optics showed his location signal moving parallel. She pushed her way off the sidewalk and into the broad entrance of the park, pleased and saddened by how beautiful places were always the least utilized in cities. She squatted on the balls of her feet on the raised concrete of the dry water feature on the lowest of the four park tiers, waiting patiently for him to arrive.

A few minutes later, Mathis entered the park at a quick step and slowed abruptly as he closed the distance to her. He stopped completely to look at the immense matrix of colourful one-by-one meter panels, framed in red oxide steel, and bolted to the adjacent tower directly behind her. Miyu had envisioned this moment thousands of times ever since Mathis had been assigned to her, but all her careful rehearsal was meaningless as he reset his attention on her and took the final steps. Her anxieties sharpened. He stopped closer than she was comfortable with, but far enough whispers would die unheard in the wind.

He started to say something, then sat down on the raised concrete, facing outward. The creeping edge of panic gripped her. Why hadn't Mia Locke been assigned Mathis? Her easy manner with men and her ability to make them do things, to give her money or access, were far above Miyu's capabilities.

Mathis reached over and placed a coffee at the halfway distance between them. "It's black. I didn't know how you took it. If you told me, I could get it right next time."

She nodded.

"I'm Mathis, but I'm pretty sure you know that already. Maybe you could start with your name?"

"I haven't earned mine yet." Telling him a number would complicate things further. Mathis might confuse *Seventeen* with her age. Her real name felt like it belonged to someone else. Rei was the one who consistently used it, and usually in anger.

He laughed out loud. "That's not what I was expecting to hear. What should I call you?"

"Whatever you'd like. It doesn't matter. I'll know when you're talking to me."

"Would it be too much to ask you to remove the mask?"

"We all wear masks. Yours just isn't covering your face. I'd rather you not judge me for anything besides your experience."

"I—" Mathis stopped himself and frowned. Eventually, he offered, "It's easier to drink coffee when you're not wearing a respirator." He smiled harmlessly. "I promise I don't have a latent strain of Zambezi. My Net contacts take real-time readings from my body. I could offer my health data if you changed your share settings."

She cursed herself for not having noticed his Net contacts. Teo had speculated about the tech's research and development, but he'd said they were years away from commercialization. It would've been disastrous had Mathis not volunteered the information before they went too far.

"Take them out, please."

He shrugged, carefully put his lenses into their case, and tucked them in his outer pocket. "I'm digitally blind now. Satisfied?"

Miyu hesitated before unclasping her respirator. It fell gently to one side of her face, hanging by an anchor point. She breathed in the early winter scent of the nature around her—the smattering of dead leaves on the barren trees had a distinct odour and carried on the crisp evening air, pushing past the dirt and congestion of the city. She wore no makeup, but her lips were flushed, and her cheeks were hot. Self-conscious and nervous, she instinctively pulled the cowl further forward.

"Don't ask for more."

"Why have you been following me?"

"Because you're about to make the world regret your decisions." She cupped the coffee close to her face, relishing its warmth, not appreciating how cold she was beforehand. She was so often cold these days.

He shifted away from her. "What do you think you know?" His tone was suspicious.

"Very little. There are better people. They were going to leave you alone, to let your wetware program go to market without interference, but you changed the dynamics."

"Did you spy on my meeting today?"

Miyu savoured a sip of coffee. When she could force herself to eat, it was always a quick shot of tasteless, nutrient gel meant for the most infirm patients to recover. "You don't have to be paranoid around me. Everyone else, yes, but not me."

"What do you want?"

"For you to have a conversation I'm incapable of. I can take you to them now if you want. But we need to disable all your digital signatures first."

Mathis held both hands out palm forward. "The only thing I know about you is that you speak with an accent, like practically everyone in the city. Why have you been following me? I'm not dangerous."

Miyu shook her head. "You're the worst type of person."

He physically recoiled, wrinkling his brow.

She vacillated on whether to point out the tiny, broadcasting, sub-dermal audio device she'd tagged him with. Miyu couldn't gauge how he'd react. She was already too vulnerable and exposed. Failing, too. Miyu gathered her courage. "The others don't know what you've committed to yet. Just me. But I don't know how to help you. I'll have to tell them if you don't give me another option, and it'll go... differently than this."

"You can't just stalk and spy on people."

Miyu shrugged, but struggled with the desperate beat of her heart and acute sensation of vulnerability.

"None of this is normal." His tone was agitated, too loud for their quiet setting.

"Okay."

Miyu attached her respirator, adjusted her cowl, and hopped off the ledge. She willed herself past crippling self-disappointment and into motion. He called for her attention as she walked away. Her eyes locked on the long shadows she was casting. Miyu desperately wanted to sprint as his shadow closed in on her, but instead, she allowed herself to be caught. He grasped her shoulder indelicately, turning her around to face him. She gave herself over to his momentum and force—a stray balloon captured by the greedy hands of an entitled child.

His expression was bewildered. "What's wrong with you?"

"Everything," Miyu acknowledged. "Please stop touching me."

He let his grip go but hovered his hand over her shoulder, like a house cat toying with a lesser creature. He may not have even realized he was doing it. She doubted he would've done the same if their size disparity worked to her advantage. Miyu wished she had her father's force or her sister's charisma to have the upper hand in the dynamic. Anything. She took two steps back, barely out of his reach. Mathis didn't have a history of violence, but frustrated men, even the ones who considered themselves kind, were unpredictable. Especially in quiet settings outside the gaze of prying eyes or recording cameras.

"Are you going to keep following me?"

She was failing her assignment and didn't know how to correct the situation. It was incomprehensible they had sent her to bring Mathis in. All she wanted was to retreat, to get away from this man who was so despicably cavalier about everyone's shared future. She tried to find stillness and courage to control her body so as not to crumble under the unfocused force he represented.

"No, you've already chosen for all of us."

His arm fell slack to his side, and his face showed the vulnerability of a guilty conscience. "What if I need to contact you?"

"I can always find you. Anyone can. You might want to do something about that."

She edged further away from him, abruptly turned on her heel, and sprinted towards the far edge of the small park. Mathis didn't move. Miyu unconsciously shook her head in disappointment before losing herself amongst the east-west stream of commuters.

4

Amrita

AMRITA WAS THE ONLY one in her section of cubicles still onsite a little before midnight at the Toronto branch of the Canadian Security and Intelligence Service. She was engrossed manipulating the output of her algorithm, and didn't have time to hide her screen when her director unexpectedly limped towards her desk.

Mason Brand's dress shirt was impossibly white, in contrast with his navy-blue suit, slate grey tie finished in a Windsor knot, and deeply wrinkled ebony skin. His head was shaved clean, his salt and pepper beard impeccably groomed, and the sour expression on his face had been refined to near perfection from a long career in managerial roles. Amrita visibly hunched up her shoulders as she recoiled. The unconscious physical reaction was less at having been caught pursuing a lead she'd been told to abandon and more for the lecture Mason was sure to inflict. She spun her task chair around to face him, risking the initiative and hoping to frame the conversation.

"Director Brand, I can explain—"

"Ms. Chopra, at this very moment, your industriously cultivated contacts in India's RAW, Russia's SVR, and France's DGSI are being called out by their superiors." Mason absently adjusted his thin UkiyoAR glasses, allowing her to digest the inevitability of her circumstance. "Of course, I expect a thorough report submitted on how you developed these contacts and full disclosure of what intelligence you've shared. I would prefer to avoid the inconvenience of a messy audit, suspension, and legal action, so I expect thorough disclosure."

Amrita squirmed under the weight of his chastisement. "Of course, sir."

Mason's unnaturally crisp British accent had resisted years of Canadian naturalization, and Amrita believed he actively practiced it in secret. While immigrants consistently tried to fit in, he wrapped himself in the Old World, and she resented the part of her which instinctively responded to it.

"Your particular mandate is to collect, share, and analyze information on terrorists with our allies, not to treat our allies like terrorists."

Amrita cleared her throat reflexively. "I recognize that, sir, but Aiden Frost has no designations in the systems."

"You've been asked to abandon your interest in Mr. Frost on a previous occasion. Either I've been too vague in my instructions, or you think yourself above them. I'll err on the side of not being sufficiently explicit. Let's try again, shall we, Ms. Chopra? Do not, under any circumstance, investigate Aiden Frost or any of his interests. Further, you're prohibited from aiding others in any such endeavour."

In her last performance review, Mason had correctly characterized her as overconfident, occasionally reckless, and overly tenacious. At least she was living up to expectations. She steeled herself for one last plea.

"Sir, Frost entered Canada on a false passport early this morning. He's trying to protect his movements with sophisticated obfuscation routines and parallel automations. Still, I managed to pattern-match his walking gait, then patched into the Toronto police drones and tracked him entering the Hikari International offices on Richmond Street this afternoon. I believe this to be of utmost importance." She cursed the natural thickening of her Goan accent as she rushed through the words, letting her passion overtake her carefully cultivated diction.

He seemed to regard her as a child fumbling her way through an adult activity. For a moment, pity animated his face. He sighed audibly. "Was I not sufficiently clear?"

Amrita choked back her protests and feelings of injustice. Canada wasn't her birth home, and she'd been spared the relentless cross-border propaganda in her formative years that generated blind spots in her contemporaries' perceptions of Americans.

"Clear, sir," she said, resigned.

Uncharacteristically, the director didn't leave after securing her acquiescence. Tension filled the space between them. She caught herself rubbing her thighs with both palms and froze in place.

"Is there something else, sir?"

"Take control of B3708. I need real-time eyes on an incident."

Mason sent coordinates to her profile without gesturing or vocalizing the action. Amrita made a mental note to figure out how he did it by interrogating her buffered Netstream recordings later. She toggled screen targets to the external display and adeptly interfaced with the drone's control systems.

"GPS shows the location as a luxury car dealership?" She searched his expression, but found it impenetrable. Pouring overtime into a property damage case was outside her mandate, especially when vandalism and theft had grown commonplace these past weeks.

She piloted the remote drone to the nearby smouldering ruin of a Bentley and idly calculated how many years it would take for her to afford it. Thirty-six gross, she quickly determined. She pivoted the camera on an ascending sweeping arc, expertly taking in the scene. The entire fleet of exotic vehicles had been similarly destroyed, sitting like dethroned despots on imported black marble floors.

The scene was a feudal expression of rage against wealth. It resonated poetic.

Despite how stretched the police services were, a dozen officers, investigators, and special liaisons were onsite. The air was buzzing with other drones.

Amrita piloted the drone to a deceptively striking *-1* stencil spray-painted white on the polished, black marble floors. Minus One. Two simple strokes to defy the upper one percent of society in another attack against unrestricted privilege. There was an elegance in its lack of pretence and blunt application.

Mason pulled up a chair and crowded the space directly beside her, directing her drone control with an urgency that felt inappropriate. As she panned, zoomed, and piloted, she skillfully implemented a custom algorithm to redirect prioritized sections of preliminary case notes from the onsite teams to her desk screen for Mason's benefit, hoping her superior skill wouldn't go unnoticed.

Amrita cleared her throat to signal his attention. "The alarms were overridden remotely, as were the onsite surveillance systems. No prints, no readily identifiable DNA, but they're scrubbing the air filtration units for particulates. We should at least get a list of people who've gained entry to the environment."

"Cross-referencing income data should narrow down the result set."

She understood the distasteful code for *rich people don't commit crimes.* "Respectfully, sir, normal people enjoy window-shopping. Besides, the type of person wealthy enough to afford those vehicles would send an assistant instead of suffering through traffic themselves."

Mason's posture straightened and he cleared his throat, as was his habit before casting judgment or making pronouncements. Amrita concealed the wince of anticipation, but her face pinched slightly in distress.

"Run the backgrounds, isolating connections to prospective legitimate buyers to rule out individuals. You're not above this, Ms. Chopra."

"Sir, I've configured an exhaustive flight pattern for the drone and have opened an API for the onsite data streams. As soon as we're done here, I'll initiate a broad search over the Net, social channels, and peer-to-peer communication, winnowing for any references to Minus One with metadata indicating that area of Toronto and a time window within thirty-six hours before the property damage." Amrita tried to mask her pride at having simultaneously engaged with the conversation while executing several advanced tasks. "At this point, sir, I think dedicating anything more than ticks of CSIS cluster processing to this incident would be pointless until I've had a chance to work with the result sets in the morning."

"This has Rochon's signature all over it. Tell me of the progress you've made against him."

It took Amrita a moment to reset from her expectation of praise to realign on Mason's request. She was confident Rochon was a false positive—just another Montreal, anti-corporate anarchist who'd served a ten-year sentence for his role in orchestrating the Mile End Riots. She wished for the days when people wore watches so she could glance at one, reminding her director it was already midnight. She sighed heavily, hoping Mason would take a hint.

"I haven't been able to pick up Benoit Rochon since he left Montreal. I've got processes grinding pattern recognition on communications and connected devices within the homes of all his known associates. I've also established cycles dedicated to street surveillance, but nothing's turned up."

"It's his work," Mason stubbornly insisted.

She gestured to her interface, pulling up Mia Locke's profile on the desk projection. "The blue-haired girl you had me investigate has no apparent connections to any anarchist organizations." Amrita shrugged. "Locke has been seen in all-white, but given her erratic behaviour, that's likely just a fashion statement. Minus One members usually wear full-face coverings in public. She might have simply consumed some Net content of Rochon's rhetoric at some point, and some of his phrasings stuck."

Mason shook his head. "Transcripts of her interrogation pattern-matched on too many occasions for it to be a coincidence. We've either redacted or corrupted

Rochon's Net content over the past decade. Her chances of finding the original, unedited content are minuscule, yet she talks like one of his disciples."

"If I might speak freely, sir? She has a history of drug abuse and antisocial actions. She's been resuscitated twice in failed suicide attempts and earns money from pharmaceutical trials. As for the transcript, we need to question the legitimacy of the entire so-called interrogation. The private contractors should've been charged under section 279 of the criminal code." Amrita didn't want to wait for him to perform a Net search. "The unlawful confinement, imprisonment or forcible seizure of another person."

"I don't buy it, Ms. Chopra. Locke tried insinuating herself in an exclusive black-tie affair for Hikari International's North American stockholders. She had no business being there."

Amrita choked back the urge to make the Aiden Frost connection to Hikari International when she caught Mason's prohibitive glare. "Locke's been charged for Net solicitation in the past. She might have been trying to turn a lucrative trick."

"I need you to keep digging. If this is anything like the Mile End Riots, Rochon's most trusted agents will be set into play as things escalate. The recent property destruction in the city is a series of trials. They'll culminate into coordinated, large-scale attacks. Locke could be the string we unravel the jumper with."

She tried to determine his angle. His uncharacteristic level of stubborn, conspiratorial insistence that something existed in this vacuum of wasted lives was difficult to fathom. Their mandate didn't include Quebecois anarchists. Her boss was flaunting prohibitions just as she'd been with Frost. They were kindred spirits of a sort—both visible minorities, hailing from other continents, trying desperately to safeguard their adoptive commonwealth country, which was constitutionally structured for vulnerability.

"I'll be more thorough in the morning, sir."

Mason brushed off her hint. "I've authorized twenty minutes with Carnivore's construct module for you. See that my trust hasn't been misplaced."

He seemed about to say more but stopped and nodded more to himself than to her. Mason took his time standing up and limped away, leaving Amrita with a mandate well above her pay grade that she was apprehensive to fulfil.

She hesitated before executing the command to generate a virtual construct of Mia Locke in a nearby meeting room. The display interface at her desk disappeared when she left the physical proximity and walked the silent columns and rows of cubicles to the glassed enclosure.

A virtual projection of Mia Locke was standing there, impatiently shifting weight from one foot to the other, fidgeting with the overlapping lateral straps of her tight, open-backed, white leather top. Amrita was taken off guard by how accurately the documented habits and mannerisms of the woman were embedded into the model. She knew the projection wasn't the real person, but the intricate humanization of the subject upheld the suspension of disbelief.

The glass automatically frosted as Amrita entered the room. The piercing eye contact from Mia's construct was unsettling. Interface displays of *probability* and *data integrity* flanked her face, rebalancing neatly fifteen centimetres above her shoulders and to the side of the cascade of her blue hair. The unnervingly pale skin and extreme eye makeup robbed any element of human warmth from the construct that was rendered and extrapolated from the last accurate surveillance footage of Mia Locke.

Amrita couldn't shake the feeling of being a predator. A Carnivore instance, having aggregated and consumed all available data points, stripped subjects of any legal protections, knowledge they were being processed, and set no limits to the information constructs yielded.

"Carnivore, set character accuracy to one hundred percent."

A disembodied female voice crisply articulated the response, *accuracy set*.

Amrita took a seat and tried to ignore the inherent violation of her actions. "Ms. Locke, tell me of your relationship with Benoit Rochon."

"Go fuck yourself."

"Carnivore, maximize cooperation."

Character accuracy at sixty-eight percent, cooperation set.

"Do you have a connection to him?"

"I was just a girl when the riots broke out. I saw how savage the police were, how the courts punished the innocent and gave a pass to all the corrupt motherfuckers. Anyone who lived through those days is connected to Benoit."

The probability and data integrity display readouts were populated at 88 and 67 percent, respectively.

"Carnivore, eliminate evasiveness, increase speculative variances."

Character accuracy at fifty-eight percent.

"Answer the question, Ms. Locke."

"Benoit is a visionary who wields a different metric on how people should be judged. It appeals to me since I don't fit in. His message of usurping control structures resonates with my low self-esteem. If those I've been trained to fear are reduced to my anguish and insecurities, I'll believe in justice. I wouldn't be motivated enough to seek Benoit out, though."

Probability: 68%, data integrity: 71%.

Her throat tightened, her stomach quivered. Listening to the construct speak impassively and candidly itself was viscerally upsetting. It felt like performing an autopsy on a living citizen.

"Carnivore, increase contextualization." She cleared her throat. "Ms. Locke, if you wanted to contact Benoit Rochon, how would you go about it?"

"I would self-sabotage before ever reaching him."

Probability: 78%, data integrity: 46%.

"If the two of you were to meet, how do you think it would happen?"

"He'd recruit me. I'm vulnerable. Especially when someone takes an interest in me for more than my flesh or sharing a fix. If he wants an agent who'll follow his biddings, especially to their own detriment, I'd be a good fit. Provided he makes me feel special. I'd be ride or die, too. It wouldn't take much."

Probability: 91%, data integrity: 76%.

"Carnivore, increase speculative variance."

Character accuracy at forty-six percent.

"Why do you think that?" Amrita probed despite her growing guilt.

"Everyone's the same. We're all insecure and self-destructive. I'm just more committed to it than most. I crave purpose but need it to be directed. Most importantly, I'm brave where others are timid because they have something to lose."

"Rochon advocates violence, but you've never exhibited those tendencies."

"I've already proven I'm willing to kill myself. I could give a fuck about anyone I take down with me."

The instance's deadpan tone sent chills down Amrita's back. *Probability: 87% data integrity: 64%.*

"You were at Hikari International's shareholder meeting. Why?"

"I couldn't tell you."

"Carnivore, maximum speculative variance. Answer the question, Ms. Locke."

"I'm an upscale escort for executives sometimes. It's the hair, the clothes, the makeup. They assume I fuck like a porn star. I'm the type of conquest those men pay for. If they buy me things, I'll go places with them. I clean up well, too. Security picked me up even before I entered the reception, though."

Probability: 42%, Data Integrity: 29%.

"Who were you there to meet?"

"Someone. Anyone, maybe."

Probability: 22%, Data Integrity: 12%.

While Amrita hadn't been trained in interrogation, it struck her that working with the Carnivore instance was a tantalizing path to a dead end. The real Mia Locke would have answers.

"Where can I find you?"

"If I'm by myself, I'll be wherever there's a warm bed, a well-stocked bio-printer and blueprints for designer drugs. If I'm with Benoit, you won't find me until people start dying."

Probability: 86%, Data Integrity: 62%.

"Tell me specific places you've been recently."

The fine hair on Amrita's arms and neck stood on end as the construct spoke from data points secured through blanket surveillance, metadata, transit logs and economic transactions. She tried implementing a custom recognition algorithm against the list of eclectic locations the construct yielded, but the output defied any set pattern. Mia Locke was a nomad, not sleeping in the same bed more than once and patronizing various establishments, from soup kitchens to Michelin-rated restaurants. Amrita cross-referenced historical data to see an acceleration of random movement and behaviour over the past several years, akin to the steady progression of a compulsive disorder.

Amrita internalized the Carnivore access Mason had provided as an invitation to finally distinguish herself, and she didn't want to come back empty-handed. This woman might be a false positive, but the opportunity wasn't—provided Mason was insulated and she didn't get caught. Her heart raced. She bit her lower lip, but the moment's excitement was intoxicating.

"What's the best way to meet you, to have you spend time with me?"

"Buy me for the evening."

Probability: 91%, Data Integrity: 88%.

5

Rei

THE MORI CLAN'S BLACK S-Class Mercedes with tinted windows had followed Rei since she'd exited Shin-Imamiya station. It surprised her how quickly they'd picked her out of the crowds as she'd gotten off the Osaka Loop line, as though they'd been waiting for her. She contemplated making a desperate run for the narrow back streets of the Shinsekai district, but wasn't prepared for a physical confrontation and had no wish to incite violence by forcing them to give chase. Besides, the tight cut of Rei's fashionable suit and fitted overcoat limited her movements more than the feminine clothes she wore professionally.

She squeezed the delicately wrapped and ribboned, long-stemmed roses she held in her hand. The thorns pricked through her thin gloves. Six months was the longest relationship Rei had ever managed, and though it felt foolish to acknowledge the half-year accomplishment, Ichika was the type to celebrate each month they were together. For her girlfriend, it was true love. For Rei, simply not pretending as much was already a sufficiently rare comfort.

The luxury Mercedes rolled to a stop beside her. The passenger door swung open, revealing two enforcers sitting opposite Akira Mori, the infamous son of the clan head, Masato Mori. She was relieved to see the older gangsters. Akira was known to use his own crew when doing things which could bring shame to his father's name. Heart racing, she waited for Akira to shift from the middle position. When it became apparent he wouldn't, she stepped into the sedan, sitting in the narrow space between him and the door before it automatically closed behind her. The lock mechanism audibly clicked.

Rei forced her face to be neutral, and while she felt naked without her mask, she retracted it as a matter of form. She wore no lipstick and only a subtle application of foundation.

"You look like a faggot," Akira laughed.

She angled to face him and ate the insult, holding Akira Mori's hateful gaze as she smiled disarmingly. "Sometimes, disguises must be adopted, Mori-*san*."

"If you get off pretending to be a dyke, that's your business. Mine is with your idiot father. Where is he?"

Regardless of the old guard in attendance, she figured any hint of defence, deceit, or antagonism would turn out poorly. She maintained a neutral expression and invested only sound into her words. "Across the Pacific, in Toronto."

Akira's face twitched before his elbow broke her nose, and her head slammed against the backrest. Rei's vision immediately blurred, and a stream of blood flowed over her lips and chin. She clenched her teeth, but didn't resist, as he grabbed her by both shoulders, slamming her into the passenger door over and again. She endured a rapid flurry of punches to the side of her face and the back of her head. It took all of her willpower not to make a single noise, to accept Akira's violence until the old guard mercifully intervened.

Akira barked a command at the two enforcers, but it was unstructured noise to her. He grabbed her by the throat. She twisted painfully in his grip to face him. His harsh words registered as angry sounds beneath the ringing in her ears. He kept shouting the same thing until she finally acknowledged it.

"I'll inform Shinoda-*sama* of your concerns," Rei croaked.

It was excruciating to speak with Akira squeezing her throat. The bruising pressure of his fingers was unrelenting. A mortal panic gripped her. She could barely see between the tears in her eyes and the blinding pain. She rasped the words again—each sound allowing Akira's fingertips to dig further.

The door to the S-Class Mercedes swung open, and Akira shoved her unceremoniously onto the curb. Her vision flashed white as her head bounced off the sidewalk. She laid crumpled, too stunned to move, with one leg still painfully tangled in the sedan. The older of the two Mori enforcers stepped out, pulled her ankle free, and lifted her to her feet as though she was weightless. Her legs buckled, but he held her firm until they started to steady. He took a handkerchief from his inner pocket and wiped some of the blood off her face—too firm to be tender, too soft to be another lesson in humiliation.

"You took your beating like a man. Your father would be proud."

The Mori enforcer fumbled with her retracted mask until he engaged the solid-state button. It slipped over her face, concealing the mess below. Rei started to bow but fell forward as she did so. The old enforcer caught her, stood her straight again, and brushed some street dirt from her overcoat. Her body was starting to go into shock, or maybe it already was. She'd been hurt before, but not like this. Akira was shouting for the old enforcer to return to the car. Blood streamed down her neck from under her mask, staining the crisp collar of her white shirt and providing an unwanted accent to her crimson tie. The enforcer frowned, adjusted the lapel of her overcoat to conceal it, and returned to the sedan. The black Mercedes rolled silently away the moment the door closed.

Pedestrians walking past her spoke in hushed whispers, and passengers in passing cars and buses stared. Rei willed herself to move, to blend in. She glanced around for the roses, finding their shape in the gutter, not knowing why she cared but committing to the action nonetheless. She reached down, taking a knee in the process of retrieving them. Her head was swimming, her vision was blurry, and her jaw was numb from clenching. She could taste the blood in her mouth and swallowed reflexively. Steadying herself with a hand, she waited until the crest of nausea passed before grabbing the roses and returning to her feet. With her mask down, the overwhelming smell of blood choked her breath. She began moving mechanically, with shaky and jarringly painful steps, along the sidewalk.

What should've been a short walk to the cafe turned into a torturous fifteen minutes. Twice, Rei had to stop to collect herself and regain control over her trembling limbs. She choked back her nausea and kept putting one foot in front of the other. Numb. The regular cacophony of street-level advertising with aggressive AR elements injecting themselves into her UkiyoAR vision increased her disorientation. She whispered the command to suspend enhanced processing, barely registering the sound of her voice over the ringing in her ears. As she neared the cafe, she caught her reflection in a shop window and adjusted the silk scarf around her neck to cover the blood leaking from her broken nose. She knew it would be better to cancel on her girlfriend, but she was irrationally drawn to the comfort of being around someone who loved her.

As she entered the cafe, the all-female staff, dressed in exaggerated maid costumes, immediately turned to face her with a synchronous greeting.

Irasshaimase!

Teddy bears of all shapes and sizes lined the pastel-coloured walls in stacked shelves above the young female patrons. Many were by themselves, sitting opposite teddy bears, chatting happily with them in immersive, Net-enhanced experiences. Most customers were high school age, and the others dressed as though they were. Murals from a famous childhood manga, *The Adventures of Keiko and Kuma-chan,* were animated on the walls and ceiling. Saccharine-sweet J-pop played loud enough to force conversation levels to be more energetic. The whole package made Rei sick, but it was all in keeping with her girlfriend's curious concept of *cute* as substance.

Ichika waved with happy exuberance from a table at the back of the packed cafe. Although only a few years Rei's junior, a change in Ichika's expression could exacerbate the age gap, making her girlfriend seem like a high school freshman. Ichika's layered, pastel-blue, one-piece dress littered with white bows, white knee socks and shiny pastel-blue shoes didn't help, either. Rei couldn't process the innocence. The incongruence felt insurmountable. Already regretting coming, she gestured discreetly for Ichika to sit, unwilling to risk a hug in public. She threaded the narrow walkway between the high-backed chairs and white linen-covered tables to hand her girlfriend the wrapped bouquet of roses as she sat.

Ichika's eyes lit up at the flowers, somehow overlooking the smear of blood halfway up the wrapping. "You remembered!"

She reached into her purse and offered Rei a small envelope liberally scented with perfume. The outside of the card was decorated with hand-drawn hearts or stars. Rei's vision was too blurry to make out the details. Given the precedent of past one-month anniversaries Ichika indulged in celebrating, the thick envelope would be filled with the painstakingly handwritten pages of another love letter.

"You can take off your mask, Rei. They're friendly here. It's okay."

"I can't stay long."

Ichika's whole face expressed her disappointment—fake eyelashes, under-eye blush and candy-floss lipstick exaggerating the sentiment. "Oh."

"Your hair's nice."

"Do you like it? Cute, right? I told the salon to style it like Ayumi from *Girigiri8*. You'd recognize her from my playlist."

Rei's face and head throbbed painfully as the shock of adrenaline started to wear off. Usually, she didn't mind listening to Ichika talk, but focusing on the conversation was making it worse, especially one incorporating inane idol groups. The relentless scent of blood drying on her face, now mixing with Ichika's floral perfume, was sickening. She tried to temper the irritation from her voice, recognizing the effort her girlfriend had put into her ensemble. It was a special day for her.

"I'm sure I'd remember if I saw it again."

Ichika's brow furrowed. "Are you okay? You don't sound like yourself."

Her genuine worry weakened Rei's resolve. In their relationship, she'd always been the strong one, never needing a shoulder to cry on or reassurance for doubts.

"I'm not feeling well. And it's loud in here."

"My place is right around the corner, and my parents should be out for the next few hours. We could go there. Or to a love hotel, if you'd rather." She bit her lower lip. "Maybe you could finally show me your apartment, and I could nurse you back to health?"

"Not my apartment." The refusal came out firmer than she'd intended. Shaking her head, the drops of blood suspended on her chin and the inside lip of her mask splattered on the clean white linen of the tablecloth.

"Is that blood? Are you bleeding!?"

"Don't make a scene, I-*chan*," she whispered sharply. She closed her eyes, took a breath, and softly added, "Please."

Ichika clutched Rei's hands tightly. "Did someone hurt you?" The anxiety in her voice kept escalating. "Should we go to the hospital? To the police?"

Rei glanced at the other patrons and staff, thankful her girlfriend's outburst had gone unnoticed. She weighed the advantage of a love hotel's anonymity with the prospect of onsite supplies at Ichika's apartment and the pharmacy directly beneath it. "Your place is fine." She tried to link her mask with the bear-shaped terminal but couldn't navigate the interface with her blurred vision. She reached into her coat, thumbed a bill from her stack, and placed a 10,000 yen note on the table. "Order us coffee and a slice of cake for yourself to go."

"I'll get it. They don't accept paper money here." Her voice quivered.

The smart thing would be to head home. Rei could always pick up things with Ichika when she'd healed and the heat was off. However, her desire to be cared for was overwhelming. She found herself unconsciously nodding in small movements before enforcing stillness.

Ichika put on cute, oversized UkiyoARs, framed in the same auburn colour as her highlights and completed a series of gestures toward the small terminal at the table's edge. Rei took a handkerchief and tried to wipe the worst of the fresh blood from the bottom of her mask and chin, discreetly palming it into the pocket of her overcoat to spare Ichika the sight of the saturated cloth. Several minutes later, one of the maid-uniformed waitresses arrived at their table with a custom coffee tray designed to appear like a swing set—one cup had artwork of Keiko and the other Kuma-*chan*. Clear plastic decorated with clouds surrounded everything and was tied off with a bright red ribbon. The handle was fashioned as a tree branch, anchoring two transparent cords for string on either side. Even with the dramatic effects of climate change on Japan, excessive takeout packaging destined for landfills was an expected premium.

Ichika slipped on a candy-floss pink overcoat and reached to hold hands as they exited the cafe. She always tried, no matter how many times Rei had historically pulled away. *Just this once*. Rei tried to convince herself it was magnanimity instead of her need for a sincere touch.

Her head pounded with every step, but her vision had cleared sufficiently to see the scowls of condemnation from people they passed on the street. Ichika was oblivious to the judgement of strangers. Her girlfriend's natural exuberance and upbeat nature returned by increments the closer they were to her home. Keiko and Kuma-*chan* swung carefree with every step, and the bouquet of roses was tucked safely under her arm.

She couldn't tell if Ichika was self-absorbed or trying to take Rei's mind off the situation by talking non-stop about anything coming to mind. She decided the girl was nervous and overcompensating. Rei settled into appreciating the one-way conversation, which only required an occasional word of response to maintain. In Ichika, she saw a dated reflection of herself and her sister. They used to act the same as children when her father had come home beaten and bloody.

She wanted to laugh and cry at the same time.

Tightly flanked by a pharmacy and Lawson convenience store, the narrow foyer of the low-rise apartment smelled the way old buildings did—technically clean but with a musty, slightly off-putting scent from decades of age. A uniformed man at the tiny reception desk smiled fondly at Ichika before eyeing Rei's masked appearance warily. His expression turned pragmatic as the suite of paid-access APIs tried to match her overall form and visual patterns to an identity. They waited patiently for the elevator doors to open and took it to the fifth floor.

The utilitarian two-bedroom apartment was typical of modest households. A compact kitchen immediately to the right of the entrance connected to a small family room with a couch facing a large monitor bracketed at eye level and several cushions arranged around the *kotatsu* between them. Rei had begged her father for a *kotatsu* when she'd been young, but his comfort had always been at the bottom of a bottle, not in the shared experience of being warmed under the insulated skirt of a low, heated table. Two digital frames hung on the walls, cycling silently through movies inexpertly captured on handhelds or first-generation UkiyoARs. They were awkwardly placed and drew attention to the deficit of design elements in the rest of the environment.

Rei's head swam with dizziness as she removed her boots and stepped into the pink slippers set out for her. She'd barely stood back up before Ichika reached to retract her mask, her face pinched with worry and anxiety. Rei wanted to push away her girlfriend's eager hand but allowed herself to be unmasked. The day was full of bitter firsts. Ichika gasped and collapsed to her knees on the cheap laminate flooring, eyes welling with tears.

"Who did that to you, Rei?"

She was unprepared for Ichika's horror and concern. A bolt of fear ran down her spine—she might be worse than she imagined. "It doesn't matter."

She hung up her overcoat, unwrapped her silk scarf, sticky with drying blood, and stepped past Ichika. She beelined directly to the washroom, needing to take stock of the damage.

Her heart quickened, and a sick knot formed in her stomach as she looked into the small mirror above the sink. Blood painted her mouth, chin, and neck. It stained the collar of her white shirt, spotted her fitted grey suit, and even dribbled from one ear where her solitaire earring had ripped the lobe, but not entirely. She was thankful the diamond remained, albeit slightly askew. It had been a gift from one of her corporate suitors, and Rei would've been stretched to replace it accurately. Her eyes were already starting to blacken, and her face was badly swollen on one side. Everything was tender or painful to the most delicate touch. So much trauma in so few seconds. It was no wonder her father, a once-celebrated legend of gruelling twenty-five-minute cage battles, came home thoroughly abused, even in victory.

She laid her suit jacket carefully over the portable washing machine. Next came her tie, pants, and knee-length stockings. She caught sight of Ichika timidly staring from the edge of the doorway, clutching the door frame as though bracing against a typhoon. Rei held eye contact through the mirror as she unbuttoned her white shirt, failing to gain strength from seeing weakness. Clad in underwear, she was vulnerable and exposed. The weakness and fear of a victim clung to her even in safety. She was frozen in place, pathetic, hating herself.

With an economy of movement, Ichika removed her clothes in the hallway. Naked, she waited for permission to enter. Rei closed her eyes. The door to the shower and bathroom opened, and the water started to run. Ichika's arms delicately wrapped around her waist, and her girlfriend's body pressed against her back. The sounds of water running, of breathing, of heartbeats. They stayed still for long minutes until Ichika unclasped Rei's bra, removed her underwear, carefully set her jewellery aside, and led her into the shower.

The water turned pink as it pooled around on the tiled floor before swirling down the drain. Rei stood under the warm water, allowing herself to be cleansed by careful, compassionate hands. There were soft, intermittent kisses to the nape of her neck or the small of her back. Vulnerable places. Reflected in the shower's floor-to-ceiling mirror, Rei was more naked than ever, utterly devoid of costume, makeup, and pretence. Ichika, usually shy and self-conscious while unclothed, moved without inhibition. Mascara streaked down her cheeks, and her matted hair clung awkwardly to her face.

Rei's remaining strength ebbed as the water turned clear. Her legs felt like rubber, her balance elusive. Standing was an exercise of will. The press of their bodies together, Ichika's gentle touch, and repeated whispers, *You're safe now, it's okay*. Rei thought the trembling was coming from her girlfriend but realized she was the source. Angry, hurt, frustrated, trembling. Weak, self-loathing, pathetic trembling.

Her stomach folded in on itself. Her knees buckled, and she would've collapsed to the tiles if not for the embrace guiding her to the floor. She cried in violent, heaving, and uncontrolled spasms. Graceless. She hated herself for it, for being a victim, for her powerlessness. Ichika crouched behind her, holding her. The water cascaded over them, somehow colder despite the fixed temperature.

Ichika removed the insulated cover from the moulded acrylic bathtub. It was tall and squat, designed for sitting, and filled with steaming hot water. She shut off the shower, helped Rei to her feet, and into the tub. As Rei eased into it, Ichika carefully folded a pair of fresh washcloths—one to cushion the back of her head and the other for her forehead. Afterward, she took the blood-stained cloth, folded it once, and placed it on the tiles beside the tub for her to kneel on. She leaned forward to delicately kiss Rei's swollen eyes, then the corner of her mouth tenderly. Ichika rested her face on her folded arms and perched on the lip of the bathtub.

"I'd never betray your trust, Rei."

Rei mouthed her acknowledgement more than speaking it. Her throat constricted as though Akira was still strangling her. She was tempted to unburden herself from her tyranny of secrets. To Ichika, she was strong. To her family, she was straight. To her targets, she was attainable. To society, she was a model citizen.

She was none of those things. There was no way out, no truth to tender without punitive stigma and rejection. She'd earned some of it, she acknowledged, but any remaining empathy would be usurped by the lies she used as commerce and wore as armour.

This painful serenity, this moment of throbbing aches, of blood and bruises and active deceit, was the clearest moment of honesty she'd lived since childhood. It was inhospitable, incalculably reductive. She could never withstand a more frequent pace of truth.

6

Mathis

MATHIS WOKE WITH A start—heart racing, clammy skin. While he couldn't remember the dream that had shocked him alert, he remained gripped in heightened anxiety. It would've been a chase dream. Probably dogs again. It took a moment to recognize there was a man sitting at the foot of the bed, staring at him as though he were a piece of mildly interesting furniture.

The stranger was dressed in an all-white, similar to the strange woman he'd met in the downtown park. Suit and overcoat, and old-school, optical correction glasses. He sported the type of short, grey beard long periods of neglect between shaving would account for. His face was like an old baseball glove—worn, stained with patches of liver spots, and deeply creased by past sorrows. Mathis' hardcover copy of *How to Talk to Your Hamster About the Coming Apocalypse* was in the man's left hand with his thumb bookmarking a page a third of the way through.

Mathis' heart lurched and he scrambled to a sitting position, holding both hands before him. He wanted to shout, but his teeth were clenched shut in panic, his body stiffened, locking in vulnerability. The man frowned, raised an eyebrow, and showed the face of the book in accusation.

Bewilderment loosened his locked jaw. "A gift from my dad."

Mathis reached for his Net contacts case on the bedside table, and fumbled to wear them. The man sighed, sounding disappointed, and waved for Mathis to continue. After some fumbling, blinking, and correction, the lenses automatically transitioned to the low-light environment of his room, amplifying visual inputs and the judgement on the stranger's face.

The man tossed the book to the floor, gestured at the stark black and white, hard-lined, modern interior of the bedroom and began speaking in a thick French-Canadian accent. "This place has no soul, no art or character. I ask myself, what sort of asshole wants to live in a home like this?"

Mathis couldn't wrap his head around defending interior design to an intruder. It was disjointed and disarming at the same time. Instinctively, he pulled the duvet higher up his chest. "I had the option to buy the model unit."

"You must be doing well."

"Forty-year mortgage," Mathis said evenly, avoiding sarcasm.

The man stood casually and turned to face the nearest wall. "I can handle this pup by myself, Hunter. Wait for me in the other room."

A giant of a man materialized in view. Mathis wasn't sure if it was a light-bending tech the military used or digital cloaking, broadcasting a false image to his Net contacts. Either way, the man was well practised at being unseen—an unsettling accomplishment since he was over two metres tall, hunched. Hunter's face showed signs of moderate gigantism. His over-pronounced jawline, prominent forehead, and sheer size were arresting. The weathered, ballistic-grade jacket he wore had irregular lumps and protrusions. Mathis heart raced as he imagined an arsenal of weapons, ammunition, and plates of reinforced armour. Two hook-shaped knives and a pair of pistol grips were visible. Despite his size, Hunter made no sound as he exited the room with an economy of motion.

Mathis recalled his stalker's words. *I'll have to tell them if you don't give me another option, and it'll go different than this.* He tried to swallow his bubbling panic.

"As I made my way here this evening, Mathis, I wondered whether I would find a kindred spirit. Instead, I found you asleep in your pyjamas while your city burns and the precious seeds of rebellion blossom in the hearts of millions. I ask myself, what type of man would turn off his mental lights on the first night of these Days of Anger?"

The incongruence between the man's calm, conversational tone and his terrifying presence were impossible for Mathis to reconcile. "Who are you?"

"I'm Benoit Rochon, and judging from your face, I can see you're a man who knows nothing about your nation's history. As for why I'm here, it's because there's freezing rain tonight. Not enough to threaten the fires consuming the excess of privilege, but sufficient to ground drones from passing overhead."

Mathis tried to contact emergency services, one of the first, imminently practical thought commands he'd mastered with his prototype contacts, but couldn't get a Net connection. There was a localized digital countermeasure in play. His mouth went dry, a rivulet of sweat rolled down his side, his heart pounded. Mathis had managed to go his whole life without physically fighting, and he doubted he could overpower Benoit, who appeared twice his age and had lived those years hard. The only thing between him and the men in his home was the thick duvet his ex-girlfriend had insisted he purchase before she'd spend the night.

"What do you want?" He grimaced, hearing his voice squeak.

Benoit walked to the window, focusing on the expanse of Toronto's fashion district. "For the world to punish the tyranny of wealth and carve collective freedom from the established order."

Mathis failed to put the answer in any plausible context. "What does that even mean?"

He smiled easily, turned to face Mathis and leaned against the windowsill. Cold, winter rain silently pelted the glass. "Not everything fits in neat, programmer-friendly compartments."

"I'm a bio-digital architect with—"

"That's one." Benoit held up a single finger in prohibition. "I was once like you but less stupid. I believed I could use technology for purpose and spent years of my life writing algorithms to capture the very essence of a person. Not this bullshit passed off by commercialized AI spamming social platforms, but the truest form of who someone was distilled from countless data sources. For years, I compromised databases, pillaged feeds from the surveillance state, and integrated new suites of variables. I even created sub-packages to generate causality between micro-expressions and environmental context."

Mathis hadn't recognized Benoit's name, but the infamy of his achievements was well known throughout the Net, spanning subcultures as disparate as AI architects, ethical theorists, and hacktivists. He shook his head, eyes widened.

"You're Adversus... You created Carnivore."

"Carnivore is their fucking abomination, perverted from the ruins of my ambition. Don't speak that name to me again," Benoit spat.

"It's a bane to privacy and human rights. Why would you create such a thing?"

"I wanted to discover the Warrior Poet King who could build an egalitarian society from the ruins of this debased culture. My years of work, dedication, and sacrifice made me realize no individual walking the face of the Earth is worthy of our collective trust. Everyone is corruptible, only possessing integrity within the finite box of their immediate opportunity."

"Seems you could've benefitted from peer review," Mathis muttered.

"That's two." He raised two fingers for effect, sneering. "You think you're clever? What do you know? You, with your middle-class upbringing, never knowing what it is to be without, never having to choose between medicine or food, never having to defend yourself. You know nothing. Your privileged life has allowed that big brain of yours to not wither from hunger and avoid getting smashed by geographical conflicts. You won the birth lottery. The hardest obstacles you've had to overcome in your life are ones systemic to this travesty of culture. You subscribe to them, empower them, and adhere to your place within them. You consider yourself elite, having earned the top percentile in your industry, and confuse rank with life's meaning. You're the embodiment of ignorant privilege. You lack the strength, resilience, and integrity to deal with injustice. You may be gifted in raw intellect, but you're unqualified to leverage it. *Tabarnak,* those motherfuckers stole my work to repress the masses. That's what will happen to your crowning achievement, your vision. It will become their most brutal, indiscriminate and pervasive weapon."

The sentiment cut into Mathis, each word pushing the metaphoric blade deeper until the ache in his chest made it hard to breathe. Benoit, dressed in crisp white, was like an avenging angel hovering a few steps away from the bed. It was surreal. He knew it wasn't a dream since his nightmares were surprisingly banal. Mathis didn't know what to say. He remained quiet, waiting for Benoit to speak.

"Dress yourself. It's like I'm talking to a child, and I need you to be more than a frightened boy in pyjamas, hiding under a duvet."

Benoit entered the kitchen. Mathis heard cabinets being flung open, contents roughly manipulating, and the careless clattering of objects on the synthetic bamboo flooring. He wondered what the old Quebec anarchist could possibly be searching for. When his large, monochromatic, abstract impressionist print made a warbling sound before crashing to the ground, Mathis remembered the wine rack. Not a drinker himself, he'd found the built-in wine rack an unnecessary eyesore and had concealed it with one of the recommended art prints which were part of the model unit. He struggled to recall whether the bottles from when he took possession of the condominium years ago were still there. The distinct sound of a cork being pulled free answered his speculation.

The seamless doors of the wardrobe retracted as Mathis scrambled out of bed, triggered by his proximity. He slipped into his basic home uniform of blue jeans, grey cotton t-shirt, and black hooded sweater, shoulder nervously checking every few moments for spying eyes. The chill synthetic bamboo flooring left ghostly impressions of heat from his bare feet as he walked to the foot of the bed and stepped into his open-backed slippers. They were shaped and decorated as bread loaves—another gag gift from his parents, but comfortable enough to be spared from donation. He cursed his habit of turning off the in-floor heating at night, and briefly considered arming himself with something, but there was nothing remotely weapon-like in his bedroom. Even if there had been, he sincerely doubted his ability to be anything more than a victim should the situation escalate. Mathis squeezed his eyes shut, willing himself past the fear paralysis inhibiting his stride. With the small, robotic steps of someone attending their execution, he put one bread-slippered foot in front of the other and forced himself to the adjoining living room.

Benoit scowled at Mathis' feet.

"They're warm," Mathis explained self-consciously.

Benoit was drinking directly from a wine bottle and gestured disgustedly at the corporate-flavoured, abstract impressionist canvases breaking the sterile white monotony of the interior. "Those come with the interior package?"

"Yep." Mathis scanned for the enormous man, growing more anxious when he was nowhere in sight. "Where's your friend?"

"The grapes in the south of France have never produced the same wine since climate change. None of the bottles in your rack are worth drinking." He scowled through another sip.

"I don't entertain. Your friend?" Mathis glanced around again.

"Hunter is no more a friend than you are, Mathis. He's a tool and comfortable as such."

Mathis crossed both arms in front of his chest to stop himself from wringing his hands. He gave one final look for Hunter. "What do you want?"

"I know you made a deal with the devil, believing you can outsmart him. You can't. When you architected wetware, you assumed its ethical responsibilities. And when pressured, you rolled over like a bitch. A coward can't be trusted to hold the fate of humanity."

"You can't pin humanity's fate on one person."

Benoit sighed audibly, shaking his head and holding up three fingers. Mathis struggled to read into the resignation and disappointment, but the appearance of Hunter stiffened him in wide-eyed panic. The man had both fists in a high guard, covering his face and chin like an experienced boxer.

"I'll give you the first shot." Hunter's voice was deep and unnervingly calm.

Mathis shook his head in a blend of fear and confusion. "I don't want to hit you."

"You think you can actually hurt me?"

"I—" The question hung in the air, an accusation of impotence, demanding to be answered, bewildering and terrifying. He hadn't been in a physical confrontation since a playground incident in childhood.

"Don't drag it out, Hunter," Benoit instructed.

Hunter shrugged and threw a combination—a left hook into Mathis' liver and a crushing right straight into his sternum. Mathis' vision exploded in a shock of blinding pain, and his body crumpled like a marionette with its strings cut. Instinct curled him into the fetal position. He gasped, coughing in uncontrollable spasms. His body wasn't responding right. Like someone was flipping the switch to his nervous system on and off. Eventually, the coughing and retching subsided, and he struggled to his elbows and knees. The urge to stop, to collapse into the smothering pain, was strong, but the sensation of being vulnerable was stronger. He willed himself to push off and turn into a seated position, his eyes scanning frantically for Hunter, but all he found was Benoit's disdain. Mathis dug in his palms and heels to push distance between them until his back pressed against the thick frosted glass separating the living area from the bedroom.

"Yet another problem with the modern age. Growing up in a nanny state, young men can't take a punch anymore." Benoit swigged from the bottle. "Consider yourself lucky Hunter spared your pretty face."

Mathis was nauseous. He searched for Hunter, dread mounting when the man was confoundingly nowhere in sight. "What do you want?" he gasped.

"Initially, I came here to try to recruit you, but I can see now it was a misguided idea. You've chosen to weaponize the future and promised a backdoor into humanity to solidify the tyranny of the status quo."

He'd been pushing the despair and helplessness far from his mind, but it welled up in a crippling torrent. "He threatened everyone connected to me. My family, friends, colleagues—"

"These are the consequences of trying to change the world."

"What would you have me do?" he whimpered.

"Are you rolling over like a bitch for me, too?" Benoit laughed. *"Criss,* you're surprisingly spineless for a visionary."

The truth hurt more than Hunter's blows. "What would you do if you were me?"

"Engage me with courage, and I'll answer your question."

Mathis tried will it of himself, but there was no reservoir to draw from. He gambled faking it. "Fine. What would you do?"

Benoit stepped closer and squatted down to share eye level, holding Mathis' gaze captive with his intensity. "I'd make each person who used wetware develop a slow, building intolerance in the face of privilege. I'd implement crippling guilt and self-loathing in those who exercised wealth without balance or empathy. I'd inoculate the populace against the greed and elitism that fouls political systems and ensures only a fraction of the world can live with opportunity." He drank from the bottle and gave a contemplative swish to the remaining wine. "While I was at it, I'd eradicate pointless scourges like homophobia, racism, bigotry, and religion. No sense in removing one tyranny while leaving others to flourish."

"So, social engineering."

Benoit grinned menacingly at the challenge. "I would make the one percent grapple with self-disgust, self-loathing, and the desire for penance each time they exercised excess privilege. If any could push past that, I'd make them flare their nostrils like a bull, bark like dogs, and twitch uncontrollably. It's time to take off their hoods, their masks of flesh, which enable these ghouls to hide amongst the living."

Mathis' heartbeat raced to match his anxiety. "You're delusional."

"No, I am fury. I am righteous indignation. I am a weapon." Benoit stood straight and agitatedly paced. "I'm not against money. Without it, how could we have labs of scientists who cure diseases, schools to teach children, or fresh produce to eat? I'm against the weaponization of treatments to enrich shareholders and rob the masses who have to choose between food and ineffective medicines each month. I'm against the rape of the environment that leaves the world toxic, poor, and beholden to enrich the few. I'm against how greed and deception have been codified, sanctioned, and intrinsically rewarded."

"You think it'll change by eliminating the one percent?"

"There'll always be a one percent. That's inescapable math. The role of Minus One is to punish and to keep punishing until a better world is created. People don't intrinsically grasp causality. They need to be taught that both the rich and poor must earn their place in society. There are no bloodless solutions, no legislative approaches. It's the moral imperative of the citizenry to destroy the luxuries of the elite, eliminate their places of refuge, and make them understand they live at the discretion of the many."

Mathis' palms were sweating, his skin itchy. "It's a negative sum game. You give people nothing."

"I'd give them a path to justice. And your vision is...?"

"To amplify people. Allow them to be as lousy or incredible as they want."

"So, giving monkeys fire," Benoit succinctly concluded.

"That's pretty much the sum of it." He didn't quite grasp the stakes he was gambling with but pressed on with half-truths and unfelt courage. "I've encoded a user's unique neural pattern to act as the core transactional key. Already, the model is sufficiently intrinsic, recursive, and unassailable to people like you and Frost. I've already baked it into the code repository, trunk, and branches. There's no rollback to a clean source without losing all the progress. In short, there's no back door for you or Frost, and there never will be."

Benoit's smile caught somewhere between anger and appreciation. "Prometheus couldn't avoid an eternity of agony inflicted upon him by the gods."

Mathis became aware of Hunter appearing in his peripheral vision. Instinctively, he took two steps back.

"The rain's easing off, and drones will be airborne shortly." Hunter gestured at Mathis. "Breathing or not?"

Benoit ignored Hunter's question, pulled a microdrive from the inner pocket of his white overcoat, and placed it on the counter. "You'll implement this code in the core architecture."

Mathis started to protest, but a glance at Hunter's alarming grip on the handle of his karambit knife made him freeze.

"Tell me you understand, Mathis."

He didn't know what else to do other than capitulate again. "I understand."

"And when we talk next, I expect you to be more."

"More what?"

"Just *more*."

7

Tatsuo

TATSUO DIDN'T UNDERSTAND WHY the plane had circled the vast airport for twenty minutes, waiting for landing clearance. Before she had left Japan for Toronto, Miyu tried to explain the ongoing flight restrictions. Something about international protocols and climate change. Or was he confusing her complaints about the state of the world? He'd grown used to his youngest daughter's attraction to causes and had nodded, agreeing with her as she rambled about the things he didn't care about.

Tatsuo nervously clenched his fists and cracked his knuckles. It had been a long time since he'd seen Miyu. His relationship with her had been less turbulent than with Rei but somehow more tenuous. She'd been slipping from his grasp for years, and he didn't know how to stop it from happening. It would never be as it had been when his girls were little, before Miyu's misdiagnosis, when his daughters expressed affection and delight when he came home. Tatsuo had long since given up trying to discover what he'd done to sour them. He'd always done his best. Maybe it wasn't enough, but it was all he had to offer.

He walked the long, winding hallways of Pearson International Airport by dozens of other well-dressed passengers who'd gotten off the mostly empty direct flight from Osaka to Toronto. As he made his way through the countless roped-off switchbacks in the vast customs area, Tatsuo unfolded the documents from his inside jacket pocket. Rei had exhaustively instructed him on why they couldn't get damaged—something about eInk—but they seemed fine to his eyes. He was proud of how resourceful and clever Rei had grown. She'd be okay after he was gone. Better off, no doubt.

People were queuing up behind a row of terminal platforms, and Tatsuo did likewise. Unlike him, everyone wore UkiyoARs. The other travellers gave Tatsuo a wide berth and kept stealing glances at his face or his incongruent fashion—a worn-out leather coat, MMA-themed sweater, and denim pants. When a terminal came free, he stepped up to it and was immediately confused by the lack of interface. He waved his hand over the platform, trying to summon a screen. Next, he tried tapping and, subsequently, banging on it. Everyone else seemed to be experiencing no trouble. He rubbed the back of his neck in frustration.

There was a digital display of what he assumed were instructions, but none of the languages were Japanese. He concluded his terminal was broken, waited for the person next to him to finish, and took their place. Again, nothing. He looked around for a human, and gestured to the armed customs officers scanning people as they passed the bottleneck between them.

"Over here! Fucking thing doesn't work."

Tatsuo didn't consider whether the Toronto customs officers understood Japanese, and there was no way he was going to wear the goofy, in-ear translator Rei had insisted he take with him. He figured the customs officers didn't hear him. He repeated himself louder and added an irritated gesture at the blank platform. One of the officers stared at him, mouthing words he couldn't hear and wouldn't comprehend even if he could. Tatsuo left the terminal and approached the officer.

"Piece of shit doesn't do anything." He tried to hand over the folded packet of travel documents.

The man said something, but Tatsuo had forgotten all the English he'd been forced to endure in high school. He'd never been any good at it and had no interest in going anywhere where people spoke English anyway. He tried to walk past the two officers, but they immediately intercepted him. Irritated, he correctly interpreted the aggressive gestures to step off to the side. One looked as though he could take a punch, but the other was some skinny kid in a uniform. Tatsuo amused himself at the thought of taking both customs officers on and making a run for it.

Eventually, a young woman approached him, dressed in the same uniform as the officers but lacking a sidearm or baton.

"Please come with me, sir." Her eyes darted between the stitches on his brow and the bruises on his face.

He laughed out loud. A brown person speaking formal Japanese in another country was unexpectedly entertaining. He nodded, grunted his response, and followed her out of the sprawling customs intake room, down a hallway, and into a smaller side room. A dozen wickets were protected by reinforced glass before a sprawl of empty seats. She led him to one, instructed him to wait, and disappeared through a side door. A few moments later, she appeared behind the raised wicket. He pushed the packet of documents at her through the slim opening in the glass. She unfolded and began processing them sequentially, scanning each into an authenticator.

"What's your purpose in coming to Canada, Mr. Yoshida?"

"Doesn't it say in there?"

"Please answer the question, sir."

"My daughter, Miyu." He tried to remember the details Rei had relentlessly coached him on. "She's sick and alone. She needs her father." He was confident he got the gist of it.

"What exactly is her condition?"

"Listen, lady, I'm no doctor. I used to fight for a living and wouldn't have left Japan if my daughter didn't need me." He gestured at the documents. "All the medical stuff is in there."

"And where will you stay?"

He shrugged. "My other daughter wrote it all down for me. She's thorough. Anything you need will be in there. I might as well sit down and wait for you to finish up."

He turned to walk away, ignoring her protests. He was tired from his sleepless transpacific flight, and the wide, padded seat in the waiting area was as comfortable as it looked. He crossed his arms over his chest, stretched out his aching legs, and closed his eyes. Thus far, he wasn't enjoying his first experience of international travel.

An armed officer approached, barking commands and standing over him an arm's length away. Tatsuo unflinchingly held the man's gaze as the officer puffed out his chest, pointed in stabbing motions, and repeated instructions in an ever-louder voice.

"I don't understand a fucking word you're saying." Tatsuo used the blunt grammar one would use to address a victim.

He closed his eyes again, ignoring the noise of the customs officer's voice. Eventually, he went away with the sound of angry footfalls. It was blissfully quiet for a few minutes.

He was certain he didn't like travelling.

"Sir. Sir? We're not done. I need you to return to the wicket to be processed."

The brown lady had returned. Tatsuo admired how she spoke. Formal, like an NHK broadcaster with their crisp Tokyo standard, but not nearly as smug. Also, she had no issues comprehending his rough Osaka dialect. "Your Japanese is good. Where'd you learn it?"

"Please return to the wicket, sir." She walked away.

Tatsuo was scanned and documented thoroughly—hand and fingerprints, retinas and face. He volunteered to piss in a cup, but the woman didn't seem to appreciate his offer. She explained his visa was temporary and conditional, and he could be removed from the country at any time. He nodded, grunting his understanding as she spoke, waiting for it to end. It was the same pattern he defaulted to whenever dealing with people he couldn't ignore, intimidate, or punch. Eventually, he was released, and made his way down another long series of hallways and stairs to get to the baggage carousel, where he retrieved his duffle bag. His knees were acting up after enduring the long flight in economy class, and all the walking increased the irritation. The exit to the public atrium was mercifully close, however.

As he walked through the automatic doors, a voice called out, *otousan*. Father. He grinned ear to ear. Tatsuo scanned the crowd for Miyu in vain. It wasn't anything like Japan. There was a bewildering variety of people—asians, blacks, browns, whites, and all the colours in between.

A skinny figure cloaked in all-white, wearing large, mirrored goggles and a polished ventilator, wove effortlessly through the assembled crowd, beelining directly to him. Tatsuo dropped his duffle, took giant steps toward her, and grabbed Miyu in a ferocious hug. She started squirming against his grip, but he was too happy to care. He picked her up off the ground, swinging her around in a circle before relenting to her sharp protests and setting her down again. She was light, a child's weight. His fingers skated over her unnervingly sharp ribs.

"Let's go." Her sharp words betrayed no emotion as she turned and entered the crowd.

He picked up his duffle and hurried to follow, bumping into people along the way. People in Toronto didn't know how to move amongst groups. They smelled strange, too. He couldn't quite put his finger on it. A subtle, unpalatable blend of sour milk, wet dog, ginger, cabbage, or curries, depending on what part of the crowd he was pushing his way through. He wrinkled his nose, glad it'd been broken numerous times in the past. After the double doors opened to the cutting chill of the outside weather, he caught up with Miyu as she stopped in front of the car service cue.

"Let's take the train." Tatsuo gestured to the iconic sign.

Miyu shook her head in response, not even looking at him, and stepped forward in the cue. He knew something was wrong but couldn't figure out what. He resolved to sort it out later, as was his habit when dealing with problems involving his daughters. After a few moments, a white minivan pulled up, came to a stop, and auto-retracted the side panel door. With no driver, the inside was spacious and configured with luggage racks. Miyu slipped in, voicing what he assumed was an address in English. She sounded cold, intelligent, and worldly. Where had his precious little girl gone? He tossed his duffle on the racks and eased back into the luxurious leather chairs. The minivan silently sped off as soon as he closed the door.

"Hey, let's get something to eat. I'm starving."

Miyu yanked an unmarked, silver foil packet of nutrient gel from her coat pocket and unceremoniously shoved it at him.

He held up the small packet uncomprehendingly. "What am I supposed to do with this?"

"It's a meal equivalent."

He wasn't used to her cold tone. He frowned with equal measures of disapproval and hurt. He'd come to expect it from Rei, but never from Miyu. She was closed off from him in her mask, ventilator, and cowl. He reached across to grab her shoulder and pulled her to face him.

He leaned closer, forcing a smile, and said softly, "Hey, don't be like that. I'm here. It's been years since I've seen you. Take off the gear, okay?"

She slapped away his reaching hand, abruptly pulled away from reach, and shifted over to create more distance between them. He felt like a dog smacked by its owner, dejected and not comprehending the burst of malice. Only his daughters could make him this pathetic. She held still for several heartbeats, sighed, and pulled back her cowl to reveal a shaved head. Unclasping the ventilator, she let it hang at the side of her dangerously skinny face, and hesitated before finally removing her mirrored goggles.

His heart sank, and tears welled in his eyes. His posture crumpled. He struggled to speak, to give voice to the desperate need to reject the mutilation of flesh and steel where there'd once been eyes.

"My beautiful little girl, what did you do to yourself?"

8
Miyu

MIYU WAS THANKFUL WHEN the taxi's doors unlocked after the payment transaction went through on the stolen banking information. She could sense her father's smothering disapproval as she put back on her mirrored goggles and ventilator, opened the door, and stepped into the cold evening air of one of the last remaining industrial zones inside the city.

They hadn't spoken ever since he'd seen her eyes.

There was no point in explaining that she'd been part of a DIY bio-hacker collective or describing the horrifically unpredictable and painful results of her failed transhuman experiment. He wouldn't understand the promise of a permanent thought-controlled Net interface, and she barely understood how she'd ended up as an abomination herself.

Tatsuo slung his duffle over his shoulder, scanning the industrial neighbourhood. A chemical stink saturated the air, double rings of razor wire menaced the tall fences peppered with electrical warnings, and burned-out street lights stood as towers for antiquated CCTV cameras to scan in slow motion. Stacks of brown brick factory buildings lay beyond the electrified perimeters, with boarded or broken windows and garbage cluttering their courtyards. The district had already been rezoned, but the ground was contaminated. The entire place had a foul odour of burning plastic and used diapers. The CCT cameras had long since had their lenses vandalized and moved as blind sentries atop the fortifications of a kingdom time had forgotten.

"If you have to pee, you should go now."

Ignoring her father's dumbfounded expression, she slipped behind a shoulder-height stack of construction waste, discarded furniture, and unmarked black plastic bags, making sure he had no line of sight. She waited, pricking up her ears to detect movement, before pulling down her leggings and squatting in a practised movement. She wished she could control the sound of her stream as it cut through the silence, sensing her father's revulsion growing impossibly deeper. He'd always seen her as his darling little girl, and now she was an unfathomable stranger, a broken degenerate, and a skeletal freak.

"There's no place to go once we're inside." She pulled up her leggings and discarded the tissue amongst the many crevices of garbage.

"I'm not a dog."

"I'm not a dog, either," she whispered.

Tatsuo recoiled, his pained expression unable to settle between hurt, disgust, and confusion. "That's not what I mean, Miyu." He gestured around. "This is no place for my little girl. Rei gave me some money. Let's get something to eat and find a hotel."

She shook her head and sifted through the debris until she found a mostly clean cardboard box filled with non-organic waste, dumped it, and broke it down into a long, folded strip. Miyu started walking along the fence line. "This way."

Tatsuo followed dumbly and stopped calling out her name when she refused to acknowledge it. A stone's throw from the main street, Miyu crouched beside a breach cut into the fence. The hairs on her arms and the back of her neck stood on end as she pinned the grounding wire of the low-tech current tester and touched the fence with the contacts. She pushed the folded stack of cardboard through the opening, waited for the current tester to signal again, and scrambled through with an ease born of habit.

"There's a pulse every five seconds. You'll need to be quick."

Tatsuo crouched down, judged the size of the opening, and frowned. "Nope."

"You'll fit, Dad. You just need to be fast." She reached through the opening, grabbed the strap of his duffle, waited for the pulse to go by, and pulled it through. It was surprisingly heavy. "What's in here?"

"Omiyage."

Miyu absently counted the seconds, toying with the idea of what gifts he'd brought her from Japan. Tatsuo's strangled grunt as he failed to make it through the opening in time snapped her back into the present. Instinctively, she grabbed his coat by the shoulders, dug in her heels, and pulled as hard as she could. The trace scent of burnt hair, plastic, and metal made it through the respirator's filter.

Tatsuo clawed clear of the fence and sat cross-legged on the cold ground. His breathing was quick, and he'd broken an immediate sweat in the chill night air. After a time, he struggled to his feet and shook out his limbs.

"That'll wake you up," he laughed, grinning for the first time since she'd revealed her face.

It would've been more convenient if he had a bad heart and had died there. There'd be some awkward explaining to do with Rei, but less than having him alive. Her father had once again proven himself unkillable. Disappointed, she tucked the cardboard under her arm, pushed the duffle towards him, and made her way to the retracted ladder of the building's rusted-out fire escape. Miyu snapped her fingers twice, and a young girl's small, dirty face emerged from a formless heap of materials easily mistaken for garbage. The ladder lowered in increments after.

"What are we doing here, Miyu?"

She ignored her father's question and climbed up the ladder. The child, dressed in a collection of stitched rags and stray materials, waited patiently with both hands in front of her. Mucus ran from one nostril onto her upper lip, but Echo didn't notice. Her skin was pale from cold, the dark circles around her haunted eyes like spilled ink. Her straw-like hair was pulled into two braids, tied off with raw string, and hanging at either side of her face. Miyu gave her two packets of nutrient gel.

"That's one for you and one for your mom."

"You shouldn't go in. Bearcat's looking for you." The small murmur of Echo's voice sounded haunted.

"I know. Be sure to only give one to your mom, okay?"

"Bearcat's real angry."

Tatsuo got to the landing and sized up the child. "Who's the street rat?"

Miyu grit her teeth, thankful her father didn't speak English. "Just bring up the ladder." She squatted down to face Echo and smiled affectionately. "It'll be okay." Even to her ears, the words sounded insincere. She owed Bearcat money, and he'd come for either flesh or blood until her debts got squared away.

Tatsuo slung the duffle over his shoulders, opened the fire door, and stepped inside. The door spring had long since been stolen, and the door slammed shut behind him. Miyu flinched at the catastrophically loud sound that would serve as a rally alarm for the building's denizens. She cursed in Japanese, touched Echo's head, and slipped in after her father. Already, half a dozen squatters armed with pipes, clubs, and knives had advanced in a loose semi-circle around him. More were scuttling up to the scene, peeking out from behind the large, graffiti-covered columns supporting the open expanse of the derelict factory.

The area was illuminated with an eclectic blend of warm and cold lighting. Barrel drum fires with jerry-rigged vents, LED hand-crank lamps suspected from makeshift wires, and sharp beams of flashlights carving the darkness to focus on Tatsuo. He dropped the duffle on the unfinished concrete floor, rolled his shoulders a few times, and cracked his neck. A smile started to form on his profile as his hands balled into murderous fists and he shifted his stance.

The crew of squatters and junkies should've already been rifling through Tatsuo's clothes and squabbling over items, but they hesitated. Her father was outnumbered, unarmed, and outmatched, but they still hesitated. Tatsuo manifested as an insurmountable force of nature—an indomitable mountain or merciless thunderstorm. She'd never seen footage of his fights, let alone anything suggesting the brutality she perceived barely contained within him. Her father had always struck her as a loser, coming home bloodied up and drunk, happily receiving the dutiful administrations of his two children. It never dawned on her to consider what he'd done to his opponents.

She rushed in front of Tatsuo, arms wide open, dropping the cardboard as she waved frantically. The flashlights' cutting illumination blinded her, and her optical dampeners were slow to engage in the eclectic lighting.

"It's okay, he's with me!"

She spun around to face her father, switching to Japanese. His focus was beyond her, a predator now, hungry and consumed with nearby prey.

"No, Dad, stop! Don't do this to me. Please!" She switched to English, pleading with the squatters. "Just back away. No one's got hurt yet. He's with me, okay? I'm responsible, okay?"

T-Ray, a lanky junkie drowning in an oversized jacket, unlaced combat boots, and knit cap pulled low on his face, lowered his length of pipe as he stepped out of the shadows. His lips were covered in blisters, his face ravaged with weeping sores. He licked his lips, showing his decaying brown teeth, fixating on Miyu.

"Bearcat wants a word with you, Ultra." His words came out mangled, barely intelligible, choked on a thick mix of drugs, desire, and malice.

She had many names in Toronto. Minus One called her Seventeen for her position within the local cell, the grinders who'd done her optics had referred to her as Alita after some obscure manga from the last century, and strangers routinely labelled her junkie, trash, or freak. Because of her eyes, Ultragirl had been Echo's suggested monicker, and it'd stuck with the current group.

"I know." Her heart was racing. She tried to keep her limbs from shaking, but the shock of adrenaline and fear was crashing over her. "That's not this, though."

T-Ray gestured with a lazy head movement, and the armed squatters moved away from the area. Murmurs of disappointment echoed as they retreated in clusters to the isolated illumination spots.

Tatsuo picked up his duffle and casually slung it over his shoulder. Miyu glowered, but was awestruck to see how he could turn the overwhelming aggression he possessed moments ago on and off like a switch. She expected him to at least comment on the narrowly avoided confrontation, but he simply pointed to a large piece of graffiti.

"What's that one say?"

"Rent is theft." Virtually every interior surface was a chaotic blend of tags, slogans, and artwork. She couldn't fathom the way her father's mind operated. "And what the hell are you thinking? You don't live here. I do. You don't have the right to come into my life and mess it up any more than it already is."

"You live in this shit hole?"

She was about to snap at him but remembered he'd been giving her money every month since she'd left Osaka, allegedly for rent and living expenses. A lot of money. There was no way to explain without making him furious. She picked up the cardboard and walked past him, carefully staying close to the wall as she did so. Her optics filtered the low light environment well, but her father kept tripping over the debris of garbage and fallen materials from the dying building. She was thankful he was at least ducking the lines of hanging clothes or veering around the furniture, demarcating the small personal boundaries of other inhabitants. A few adults greeted her as she passed, and all the children, but others, immobilized from drugs or lying strung out on salvaged mattresses, stared with their hollow eyes.

She ducked under the dead branches of her potted Japanese maple, placed strategically to alert her of potential threats through the tangle of small bells she'd secured on the wide-reaching spindling branches. Tatsuo walked through them, causing a cacophony of tinkling. He bumped into the empty stack of crates blocking access from the other side, knocking over the broken glass she'd set atop them. It didn't matter, she acknowledged, resigned. Bearcat already knew of her return, and there was no escaping the inevitable confrontation.

Miyu assumed anything of value left behind would've been immediately stolen, and a quick scan confirmed the fact. Why someone would take her small stack of Japanese books was beyond her, but anything someone could theoretically sell or fence was fair game without Bearcat's protection. Her naked mattress had been slashed and searched as well. Disappointed but unsurprised, she unfolded the cardboard into a long strip and flipped the single mattress over. She affixed the small flashlight she carried in her coat pocket to a hanging wire, adjusting the setting before turning it on. A diffuse cone of soft light provided barely enough illumination to cover her area. She gestured to the cardboard.

"That's your bed, the mattress is mine."

Tatsuo furrowed his eyebrows, hesitated, and took a half step closer. "Miyu—"

"Don't."

His shoulders sunk as though under the weight of disapproval, sadness, and assumed responsibility—a man collapsed, a father finally comprehending the extent of his failures. She took off her ventilator and goggles, placing them carefully in the eclectic stacks of empty boxes. Miyu regretted hanging the light, knowing it served to exacerbate her weight loss and illuminate her pathetic state. She edged back, but couldn't escape the spotlight.

She wished she could close her eyes, but they were always on.

Tatsuo put his back to the wall and slid down it into a seated posture. They sat in a heavy silence, neither having words to push through the drudge and oppression of years of shame and regret. After a time, he sighed heavily, reached into his duffle, and carefully placed items in the narrow strip of space between the cardboard and ruined single mattress she sat on. Four packages of *Peko-chan* milk-flavoured caramel candies, a small stack of manga comics, and a bottle of twelve-year-old Yamazaki.

He opened the whiskey, setting it between them. *"Omiyage."*

She pushed the bottle towards him. "I could never drink the hard stuff."

He shrugged and drank straight from the bottle. "I don't know what these are. I asked the woman to give me manga popular with girls."

"I'm not a girl anymore, Dad."

He didn't respond. She opened one of the *Pecko-chan* packages, unwrapped the candy, and savoured the chewing of it. A flood of memories from her childhood hit her. The three of them competing for space on the couch while streaming a movie, her father holding her hand as they walked through the cherry blossoms in Osaka castle park during *ohanami*, and slurping ramen over used manga novels while they were hiding out in 24-hour Net cafes. Simple memories from when she looked upon him with love, pride, and happiness. She was overwhelmed with both the ruins of her life and the impossibility of turning back the clock.

The bells tinkled. Well behind Bearcat, she could make out T-Ray—his lower jaw constantly moving, set in motion by whatever drug he'd been given as a reward.

"Turning tricks here will cost you, Ultragirl." Bearcat gestured at Tatsuo with the short-barrelled, 3D-printed shotgun. The glint of a machete blade could be seen from inside his overcoat. His goggles concealed half of his face, but years of cheap drugs and fringe living had left his visible skin riddled with pockmarks and scars.

Tatsuo set down the bottle on the concrete floor, and slowly got to his feet. "Tell that asshole he's got three seconds to leave."

Miyu desperately hoped Bearcat didn't have an active language parser to translate the Osaka slang. "He's my... He's not a John, Bearcat." She turned to her father, begging him in Japanese. "Please, Dad, don't do this."

Bearcat stepped forward and pushed the barrel of the shotgun into Tatsuo's chest. "The money, Ultragirl."

Tatsuo angled and slapped aside the barrel as the shotgun fired. The deafening crack of two heavy gauge shells made Miyu's ears ring and sent shards of brick ricocheting around her. Her father scooped Bearcat's leg, turned, and tackled him to the ground. In a connected movement, Tatsuo straddled Bearcat's waist, pinning him helplessly to the floor, and torquing his powerful upper body, rained monstrous elbows down on Bearcat's face.

Miyu grabbed her father by the shoulders, trying to pull him off with all her strength, alternating between shouting and begging him to stop, but it was useless. He'd only stop when he was finished, and that wasn't yet. Bearcat's strangled screams fell silent, his flailing arms dropped seemingly lifeless at grotesque angles, leaving only the wet impacts of Tatsuo's blows. After a time, her father stopped, pushed himself upright, and surveyed the mess of Bearcat's face, satisfied.

It was all her fault. She wanted to throw up and choked back the retching as her stomach quivered. She couldn't tell whether her father had murdered Bearcat but knew he'd be disfigured for life if he wasn't. If her surgery hadn't destroyed her tear ducts and eyes, she'd be crying.

Inconceivably casual, her father asked, "What did he want?"

"Money." Miyu was barely able to sound the shape of the words. "I owed him. For drugs."

Tatsuo reached into his coat and tossed his wallet to Miyu. "Rei put paper money in there. Give me what you owed him."

"Is he..." she trailed off, afraid of knowing. Mechanically, she sifted through the wallet, removed three bills, and handed the wallet and cash to her father.

He laughed. "Hardly worth an ass kicking."

He added two more bills, folded them, and tucked them in Bearcat's coat pocket. Tatsuo patted him down, removed a handful of shotgun shells, and disappeared them into his coat. He yanked up Bearcat's head, slapped him twice on the cheek with force, and shook him until Bearcat groaned in acknowledgement.

"There's a way to ask for money, and that's not how you do it. My daughter's paid out. Tell him, Miyu."

Miyu obeyed, dutifully repeating the words in English, but knew they wouldn't be understood. Blood concealed most of Bearcat's distorted features. His head lolled back, and his ruined mouth gasped open, exposing ragged splinters of broken teeth.

Her father grunted, satisfied the transaction was complete. He stripped Bearcat of his machete, grabbed him by the collar, and dragged him off into the darkness, shouting a warning to everyone. While his words were wasted, the ferocity of his actions wasn't.

Eventually, Tatsuo made his way back to her area. Blood was splattered on his face, neck and jacket. He eased himself down, sitting cross-legged on the cardboard facing her, and took a long pull of whiskey. He offered her the bottle. She took it and managed a tentative sip. It tasted harsh in her mouth. Overwhelming, saturating. She couldn't understand how people enjoyed the stuff. Making a face, she shook her head and returned it to him. He leaned back against the wall, rubbing his elbow absently in the silence.

"You know, your mother died in a place like this." Tatsuo took a long drink and held the whiskey in front of him, pensive. After a few moments, he frowned, exhaled slowly and set down the bottle. "For years, I tried. I brought her food and medicine. Sometimes even doctors, but she was out of life long before she passed." His words came out ponderous and troubled. "They say these types of places don't exist in Japan, but they're everywhere people run out of options."

The unspoken question hung in the space between them. Miyu couldn't recall a single time he'd discussed her mother. She unconsciously pulled her knees to her chest, making herself as compact as possible.

"Her name was Kaiyo. She was a good person despite what you might think. Able to see worth in someone like me, but no more a mother than I was prepared to be a father. What did we know? With boys, it would've been easy. I could've taught you to fight to survive. But you girls?" He shook his head sadly.

"We have to go," she whispered, forcing the words past the lump in her throat.

"You're safe now."

"You don't understand. It'll get bad soon."

He touched her cheek—just like he'd done in the past.

She swallowed reflexively, trying to choke back the words but unable to withstand the desire to be protected after years of vulnerability and exposure. Miyu searched his expression and couldn't fathom why he wasn't angry with her. She'd seen the depth and capacity of his rage moments before. It hadn't been purely the conditioned response of a fighter but the fury of someone who would shatter the world without thought for consequence. Yet there he was, gazing at her as though she were an innocent little girl. She struggled to find her voice.

"I really fucked up, Dad."

He smiled sadly. "I know a thing or two about that."

Before she knew it, words started crashing out of her mouth. Rapid at first, then in fits and starts. She jumped from the state of her debts, her dire alienation and shattered hopes after the biohacker collective, her addictions, and being trapped inside a terrorist movement. Eventually, they were quiet, and he stroked her head, holding her tight. The smell of blood sickened her, but she was so thankful to be in his arms again that it didn't matter. The fact her father, for all his strength and protective fury, was utterly powerless to help her didn't matter either. The tantalizing illusion of safety was enough for now.

9

Amrita

INSTEAD OF WORKING IN a war room at CSIS, hopped up on legal stims with an overnight bag, Amrita was pushing her way through the interior of The Mission. The converted church turned raucous alt-club was densely packed with frenetic lighting and overwhelming music. Onstage, a performer hung suspended by silken threads while singing, dangling precariously over the converted altar. Masked band members—a skull, a rabbit, and a former prime minister, respectively—wore ill-fitting nun outfits and laid down a mix of dark techno and black metal. Dancers wearing little other than high-heeled boots and leather straps were suspended in stacked glass enclosures across the length of one wall or glided on invisible tracks overhead. Digital overlays saturated her UkiyoAR vision, creating light echoes of movement cascading into each other. Amrita hadn't been as bewildered and out of place since first arriving in Toronto during an infamously cold Canadian winter.

Her black attire of finely cut wool and black overcoat, a solid generic uniform to blend into the city's night scene, proved about as inconspicuous as wearing a business suit. Amid the crash of pleather, latex, and extreme makeup of The Mission, she felt intensely unwelcome. Many who wore digital masks had -1 emblazoned large in eInk, pulsing to the frenetic rhythm of the environment. Clusters dressed in all white, though lacked the signature masks and respirators of official members.

The Minus One movement and their Days of Anger were swiftly becoming a phenomenon. A blunt rallying cry for the disaffected, an aspirational example of counterculture. Globally-coordinated signature acts of destruction had already emboldened sympathizers worldwide, spawning copycat sabotage and vandalism.

Amrita should've been trying to feed Mason information to filter to stunned politicians flooding the channels with insipid entreaties for calm. Instead, she tried to identify commonalities in the crowd and inexpertly mimicked the patrons' shoulder rocking or head movements. She felt idiotic, despising the music's volume and intensity. Claustrophobic, she pushed her way through the press of bodies. Even with a live broadcast of her location coordinates, it was inconceivable Mia would find her. A terrible realization dawned on Amrita—she couldn't pull off her assumed character. She'd never been a natural liar. She should've stayed at home and left the investigation to trained professionals.

She squeezed her eyes shut, clenched her fists tightly at her side, and steeled her courage. This was finally a chance to distinguish herself.

She slipped past the shoulders and limbs of the alt-club patrons, sacrificing grace of movement for minimal contact, and made her way to the bar. The bartender, dressed in a chainmail shirt, eclectic leather straps, and a replica army ventilator from early last century, stood between a display of pills and shelves of clear, unmarked bottles. She didn't know the etiquette. Amrita glanced in vain for a Net terminal. She swallowed her trepidation, shouting above the crowd's din and music's driving pulse.

"Something strong, a double!"

As the bartender nodded, the filtration canister at the end of the ventilator sparked on her UkiyoARs as being the terminal interface. She couldn't help but make a face at the price. Including a tip, it was enough to feed herself for a week. As he free-poured from a clear, unlabelled bottle, she glanced behind as a patron bumped into her. Using her arms as a protective cage, she cradled the incredibly expensive drink, stood on her toes to glance around, and gingerly made her way to a narrow, empty wall section in front of the caged dancers. Shooting scowls, patrons gave her even more space as she pressed her back against the wall and sipped her drink nervously in small, staccato movements.

As the minutes passed, a warm sensation swelled within her chest. She opened her jacket reflexively and, moments later, took it off and folded it over her arm. Her heart rate accelerated, and she broke out in mild perspiration. Her eyes started to hum, and even after removing her UkiyoARs, her sensitive vision kept tracing echoed arcs of light in the otherwise dark environment. Her paranoia blossomed as she envisioned getting fired from CSIS for failing a controlled substance test but receded as a slow-building euphoria took its place. She tugged open the top two buttons of her shirt, set her overcoat on the floor, and started unconsciously swaying to the music. Initially by minor movements of her head but progressing to her entire body.

Amrita lost all sense of time. She'd seen places far less exotic than The Mission in cinema and had always secretly wished to go to one sometime in her life. Now, she was living a long-suppressed dream and was amazed it wasn't the rebellious, guilt-ridden, degenerate activity branding her forever an outcast. It was exhilarating.

The singer at the altar wrapped herself in thick red ribbons suspended from the ceiling and gracefully danced in the air, arching and twisting herself in all directions before suspending herself in an inverted T five metres off the ground. The haunting grace of the singer belied the driving, aggressive music Amrita had previously considered unpalatable but was now entranced with. Just as she finished what little remained of her drink, she caught sight of Mia Locke, standing in the middle of the crowded floor, staring at her. A static figure among a crashing, frenetic sea of people.

Amrita smiled wide, unexpectedly elated at her arrival, and eagerly waved for Mia to come over. She was exactly how the Carnivore construct module had presented with her tangle of vivid blue hair, a magnificence of irregular white leather straps, and an irresistible expression cast somewhere between amusement and judgement. Frustratingly opaque white Net lenses concealed Mia's eyes, but Amrita imagined them shining blue, sparkling in contrast to the heavy black eyeshadow and mascara the construct had primed for her.

With the patience and grace of a predator, Mia stalked the distance between them, effortlessly evading the patrons' movements, walking to a rhythm entirely her own.

Amrita wanted to hug her instinctively but managed to resist the irrational urge. "I'm Amrita," she yelled exuberantly. "Can I see your eyes?"

"You're high as fuck."

Grinning at being acknowledged, Amrita gestured to her ears. "I can't hear you!"

Mia leaned in close, her scent an exotic blend of orange and lychee.

"You're not a corporate exec."

"No, I work for the government!" Why weren't all her interactions so easy, straightforward, and enjoyable? She'd constantly worried about what to say and how to say it. The liberation from cultural, societal, and professional pressures was joyous.

Mia picked up Amrita's discarded overcoat and rifled through the pockets until she found the CSIS digital security token and disappeared it into the folds of overlapping leather straps covering her upper body. She ejected the microdrive from Amrita's UkiyoARs and likewise concealed it. All the while, Amrita took in her movements, intoxicated with Mia's grace. Unceremoniously, Mia folded the coat over itself, handed the glasses and coat to Amrita, and stepped back into the crowd of patrons.

Amrita hurried after Mia through the press of bodies on the packed floor of The Mission. The jostling human touch was revitalizing, connecting. She welcomed it. She caught up with Mia as she was zipping the front of her white, high-necked jacket. It constricted to match Mia's exact form.

She put a hand on Mia's shoulder, grinning ear to ear. "Where are we going?"

A frigid gust of wind buffeted her as more people entered The Mission. It was crisp and refreshing, instantly cooling her overheated body.

"We're not going anywhere together."

Amrita shrugged off the coldly-delivered rebuff, and chased her out the door onto the dimly lit section of Queen Street East. A black, driverless sedan pulled up, audibly unlocking its door as it stopped.

"You accepted my offer. We still have four hours together." Amrita was confident in her recollection of the contract.

"No, an executive from Hikari International paid for my time, not a government pawn. I don't fuck oppressors."

Amrita recoiled, dumbfounded by the cutting accusation. She vigorously shook her head, causing a cascade of light patterns from the overhead street lights. She couldn't reconcile Mia's scorn with her own incredible exuberance.

"Let's go back inside, okay? It's amazing there."

Mia shook her head. "You have no idea."

Mia stepped into the car. The door closed automatically behind her, and the windows tinted. The sedan merged into traffic, glided effortlessly to the intersection, and disappeared as it turned the corner. The lingering streaks of light soon dissipated, leaving Amrita stunned at the curb's edge, lost in a conflicting tangle of competing sensations.

She was about to head back inside The Mission but recognized she couldn't without digital authentication of her cover fee. All the proximity-enabled profile applications and commerce were gone with her UkiyoAR's ejected drive. She couldn't get on public transit, take a taxi, or even unlock her apartment.

A bubbling panic growing in increasingly tumultuous waves drowned her prior euphoria. Retinal patterns secured her banking, citizenship, and health information. With her CSIS security token also stolen, her personal and professional identities were primed for catastrophic compromise.

She needed to get somewhere to straighten herself out. She couldn't afford the time to cue for a counteragent in the emergency intake at St. Michael's hospital, and waiting out the effects of whatever narcotic she was on seemed a recipe for disaster. Amrita closed her eyes, mentally indexing family, friends, and acquaintances, but disqualified everyone either on trust or cost. Eventually, she remembered her black sheep, younger cousin, Ajay, who was only thirty minutes away by foot.

Circular, eviscerating thoughts plagued Amrita at each step. She paid no attention to the people she passed on the sidewalks. Automated cars screeched to a stop as she walked across intersections against the traffic, aggressive marketing of consumer services projected unseen around her as she made her way to her cousin's place. She was sweating profusely despite the cold but otherwise returning to her natural self—anxious, trapped, and fearing the worst.

Before long, she was in the small entrance enclosure of a converted bank, rapping on the door, struggling to get the condominium concierge's attention. She spoke in a fast-paced Konkani, repeating her cousin's name with bursts of English, playing up the immigrant card Canadians were reluctant to deal with. Even after she'd been asked to leave twice, she kept banging on the security glass, shouting her cousin's full name, and pointing upward. She channelled her mother's entitlement, her father's relentlessness, and her family's legendary stubbornness until her cousin's bewildered, lanky figure crossed the foyer, apologizing to the concierge the entire distance to the security door. Ajay wore a two-toned hoodie with a large -1 emblazoned on the chest.

"I changed your diapers when I was a child, Ajay. Now open the damn door and let me in!" She was amazed at how easy it was to yell at family, even when she desperately needed their help—the energy of fear flowing seamlessly into prerogative.

"Please don't cause a scene!" Ajay held both palms out, his young man's features regressing to boyishness amidst his pleading.

As soon as the door unlocked, Amrita marched past him through the near-silent foyer and directly to the elevator bay. He scampered up to her, disabled the security lockout on the elevator interface, and waited beside her for the elevator.

She spun on him the moment the doors closed. "Why are you wearing that Minus One nonsense? Tell me you haven't done anything so stupid as to become involved."

"I'm not involved!" he protested, instantly flushing with embarrassment.

She instinctively adopted the tone of inquisitorial judgement her family was famous for. "So, why would you wear such a thing?"

"Because it's cool! They're cool. The rich are finally getting a taste of what it's like to have something taken away from them." He squirmed under her gaze. "And besides, it's eFabric. I can change the pattern anytime I want. And not that I'm ashamed, but I haven't actually gone outside since updating it. No one's seen me like this." He shuffled nervously under her gaze. "I just wanted to see what it'd look like. You know, because everyone's doing it."

"You're an idiot, Ajay," she snapped.

She shook her head and watched the numbers light up until the doors opened on the fourteenth floor.

Amrita followed her younger cousin down a tired hallway of densely packed doors, hoping she had never been as awkward. Even the way he walked was hesitant and unsure, as though he was still fleeing the spectre of condemnation...

which she had instinctively brought with her. Amrita chided herself, remembering she was at his mercy.

Ajay's studio apartment was small by any standard. A bed, a single chair, and a narrow desk covered with dirty dishes, half-empty glasses, and a mess of technological gadgets. The walls were painted in rental-beige and peppered with patches of unsanded drywall compound. The small kitchenette was filthy. Stacks of dishes peeked out from the lip of the sink, the two-burner stove was covered in pots, and the countertop was littered with empty energy drinks and takeout containers. The apartment had the damp stink of used clothes, sour curries, and dirty linens. She was nauseous breathing the air, and tripped over some lightweight dumbbells on her way to open the windows. She drank in the luxurious scent of city air, ignoring the frantic clatter of activity behind her as Ajay swept whole surfaces clear into a garbage bag.

"What's with you, Amrita? We haven't spoken in years, and suddenly, you come charging in unannounced."

She brushed off Ajay's petulance, considering what to tell him, recognizing her words couldn't be taken back. There was a thin chance it wouldn't turn out as badly as she feared. "You're not broadcasting or recording now, right?"

"You think I want people to see this?"

She swallowed her pride. "I'm in trouble but don't know how bad yet."

"Can't be any worse than spending your sixteenth birthday getting convicted in front of your extended family." He laughed self-deprecatingly but grew excited at Amrita's grave expression. "No way! What'd you do?"

A pair of industrial UkiyoAR goggles, typical of construction workers, were lying on the table. It'd only take a minute to figure out where she stood. Maybe only thirty seconds. She deftly put on the goggles as Ajay lunged forward to take them from her. It took her a disorienting moment to recognize her vision was filled with a zoomed-in vagina. The goggles were stripped from her face a second later.

"Eww, gross! What the hell, Ajay!?"

"Shut up! I wasn't expecting—You shouldn't snoop!" Dejected and humiliated, he sat cross-legged on the floor, shoulders stooped and looking down. He folded the goggles, and tossed them on the bed. "I get unlimited data from my work," he mumbled.

"You could get fired for misusing city gear."

"I run in stealth mode, spoof the metadata to show usage from today's job sites, and corrupt the timestamps of outbound packets."

Half impressed, she evaluated him critically. "You know, I have a dozen subroutines at CSIS to ferret out those discrepancies."

"No one is going to investigate me for skimming a little bandwidth. I'm a nobody, a power line technician. There's nothing special about me. What do you want anyway?"

"I need—" She bit her lip, considering how little she could get away with saying. "I need to use your Net connection but have to do a full reinstall from my cloud backup. And before you say no, remember I defended you to the family after you got arrested. I was the one who explained digital harassment wasn't a big deal, especially as a young offender, and that you'd been badly bullied."

"It was a big deal, though!" He sprang to his feet, rapidly shaking his head. "Everyone at home cut me off. You included. It doesn't matter that I don't have an adult criminal record. Instead of going to university, I got kicked out as soon as I turned eighteen, had to learn a shitty trade to support myself, and am stuck working an even shittier job. Everyone hates me there, Amrita. They call me the Squirrel because of the way I climb. The real world is no different than high school. No matter what I do, I don't fit in. Only now, it's forever."

Amrita didn't have time to relitigate the past, or feign concern for her cousin's state. She forced herself to stop wringing her hands, and held his gaze hostage with impatient intensity. "Let me use your Net glasses, Ajay. Please. I've been drugged, had my things stolen, and am locked out of my own home. I don't even know how bad things are yet."

He hesitantly reached to the counter and passed his personal UkiyoAR glasses to her. Amrita navigated the settings, reset the gear when Ajay's voice authenticated her request, and selected her Net backup to reinitialize. His glasses were two generations older than her own, and it was doubtful she'd have the full support of the applications in her profile, but they were better than nothing.

As her familiar interface overlaid her vision, she scanned a backdoor one of her contacts had given her for American inter-agency alerts to find her name flagged with critical status. She was wanted for questioning in the most significant single act of cyber terrorism in Canadian history. She would be publicly denounced as a fugitive, a traitor...

Her legs started to give out from under her, but she kept herself from falling. Heart lurching, she scrambled past Ajay to the tiny three-piece washroom, holding the vomit in her bulging mouth until she crashed to the tiles beside the toilet. She retched until her quivering stomach stopped spasming, waving away Ajay, who lurked concerned at the edge of the doorway.

When there was nothing left to throw up, she rinsed her mouth with tap water and splashed her face. She had to clutch the small countertop with both hands between each action to steady herself. Amrita's whole world was crashing down around her. It was all her fault. As she walked out of the bathroom, Ajay was standing, searching her blank expression for insight. He offered her a cup of instant chai, but she waved it off. Her vision started blackening at the periphery, and her limbs went rubbery. She wasn't having a heart attack—there would be no such easy escape from consequence. Amrita put her back to the wall and slid into a sitting position—helpless, overwhelmed, saturated.

Ajay waited patiently for her to say something. He goaded a response by widening his eyes and wagging his chin. She was staring in his direction but not seeing him. Ajay crouched down beside her, touching her gently on the shoulder.

"So?"

"So, you're no longer the family's black sheep." Her words were mechanical. It was someone else speaking. A stranger from a different world, an alternate life, existing in a competing and flawed timeline.

He angled his head, brow furrowed in confusion. "What are you saying?"

"Apparently, I—" She swallowed the sick knot in her throat. "It seems I just took down all the RCMP, CSIS, and INSETS processing clusters after corrupting their data centres. Oh, and data theft. Like, a spectacular amount of classified data." She choked back her blossoming sickness and disorientation. "I'm probably the most wanted criminal in the nation."

10

Rei

Rei at first believed her father's micro apartment had been ransacked but soon realized the litter of items chaotically arranged on the bare wooden framing or scattered across the half-width futon dominating the floor space of the single room were thoughtless rather than deconstructive. Tatsuo lived in a windowless room a little larger than her modest bathroom. It was saturated with the mouldy odour of badly dried laundry, sweaty training gear, and the pervasive oily stink of *okonomiyaki* from the mom-and-pop restaurant below. Clothes were stacked in clumps and triple-layered on irregular pegs or thin, dry-cleaner hangers. A pair of suit bags, hermetically sealed, hung from a naked pipe above the bed.

Her heart broke yet another increment as the door clicked shut, temporarily trapping her in a darkness warded off by the fragility of a single, naked bulb and the isolating ghost of thankless suffering that allowed Miyu to enjoy her princess lifestyle in Toronto.

Rei trembled under the swell of humiliation, shame, and anger her father should have, engaged her UkiyoARs and tried to connect with her wayward sister. She was flagged as offline, but Rei had never known her to be disconnected. If anything, Miyu's accursed avatar would auto-respond. She engaged a Netstream of the environment, sending the video feed as she spoke in harsh Osaka slang.

"This is what your entitled lifestyle has reduced Dad to, Miyu. If I find out he's paying for anything while he's staying there, I promise you'll regret it."

Rei ended the Netstream, sent the message, and wished she'd paid more attention when people around her made threats. Hers had been toothless and hollow to her ears. She retracted her mask, wincing against the unfiltered foulness of the air, appreciating how trapped and pathetic his life had become. She pushed aside a heap of laundry to sit on the futon and forced herself to take in the details of the environment no one was ever supposed to have seen.

The unfinished framing studs were littered with pictures and eclectic keepsakes. Cut magazine photographs of his glory days as a fighter haphazardly tacked to the bare plywood walls facing the other side, images of Rei and Miyu in cheap hundred-yen plastic frames and a single damaged, dog-eared and subsequently laminated photograph of a young woman Rei presumed was her mother.

The woman was smoking, ignoring the camera, sitting at a table covered in drinks and the small plastic dishes typical of cheap *izakayas*. She was wearing an inappropriately low-cut blouse, showing the hint of a tattoo, jewellery too gaudy to be real, and black hair folded into a simple knot with an elastic at the back of her head. It was the lazy, casual hairstyle of someone who'd forgotten to care of themselves or had lost interest in their appearance. Long, stray locks hung listless at the side of a face eerily resembling Rei's own.

Rei stared at the photograph, waiting to feel something more than detached curiosity before finally abandoning the impulse.

In a thin box beside the futon, she found a stack of print-outs from Rei and Miyu's report cards bound by a single elastic band, two small, unmarked glass bottles of baby teeth and a well-worn shoebox of handwritten cards she and Miyu had made for him for Father's Day over the years. She was ashamed at how few were hers and how short and generic the messages were. The sensation grew more acute when she noted the last letter she'd given him was when she was ten years old. Miyu had continued writing Father's Day cards until she'd left for Toronto.

She ached in every way there was.

She zoomed in on the photograph of her mother and captured a high-resolution image with her UkiyoARs. When her father returned, she'd talk to him about the mysterious woman in the way a daughter should. For now, the woman would exist in ethereal ones and zeros, offering no more substance than she had throughout Rei's life.

An alert flashed in her vision. She had to leave shortly to make her appointment at *Aki no Sora* with Shinoda. Some messages were too sensitive to send over the Net and Akira Mori had left little room for interpretation. She took a final recorded inspection of Tatsuo's room, vowing never to allow him to return to the lonely squalor, before locking the door behind her and taking the narrow concrete staircase to the dizzying backstreets of the Minami district. As was her habit, she scanned the immediate vicinity for potential dangers by engaging a suite of recognition algorithms and winnowing results for known criminals, Mori gangsters, or members of rival clans.

Within a few quick turns down tight laneways, she confirmed a solidly built man in a dark overcoat was following her. He had a black scarf covering his face from the bridge of his nose down and the remainder concealed with oversized goggles. The man had digital suppressors active since nothing was displayed in her augmented view of him.

Fear gripped her, an invisible hand mercilessly squeezing her intestines. She broke out into a run, veered into a small restaurant and dashed through the back exit, leaving a startled staff cursing in her wake. Her breathing, already compromised by a broken nose, became ragged and irregular. She lost her footing on debris in the alley as it intersected with a narrow street jammed with salarymen and career women on their way for after-work drinks. Her ankle throbbed. Rei slowed her pace, trying to blend in, insomuch as a fully masked individual could, and activated the razors in the fingertips of her professional gloves. She'd already endured Mori clan's first message without struggle. Anything further would need to be met with whatever resistance she could offer.

When she shoulder-checked, she caught sight of the man again. He kept a fair distance, drifting an unhurried twenty-five metres behind, but remained dialled-in as though he was following the GPS trail of her Net connection. The nearest solace was *Aki no Sora*, a place no clan would violate due to a secretive agreement made amongst all the clan heads and the implicit threat of Aki's numerous, well-connected admirers. But Rei was meeting her yakuza boss there, and endangering him was borderline treasonous.

Rei conferenced Shinoda as she quickened her pace.

"Shinoda-*sama*, I won't be able to meet you."

"It's unlike you to disappoint."

"I'm being followed and can't lose him."

"We have an appointment."

She cursed aloud as he terminated the communication.

Rei pulled up a map overlay of the district and planned a last-ditch effort to evade her pursuer. She disengaged the razors on her gloves and burst into a sprint, as fast as she could hazard with her tall, heeled boots and sore ankle, weaving recklessly between people, digital signage and analogue street placards. She wrapped around corners, jostling through startled pedestrians, to duck into stores she'd previously flagged as having back exits on her personal map settings. She was perspiring from fear and effort, her mouth-breathing unsettlingly ragged, but she didn't slow or glance back.

Five more turns. She counted down as her lungs burned from effort and her face turned numb from the painful shocks of her heavy footfalls. She shouldered, pushed and squeezed through shocked pedestrians and advertising-cluttered streets. *Four*, she said aloud as she rounded a corner into a broader avenue and had to adhere to the conventions of a sidewalk to avoid the autonomous vehicle traffic.

She knew she was being flagged for abnormal behaviour by police and municipal surveillance systems but trusted any direct-recognition software would be thwarted by her mask, evasion tech, and uncharacteristic movements. Slipping through the partially opened automated doors to the office building, she ran through the foyer and exiting out the side, leaving a bewildered security guard with a breathless *three* in response to his demands for her to stop.

It was a two-hundred-metre straight shot down a narrow, single-lane street before a pair of turns to *Aki no Sora*. She willed herself into a final burst of speed, whirling past the glut of salarymen and career women, gasping as she rounded the final corner to encounter the man she'd been desperately trying to avoid standing directly in front of the *izakaya*. She lurched to a sudden halt, near enough to see her reflection in his mirrored goggles.

She blinked the stinging perspiration from her eyes, suppressed her fear, and engaged the razors on her gloves, determined to bleed him before she fell. Instead of advancing on her, the man gave her a small bow and walked a dozen paces to the left of the entrance. Rei remained frozen until he gestured to the doorway. Apprehensive, she walked forward, confusion mounting with each step. He wasn't even facing her anymore.

The black-lacquered, wooden door to the *izakaya* retracted at her proximity. Aki was performing on the small stage at the back of the bar. Her mournful voice, haunting shamisen strings, and tragic lyrics of the *enka* song pierced the hearts of the dozen salarymen who crowded the tables and stools, vying for the privilege to be closest to the ageing queen in her vibrant, young woman's kimono. Never missing a beat, Aki made eye contact with Rei and discreetly gestured to the rear-most table—always reserved, virtually never used and mostly concealed behind a series of paper-screened panels. Rei bowed low with gratitude, made her way past the translucent veil, and bowed reverently to the seated figure of Shinoda.

Handsome in a way few older men she encountered were, he had a recognizable strength of conviction, with hard lines on his face and slight knots of muscles above his brow earned from intense scrutiny. His countenance conveyed familiarity with the exercise of power and a spartan quality prohibiting excess. Clean-shaven head and face, wearing a classic black double-breasted suit, white shirt and simple black tie, Shinoda was the man she wished her father had been. Even how he held his body, sitting cross-legged on the cushion in front of the low table, spoke of discipline.

"Shinoda-*sama*, you need to secure backup and an exit. I couldn't evade my pursuer."

"You did. He just knew you'd be coming here." He smiled with one corner of his mouth, gesturing for her to sit opposite him. "I'm sure Hiroshi expects strong words on how a young lady in heels managed to escape him."

"Kono-*san*?"

"Your father's partner, yes. I tasked him with keeping you safe after your encounter with Mori's son. He's been following you since you left the apartment in Shinsekai." Shinoda poured her two fingers of whiskey from a special reserve bottle the clan kept behind the bar, filling his own simultaneously. "Take a seat."

"I'm not yet presentable." Vulnerable and exposed, she stepped back toward the restroom. If they had known she had gone to Ichika's, she might have been outed already, and Rei wasn't prepared for those consequences.

"Don't make me repeat myself."

Reticently, she retracted her mask, noting he wasn't surprised at her broken nose, blackened eyes, or the mess of lacerations and swollen bruising on her face. She put on near-opaque UkiyoAR sunglasses with thick, rounded frames, complimenting the delicate strings of black pearls she wore around her neck. She removed her boots, stepped onto the tatami mats and sat opposite him. Shinoda slid a tightly rolled, damp hand towel towards her and looked aside, allowing her a break in etiquette to wipe the sweat from her face and neck.

"You know, half my scars came courtesy of your father. Most were from when we were just boys." With a ponderous gravity, he gestured to a series of thin lines affording additional character to his cleanly shaven head. "You accounted for yourself well today, I hear."

Rei swallowed the validation, careful not to let it play out on her face. It was the first compliment he'd given her in all the years she'd brought revenue to the clan. She waited for him to continue.

"I spoke to the elder Mori. He extends his apologies for the *misunderstanding* with his son earlier today."

A sneer partially subverted the intended graciousness of her smile. "I'm pleased to hear you've had the chance to establish a new understanding."

He raised his glass of whiskey, waited for her to do likewise, and finished his own. She did as well—slowly, ensuring Shinoda would notice she wasn't forcing it. The whiskey he was serving, a twenty-five-year-old Macallan, was too precious to be seen to go to waste on an uneducated palate. She didn't particularly enjoy it, though. Drinking was simply a professional function or a habit abused to unwind.

"It's similar to the eighteen, but considerably more full-bodied. Thank you, Shinoda-*sama*. I'll treasure the experience."

He leaned forward, showing uncharacteristic interest. "What's your preference?"

"The Hibiki twenty-one for special occasions, or the Yamazaki twelve otherwise."

Shinoda smiled. "Japanese whiskies are the best."

Then why didn't you stock one here? She knew the answer, though. The Macallan was to impress those who were impressionable. "My father would often take me to the Yamazaki museum, a little past Takatsuki, when I was a child and sneak me one of the free samples at the end of the tour. Everyone knew what he was doing, but it was a different time, and no one wanted to confront a prize fighter."

He sighed long and deep. "Your father, he can be the source of trouble."

Rei patiently waited for Shinoda to continue. She adopted a concerned tone when it became obvious etiquette required her to prod. "Has the *misunderstanding* not been sufficiently settled?"

"There will be an accounting, but I don't believe a child should inherit a parent's sins."

Rei was actively losing respect for the man she'd held in high esteem. She knew what he was expecting but wouldn't thank him for not holding her accountable for an unprovoked and merciless beating.

"Yes," she acknowledged.

Shinoda held her gaze for a long moment, testing or challenging. He poured himself another measure of whiskey and filled her glass with half the amount.

"Tell me of your progress with Hikari International. You've invested considerable time and more of the clan's resources than any of your other schemes, but there's still nothing to show for it."

Rei forced her expression to be neutral while scrambling for an angle to spin her failures. "Your investment has already yielded a thirteen percent growth in stock value, Shinoda-*sama*."

"It's not real money if it's locked in," he countered. His eyes narrowed with the greed that lures men to overlook the value of relationships. "You're supposed to have gotten information we can use against them already."

"Hikari is on the verge of a major breakthrough coming out of Toronto."

"Which is why now's the time to apply leverage."

It galled Rei to be told how to do her job. "I understand, Shinoda-*sama*."

"What about your source in that city? You promised they'd provide valuable intelligence." He scowled at her. "Why are you taking so long?"

"I was supposed to meet the chief technical officer today, but I had an unexpected setback." She gestured to her face.

"Does he love you yet?"

"Powerful men don't afford weakness to women they can easily conquer."

"Mori-*san* has agreed to cash instead of territory to keep the peace. I'll not pay a single yen from our remaining coffers to cover off your father. Close Hikari or make good on one of the other scams you're running. I may not be able to convince them to lose interest in you if it takes too long."

Over the years, Rei had heard corroborating whispers suggesting her father's fighting career had been ruined by Shinoda pressuring him into taking a dive in her father's fateful championship match. To hear the man who'd gained from her father's miseries balk at ensuring his safety with mere yen made Rei involuntarily clench her teeth hard enough to hurt.

"I'll adjust my timelines accordingly, Shinoda-*sama*," she said politely once she could loosen her jaw.

11

Tatsuo

THE TIME ZONE DIFFERENCE and the potential threat of repercussions ensured Tatsuo had shallow, brief periods of sleep. Miyu, exhausted from the stress of conflict and outpouring of emotions, had nodded off like she used to as a child—slowing the pace of her speech until sleep overtook her mid-sentence. Her face had softened around the weirdly convex metallic lenses, ruining the image of his emaciated angel. All her anxieties, loneliness, and grief had temporarily been erased in his protective embrace.

Tatsuo hadn't understood most of what she'd said but knew better than to interrupt. Unlike his daughter, he'd always been immune to the lure of causes, technology, or hope. The world was already complicated enough to make the living of it a daily challenge. Who needed the extra burden? He'd tried to listen, nodding or grunting appropriately, allowing the stream of his daughter's unfiltered troubles wash over him like a river breaking on rocks. As the minutes had slipped by, the sentiments had worn him down and smoothed out the hardness of his character, leaving him without the edge or defence. Her miseries and despair flowed into his heart unfiltered. Of course, he'd never been able to emotionally protect himself from either of his girls. Tender Miyu, most especially.

She'd been running hot all night with a fever too strong for her delicate, withered frame. Like when his daughters were little, Tatsuo didn't know how to diagnose or treat the condition. There was no school to keep her home from and no television or junk food to appease her until time ultimately proved a remedy. As the first rays of light provided a ghastly illumination to the cold, bleak environment, he could better appreciate the terrible composite of desperation, extreme poverty, and degenerate addiction his daughter had made her home. His heartbreak made him restless.

His knees still ached from the cramped economy seats on the transpacific flight, and the discomfort was compounded by decades of cage-fighting injuries. After inspecting the 3D-printed shotgun for telltale fatigue cracks, Tatsuo methodically loaded shells into the twin barrels, tucked the several remaining shells in the outside pocket of his duffle bag, and closed the breach.

With patience and care, he balled up his jacket, gently lifted Miyu's head from his lap and set her down without waking her. He stretched as he stood—the crackling pops of damaged joints testified to a life of hardship. His elbows still throbbed dully from the conflict with Bearcat.

Gun held lazily by the shortened stock, he walked to the area of the previous evening's conflict and continued along the drag marks to where he'd deposited Bearcat to find the man breathing but unconscious. Given the disfiguration, he wasn't sure if it was sleep or a coma. Even from the caked blood, Tatsuo could see evidence of broken orbital bones, a collapsed cheek and a broken jaw. If it'd been a competition, he would've felt remorse for the savage state of the man, but Tatsuo reminded himself Bearcat had poisoned his child with drugs, held her hostage and had probably tried to rape her as well. Reflexively, Tatsuo gave Bearcat a hard kick in the ribs. The man groaned and sputtered.

Several denizens of the warehouse were watching the scene play out. They resembled the quietly disenfranchised people who haunted the fringes of society rather than junkies who'd given themselves over to addictions. Their faces held the stunned expressions of a hostage citizenry who'd seen a tyrant deposed—not trusting in the newfound safety, waiting anxiously for a new tyranny to be inflicted upon them. He paced frustratedly, staring them down as a group.

"Any of you could've done this!"

A small figure emerged from behind the protection of a graffiti-covered concrete support column. It was the strange little girl from the previous evening who had lowered the fire escape ladder for them. She shuffled across the dirty floor, gaze held carefully not to meet his own, holding a stack of paper books. Tatsuo caught sight of the plain paper wrappings typical of the protective slips Japanese bookstores once offered. The girl whispered English words and held out the stack of books with trembling hands. He didn't know whose eyes were more disturbing—his daughter's pus-encrusted, technological mutilations or Echo's blackened, haunted, near-soulless eyes. They were his dead wife's eyes worn by a little girl.

Tatsuo lowered himself to one knee and tried to smile reassuringly. "You're a good kid."

More nonsense English delivered in hesitant whispers. He wished he was smart like Rei or bilingual like Miyu but couldn't even remember the basics of English he'd been forced to learn in school. He opened the shotgun breach, exposing the brass primers of the two shells, snapped it shut and aimed at an imaginary foe.

"You squeeze the trigger at the next asshole who tries to make your life hell."

He gripped the weapon mid-barrel and handed it to her. Echo shook her head vigorously, crouched down to place the stack of books reverently at his feet and shuffled an additional arm's length from him. All the while, she made hurried sounds in her impenetrable language.

Tatsuo set the shotgun on the concrete floor and gestured to the girl to stay. She could've been either of his daughters if he'd left the many times his wife had given him cause. He riffled through Bearcat's jacket pocket, finding the bills he'd put in there the previous evening. He peeled two off, ensuring the three remaining would settle Miyu's debts, and offered them to the girl with an outstretched hand.

"Make sure you get something to eat, okay?"

She took the money, disappeared it into the layers of rags she wore as clothes and scampered out of view. A pair of onlookers followed her while the others advanced cautiously forward—carrion circling a lion's kill, waiting for Tatsuo to leave. The impulse to follow Echo flickered briefly, but he couldn't risk his daughter's safety. He picked up the shotgun and stack of Japanese books before returning to Miyu's corner. Tatsuo didn't need to look to confirm the desperate squatters were clamouring over Bearcat's belongings. He'd signalled the body was there to be picked at by distributing the first spoils.

Miyu was awake, already concealed in her oversized goggles, respirator, and startling white clothing. She packed her few remaining items into his duffle bag with small, rapid movements. Pausing, she shot Tatsuo an anxious glance.

He offered her the books. "The kid—"

"You shouldn't have let me sleep." She grabbed the volumes from him, shoving them in the duffle.

"There's nothing to worry about. The asshole's still stretched out where I left him."

"You don't know how places like this work. We have to go. Now."

He put on his coat, slung the duffel over his shoulder and followed Miyu as she snaked through the clutter of squatters' areas. No one made a directly threatening motion. Hungry, overly interested eyes followed them, but Tatsuo started to pick up Miyu's anxiety. Scanning for danger, he bumped into obstacles she wove through and tripped on debris she glided past. The heavy fire escape door was twenty metres ahead but crowded with half a dozen armed squatters.

Miyu stopped in her tracks as T-Ray, machete in hand, shouted something, the rough words mutilated by the effects of competing drugs. Stimulants made him twitchy, but his dilated, unblinking eyes were dull. The air hung heavy with the treachery of a fresh kill and the restless anticipation of a new pecking order. T-Ray was pointing at them. At him specifically. More armed squatters were starting to hem in the periphery. The group fanned out as Tatsuo aimed the sawed-off shotgun at T-Ray.

"Tell that faggot he's got three seconds to get out of the way," he told Miyu.

When she didn't acknowledge him, he followed her fixed gaze to the small, crumpled body he'd initially overlooked as another pile of trash in front of the fire escape door before recognizing the form as Echo. Tatsuo's public gift of Bearcat's money had murdered the girl as surely as if he'd killed her himself.

He was in motion, already closing half the distance. His vision was bleeding red, dark at the edges. Anger, unfettered and overwhelming, powered his headlong charge toward T-Ray. The other squatters broke rank in panic.

Reflexes saved him from the worst of the machete's blade as he used his left arm to protect the side of his face. The arc of his block blunted the cutting impact, but the blade sheared through his leather jacket and bit into the flesh of his forearm and shoulder. The pain cut through his bloodlust just enough to remember he had a gun. Too late to stop the furious charge, he used his free hand to grab hold of T-Ray's face, forcing it back as he drove them into a bone-rattling impact against the graffiti-covered wall. Tatsuo jammed the barrel of the sawed-off shotgun into the crook between T-Ray's chin and neck and pulled the trigger.

The deafening blast reverberated in his ears. His face was wet. The smell of blood and cordite was choking. T-Ray's body hung limp to the side, but his head, pressed against the wall by the force of Tatsuo's grip, remained in place. He spun around to face the squatters, dangerous as a wounded predator, ferociously yelling to hear something outside the ringing in his ears. His teeth gleamed white, his face painted in blood and fragments of flesh. He tossed T-Ray's body towards the nearest of the gang. The half dozen armed squatters froze in their tracks. Tatsuo discarded the shotgun in favour of T-Ray's machete and advanced on them.

He had become a death collector, a nightmare manifest.

Miyu scrambled between them—face animated, mouth rapidly moving, arms gesturing frantically at the crowd. Tatsuo caught sight of two squatters in the distance starting to go through his duffel bag.

"Leave it!"

With her attention on the gang, Miyu planted a palm against his chest to stop him from going after his bag. She was pleading. Blood-drunk and wired from near-death adrenaline, he blinked his stinging eyes and shifted his weight from left to right, knowing he could close the distance faster than the squatters could raise their guard. His hand relaxed his white-knuckled grip on the machete. Loose was faster.

The rapid pantomime of alternating words and gestures playing out before him was bewildering. A deal was being brokered. Miyu didn't see the victory he was poised to seize. He was unstoppable, a champion facing a rabble. He could hear the crowds chanting his name, a chorus of tens of thousands, the memory of a packed Osaka Dome on fight night. *Yoshida! Yoshida!* He drank in the familiar scent of blood, breathing deeply, pouring oxygen into his muscles. Unlike every other moment in his current existence, he was alive now. Electric. Soon, it would all be over, and he'd either be dead or forced back to the death of a life he'd made for himself. Everything had become binary, a warrior's reality of absolutes held momentarily in check.

Miyu spun to face him, mouth moving, but the ringing in his ears drowned out her words. She pushed him towards the door with all her might, but he didn't budge. She slammed her tiny fists against his broad chest, pleading as she desperately pushed.

It's finished! Miyu's shout pierced the deafening tone like a bell at the end of the round.

"My stuff." He gestured with T-Ray's machete at the pair of squatters going through the contents of his duffel bag.

She shook her head, pushing again in vain. She switched tactics to grip his left arm, tugging forcefully towards the fire escape. The sharp throbbing in his shoulder and forearm spiked signals of pain he'd spent a lifetime conditioning himself against. Her desperate urgency helped disrupt the red tint from clouding his vision, leaving him trembling with a shock of adrenaline and no outlet for it. Hot spit formed in his mouth. Tatsuo allowed himself to be led past T-Ray's body, past the corpse of Echo and through the heavy fire escape door into the cold morning air and cloudless daylight.

As soon as the heavy door slammed shut behind them, the enormity of his actions drowned him. He lurched to the guardrail, leaned over and threw up violently. The machete clattered off the side of the building and lay inert on the ground, robbed of all intent, transformed into yet another piece of garbage littering the area.

"We need to go, Dad." Miyu's urgency was bereft of judgment.

Through the diminished ringing in his ears, he heard the fire escape ladder lower. His head swam in thick disorientation, making even the simplest tasks difficult.

"Can you make it down by yourself?"

He grunted his response, not having any of the conviction he faked. Miyu gracefully descended the ladder and stared up at him. He remained poised on the top, not trusting his body to react as needed. It was a basic action, but the mechanics of starting the descent were unfathomably awkward for him to process. His hands were slick with blood, and he slipped down the first few iron rungs before a desperate grip saved him from freefall. The violence of the abrupt stop wrenched his shoulder. Pain made his eyes tingle. He continued down cautiously, one rung at a time, relying on the stability of his right arm.

At the bottom, he turned to face Miyu, seeing himself in the mirrored lenses of her oversized goggles. Blood and bits of flesh lacquered his face, neck, and upper body. He started trying to wipe clean his face in increasingly frantic movements, but only succeeded in making more of a mess of himself. The sleeves of his coat did no better. He shrugged out of it, pulled off his hooded sweatshirt, and used it to desperately wipe away the worst of the sickening mess covering him. His t-shirt was drenched in sweat, his body steaming in the chill air—thicker from the wounds on his shoulder and forearm.

"Dad, stop."

Miyu grabbed his wrists with her slender fingers in a grip he could've easily shrugged out of but allowed to govern him. He dropped his arms, discarding the sweater. His stomach heaved again, and he dropped to his knees, skin raw from forceful scrubbing. Careful not to get blood on her white clothes, Miyu rolled up her sleeves, pulled on a pair of thin latex gloves and picked through his coat pockets. She delicately removed his wallet and the folded bundle of travel documents. Afterward, she found relatively clean areas on his hooded sweatshirt to cut strips from with a small blade concealed in her coat.

She took his hand, guiding him away from the warehouse, across the desolate courtyard and towards the breach in the electrified fence. She shoulder-checked at several intervals, slowing their pace by increments. By the time they made it to the breach, they were at a shuffle. Unprompted, he sat on the ground as his daughter wrapped his forearm in sweater strips. He couldn't grasp why she was being kind and wished he could see her face for some hint as to her motive, but it was entirely obscured between the goggles, ventilator, and high collars of her impossibly immaculate white coat. He resigned to her administration, trying to control his shivering. He wasn't sure if it was from the cold or excess adrenaline. She exhausted the remaining strips on his shoulder, affixed them with a tight knot, and crouched opposite him.

"Was that your first time?" Miyu's question hung heavy in the silence.

He closed his eyes, involuntarily replaying the scene in his mind, and nodded.

She stood up, turning her head to take in their surroundings. "A friend will pick us up in about twenty minutes, okay?"

He cleared his throat. Voice hoarse, he asked, "Why are you being nice?"

She pressed her lips tightly together, and glanced around.

"Miyu?"

"I received a Netcast from Rei."

"What did she say?"

"It doesn't matter." Miyu seemed to weigh the situation. "But you shouldn't call people faggots."

Nothing made any sense to Tatsuo, least of all what his daughter had just said. He'd been in this terrible country for less than twenty-four hours, and it had come close to costing both of them their lives. He stared at the savagery of his reflection in his daughter's mirrored goggles.

"Promise me, Dad. Promise you won't say it anymore."

He didn't understand his daughter's odd insistence.

"Yeah, okay."

12
Mathis

After Benoit had left and the fear-based adrenaline pounding through his bloodstream finally subsided, Mathis glued himself to newsfeeds until the early morning hours. The constant sirens relentlessly echoed off the downtown skyscrapers, keeping him alert even in exhaustion. The scale of global property damage signalling the start of the Days of Anger was incalculable, and the scope of Minus One agents or sympathizers defied comprehension. It made no sense how a sustained, widespread attack wouldn't have been shut down immediately. There were too many people, too many plots, and too much damage. Perhaps an attack on the very concept of wealth was sufficiently preposterous to evade pre-emptive arrests.

As he consumed Net content, Mathis obsessed over his fundamental inability to protect himself. Aiden Frost or Benoit Rochon were modern-day boogeymen—spoken of in conspiracies, often inferred into terrible outcomes, but virtually never encountered firsthand. Reports of the more spectacular, marquee Minus One destruction failed to push past the intimacy and immediacy of his fear. Mathis weighed the value of getting his parents' typically well-reasoned counsel since they'd always been able to guide him to solutions when he found himself trapped. The fact they were infamously early risers sealed his decision.

"Call home."

His helper AI initialized the conference request and spun up the camera bee. The device flew to his preferred vantage point—slightly to the right and angled down a few degrees to avoid showing his nostrils—and bathed him in a secondary filler light. The alert rang several times before his mother's heart-shaped face filled the screen a little too close.

"Oh, good morning, bunny! What an unexpected surprise!" She turned her attention to the right. "Casper, look who's on the refrigerator! It's Mathis."

"What's he doing up so early?"

She leaned into the display, "Did you sleep? Are you feeling okay?"

"Mom, can you accept my encryption key?"

"I don't think I know what that means. No, wait. A box popped up on top of your picture. You were so handsome in the award ceremony, did I ever mention that?"

"Yes, Mom. Can you hit okay?"

"There's some sort of error. Casper, can you read this? I don't have my glasses on."

Ingrid opened the fridge door, wildly swinging the fixed point of view past where his father was sitting to focus on the over-stacked china cupboard. His father came into view, dressed in the same navy-blue pyjamas as his mother, approaching the fridge as though it was an alien to be investigated. He cocked his head, took the glasses from his pyjama's breast pocket, and set them on his face.

He stroked his mostly grey beard pensively. "Yep, definitely an error."

Mathis failed to recall what brand of appliance they had from his last visit in the summer, remembering it only as generically stainless steel. "What does it say?"

"I don't know, buddy. There's a big white X in a red circle, and the rest seems like it's in another language. There are all these characters with funny symbols in a box. Below that is a cancel button."

Now also wearing glasses, his mother crowded his father away from the screen. "Oh, look, Casper. There's an upside-down question mark! They have those in Spanish, don't they?"

"Why would our Korean refrigerator speak Spanish, dear?"

Mathis unconsciously rubbed his eyes. The pressure overexposed and warped the Net-contact display of his parents hovering around the refrigerator's digital console. "It's not Spanish, Mom. It's encrypted."

"Your dad thinks it's Korean," she chided.

"Just hit cancel, please," Mathis sighed.

"Okay, it's back to normal now. It's nice of you to touch in. Now tell me, what's keeping you up all night?"

Mathis struggled to find the words without endangering them. Hesitantly, he asked, "Have you ever been in a situation where someone stalked you?"

"Is she cute?" Casper grinned.

"Getting stalked is an extremely serious matter, Casper." Ingrid gave him a little shove. "So, what's her name?"

They both glanced at each other mischievously and giggled. In a way, Mathis was happy the encryption failed since speaking the truth directly would traumatize them.

"What would you do if someone could intercept you where you lived, worked, and went?"

The smile faded from his father's face first. "I suppose we're to understand you can't go to the authorities, for whatever reason—"

"Because talking to the police would be the best thing to do in this situation," Ingrid finished.

Mathis nodded. "No police, but I don't want to be surprised again."

"Can this person be reasoned with?"

Mathis shook his head at his father's question. "They're beyond reason. And I don't want to confront them."

Ingrid cut in anxiously, "Are you in danger?"

"I'm okay, but not sure what to do."

"Well, not long before you were born, a student stalked your father. The little tart followed him everywhere! She became obsessed and even tried to run me over once!"

Casper nodded sombrely. "Not quite, but close enough."

"Anyway, she was young, and Casper didn't want to ruin her academic career—"

"Daddy issues," his father explained dismissively.

"Regardless," Ingrid continued, "we changed our schedules and routines dramatically."

"We pretended to be spies!" Casper clapped his hands, delighted. "We made up these complicated backstories and sometimes even carried props. It was awesome!"

"We did make the best of it, didn't we?" Ingrid gazed lovingly at her husband.

"Needless to say, you were born nine months later."

"Casper!" She swatted at his shoulder.

Mathis smiled, easily imagined their ham-fisted acting and playful companionship. "How did it resolve?"

"The girl gave up when your mother started showing." His face turned serious. "You see, buddy, you can never control anyone. Your life will always be punctuated by people who want different things for and from you. Deep down, though, you'll always know what is most important. That's what you have to protect."

"And yourself, too, bunny. But not just your safety, your real self. If this situation makes you into someone you're not, whoever it is has already beaten you. You've always had the most beautiful moral compass. Let it guide you in the right direction."

"And what if it puts other people in danger?"

"It wouldn't be you. It'd be some outside individual beyond your control who's culpable. You need to trust yourself. You're sensitive, thoughtful, and compassionate, like your mom."

"And handsome, like your father," Ingrid chimed in.

Casper cocked an eyebrow. "Less fun, though?"

She regarded Casper with adoration before turning her attention back to Mathis. "We believe in you and know whatever decisions you make will be for the best. Not all of life is smooth, but with the right attitude, the very best things in this world can come from troubled times."

"She means you need to find a girl to play sexy spy games with, buddy." His father dramatically pantomimed finger guns.

"Casper!" She swatted him again before addressing the monitor seriously. "We meant you."

Mathis was humbled by the affection and support he'd always had access to. "Thanks. I love you both."

"We love you too, bunny. Now, go and try to get some sleep before you have to start work."

His father had already walked out of frame towards the kitchen table. "Try to have fun, buddy. Don't overthink it!"

Ingrid's finger blotted out the console's camera, repeatedly jabbing at the screen. "Casper, how do I—"

The conference terminated. The filler light from the camera bee switched off, and it returned to its recharging station.

Mathis tried unsuccessfully to place his challenges within his parents' blind advice, but there had still been enough overlap to have taken the edge off his desperation. He was calmer now, able to focus. He sent a message to Evy Carter, requesting an emergency meeting. Almost immediately, Evy injected an eight-thirty physical meeting into his calendar rather than a video conference. Mathis followed her lead and injected an 8 am onsite appointment for Logan.

With time to kill, Mathis logged into his social profile and skimmed content from *TheChivalrousArab* with disappointment. All of Tariq's protest Netstreams were still live. Mathis grudgingly admired his colleague's social game. It was amazing how consistently handsome, compelling, and important he could appear—especially when an equally attractive, seemingly ardent, and aspirational woman was sharing the frame. Mathis couldn't help but scroll through Tariq's feed and was arrested by a series of him with Mathis' ex-girlfriend, Marisol. The dates of the posts overlapped with the time Mathis assumed they'd been together.

Regret outweighed Mathis' feelings of betrayal. Her easy laughter to Tariq's carefree banter haunted Mathis like the Ghost of Christmas Yet to Come—offering a vision of a solitary, loveless future. He toggled to his professional avatar and composed a short message.

Please take down the protest content, Tariq.

He vacillated on whether to send it, fearing it might usher in the type of conflict Mathis loathed, but he decided losing a talented developer for a PR infraction didn't serve anyone.

Next, Mathis discovered and subsequently scanned Logan's social account, *BoBobosActualNoseHair*, for anything that might be incriminating. While there was nothing involving the protests, he found a frantic pace of eclectic content ranging from pedantic cosplay takedowns and furiously petty arguments on the powers of obscure anime characters to pissing on emerging consumer gadgets or creepily invested comments on food porn. The frequency of posts was approximately every fifteen minutes, often punctuated with a set spammed in quick succession. Peppered throughout were ardent, early-access reviews for a beta platform, Skeleton Crucible, that came across as paid advertisements. Against his better judgement, Mathis' curiosity won out, and he played the short pitch.

Imagine a platform where you can battle to finally be who you truly are! Character exclusives earned through combat brackets! Victors claim both likeness and bragging rights in our Hero's Convention! Skeleton Crucible is equal parts Comicon, Battle League, and social network! Select from our incredible catalogue of characters! Skeleton Crucible has every childhood favourite to one-off characters from rare mangas. If you could be anyone, why be yourself? Join the growing ranks of Skeleton Crucible!

The video was thirty seconds of jump cuts from as many anime series, overdubbed with Evy Carter's voice. Logan must have sampled her content and fed it through an emulator. Mathis rubbed his eyes, consumed with the proxy shame Logan should've been crippled with. It was bad enough his lead developer had been leaking corporate secrets to the CCP, but if Evy ever found out about her voice getting hijacked, she'd eviscerate Logan before coordinating a binding class-action lawsuit to economically cripple him in perpetuity. Mathis considered sending a message, but Logan's profile was already too toxic to risk further association with.

He packed a virgin carry-on suitcase he'd purchased years ago for when affordable and approachable air travel resumed. He confirmed his passport was valid before packing a week's worth of undergarments, several days' worth of clothes, and toiletries. After tidying up, he dressed and did a final shoulder check on his place from the door. With the exception of Benoit Rochon's microdrive laying abandoned on his kitchen counter, it still looked like the model unit. It could've been anyone's home, but anyone else would've left some essence of themselves behind, whereas he was just leaving it empty.

The walk from his building to Toronto's Hikari International office was forty minutes at a leisurely pace. With no press of commuters filling the snow-dusted sidewalks at six forty-five in the morning, he could take in the relative stillness of the city. Sirens wailed in the distance, but their sound was drowned out by the chill wind forced through the tunnels of office skyscrapers and condominiums.

The scent of burned wood and rubber carried on the wind. A light dusting of snow had fallen on the city as the temperatures fell overnight.

Unless he stretched or tried to move quickly, he could ignore the ache from Hunter's beating. Aggressive, deep purple bruises had already formed on his lower right rib cage and below his solar plexus. Mathis had no context to put his discomfort in. It might've been bad, but his expectations had been crippling, and he wasn't. He counted himself fortunate as he stepped into a cafe, got a large coffee, and sipped it as he continued walking to his office.

Mathis didn't engage his Net connection with his contact lenses, fearing he'd leave a direct trail of metadata. He took in the city with eyes unpolluted by data overlays and distractions. It was surprisingly banal and dreary without the constant visual chatter of augmented vision enhancing or distracting from it.

City vehicles were out in force, cleaning up after what might've been a riot. Numerous burned-out or badly damaged luxury vehicles littered the sides of the street, and others had their windows smashed or tires slashed. The financial district was a mess of garbage, graffiti, and broken windows. Firetrucks and firefighters lingered, exhausted from battling arson throughout the night. A handful of police cruisers were blocking the street, and the officers were redirecting vehicle traffic. Bloodstains were cordoned off by police tape in several locations. The ferocious transition from mass protests to the Days of Anger made it seem he was on the cusp of living in a failed state. It all felt underwhelming. He recalled photographs of kids playing in the rubble of their neighbourhoods after air raids, how easily violence and destruction could be normalized.

More people were on the streets now, bundled up against the cold and heading in early for another long day of white-collared labour, uninterested in the legacy of the evening's carnage. Everyone wore UkiyoARs of some variety, giving a fraction of their attention to their surroundings. Eyes and minds divorced from context, bodies propelled forward by the imperative to trade task and time for food, shelter, and distraction.

Hikari International's office building had been spared any damage due to geography. It was a couple of streets east of the financial district and wasn't in the hot zone of protest or terrorist activity. Maybe it would be tonight. He went through the biometric security scans at the front and offered his digital key to access the elevators. He rode to the thirty-fourth-floor cafeteria for another coffee. Hikari, true to the Japanese namesake, was always brightly lit.

Mathis still had plenty of time before his first meeting. After exchanging rote pleasantries with a handful of night shifters who wanted to earn his attention, he made his way to the development department's meeting room to run an obfuscated backup of the version control server and prepare for the insertion of his recursive encryption algorithm. Thereafter, he started reverse-engineering and cataloguing Logan's activities, growing increasingly frustrated with himself for not detecting his subordinate's scams that had accelerated Frost's timetable and prematurely dumped the whole mess in his lap.

Fifteen minutes late for their scheduled meeting, Logan pushed into the room, huffing as though he'd run a marathon. "Do you know how hard it is catching rush hour traffic coming in from Dufferin and Lawrence? And what's with the suitcase?"

"Never mind the suitcase. We've got a lot to cover, and I'm already running thin on time."

"Technically, I'm not supposed to start for another forty-five minutes. Accepting your meeting shows how much I admire you." Logan slung himself into a chair opposite and angled to Mathis. His body lurched, gracelessly self-correcting against his momentum. He slapped the tabletop with his meaty palms. "So, what's up, boss-man?"

"I'll save you the public record if you spare me the deceit. I know you're outsourcing your development sprints to an AI code generator made by a hacker collective." He was cautious to meter his tone and pacing despite the increased heart rate and agitation. "It's all Chinese state-sponsored, you idiot. You even gave it access to the secure repository and spoofed all the source check-ins to look like it'd come from your home IP address."

Logan opened his mouth, but no sounds came out. He adjusted his oversized UkiyoARs. Beads of sweat started forming on his brow, growing more saturated throughout the awkward silence. He swallowed audibly, licked his lips and leaned forward, a desperate zeal in his eyes. "Is this off the record?"

Mathis' head already ached from dealing with the confrontation. He started rubbing his temples unconsciously. "Don't embarrass yourself."

He reflexively glanced over both shoulders. "But is it?"

"Maybe."

"I can cut you in. Retroactively, too. You could be a silent partner in my side gig, considering you kind of funded it."

"Skeleton Crucible?" He shook his head at the mistake of saying the name out loud.

"Ah... yeah. That one."

"It's an absurd idea destined to get shut down for copyright infringement, and Evy's going to murder you when she discovers you hijacked her voice."

"Okay, okay. I'll take down the posts as soon as we're done here. I swear." He leaned forward, whispering conspiratorially, "But aren't you even a little bit interested?"

"What's wrong with you?" He searched Logan's eyes for a hint of shame but found only scheming. Sickening. "It's over, Logan. I've already got IT to revoke your access credentials, flagging them as maliciously compromised. They're taking half of Hikari's systems offline for audit and remediation." He grimaced at the conviction in his own voice and the need to exercise his authority. "And before you ask, I can't cover for you and wouldn't even if I could."

"Mathis, buddy..." He trailed off under Mathis' hard stare. "Does Evy know? About the code generator? Are you going to tell her? I saw the calendar appointment in your schedule."

"You'd already be getting tortured in a black site if Evy even suspected."

"I'll assume that's a no on telling her about the Skeleton Crucible stuff, too. Thanks, boss-man! I definitely owe you." Logan finger-combed his hair. "So, should I just get IT to issue me new credentials?"

"You're not taking this seriously." Mathis wasn't certain who the bigger idiot was—Logan or himself for having gone to bat for his subordinate. His frustration was boiling over, spilling into his voice. "You outsourced proprietary code I've dedicated a decade of my life towards to a state-sponsored hacker collective. Ten minutes of Net searching was all it took to figure out the connection to the AI code generator. I can't say whether I'm more upset at your laziness or greed. You need to make this right."

"Buddy, it'll all be okay. I mean, I get it. I could..." He checked over both shoulders before whispering, "I came across a type of trojan on the DarkNet. If you could get IT to enhance my permissions, I could install it on the Hikari servers—"

"No more foreign code on the infrastructure and no more shortcuts." He stared at Logan hard, trying to convey the point. "I have to meet Evy now. I need you to run through these items by the time I'm done." He slid a folded piece of paper across the desk.

"Whose credentials are these?" Logan's interest was piqued. "And what sort of spy shit is this?"

"Maybe the type with continued employment. Tear it to bits and flush them down the toilet when you're done."

"But what if—"

Mathis shot a finger at Logan. "Just do it, Logan. Follow the instructions to the letter and get rid of the list after." Mathis couldn't believe he was trusting Logan with something essential, but didn't have a lot of options. "Don't screw this up. I won't serve time in prison for you."

"Prison!?" He chuckled nervously. "You've got to be joking, right? Right, Mathis?"

He shook his head.

"Listen, buddy. I'll do whatever you need. You've got to help me out here."

Mathis pointed to the paper and walked out of the department meeting room, feeling dirty from both dropping the hammer on a colleague and for his own corporate sabotage. His pace quickened. The wheels of his carry-on suitcase rolled audibly on the marble floors, skipping predictably on each seam. The influx of day shift colleagues regarded him with curiosity but didn't comment. He dropped his luggage off at his desk, ensured the biometric lock was active and made his way to the management wing of the office tower.

The frosted glass door to Evy's office was slightly ajar when Mathis got to it, as was her custom when not engaged in a conference call. He'd interrupted her plenty of times in the past without any anxiety, but this time was intensely personal. His found his body was already starting to turn away from the door. Mathis paced nervously, unsure of how he'd navigate the conversation.

"Are you planning on coming in?" she asked from behind the frosted glass.

He cursed quietly and willed himself through the door to find Evy composed, seated at her desk.

"Christ, Mathis. You're not wearing a tie, and your shirt looks slept in. What if I need you to go on a conference?" She opened a desk drawer and threw a neatly rolled tie at him. "It's black, like my mood with half our infrastructure offline. And don't give me any of your special contract status bullshit. Make yourself presentable while you explain why you've crippled our production capacity."

"Thanks." He smiled awkwardly and started putting on the tie—a Hermes. "Logan's credentials have been compromised."

Her eyes narrowed. "Remind me, what does he have access to?"

"A branch of the current dev repository, but not the master. File servers, basic accounts for his profile and intranet. He's pretty locked down for edit and execute permissions, but I figured it's better to be safe than sorry. After completing their remediation and interviews, you'll get a report from IT."

"Fine." Her previous agitation noticeably slimmed down to irritation. "Would it kill you to run a comb through your hair?" Not a single lock of hers was where it wasn't supposed to be.

The imperative for being well groomed felt surreal to Mathis. He suspected something was afoot. "Evy, I need a big favour."

"Is this about yesterday? If so, I can't help you. Frost is above my pay grade, and head office explicitly instructed us to play nice with him."

"I need to get off the continent."

She paused, appraising him critically. "We're already falling behind development targets. Ones you established and I backed you on, Mathis. This morning's infrastructure outage is going to impact those timelines further. You may not recognize it, but Hikari has put incredible momentum behind your program and is using it to shore up investor expectations. Delays in hitting these milestones will impact the stock price, and if that happens... Well, let's just say we all should avoid that." Evy sighed and leaned forward. "I know you haven't taken any days off these past few years, but now's not the right time."

"Can you arrange for me to work at head office for a couple of weeks? At most, a month."

"Why do you suddenly need to go to Osaka?" Her eyes flickered wide with unease, before falling back into her usual composure. "What's all this about?"

Mathis weighed the options. Evy was far too savvy to misdirect in any non-technical matter, and while she wasn't as proficient as she once was, she retained her ability to see into the heart of even the most complex technical issue. Also, she was dressed for combat in her conservative business attire, defences primed. Something was definitely going on behind closed doors.

"After Frost paid us a visit—"

"I told you, I can't help with Frost."

"It's not Frost. It's Benoit Rochon, the guy at the head of Minus One."

She raised her chin. "The terrorist? What about him?"

"He broke into my place last night and... interrogated me."

"Well, what did you tell him?"

It wasn't the response he was expecting. "Nothing to put me in breach of contract," he lied as evenly as he could manage.

"It's a matter for the police, then. Have you reported the incident?"

"The police aren't equipped to deal with him. They can't even stop commonplace protestors from burning the city. I'm pretty sure they've got their hands full without babysitting me."

He wondered idly whether Evy would've lost any sleep from the fires and rioting in her upscale, uptown neighbourhood last night, but he knew she wouldn't bring it up. She was too professional to reveal anything about her life and expected the same courtesy from him.

"You think you'll be safe in Japan? They've had Minus One incidents there, too."

"Yes, but *he* won't be there."

Mathis pulled up his wrinkled button shirt and turned halfway around, exposing the ugly purple bruise on his lower ribs. He angled to show the one on his sternum. Her jaw clenched, but she didn't betray any further emotion.

"Rochon promised to pay me another visit. I won't get anything accomplished if I stay in town. I know you need me to hit my milestones, and I'll stand behind them, but I need to be somewhere safe to function. Halfway around the world seems like a pretty good option right now."

"I get it. Now, cover up." Her fingers were manipulating the gesture interface of her UkiyoARs. "And you need to be more realistic. I know everyone believes you're some professional rockstar, but you're not an actual rockstar. I can't get you on a charter."

"Hikari could if you gave them a compelling enough reason."

"Such as?"

"Final development of their go-to-market wetware security model needs to be confined to a LAN at head office?"

"Your excuse is a local area network?"

The intensity of her brown eyes and cold tone cut through him. She stood up, automatically smoothing a wrinkle in the line of her skirt and walked up to him, never breaking eye contact. He could see himself shift awkwardly in the translucent reflection of her UkiyoAR glasses and straightened his posture reflexively.

"If I get you on a plane, make sure you sell it when you're onsite. And it'd better justify all the hassle, special treatment, and expense."

"Understood."

"Do you at least own a decent suit and pair of shoes?"

"They'll be the first thing I get there. Promise."

"Are you packed?"

"Suitcase at my desk."

She was uncomfortably close, and her gaze had lost none of its intensity. "Don't fuck me, Mathis. I mean it."

"I know. I won't. Fuck you, that is."

He sighed at how awkward his words sounded. His ears were hot, and he could imagine them flushed red. Stopping himself saying anything further, he opted to endure her lengthy scrutiny in silence. She stepped back to her desk, sat with her back straight, and turned her attention from him.

"Close the door on your way out."

13

Amrita

AMRITA HAD BEEN WALKING the streets for the past number of hours, numb from cold and the shock of her disrupted life. She was trying to wrap her head around her imminent national infamy. It would be impossible to distance herself from the historic data breach and extensive cyber crimes by pleading innocence. There's no way she could return to CSIS, either. Mason would exercise his considerable influence to expedite her prosecution. She'd been too involved in the nation's security apparatus to think there was anything less than endless hours of interrogation without representation waiting for her when the authorities eventually detained her.

The security of partnered nations had been compromised, and the trust of international relations affected. She was certain her name was already synonymous with this catastrophe, her face plastered across the Net and prejudged as the culprit, but Amrita had no safe way to check. Ajay had offered her his personal UkiyoARs, but she'd refused, unwilling to jeopardize him further. All she'd taken was a scarf and the small amount of physical currency in his apartment before leaving.

As the Bloor Viaduct came into view, she took inventory of her situation. Clocks outside corporate buildings showed it was just past nine. Her cousin was undoubtedly on the line with an investigator now. The protocols would be to effectively seal off the city from her egress with facial and movement recognition nets. She assumed the skies were swarming with drones, but there was a surplus of crime in the city to catalogue. She knew she shouldn't be outside, but there was nowhere else to go and being somewhere warm cost money—which she had precious little of. She'd wrapped Ajay's scarf around her lower face and neck, pulled her hat low above her eyes and changed the rhythm of her walking stride, hoping those basic tricks would buy her some time.

Amrita remembered the Bloor Viaduct, the half-a-kilometre-long arched bridge system linking east and west Toronto over the Don Valley, used to be the second most popular bridge for suicides throughout all of North America. Years ago, the city had installed thousands of steel rods at intervals too close for a child to slip through, naming the barrier system the Luminous Veil. She'd always been fascinated by the name and imagined it as a nod towards all those who'd successfully escaped their terminal anguish at the location. As she walked over the viaduct, the seductive urge to throw herself into the river, forest, or multi-lane expressway far below tugged at her. Only the shame her suicide would inflict on her family prevented Amrita from killing herself.

She could practically hear her Auntie Priyanka chiding, *why cry when the birds have already eaten the whole farm?* There was a steadying assurance in knowing things couldn't be any worse.

She leaned on the cold stone of the thick balustrade, closed her eyes and gave herself over to the white noise of traffic all around her. A half dozen lanes far below, the rumble of trains running beneath her feet, the vehicle and bicycle lanes behind her, and the intermittent press of pedestrians. She couldn't remember the last time she'd been still enough to take in the sound of movement. She let the chill air wash over her, gently blowing away her most aggressive concerns and sense of self until only emptiness remained. Eventually, her chattering teeth brought Amrita back to her terrible reality. She had to move. Willing herself to walk west along the bridge, she headed back toward the downtown core.

A blue-haired woman dressed all in white was leaning up against the first balustrade on the opposite side of the viaduct, smoking a real cigarette. Amrita's heart pounded at the sight of Mia Locke. Stomach lurching, she rushed headlong across the five lanes to the other side of the viaduct amid a cacophony of horn honks and angry shouts. Mia, about one hundred metres away, stubbed out her cigarette, and started walking away. Amrita hurried after her, trying to close the distance.

When she got to where Mia had been standing, she found four spent cigarettes lined up in a neat row—dark red lipstick ringed the white filters, the acrid stink of extinguished tobacco lingering. Around Castle Frank subway station, she was close enough to be heard but hung back several metres, adjusting her pace to match Mia's, walking amongst some of the most costly real estate in that area of the city. The scent of burnt buildings, of a night filled with anger, hung thick in the air.

Though she was no longer under the spell of whatever drug they'd put into her drink at the alt-club, Amrita couldn't help but marvel at Mia. The easy rhythm to her walk despite the height of the platforms on her white leather boots, the impractical clothes affording only style against the chill early winter weather, and even the slight sway of her unkept blue hair as it kept tempo to aggressive music emanating from her over-ear headphones.

Mia cut through the path where Castle Frank road came to a bend, heading straight towards a park Amrita didn't know existed. A little further down the road, there was police tape and pools of mostly frozen water. The smell of burnt wood, plastics, and rubber was more prevalent, carried by the chill breeze. She followed Mia down a narrow path between luxury single-family homes until a thirteen-acre park opened up with well-maintained paths running between mature trees.

Mia slipped off her headphones, stopped, and lit another cigarette. Amrita circled to face her, keeping deliberately back. Close enough to talk but not enough to whisper. She had everything to say but was paralyzed at where to start. Mia met her scattered attention with cold, impassive eyes lined in heavy, irregular makeup.

"Say what you're going to."

"Did you know what would happen to me?" Amrita's voice sounded pathetic and disgusting to her ears.

"More or less."

"And you could still do it?"

"You destroy people all the time, but I doubt you carry any guilt." She took a long drag on her cigarette, exhaling as she spoke, "But that's not what you want to know."

Amrita blinked against the tears in her eyes and wiped them reflexively with the fabric of her sleeve. "What am I supposed to do now?"

"There it is." She started walking again, slowing to let Amrita catch up. "You know, I've lived in the city my whole life and never came here before. It'd be a shit place in good weather, polluted by toxic locals, but it's decent enough now."

"I've lost everything."

"There are so few places left in the city to feel like you've got space. Even the public spaces are crowded with people trying to scavenge their shred of peace." She took another long drag off her cigarette, exhaling through both mouth and nose as she spoke. "It's exhausting trying to find comfort."

"I'm scared."

The two walked together in silence while Mia veered towards a park bench. There was a dedication on it—*In memory of Wilhelmina | For your fierce strength, love and | showing us how best to live life.*

Mia brushed some frost off the plaque, her fingers gliding over the inscription with tenderness. "There's not a single dead person who wouldn't trade places with you."

The deadpan delivery could've been humanized with even the hint of a smile, but was left nebulous without. It was as though Mia's face was exhausted from expression. Amrita sat on the far end of the bench, angling space between them.

"I don't know if you're trying to chide or comfort me."

Another drag, another exhale. "You paid for my attention last night, and you have it now."

"Why were you following me?"

She leaned closer. "It's like watching a train derail and the frantic search for survivors. You don't know anyone on board but become invested. Despite what you did for a living, you don't seem awful." She shook her head slowly. "You shouldn't have tried to meet me, though."

Amrita viscerally reflected on the praise and distinction she'd sought, and how spectacularly her initiative had backfired. "I... I know."

"You used your own money to secure me, and it was clear you didn't know the first thing about what you were doing or even why you were doing it. It's been a long time since I've encountered such naivety. Most people judge and are already halfway to implementing an agenda before I ever get face-to-face."

"Pretty sure I was drugged."

"You were an easy mark."

"I have nothing now." The nagging anxiety Amrita had been trying to keep at bay swelled into despair as her mind registered her statement.

"You already had nothing of consequence. You live alone, work alone when not under duress, are isolated from your family and operate as an acquaintance to friends. You partake in insipid online conversations to trick yourself into feeling connected and placate yourself with trinkets until your next achievement marker is obtained."

Amrita was stung to her core. "That's unkind."

"Think you're the only one with access to Carnivore? Benoit wrote the damn thing."

The name of Benoit Rochon dragged Amrita deeper into the pathos of her situation. Mason had been right all along, and her own arrogance had sacrificed caution to ambition. She wasn't having a heart-to-heart with a sympathetic stranger, she was engaged in conversation with a terrorist who'd already stripped her in advance of any protection, excuse, or justification. She was naked and exposed, stunned at the level of violation and hurt there was left to experience.

"I…" Amrita trailed off, not knowing how to process it.

"Your digital construct confirmed, with high scores in accuracy and integrity, that you're earnest, not clever, and eager for approval. *Unremarkable* was the term it used. Sucks when you betray yourself." Mia took a thoughtful drag on her contraband cigarette. "Do you know why he made the damn thing? To find a Warrior Poet King worthy of people's trust."

"That makes no sense."

"No, it doesn't. Everyone is corruptible. And even if it weren't the case, directives would get twisted, coerced, and mutilated through the inevitable greed of gatekeepers." She shook her head, blue locks glancing off her face, partially concealing her eyes. "The way forward is through a sustained expression of anger."

Amrita immediately recognized the quote from all the times her boss Mason had cited it. "You're saying Rochon's words."

"He's smart enough to know counterculture movements self-immolate in purges, trying to outdo each other in some ideological purity contest. They get caught, get stupid, kill their darlings and do the work of the one percent for them. Minus One is different. There's no status to aspire towards, no courts or tribunals, and no asking permission. There's only action and outcomes."

"Why are you telling me this?"

"Years ago, your cousin posted a video of your family celebrating your job at CSIS. You said you wanted to *work within the system to change the system*. Your digital construct verified it was a long-held but forgotten ideal. You're indoctrinated into the status quo now, but not irredeemable." Mia leaned uncomfortably close, exhaling smoke with her words. "So, do you want to change the system?"

14

Miyu

AN OLD, WHITE DELIVERY van with rusted steel rims and bald tires pulled up to where Miyu and her father were laying low. They hadn't talked in the time they'd been waiting, each consumed with thoughts too daunting and perilous to confront or voice. When the side cargo door of the van slid open, the diminutive figure of Teo Hagen emerged, dressed in layers of mismatched white garments with pockets bulging with tech. Whatever style or design the clothing once had was now subverted with the careless application of utility. As Miyu and her father stepped into the open, Teo's carefree smile transformed into a scowl, gaze locked on Tatsuo's imposing and bloody appearance.

"No, no, no. Seventeen, you can't bring some bleeding musclehead." He shook his head vigorously. The welder's UkiyoAR goggles he wore blackened automatically, and he yanked his hood deep over his face, further concealing himself.

"He's my dad, Teo." Miyu used his name instead of his Minus One assigned number.

"Why's he wearing a t-shirt in winter?"

Collecting favours was always difficult for her. Channelling what Rei would do, Miyu unhooked her ventilator and took off her mirrored goggles, knowing his interest in both her and her surgery. It was dirty, but also arrested him.

"Just please, Teo," she softly implored.

He paused midway through closing the cargo door and sized up Tatsuo critically. "Who did he piss off?"

"No one." She stole a glance at her father. "Everyone," she corrected herself. "But he's my dad, and I need to get him help."

Teo hid most of his small body behind the van frame, peeking out a head and shoulder in the cargo door opening. "Benoit won't like it. He's already put out word you need to be brought in. You know how he can get when people go AWOL."

She sighed, already feeling the tentacles of the Minus One movement constricting her. "I know."

"What's his problem?" Tatsuo's delivery made the question sound like a statement.

Again, thankful few people in Toronto spoke Japanese, Miyu answered while not breaking Teo's gaze. "It's fine, Dad. Let me handle this, okay?" She switched back to English. "I can't exactly bring him to a hospital. He needs a few minutes with Rodrigo, and then I'll get him out of the way."

Teo shook his head. "Nope. I'll go as far as dropping him at a walk-in. The one at Moss Park is on the way and doesn't ask questions."

"I'm not going to dump my dad there, Teo. That whole area is nothing but junkies, dealers, and pimps. Either bring us to Rodrigo, or I'm not coming."

"It's not that bad. Just tell him not to make eye contact and stay away from their tents."

Miyu took a step back, closer to Tatsuo. "No."

Teo held a frown in silence. "I'm going to have to call this in." He shut and locked the cargo door.

Tatsuo turned to face Miyu. His shivering was discernible but controlled. "How do you know that asshole?"

"It's complicated."

"You didn't, you know..." He winked, smirking with one side of his mouth, mirth becoming the dominant expression on his bruised and blood-smeared face.

"No, Dad! Don't be gross."

Again, Miyu didn't understand her father's ability to switch mindsets. If she were him, she'd be consumed with the killing or their terrible situation, but somehow, he was impossibly able to live in the moment. His lips were starting to turn blue, though. He crossed his arms across his chest, tucking his hands under his armpits, and shifted his weight from side to side but otherwise, betrayed little discomfort. The cold wasn't registering at all in his voice.

Her father shrugged. "Probably a good thing. He looks like a f—" He caught himself. "Like a pussy, that is."

Tatsuo appeared to be seeking acknowledgement for keeping his promise, and Miyu nodded cautiously in recognition of his effort. *It was always about body parts and sexuality with men...*

The cargo van door slid open noisily. Teo's goggles were transparent again, and his cowl was thrown back. "I have to scan him."

She exhaled, her tensed shoulders dropping in relief. "He doesn't carry tech."

Teo let out a nervous chuckle. "Hunter would kill me if I didn't."

She knew he was trying to joke, but the statement had a non-zero probability of truth. People whispered stories in stolen moments—that Hunter had murdered his commanding officer in Canada's elite special operations force, JTF2, that he'd *disappeared* Minus One associates, and that he had an active ledger on everyone. Hunter's black-and-white enforcement within Minus One was universally feared, and terrified members fell silent in his presence. He'd once unexpectedly approached Miyu, expressing awkward condolences for the death of a cat she'd been trying to nurse back to health. The mere thought of the unnervingly ardent encounter, the one time she'd seen Hunter in a non-transactional verbal exchange, remained chilling.

"Fine, but don't be weird about it." To Tatsuo, she said, "He needs to do a quick check for weapons and devices."

"Tell him to get fucked."

She pursed her lips, agitated. *He always had to make things hard.* "It'll be quick, like the police in Japan."

The comparison brought forward the kindly image of Officer Matsumoto all those times her father had been taken away, and Matsumoto had stuck around to comfort her and Rei until the social workers came. Miyu wondered if he was still on the force or even alive.

Teo kept a wary distance from Tatsuo, circling close enough with a handheld scanner to complete the action. He took two steps backwards before putting away his kit and addressing Miyu.

"You can ride up front with me, Seventeen."

She didn't relish the prospect of sitting beside Teo but also didn't want to face her father's inevitable litany of questions if she stayed in the back with him. "You'll have to go in the cargo area, Dad."

"Where are we going?"

"Some place safe to get you stitched up." She didn't wait for his response and climbed into the front passenger seat.

Teo's face pinched in consternation. "Hey, your eyes are pretty, uhm..."

She angled her face away. "Infected. Yeah, I know."

He angled, inspecting them closely. "You might want to get Rodrigo to check them out."

She nodded, uncomfortable under the intense scrutiny of his magnified vision. Most people tried to avoid staring at the botched transhuman procedure, but her eyes had always fascinated him. Either that, or he took some alien comfort in being around another freak.

"Seems like you haven't been eating, either."

"I will." Miyu couldn't stomach justifying herself or her state to him. She forced herself to be upbeat. "Are you still making music?"

His face lit up. "I've been tweaking my algorithms to produce some mathy, progressive grindcore. There's no vocals yet, but—"

"Why don't you put it on?" Miyu offered him a disarming smile, hoping she'd successfully channelled some of her sister's charisma. Her face felt weird trying to be charming. A disfigured plastic mould. She turned away as her expression soured, catching her translucent reflection in the window—partially present, easily overlooked, and lacking substance. It struck her as holding a greater truth of self.

As the chaotic, aggressive, and discordant music started after the engine turned over, she prompted herself to feign renewed interest, edging up the volume to drone out his conversation, and her father's complaining from the back. She tried to lose herself in the chaotic sounds as the van took them away from her squat and the carnage therein. Her father soon stopped his grumbling, and later, Teo's words ebbed. Eventually, even the music stopped, leaving the dull sounds of commuting traffic. Stops and starts, the stutter of the antiquated combustion engine, the soft squeal of brakes needing service, the cacophony of the outside world muted behind a layer of tempered glass and rusted steel.

The beaten-up, upholstered bucket seat was remarkably comfortable. Miyu had drifted off by the time they'd arrived at one of the few non-descript industrial buildings not converted into an evangelical church, off Victoria Park on Sunrise Avenue. The parking lot was crowded with e-bikes, scooters, cars, and commercial trucks. She'd never seen more than a handful of vehicles at the place before. Teo angled the cargo van behind one of the far trucks, cut the engine, and jumped out of the vehicle.

She put back on her goggles and ventilator before pivoting to see her father—a pending calamity sitting cross-legged in the gap between the wheel well and rear doors.

"Try not to say anything when you get inside. The less they know about you, the better."

Teo was gesturing animatedly toward Hunter's massive, black-clad figure. A sick knot of anxiety filled her stomach. She couldn't make out what was being said between the two but knew it wasn't good if Hunter was part of the welcoming party.

Tatsuo got to a crouch, poised one knee down, one foot planted. "What's going on, Miyu?"

"Nothing. Don't worry about it."

"Are you in trouble?"

When am I not? "Just don't embarrass me, okay?"

She didn't wait for a response and stepped out of the cargo van, closing the door behind her. Tatsuo opened the rear doors from the inside and got out before Teo or Hunter closed the distance.

"Where do I know your dad from?" Hunter asked Miyu, angling to intercept Tatsuo.

"Nowhere. He's never been overseas."

"No, I recognize him from somewhere. He's got some muscle on him, huh?"

"Please, don't, Hunter. He's... he's like you."

Miyu didn't know a better way to express it, but it didn't matter. Hunter's interest was unnerving, and he'd already walked past her. The two men were sizing each other up, as though prize fighters at a stare-down, each stepping forward until they were no further apart than the distance of two hands. Hunter was taller by twenty centimetres and much broader. Her father didn't exhibit a fear response.

"Tell this asshole he's going to get smacked if he doesn't back off."

"Dad!"

Hunter didn't break eye contact with Tatsuo. "Translate, Seventeen. Word for word."

There wasn't space to come between them. Panicked, Miyu dashed towards her father, her tired and feverish mind scrambling for a way to de-escalate the confrontation.

"Dad, he's a friend!"

"Oh. No hard feelings, huh?" Tatsuo clapped Hunter on the shoulder and immediately snapped back at ease. He turned away to face Miyu, acting as if Hunter wasn't there. "You should've said something," he casually mentioned.

"I shouldn't have to!" Miyu was trembling with fear-based adrenaline at the narrowly avoided encounter.

"Tell him I'll buy him a beer or something."

Hunter hadn't yielded any ground and was maintaining the same intensity. "What did he say to me?"

"I told Dad you're a friend. He apologized for the misunderstanding and said he'll buy you a beer."

"Hmmn." Hunter caught and held Miyu's gaze, carefully weighing her words before letting go of his confrontational posture. "Benoit wants to see you."

If Miyu had proper eyes, they would've betrayed her. Icy chills ran down her spine as Hunter fell in behind her and Tatsuo. Her father didn't appear the least bit concerned about having a killer at his back.

"Place looks like a shithole." Tatsuo was trying, in his particular way, to make conversation.

"Why are you being like this? So bloodthirsty."

Tatsuo frowned. "This city is like fighting in an opponent's hometown. You don't know which of the local fans will throw something at you or try to take a shot." He stopped walking for a moment and turned to face her. "And you surround yourself with assholes."

There was nothing Miyu could say to the truth. She silently walked the rest of the way to the entrance. Teo was holding the door open for them, unconcerned about letting in the cold air, not appreciating warmth as a privilege.

As they got close, the crash of voices competed with the pounding base, clever keys, and slick bars of old-school Quebecois hip hop. Commands shouted, the general din of elevated conversation. Entering the building, she was hit by the warmth and unpalatable scent of people. The musty odour evoked hated memories of packed train cars without AC in Osaka's humid and sweltering summer months. Scores of Minus One followers dressed all in white were rushing amongst ramshackle desks and working projected screens in the open space of the warehouse area.

The walls were crammed with racks of shelving, holding tools, stacks of various uniforms, professional accessories, and unmarked wooden boxes filled with different generations of tech. In the spaces not already occupied hung banners, painted graffiti, or posters for the cause. Stencilled artwork was spray painted on both the floor and walls. Emblems of –1 were everywhere. Dozens of languages were spoken within earshot—to each other or confederates worldwide. The Minus One headquarters was chaotic and, on the surface, unfocused, but the air of victory was unmistakable.

No one paid them any attention.

The movement was more extensive than Miyu knew, but she'd never envisioned as many vetted members in Toronto. Assembling in one space was as reckless as it was impressive. The Days of Anger had brought them together to change the world, but she didn't share any of her confederates' intensity or excitement.

A projector painted statistics in coloured light on a bed sheet draped over the catwalk suspended five metres above the unfinished concrete floor. Three hundred and twelve cities participating, constantly updating tickers of cumulative damage estimates, plus the numbers for activists incarcerated, hospitalized, or killed. The sheer scale of havoc was mind-numbing. Four hundred billion in damages, with thousands jailed or hospitalized and twelve hundred confirmed deaths.

"What are you mixed up in, Miyu?"

Her father was barely audible over the chaotic din of the environment. Miyu pretended not to hear him. It was all escalating so fast. A rogue simulation. Her breathing grew shallow and rapid. She caught Teo's eyes and nodded toward the triage area.

"Teo will take you to the doctor, Dad."

Tatsuo shook his head, concern etched on his face. "I'm sticking with you."

Miyu felt like a leaf being swept along by a river's current, soon to be sucked into the inky blackness below or ejected to lay ruined at the periphery. "I'll be fine."

She beelined to the industrial metal stairs leading to Benoit's overseer's office. Her legs were shaky climbing the stairs, weak either from anxiety or her growing fever. The door at the top was open. An invitation she desperately didn't want to accept, holding an expectation she couldn't fulfil.

From the railed landing outside the opened door of the office, she observed Benoit sitting alone at his desk, dressed in a white suit and tie, consumed by the weak illumination of an old handheld device. Temporarily caught between not wanting to disturb him and being driven by his imperative, she slipped in, careful not to make a sound.

"Close the door behind you."

"Yes, Monsieur Rochon," she replied.

He gestured at her with a discreet wave of his finger. She'd been trained to wait for it and stepped forward as instructed.

"Where were you last night, Seventeen?"

She wanted to speak, to lessen his disappointment in her, but had no words. Benoit didn't countenance excuses, and there was no legitimate reason to offer. She bowed her head, wishing she could close her eyes.

Benoit closed in. One hand grasped her by the back of her neck, and the other roughly stroked her shaved head. His fingers and thumb dug in below the back of her jaw, squeezing and guiding her face up, lifting her to her toes and arching her back to try in vain to escape some of his force. She gasped involuntarily. The pressure tightened further, not allowing her to close her mouth fully.

"I was with my dad," she whimpered.

Benoit used his free hand to unclasp her ventilator and pull back her goggles, exposing her fully. The harsh industrial lighting cast deep shadows on her gaunt and unnatural expression.

"You foreswore your blood family."

"I didn't have a choice."

"We always have choices. You returned to the life you swore to reject on the most important day for the movement."

Miyu was writhing from the pain of his grip. "I didn't want to. Please!"

Benoit relaxed his pressure, but she remained trembling. He leaned closer, his breath hot on the nape of her neck.

"We've worked hard for this. Suffered. In the moment when we needed to be unified, you were nowhere to be found. You abandoned us."

"I'm sorry." She began speaking quicker than she could process. "I didn't want him here. He was never supposed to leave Japan. I was never supposed to see him again. Before last night, I hadn't spoken to him in years. Please, Monsieur Rochon, you have to believe I never wanted him. I don't even like him."

An unwanted and instinctual sense of self-preservation surpassed Miyu's shame. He wrenched her neck back, forcing her to face him. The angle of her vision was odd and disjointed but captured his menace in full.

"You made me a promise. In front of all your brethren, you swore your past had no future and were fully committed to the movement."

"I am." The pressure of his grip increased, growing into a crushing force. If she had eyes, they'd be watering. Her right leg spasmed violently. "I'm sorry," she whimpered again.

"You've disappointed me."

Benoit let go. She immediately fell to her knees before him.

"Tell me what I can do to make it better. Please."

He bent down to give a final rough stroke to her shaved head and walked back to his desk. A predator stalking wounded prey. She remained kneeling on the unfinished concrete floor before him, the weight of his judgement crushing her.

"You'll perform penance and confess to all the members."

Miyu knew Minus One was a movement of vengeance, not forgiveness, and confessions were precursors to disappearances. She swallowed the her desperate pleas. "I understand."

"Now, there's the matter of what to do with your father."

"He's no one. Just a punch-drunk idiot." Her voice cracked with emotion as she recognized some of what he meant to her. "Please, Monsieur Rochon, he's harmless."

"Only a daughter would say such a thing about that man." He poured himself two fingers of whiskey and finished half of it, maintaining eye contact with Miyu. He set the plain rocks glass down carefully. "You were the one who brought Hikari to my attention and even earned your name from it. Mathis Grenier was your task."

"He was." Her voice was barely above the sound of a whisper.

"You failed to recruit him."

"I failed," she echoed.

"He's boarding a flight to Osaka as we speak." Benoit let the silent tyranny of expectation consume the room. "You have connections there."

"Yes."

"Then they'll need to do what you could not."

Miyu's body crumpled onto itself. "Please, Monsieur Rochon. Anything but that."

"You defy me?"

"No, It's just—"

"No more excuses, Seventeen."

"I—" She grimaced, disgusted with herself. "I understand."

He reached into his desk drawer and pulled out a rectangular leather-bound kit. Unzipping it, he held a syringe half-filled with an amber liquid for her to see. "How is your pain?"

"It's awful," she whimpered.

"Your connections in Osaka need to get Mathis onboard within two days. For your father's sake."

"You'll spare him?"

He hesitated. "Conditionally."

"And me?" She mouthed the words more than speaking them.

"No, never you, Seventeen."

15

Tatsuo

TEO THREADED EASILY THROUGH the erratic movements of dozens of Minus One associates as they darted back and forth across the gaps between tables and makeshift workstations. A veteran of narrow and crowded Osaka laneways, Tatsuo followed without losing a step. The unfocused noise and raw expression distracted him. People were loud in the West. Desperate to be heard but also never seeming to listen. Most members he passed were barely old enough to be charged as adults. Their zeal and self-importance were as much of a uniform as the fancy all-white clothing.

As Teo and Tatsuo approached the triage area, clusters of battered and bandaged members lingered, sitting cross-legged on the unfinished concrete floors or leaning against the graffiti-covered cinder block wall. Men and women both, their wounds making them look even younger. Like hurt kids unable to reconcile the implications of their actions. Those same impractical white clothes were stained with blood from haphazardly treated injuries by those still awaiting medical attention. They were the wounds of trudgeons, rubber bullets fired point-blank, or proper gunshots. At least one pale figure wasn't moving—eyes open, mouth slightly parted, and with enough blood on the floor around her to confirm she'd bled out. The cries of pain from those behind the door were audible above the chaos of the environment. Tatsuo was curious why he hadn't registered the agony earlier.

Teo opened the door enough to slip through and disappeared. Tatsuo hesitated, contemplating whether trying to find Miyu and getting her out of the situation would be worse than her inevitable rejection and the complications he'd burden her with. It was always a crapshoot with his daughters. He stayed still, weighing options, until Teo opened the door and shouted something over the cacophony of chaos. The kid was trying to be authoritative but came off sounding like an angry mouse. Tatsuo chuckled to himself and, lacking a clear direction otherwise, decided to follow.

The large triage area was overflowing with wounded crying out for help, crying in pain, or just crying quietly. A neat row of bodies was arranged at the far end of the room. Amid the suffering, a handful of doctors and nurses were trying their best to attend to the most desperately in need. Glancing around, Tatsuo recognized his wounds were nowhere near as urgent as anyone else's.

Teo marched directly to a surgical table, squeezing between a patient being operated upon and the doctor. Both the attending nurse and the doctor started hurling abuse at Teo, but the kid didn't budge and tried to force a small box into the doctor's hands. Tatsuo didn't understand what they were saying, but *Rochon* was repeated multiple times. Exasperated, the doctor snapped off his bloody gloves and threw them to the floor with disgust as he gave hurried instructions to the nurse who had been assisting him. He took the box, though.

As he strode angrily towards Tatsuo, the doctor tore off his mask, uncovering a full beard framing an agitated, tanned face. He flipped up and off his headlamp in a practiced gesture. Blood streaked the teal surgical scrubs with hints of spray dried on his face above the mask line and under the surgical cap. Teo shuffle-skipped around obstacles to keep up with him, speaking in rapid, incomprehensible language the whole time.

Without hesitation, the doctor grabbed Tatsuo by the forearm with a surprisingly firm grip. "Come with me."

"Hey, you speak Japanese!" Tatsuo reflexively broke the grip.

"Amongst a dozen other tongues." The doctor again grasped Tatsuo's forearm, gentler this time. "Now, come."

Teo was plaguing the periphery, barking instructions in his angry mouse voice. The doctor didn't turn to address him but said something to stop Teo from following as he led Tatsuo towards a lit doorway at the far wall beside the rows of bodies. Tatsuo allowed himself to be guided past the suffering, dying, and dead into a cramped storeroom filled with medical supplies. The doctor gestured for Tatsuo to sit on a box, closed and latched the door, and pulled one of the unmarked plastic pails from below the bottom shelf for himself to sit on. Face to face, they were practically touching knees.

"My name is Rodrigo Joaquin Carrasco. Tell me, what have you done?"

He searched the doctor's eyes for a hint to contextualize the question. "I don't understand."

"Listen—" Rodrigo pointed at him.

"Tatsuo."

"Listen, Tatsuo. I don't have time for bullshit, okay? The sooner we're done here, the quicker I can get back to saving lives. I need to know what you've done."

"You mean this?" Tatsuo gestured to his shoulder and forearm.

"No, for me to put an explosive in you."

His fists were already clenched. "The fuck you are."

Rodrigo seemed oblivious to the terrible violence Tatsuo could unleash on him. "Whether it's me or someone else, it'll happen. Worse if not by me since no one else has any real medical training here. I'm offering you a courtesy, and you'd be well advised to take it."

"I don't know anything about you guys. I just arrived yesterday."

"Who does he control with your life at his fingertips?" When Tatsuo didn't immediately respond, Rodrigo sighed. "Is it Seventeen?"

Tatsuo squinted, his head at a slight tilt.

"Seventeen," Rodrigo repeated, as though sufficient. "The one with the strange eyes."

"My daughter's not a fucking number. Don't call her that."

"Fine. Unfortunate, though." Rodrigo frowned. "She's a sweet girl."

Rodrigo took a pair of angled sheers from his coat pocket and pulled Tatsuo's wrist towards him. In a swift movement, the blades cut through Tatsuo's clothes before Tatsuo processed what was happening. Two more travelling cuts exposed the untreated wounds, and Miyu's improvised bandages fell to the floor. Rodrigo shoved them aside with a sweep of his foot and started pulling items from the shelf.

"I know how this works, even if you don't. It's you or both of you." He stopped rummaging for supplies and turned to face Tatsuo, evaluating him carefully. "It'll be hard on her if you fight. Besides, you don't strike me as someone who would sacrifice their child. Your wounds aren't bad. Do you want me to stitch you up before or after?"

Rodrigo stared at him, impossibly detached, expecting an answer. Tatsuo's heart raced, his mind skipping between the madness of Rochon's imperative and Miyu's vulnerability. He couldn't see a way to win. Outclassed in a rigged match, he traded his suffering to lessen his daughter's exposure.

"After, then. Shouldn't we be out there, Doc?"

"Just Rodrigo. I never finished my training. And no, not out there. You can imagine these things are difficult to explain. People would ask questions."

Tatsuo allowed the doctor's sheers to slice through the fabric of his shirt. The garment fell in two pieces to the floor. "You're different from the street docs from Osaka."

"We're not in Osaka." Rodrigo edged closer, staring critically into Tatsuo's eyes. "You look familiar with pain. You can appreciate that I can't spare anesthetics for people outside the movement. Do you want something to bite on?"

Tatsuo shook his head, apprehensive.

Rodrigo set up a makeshift instrument area on another cloth-covered plastic bucket, carefully placing a scalpel, a semi-rigid tube with a boxed digital interface, a pair of long clamping instruments, and disinfectant with fresh swabs. After adding a set of curved needles and thread, he poured some disinfectant into a shallow dish. Lastly, he carefully opened and set down the small metal box Teo gave him, exposing a mechanical device about the size of a child's fingertip nestled into black foam rubber.

"I'm going to perform a modified version of thoracoscopic surgery. I won't lie. With no anesthetics, it's going to hurt. A lot. You'll need to keep still so I don't kill you." He threw a cloth on Tatsuo's lap. "You can press this against your abdomen to mop up the blood, but don't move around. Any questions?"

Of all his questions, one mattered most. "How'd my little girl get mixed up with you guys?"

"Seriously?"

Tatsuo nodded.

Rodrigo scowled, flipped down his headlamp and synced his medical glasses to the tubed instrument. He snapped on a pair of surgical gloves, disinfected the area between the second and fourth ribs on the left side of Tatsuo's sternum and picked up the scalpel.

Tatsuo's teeth were already clenched, his hands balled into fists, preparing for pain. The deft stab of the scalpel penetrating the cavity between his ribs shocked him. His muscles constricted, and he started to sweat immediately. Rodrigo used one of the long instruments to spread open the small incision and inserted the tubed device. The pressure and probing were unlike anything Tatsuo had experienced. He lost colour in his face, and a shock of sweat covered his body. Blood was flowing out of his chest—thicker at the heartbeat.

"If you're going to be sick, tell me." Rodrigo grabbed Tatsuo's free hand and guided it to the spreading instrument. "Hold this. It's okay you're trembling now, but when I tell you to stop, stop."

Tatsuo squeezed his eyes shut, trying desperately to regulate his breathing. The scalpel worked left and right, finely cutting through fibres of his flesh, going deeper by small increments over the top of his heart. He'd never been this close to being murdered before. Whether from shock or novelty of sensation, the pain muted to a jarring level of discomfort.

"You're doing fine." Rodrigo used another long instrument to carefully remove the small mechanical device from its foam rubber housing and dropped it in the shallow dish of disinfectant. He turned it over twice and brought it closer to the incision. "Now, you need to stop shaking and hold very still."

Tatsuo wasn't aware he was moving, but the hand holding the spreading instrument was practically spasming. Rodrigo's brown eyes were staring at him, impatient and expectant. Tatsuo tried his best to suppress the sensations he was experiencing. He started counting back from ten in his mind, and when he hit zero, he nodded stiffly to Rodrigo.

"You're going to make me kill you!" Rodrigo let out an exasperated sigh, and shook his head. Grudgingly, he took the cap off a pre-filled syringe and injected it without hesitation into the muscle of Tatsuo's shoulder.

"What was that?" Immediately, his anxiety lost its urgency, and the desperate strain on his body relaxed.

"Another person's suffering. Don't make me regret squandering what little I have on you." With an economy of movement, he inserted the small explosive into the tubed device, mechanically pressing it deeper into the incision, but stopped abruptly. "Hey, don't make me kill you."

Tatsuo did his best to clear his mind from the conflicting sensations of sedation, pain, and hyperawareness. He closed his eyes and tried to summon a mental image of his daughter, the one he knew from Japan, but was haunted by the vision of Miyu's shaved head, near-skeletal body, scornful expression, and those strange convex discs she wore for eyes, surrounded by junkies and homeless. He didn't know how he'd gone so wrong, done so poorly as a parent, to have his little girl end up like that. It hurt worse than losing his wife to a similar fate, trying to pull her back from the edge but watching her disappear in stages. *What about him drove the women he loved willfully into oblivion?* Time blurred in his intimate agony. He was vaguely aware of having his body manipulated, of complying, but his emotional saturation overwhelmed him and inhibited focus. He was fairly certain he blacked out at one point but found himself seated when his consciousness returned.

"You did well." Rodrigo completed the last of a small band of stitches to close the narrow incision in Tatsuo's chest. He snapped off his bloody surgical gloves, threw them into a garbage can and took one of the clothes off the shelf. He gently wiped the tears from Tatsuo's cheeks. "Use this to clean yourself up. We'll get to the other wounds after you take a moment to collect yourself."

Tatsuo blinked the last tears from his eyes, wiping them off with the back of his forearms. The sweat made his eyes sting and water afresh. He used the clean cloth to wipe down his body, only managing to spread the mess of blood and sweat across his chest. Rodrigo gestured to the garbage and patiently waited with a fresh cloth as Tatsuo threw both bloody ones into it. His chest was throbbing, but the drugs coursing through his body made the pain manageable. Fresh sweat was met with another wipe-down.

"Tssk. Careful around the stitches."

"About my daughter, Doc."

Rodrigo shook his head. "Still not a doctor. Are you going to be sick?"

Tatsuo squared his shoulders. Years of combat sports had taught him how to trick a referee into letting a fight continue, and this felt oddly similar. "I'm fine."

"First the forearm, then the shoulder, yes?"

Tatsuo nodded.

Rodrigo put on a fresh set of surgical gloves and spoke as he disinfected Tatsuo's wounds. "I don't know how Seventeen came to the movement—"

"Her name's Miyu."

"Noted, Miyu." Rodrigo lingered on the name, reflective. "No one knew where she'd come from. I remember first seeing her outside, trying to entice a stray cat with food. It was a pitiful thing. Skinny, cold, dishevelled. As was she. I remember watching her from my office, thinking a bit of food and comfort wouldn't improve its chance of survival, but the quiet little drama played out for the better part of an hour." Rodrigo threaded a needle and started to stitch up Tatsuo's forearm carefully. "As a Chilean, class struggle is part of my DNA. I'm practically hardwired to believe in the righteousness of the cause. But quiet little Miyu was different. Always on the outside, hanging around the periphery. She'd never cause trouble, though. She tried to be overlooked, and people got used to her being around. Like the stray cat, she'd trained us to give her what she needed, believing it was our idea. Weirdly, even Hunter softened to her."

"The big guy?"

"Hmmm. Maybe *softened* wasn't correct. I don't know what the right word is in Japanese. Hunter barely tolerates people, but he always seemed okay with Miyu. He'd discipline her as required but stop short of where he'd go with others. He's complicated, and I don't pretend to understand him. But he's different around your daughter. Benoit took an interest in her, too. From my office, I'd often see them together. Nothing sexual. It was mainly him talking and her listening. Benoit likes broken things."

"She's not a thing."

"We all are to Benoit. An agent, an objective, a number. Things. An effective leader can make those distinctions." Rodrigo tied a knot and cut it off, leaving an elegant row of tight stitches concealing the ragged cut from T-Ray's machete. He rethreaded the needle and started working on Tatsuo's shoulder with the same incredible speed and clarity. "Sometimes Miyu would come to my office, and we'd talk. There was nothing I could do about her eyes, though. They cause her tremendous pain. I can see where she gets her tolerance for suffering from now. For a while, I could sneak her hydromorphone. She'd never ask for it directly, but I could tell when she was at the edge. Sometimes, she'd come with the most ferocious infections, and I'd do my best to treat her. I started stocking drip antibiotics for her when the orals didn't prove sufficient. You see, in her quiet and clever way, she'd made me adopt her, too. The closer we got to today, the more difficult it was to deplete our limited stocks of opioids and antibiotics. We'd been expecting wounded in the uprising, but not this many... I don't suppose it would've mattered if I'd given her another few doses."

"You made her into a junkie." Tatsuo solicited the acknowledgement without accusation.

"No, she had plenty of track marks from long before I met her. I offered her something less poisonous than what she could get on the street. When I couldn't manage that, I gave her nutrient gel packs to keep her weight up. I even treated and shaved her head when she came in riddled with lice. I don't know why she keeps her head shaved now, though. It's curious. I tried to convince Benoit to allow her to stay here. She'd keep coming in sick or infected if she remained wherever she was, but Miyu refused even after he'd finally agreed."

Tatsuo's heart was breaking, each detail Rodrigo provided making it worse. "Why wouldn't she?"

"It's like asking why a stray cat won't stay inside. It just won't. For a time, it might, but ultimately, it'll leave. You hope it finds a home, but you know it'll die of sickness or predators or get hit by a car. Maybe it'll freeze to death, or the authorities will pick it up, but that typically ends with euthanasia. It's a short and terrible life for strays in Toronto. Sometimes, all you can do is offer them comfort without expectation."

Tatsuo watched Rodrigo tie off and cut the thread, leaving another neat row of tight stitches. "You're good, Doc."

"Again, just Rodrigo. And no, I'm not good. I put a remote-triggered explosive next to your heart."

Tatsuo was ashamed—for not having been able to care for his daughter, of not even being aware of her suffering, loneliness, and hardships. Of failing so completely as a father. In front of him was a man who'd tried to care for Miyu in his absence.

"Still."

Rodrigo held still for a moment, looking down, and then applied clear bandage adhesives to the three sets of stitches. "For what it's worth, I'm sorry I had to do this to you."

Tatsuo cleared his throat. "Just do me one favour, Doc."

He hesitated. "What's that?"

"Keep an eye out for her after I'm gone."

16

Amrita

Amrita was still sitting on the park bench Mia Locke had left her on to consider a future as a prospective terrorist. The realities of inequality were far more nuanced, pervasive, and intractable than the pitch Mia had put forward. The world *was* fundamentally broken. There *was* too great a concentration of wealth. Society *was* designed for systemic oppression, with too few having access to prosperity. Most people's scant wealth would be stolen at the end by the machinations of corporatized medical institutions instead of helping soften the hardship of life for the next generation. It was a system explicitly designed to extract value and to have everyone start from zero. Except the wealthy.

Amrita could at once accept all these truths and still reject the terrorism crippling the city and spreading like wildfire across the globe. The Days of Anger only worked if the cycle of violence was perpetual, making it worse than the quiet, pervasive economic and cultural violence of the status quo.

She could practically hear her Auntie Priyanka chiding, *to control the mind is like trying to control a drunken monkey that's been bitten by a scorpion.* She was no closer to a course of action and had wasted hours freezing in the exposed elements, competing truths into greater misery.

With fingers numb from cold, she counted the weirdly crisp, plastic currency Ajay had given her, figuring the money would be enough to get some burner UkiyoARs from a pawn shop. She knew of one off Jarvis, not far from the tent cities of Moss Park that CSIS kept under observation. It was a risk, but the prospect of a quick 'cash, no questions' transaction balanced the danger of being caught, and the pawn shop was less than half an hour away by foot.

She stood up stiffly, stretching the constricting tightness from her joints, realizing how bone-cold she was by her trembling. She forced herself into motion, retracing her steps with increasing speed as her body warmed. By the time she returned to Bloor Street, she could blend in with the near-double-time of the other pedestrians. She turned her face against the buffeting, chill wind tunnels of downtown towers until she got to Jarvis Avenue and headed south towards the pawn shop.

Amrita walked past by Allen Gardens, the once beautiful botanical oasis with a celebrated legacy of free admission for urban tranquility. Most of its windows were boarded. The entire park surrounding it had been overrun with tents filled with junkies and the desperately poor. Even in winter, the stench of urine, vomit, and feces was overwhelming.

Desperate eyes followed her, but she hoped the speed of her movement would discourage any interactions.

She eventually slipped down an alley with a hand-painted sign dangling slightly askew over a nondescript doorway. Bargain Traders. The two windows on either side of the steel door were barred and boarded. A little further down the laneway, two sets of legs were poking out from an inset doorway—telltale stains of dried urine pooled from under them. One set was small and skinny, ending in mismatched children's shoes. It took Amrita a moment to process it, and when she finally did, there was nothing for her to do with her understanding.

She gathered her courage and pulled the oversized handle of the steel door. It didn't budge. An antiquated domed camera pointed at her. She pulled back her hood and smiled awkwardly. A moment later, the lock buzzed, and she pulled the door open, stepping immediately into a cage with bars running to the high ceilings. The heavy steel door closed and locked automatically behind her. Amrita was mercifully bathed in the warmth and musty odour of the inside.

An elderly lady dressed in a vintage burgundy suit, unfashionable even for its generation, was evaluating her critically from behind a glass counter filled with small boxes and ornamental trinkets. Alert brown eyes glinted behind a tired face carved with wrinkles and a dour expression. Beyond her, the pawn shop resembled the cluttered home of a geriatric hoarder. In the far corner, an elderly man stared at a section of photographs in antique frames with his mouth agape, oblivious to Amrita's entrance.

"You don't seem like you should be here, young lady." The old woman's gravelly voice was unnaturally low.

"It could be the cage, ma'am," Amrita innocently ventured.

The lady laughed heartily but stopped to cough. "What do you want?"

"I'd like to buy some Net gear, ma'am." She scanned the rows of shelves within view and found nothing remotely technological. "That is if you have any. And you're willing to sell."

"My late husband, God rest his soul, always used to say, *who am I to judge where things come from provided they get to those who truly need them.*" She pressed a concealed button, triggering a buzzing sound and the click of a remote lock. "Come on in and warm up for a while. You look practically white from cold."

"Thank you, ma'am." Amrita stepped out of the cage, relaxing into the environment's warmth and complex blend of gently competing smells.

"I know how old I am. No need to remind me with all the ma'am shit. Call me Maryam." She turned her head and raised her voice, "Benny, go get the gin."

The old man wandered out of sight, hidden behind one of the many shelves of antiques.

"You do like gin, don't you, girl?"

Amrita had never had gin and rarely drank alcohol. "Maybe?"

"Well, first thing's first. How much money do you have?"

Amrita counted out the currency on the table.

"A hundred and twenty-five dollars wouldn't even buy you an ass kicking in these parts," Maryam grumbled, frowning.

It might as well have been all the money in the world for her inability to acquire more, and it still wasn't enough. She unconsciously scratched the side of her neck, embarrassed, as she looked for an angle. "Could I use the Net gear for a bit and return it to you?"

Maryam leaned closer, scrutinizing her for long moments. Amrita resisted the urge to squirm under such intense observation.

"You wouldn't be able to leave."

"That's fine. I don't need long. Ten minutes, tops," Amrita added hastily, trying to sway the old woman.

"Wait here, but if Benny comes back, don't let him drink straight out of the bottle." Maryam disappeared through a barely noticeable slit in the curtain behind the counter.

Amrita tried to distract herself with the neatly organized rows of costume jewellery, low-end watches, and a hodgepodge collection of coins and stamps. On the closest shelves were painted ceramic figures, Tiffany lamps with stained glass designs spanning from garish to modern, and all manner of display knickknacks. Further aside, LP records were stacked neatly beside an antiquated sound system from long before Amrita was born. The walls were cluttered with an eclectic blend of art styles, with elegantly framed pieces crowding each other for space in a Tetris-style layout. The far wall, where Benny had been, was filled with photograph portraits in decorative wooden frames in crowded, stacked layouts. It was all pretty worthless to her, but an informed buyer might find something of value.

"Anything catch your eye?"

"That's all the money I have." Amrita smiled and politely gestured to the modest amount of colourful bills on the countertop.

Maryam placed a blue and white rhinestone-encrusted case on the counter with the name *Julie* written in cursive. "This one just came in. I've already logged you into the account and set a limit of ten minutes of Net time for you."

"Thank you."

"There's a chair near the hi-fi you can use. I'll make sure Benny doesn't bother you."

"Again, thank you, Maryam." She retreated to the relative privacy of an old leather chair beside the sound system. She put on the recent UkiyoAR model, initialized the guest profile and pulled up the terminal. She whispered a handful of shell commands, and the terminal output a screen full of running application threads.

"Maryam, you've got keyloggers, screen recorders, and iris extrapolators running."

"Just turn off whatever you don't want," she replied sweetly in her rasping voice.

Amrita quit all threads, hunted down what little data had been captured and purged the system trash. She initialized the Net connection. Suspecting her CSIS credentials were burnt, she logged into a personal messaging service under a ghost account and sent a conference request to Mason Brand, flagging it as *URGENT! Amrita Chopra: 8 Minutes to Connect!* Afterward, she started up the Net conference app and shut down the display of the preconfigured, sexually explicit avatar for the original owner.

Amrita found herself furiously pacing throughout the three agonizingly long minutes before a guest, *Mason B.,* requested access. Mason's video avatar was the same as his profile in the CSIS offices, but it wasn't his government account. She wasn't sure if it was a lack of imagination or an olive branch in this context.

"Miss Chopra?"

"Mason, thank god. Yes, it's me. I have less than five minutes before the Net connection terminates. I have nothing to do with Minus One or the breach at CSIS last night."

"Curious you'd lead with that. I've had a drone follow you all morning and watched you meet Mia Locke."

There was no getting out of it. The black pit of fear gnawed as it grew. She pressed her stomach with both hands, grimacing as she decided to plunge recklessly forward. "They're trying to recruit me now that I've been painted as a criminal."

"You're rogue and need to come in," he said evenly.

"Sir, I wasn't part of the data breach. Mia stole my credentials."

"And how exactly did she manage to do that?"

"After the Carnivore session, I pulled threads on the DarkNet and set up a meeting. I wanted to come to you with a win."

"Are you a field agent, Ms. Chopra?"

"No, sir, but—"

"You're not even qualified to sit the candidate exams."

"Yes, I know, sir. But I wasn't—"

"And what exactly made you think you could—"

"Sir! Stop, please, just stop! You can dress me down later, but for now, I have four minutes of borrowed Net access, no money and no options."

Mason fell silent for a pregnant pause. "What do you want?"

"I need your help in getting my name cleared. I had nothing to do with the data theft."

"Were those not your credentials?"

"Fire me with cause, charge me with negligence, but for god sake, Mason, I'm not a terrorist!"

"You're behaving irrationally and irresponsibly. You need to come in to get properly debriefed and processed."

She shook her head, aghast at how little emotion he'd invested in the directive. Stiff, formal British. She was certain beyond reason that she'd be interrogated and incarcerated if she went back to CSIS without actionable intelligence. Her family would be condemned to a lifetime of shame with her inevitable prosecution. "I know you've been trying to get an agent close to Minus One for ages. What if I could make the most of the opportunity."

"Again, you're not a field agent."

"Beggars can't be choosers?"

Even Mason's heavy sigh sounded like it had an accent. "This isn't some lemon for you to make into lemonade."

"I can't come in until I make things right." She resented the power imbalance, creating a scenario wherein she was forced to gamble everything, and the best she could realistically hope for in return was prospectively nothing.

"You have neither the power nor the authority to make things right, Ms. Chopra. There are consequences for going rogue. The longer and further you go afield, the worse it'll be for you, and it's bad enough as it is. Don't make it any harder for yourself."

She had no leverage to match the weight of her desperation. "I'll reach out as I can, but if I die, promise you'll clear my reputation posthumously. My family can't have their names dragged through the gutter with mine."

"You're burying yourself here. Stop before you do anything truly stupid."

"Mason, please! Just promise you'll clear my name if I die."

Another pregnant pause. "I'll go on record with this conversation. That's all I can offer."

It wasn't much, but it was something. "I have to go now."

Amrita terminated the conference and immediately started going through the complex web of protocols to get her onto the DarkNet. She logged into her alias, glanced at the timer ticking down her remaining seconds of Net connectivity, and sent out a message to Mia Locke's account. *I'm at Bargain Traders, near Moss*

Park. I'll wait one hour either inside or in the alley. Please come and get me. PS: I won't have Net access going forward.

She sent the message off and logged out of her account and the DarkNet as the timer ran to zero. She was spent from the exhausting regret of staking everything on a longshot. After carefully purging her activities from the device, she packed the UkiyoARs neatly back into the rhinestone case and returned them to the front counter.

"Thank you, Maryam."

"Here, take a drink. You look like you could use it. Also, you can wait longer than an hour if you need to, Miss Amrita Chopra." She smiled and pushed forward a shot glass-sized, disposable cup of gin.

"You saw everything!?" Amrita was horrified. Her exposure was absolute, her vulnerability unlimited.

Maryam grinned and tapped on what Amrita had assumed were reading glasses. "Linked display running in a subroutine off the kernel on the admin account."

"Ah." Amrita cursed herself for assuming the old lady wasn't technically savvy.

"Your boss sure sounds like a righteous prick."

"He is." She tentatively lifted her gin, still uncertain her trust wouldn't be abused, but not seeing any flags that would indicate otherwise.

"You sure there's not something in what he's saying, though?"

She shook her head. "Thank you for letting me stay."

"You can take this back, too. A respectable girl can't exactly go around with nothing in her pockets." Maryam pushed the modest stack of bills back towards Amrita. She drained her gin in one gulp and firmly set down the small cup. "And if you end up dead and your boss screws you, I'll send the Netcast recording to the media."

The old woman's generosity took Amrita aback. "Why are you being so kind to me?"

"It's a tough world, kid. Too hard to always go it alone. If we don't look out for each other, who will?"

17

Rei

Despite how thoroughly exhausted she was, Rei couldn't sleep more than a few hours. Everything ached—even places with no reason to. She checked the time, regretfully acknowledging it was five in the morning and there was no way she'd get back to sleep. She probed around the side of her face and head, wincing as she felt the swollen skin and firm, lumpy protrusions under her hairline. She should've spent more time icing her wounds yesterday.

She ran her finger along the bridge of her nose, wincing at the touch. It was slightly crooked. Rei and Miyu had watched their father set his nose a dozen times when they were children. She took a deep breath, put her thumbs on either side of the bridge of her nose and clenched her jaw tight. With swift, decisive force, she snapped the cartilage back in place. An involuntary scream escaped her lips. Rei found herself gasping in pain. Her father had always made suffering look easy, not even flinching any of the times he'd done it in front of them.

She rubbed the tears from her blackened eyes and gingerly stood up from her futon. Her feet easily found the slippers at the bedside and spared her from the chill floorboards of her modest *manshon* apartment. She had slept in the oversized, white button shift from Ichika's father and her favourite pyjama shorts.

Her nose ran uncontrollably, and Rei wiped it with a bedside tissue. It came away saturated with more blood than mucus. She stepped into the small, Western-style, three-piece bathroom and saw a stranger in the reflection of the mirror—a battered, misshapen face defying symmetry, mascara streaks down both cheeks and blood leaking from one nostril, about to crest her upper lip. Her hair was a tangled mess, both eyes blackened, and her nose was half and again as wide as normal. It was the hijacked body of domestic violence. It wasn't truly her, Rei told herself.

She carefully inspected her teeth, ensuring none were cracked or broken, and checked for cuts concealed by her hair. As she catalogued her other injuries, a serene disassociation settled in. Skinned and bruised knees, bruised right hip and shoulder, and a swollen left ankle from when she was thrown out of Akira Mori's Mercedes. It was hard to rationalize the visual progression of her body's injuries. It'd take weeks to heal. Maybe she'd finally invite Ichika over. She could pick up some medical supplies, whiskey, and snacks on the way. It would be nice to be nursed a little. Rei involuntarily smiled, remembering how happy her father was when she and Miyu tried to out-doctor each other in those simple, early days of childhood.

She wondered whether Miyu was taking care of him and how he was doing on his first time outside Japan. While it was pathetic to worry about her father as though she was the parent, she resolved to connect with Miyu as soon as she'd made herself presentable.

Rei delicately washed her hands and the tear-streaked mascara from her face. She combed her hair and gently brushed her teeth on the softest setting. One side of her mouth near the jawline was tender and made her wince even with the gentlest touch of the electric toothbrush. Despite appearing worse, it didn't feel as bad as it had yesterday. Her pain was muted—or perhaps she was. She'd had a lot to drink, and some alcohol was probably still in her system. She carefully folded Ichika's father's shirt, setting it aside neatly on her desk before slipping on a sports bra and a long-sleeved cotton shirt to compliment the comfort of her pyjama shorts.

Rei made herself a black coffee and sat at her modern glass and steel desk, growing more composed as she followed her regular morning routine. Sparing herself the discomfort of UkiyoARs on her swollen face, Rei checked her handheld, her attention caught by a series of alerts. A message from Kazuo Ogawa, the elusive chief technical officer of Hikari International, and one from her sister. It had been years since Miyu had reached out first. Of course, Ichika had sent numerous messages, but affection and self-care always took a back seat to duty. She opened Ogawa's message.

While I certainly won't complain about being gifted an 18-year Yamazaki Mizunara, I was surprised it arrived in your stead. Your calligraphy remains exceptional and a consistent delight to enjoy. I'd been looking forward to discussing a unique incentive Hikari may be prepared to reward the faith of special investors such as yourself, Miss Yoshida. As you've so often said, some things are best discussed in person, and I'm afraid your lack of availability for the next two weeks may limit the opportunity. Of course, I'm just a dressed-up tech guy, and there may be an exception made if you'd reconsider your existing investments. Perhaps we could even open the Yamazaki together then. I promise to not pry on the competing interests that unexpectedly robbed me of your company last evening.

Rei cursed aloud. Ogawa had effectively doubled the buy-in and was stringing her along with non-committal offers. It was eerily similar to how she tightened the noose around her suitors. There was no more money she could access from the clan, and her personal funds wouldn't cover a fraction of the amount needed to keep the game afoot. Unless something changed, there'd soon be insufficient income to pay the monthly stipend for the clan's rank and file. Rei was bringing about the clan's downfall more surely than any clan war or internal betrayal.

Rei held her breath until her chest throbbed, then let it out slowly. With her eyes closed, she focused on trying to control her breathing and emotionally insulate herself from the causal outcomes of her hubris.

She checked Ogawa's message and disappointedly confirmed it'd come from his corporate address rather than a personal one. She'd be forced to navigate the near-impossible gauntlet of Fumiko Inoue, Ogawa's personal assistant and the Great Filter who'd been thwarting Rei's progress for months. The woman offered no empathy to leverage and no personal angles to exploit. She was like an android programmed to thanklessly pre-chew morsels of opportunity until they were tasteless gruel to be passed onto Ogawa. Rei cursed again and resolved to plan another assault on the fortress Inoue had built around her boss after dealing with her sister.

Miyu's recorded message employed the infuriatingly stylized avatar she used on all her social accounts. Its eyes were practically Western in shape and tinted green. Other features were enhanced, curves exaggerated, and imperfections smoothed out. The willful deception infuriated Rei, despite acknowledging the rich hypocrisy. Rei *had to mask*. It would be catastrophic if her ties to the yakuza or her sexuality were exposed. Miyu, on the other hand, was pretty enough to begin with and already living a dream life overseas in a cosmopolitan city, freeloading off their gullible father.

She trembled in anger.

Rei took a few minutes to settle down before initializing the conference request. The camera bee automatically detached from her handheld and hovered at eye level near the back of the desk, projecting soft, filling light. Rei considered toggling her visuals to an avatar but her vitriol towards her sister for using one forced her to present her awful truth instead.

Her sister's cute avatar winked into existence, leaned close and chirped, "Hi, Rei! Thanks for getting back to me." The modulation made her sister's voice overly saccharine, like an anime character.

"Turn off the damn avatar."

The avatar made an exaggeratedly confused face. "Not sure what you mean, sis."

It took all of Rei's self-control not to throw the handheld across the room as a proxy for her sister. "Now, Miyu."

The avatar pouted, lower lip curled down. "It's still me, Rei."

"You're very nearly dead to me already. Don't make me vengeful."

"Nothing you can do could hurt me anymore," Her voice sounded eerie, even autotuned and upcycled.

"Did you already run through all of Dad's money? You can tell him I changed his banking access explicitly to cut you off."

"That's not it."

"Then do you want, Miyu?"

"I need a favour."

"You don't have any shame, do you?"

Rei terminated the conference, stood up abruptly and furiously paced her small apartment. Only family could make her this angry. Her handheld was chiming a conference alert. She stared at the device like it was a tyrant, hesitating before finally sitting back down and grudgingly accepting the request.

She was met with a black screen.

"It's important, Rei."

Miyu's audio came across without modulation. Her voice sounded thin and fragile—a broken object tenuously held together with tape.

"If it's that important, show me your goddamn face."

There was the sound of jostling and the clatter of something falling. After a minute, the video blinked in, showing a white-hooded figure with oversized mirrored goggles and a highly polished lower-face ventilator. Not even a sliver of skin was visible. The shadows were harsh since there was no natural light wherever

Miyu was. Her back was directly up against a shelf stacked with irregularly shaped boxes.

Her sister's voice was stamped down from the ventilator's low-quality output. "This is important, Rei. It's about Dad."

"Is this some sort of game to you?" The indignation Rei had been trying to suppress worked its way out. "I'm not going to engage with another one of your disguises."

Miyu hesitantly unclasped the ventilator and let it fall to the side, revealing a near-skeletal face with skin pulled taut over bones. Next, her sister pulled back her deep hooded cowl, exposing a shaved head and the telltale marks of old scars. After some delay, Miyu removed her oversized mirrored goggles, exposing weirdly convex metallic discs substituting for eyes resting deep in her sockets. Pus was leaking from areas of irregularly swollen skin overgrowing the edges of the discs. The harsh glare of light made her seem like a desiccated corpse.

Rei gasped. Miyu appeared barely human. A spent object destined for landfill.

"You don't look so great either, Rei."

"I caught a beating meant for Dad," she stammered, trying to reconcile the sister she thought she knew to the horror of what she was seeing. "What happened to you?"

"I made some bad choices," Miyu responded, ethereally thin. "Someone's landing in Japan around noon, your time. Itami, not Kansai International. Mathis Grenier. He's the bio-architect leading the wetware initiative for Hikari International. They have a tower in Umeda. You might get him there if you can't catch him at the airport."

"What the fuck, Miyu? I've been begging for updates on Hikari for months to protect Dad from—"

"You're the only one who can protect Dad now. You need to convince Mathis to join Minus One."

"Why are you talking about those terrorists? And why are you dressed like one? You're not making any sense. What's going on? Where are you?"

"I'm in a closet. Hunter's searching for me, and he's good at finding people. They have Dad, Rei. They—" Miyu started convulsing in racking sobs, but with her disc eyes, it seemed like a corpse twitching from having an electrical current run through it. "I brought him here to get help, but they put an explosive in him. In his chest. If you can't convince Mathis, they'll execute Dad. It's my fault. I couldn't make Mathis join. I didn't know how. I wasted so much time not knowing what to do. I'm not like you. But you can do it, Rei. Men always do what you want them to."

Rei didn't know how to process the disjointed fragments, her sister's ghastly appearance, or what part of what was being said was even true. Her heart pounded, agitation and confusion threatening to spill over. "Put Dad on."

"They won't let me near him now. I freaked out on Rodrigo, and Hunter came, so I ran."

"You're not making sense. Put Dad on."

Instead of providing an answer, Rei was presented a Netcast of someone's point of view, presumably Miyu's, walking through a doorway of a large room overcrowded with patients on ramshackle beds or leaning against the walls. Everyone was wearing white except a handful of doctors and nurses flying past the field of view in their teal hospital scrubs. The edges of the video were fried with pixel noise, and even the focus was laggy and distorted. She squinted against a headache's onset, shifting restlessly and breathing rapidly, as she watched on the small screen.

"What are you showing me?"

"Just keep watching."

It took Rei a moment to comprehend that the muscular figure coming into focus, dressed in blood-soaked pants and no shirt, sitting slumped forward with his back to the wall, was her father. Bandages covered his forearm, shoulder, and chest. She wasn't sure if it was the quality of the poor video feed, but he looked ashen from blood loss. His chest was smeared with it. Similar to the many times in childhood when he had come home after a punishing fight, her father's whole countenance brightened, and a hard-won smile formed on his lips. *Hey, kiddo,* he said, as though he didn't have a care in the world, but the spark was missing from his eyes.

What's with your chest? What did they do to you, Dad?

Oh, this? It's nothing. You know me, I'm okay. We'll always be okay.

The vision feed yanked around, scanning the environment, with Miyu shouting the name *Rodrigo* repeatedly, increasingly frantic. All the while, her father kept trying to soothe her with comforting sounds and dismissive words. It was her childhood framed through the imperfect lens of pixel noise and lagged playback. Back then, it'd been Rei's name Miyu cried for.

The tragedy of what she was witnessing, the horror of her sister's life, and her guilt for sending her father to his death were too much. Saturating.

Overwhelmed, she whispered, "Stop it, Miyu."

The video feed ended abruptly, and Miyu's ghoulish face was back in the frame. "It's bad, Rei."

"What the fuck did you get Dad mixed up in?"

"It's all my fault. He tried to rescue me. I... I deserve all your hate. But you don't have to. I hate myself more than you could ever know. But that's not going to help. Mathis Grenier can fix this. Benoit said he'd spare Dad. Conditionally. Mathis is the condition."

"How can you expect me to do this?"

"I don't know. You're always able to get people to do what you want. I don't know how you do it. Please, for Dad, you have to."

"You're asking the impossible. My English is terrible, and I know nothing about Minus One. Go back to where Dad is and put him on. I need to talk with him."

Miyu snapped her head to the left and pulled the handheld to her face. She whispered urgently, "Hunter's close. Remember, noon your time, Itami, not Kansai International, okay?"

"Miyu—"

"Shhh, please!"

The screen was momentarily bathed in white light before the video's visual dampeners autocorrected to show Miyu fully lit, recoiling in terror.

A baritone voice rumbled, "You know better than to hide."

A hand seemingly as big as Miyu's head wrapped around her slender neck and lifted her. The video spun as the handheld fell. The sound of impact drowned out Miyu's strangled scream for a moment. The Netstream showed a towering monster of a man dressed all in black staring down at Rei's face on the other side of the video conference. A split second later, his boot shattered the display, and Miyu's video connection terminated, leaving Rei stunned and alone in the quiet of her room.

Rei held her position, unblinking, failing to digest what she'd experienced. Her throat was tight, her mouth dry. The handheld threw up an alert, prompting her to engage it, or the program would auto-terminate the open conference in thirty seconds. The time ticked down, her eyes locked in until it reached zero, ending both the session and her irrational hope something would change. The camera bee went dark and silently docked itself on her handheld.

She'd seen her father far more battered after cage matches or getting released from the police station. Rei had rushed him to the hospital numerous times, but there'd always been an unbreakable core in him no amount of bludgeoning could assail. In the video Miyu shared, he seemed *weak.* It might've been from blood loss, the resignation of his voice, or his dulled eyes. Rei couldn't put her finger on it. Diminished, he wouldn't be strong enough to fight his way out of whatever situation they were in. The horrifying truth gripped her—whatever was left of him wouldn't be enough.

She wiped away her tears with her shirt sleeves, wincing as she made contact with the bridge of her nose. The more she wiped, the more that came. She was coming apart and didn't know how to hold herself together.

18

Mathis

"You fucked me, Mathis." Aiden Frost's tone hung between resentment and an eerie note of appreciation.

Frost's image unexpectedly took over the display of Mathis' in-flight headset. Shocked, Mathis dialled back the display's opacity, frantically scanning to see if the other passengers were reacting to the unexpected intrusion, but found them sedated with uninterrupted entertainment.

"Mr. Frost, I'm not feeling well, so—"

"Spare me the bullshit. I picked you up changing flights in Narita. I've already got Logan in custody and I assure you he requires zero pressure to talk. Or to sweat. The man sweats like a pig."

"He didn't have anything to do with the recursive encryption. I had his accounts frozen by IT before I left."

"He admitted to using unauthorized credentials, and I need a fall guy to keep you in play. Logan had no problem signing whatever confessions I put in front of him."

"You can't wrongfully convict him, that's—"

"Immoral? No shit. And so's breaking our agreement. So's encrypting the trunk, branches and offsite backups of the version control system. You're forcing my hand, Mathis, and I don't roll well when force is applied to me."

"I had to do something drastic once I learned about the data breach. The asymmetric encryption algorithm should've poisoned the servers and systems of the Chinese state-backed hacker collective."

"Another lie, and your buddy, Tariq, goes from a local black site to one in the Middle East."

"It's not a lie," he protested, struggling against the responsibility for his colleagues, friends, and family's lives. "Any systems synchronized to the version control—"

"I won't get drawn into a semantic argument with an academic. Send me the private key for the encryption."

"I—" Mathis winced. "I deleted it."

He exhaled, slow and audible. "You're telling me there's no key to unlock the servers?"

Mathis possessed the bravery afforded by ten thousand kilometres of distance. "Yes."

"Now you've gone and properly fucked yourself."

"I'll restore the full backup on Hikari's servers at head office."

"You think jurisdiction is going to save you?"

A jolt of fear struck him as grasped how deeply flawed his plan was if Frost had agents in Japan. "No, probably not."

"All you've done is inject a delay and ensure Evy Carter's life is ruined, too."

"Evy didn't have anything to do with it."

"She deeply regrets aiding your escape and recognizes the consequences of her complicity in your criminal activities. She's a remarkably professional woman. I hardly had to explain anything to her."

He squeezed shut his eyes, pressing forcefully on his temples with both hands. "What do you want?"

"When you get off the plane, you'll go with the men who come to collect you. You'll do everything they say until this situation has been remediated to my satisfaction."

Mathis clenched his teeth. "I don't think—"

"You have a skewed grasp of the situation. You've traded a couple days' worth of delays for the lives of your colleagues."

He took a deep breath, and tried to control his voice. "What would make you... satisfied?"

"To not have to deal with a bitch prima donna. Half the cities in the industrialized world are burning. With your tech and my backdoor, I could shut that shit down in a heartbeat."

"It's immoral."

"There you go with that precious virtue of yours. Let me ask you, is it moral to have thousands of impressionable kids shot in the streets or imprisoned? What about violence perpetrated against families whose *crime* is doing better than some asshole liberal arts dropout with a chip on their shoulder. Or all the people who have no job to go to since the building's been set on fire, or the first responders who risk their lives to stop the chaos from spreading? Does any of this factor into your moral equations?"

"I don't have anything to do with those terrorists."

"You're planning to empower them. With your brain chip—"

"Wetware." Mathis immediately regretted the correction.

"Your *wetware* would make terrorists near unstoppable. Today, it's Minus One. Tomorrow, it'll be a rogue nation or some religious shitheads. You're guaranteeing an uncontrollable arms race. This isn't some game where you get another chance. Its winner takes all, each and every time." Frost shook his head. "You know what's more infuriating than trying to get you to grasp the gravity of the situation? Nothing, actually. You're just some smug fucking academic with a useful idea. Let me put it to you simply. Your colleagues are already sitting in underground cells with bags over their heads. Next, it'll be your parents and whatever pathetic excuse for a social circle you have. The longer you take, the worse it's going to be. Get with the fucking program."

The connection terminated, and Mathis' inflight entertainment resumed, but he couldn't process any of it. He was overwhelmed by the misery assigned to his decisions. The choice between condemning everyone he cared for or usurping the agency of future generations was sickening.

No longer vigilant against minimizing data transactions, Mathis traded the cumbersome airline headset for his familiar Net contacts and handheld. Mathis logged into his social profile to lurk on Logan's to see if Frost was lying about his colleague's incarceration. There had been no activity on Logan's aggregated feed since the time he had flown out of Toronto. A quick winnow on content related to Skeleton Crucible showed the pitch videos had been flagged as private. Given Logan's compulsive social history, Frost really did have him.

With increasing anxiety, he checked on Tariq's feed and quickly confirmed all the protest Netstreams had been removed, as had the ones with Marisol. At the top of his feed was a Netstream flagged with private permissions, set to unlock only for Mathis' profile. It'd been uploaded that morning. With trepidation, Mathis played it.

Mathis, you've always treated me like a brother and fought for me more times than I've had the grace to acknowledge. Since you saw my protest Netstreams were still up, you must've seen others that I should never have posted. Ones with Marisol. And still, you took the time to try to protect me.

You may never understand this, but I want to come clean. In my home country, I'd been well-celebrated for my skills and accomplishments, but you changed my life. More importantly, my worldview and sense of self. You effortlessly allowed me to understand I wasn't all that gifted. I'm not even in your league. It was humbling but also inspiring. You made me want to be better, to try harder, and while I am tremendously grateful, I was also slowly poisoned with envy.

I can never be your equal, and that realization hurt. I suppose I wanted to have someone who cared for you look upon me with equal favour. Marisol is intelligent, caring, fun, and beautiful. I adore her still, but I was never who she wanted. She deserved a finer quality of man, and I should never have complicated things. I'm begging for your forgiveness and the opportunity to prove I can become the person you've always given me the courtesy of being.

The Netstream ended, leaving Mathis conflicted, unconsciously shaking his head against his own deficits.

His colleagues' unjust incarceration created a sharp focus on Aiden Frost's threats towards his parents. It was approaching midnight back home. Mathis initiated a conference connection on his handheld, piping the video stream to his Net contacts. The longer the call went unanswered, the more anxious he became. His fingers drummed on the armrest, his left leg bounced restlessly. The call was finally accepted, and his father's squinting, salt-and-pepper bearded face appeared bathed in the cold light of bright pixels in their dark bedroom.

"Jesus, buddy. Do you know what time it is?"

"I know, Dad. Sorry."

"Well, that makes one of us. Can't read anything without my damn glasses. Hold on a sec."

The vision went black as the antiquated tablet was dropped face-down on the bed.

"Who's calling so late?" Mathis' mother asked sleepily from off-screen.

"It's your son."

"Our son, silly. Doesn't he know what time it is?"

"He's the only one who does."

His mother picked up the tablet—blond hair tangled, heart-shaped face anxious, and hastily worn glasses slightly askew. His parents were wearing matching red and black flannel pyjamas.

"Are you okay? Did something happen to—hey, where are you?"

"I'm on a plane, Mom. In Japan. Can you accept the encryption?"

"The what?"

"Just press okay on the dialogue box."

His father's hand blotted out the integrated camera for a moment. "Alright. It didn't do anything. Are we supposed to see something?"

"No, we're good now, Dad."

His mother fretted, smoothed out her hair with her fingers and fixed her glasses. "You haven't visited us since the summer, and suddenly, you have time to vacation across the world?"

"Is it a work or spy thing?" Distracted, his father added, "Do you know where my glasses are, honey?"

Mathis didn't know how to approach the conversation and opted for directness. "You guys need to stay with Uncle Anton for a while."

"No way, buddy. I saw him in the spring, and that's enough Anton for one year, thanks."

"Casper!" Ingrid chided in exaggerated outrage. "He's not that bad."

"He smells like a horse."

"For the hundredth time, it's because he rides horses!"

"It's not like he rode a horse to Dorthy's anniversary, and he stank there, too." Casper playful bumped his shoulder into Ingrid. "See, son? You've upset your mother."

Mathis swallowed the sick knot forming in his throat. His parents were two of the most unprepared people in the northern hemisphere to endure unjust incarceration. Willfully oblivious to danger. "Dad, this is serious."

"Look at him. Mr. International, assigning cryptic missions. Our son might be a proper spy! Also, glasses?"

"Check under your book, dear." Ingrid angled the tablet to mostly exclude her husband. "What sort of trouble are you in?"

"The type making it dangerous for you to stay at home. Please! Pack up and leave for Uncle Anton's tonight, okay?"

"Not under the book, honey," complained Casper.

"How am I supposed to know where you forgot them? Check the floor beside the night table." Ingrid shook her head. "Oh, and I don't think so, bunny. You see, Anton gets a little persnickety with unannounced visitors."

"I never ask you guys for anything, but I'm begging you. There's a good chance people will come for you."

"Take it down a notch, buddy. What rogue nation is after you?"

Mathis weighed the consequences of telling the truth, knowing facts would confuse his parents, but decided to be forthright. "Ours."

His father laughed. "Alright, good luck with that, kid. Still don't know what the time is or where my damn glasses are, but it's late here. Let's catch up at a reasonable hour, okay?"

"Wait, you've got to believe me!"

"Dear, if it's really the government, we have nothing to worry about. You have a pleasant little adventure in Japan. Don't spend the whole time working, either. Live a little. I hear the girls there are very nice and very pretty."

"Mom!"

"What? We're getting older, and so are you. It might be time to focus a little less on work and a little more on... You know."

"That's mom code for *I want a grandchild*."

They both giggled.

Mathis' frustration was boiling over. "Promise you'll get somewhere safe," he pleaded.

His father grinned mischievously. “I’ve learned the hard way to never make promises in bed.”

“Casper!” Ingrid shoved him playfully. “Goodnight, bunny. We love you.”

She ended the conference as his father made a dramatic finger-gun gesture.

Mathis tried reinitiating the conference, but their status was already flagged as offline. He imagined their short, bewildered conversation before returning to sleep, and hoped it wouldn’t be too late to try them again in the morning—provided he wasn’t apprehending as soon as he landed by Frost's agents. Mathis picked up the AR cue from the back of the seat-rest ahead of him to overlay the flight monitor on his vision and began counting down the minutes and kilometres he had left as a free man.

When the plane landed, the sickening knot of fear in his stomach tightened. As the aircraft completed its slow taxi to the gate, he was paralyzed in his seat, dreading the prospect of getting off. A flight attendant eventually approached him, speaking pleasantly but firmly in Japanese. She reached up to get his hard-shelled, carry-on bag, set it down in the aisle and lifted the telescopic handle for him. Mathis nodded his head, mumbled his thanks and walked down the aisle. Four flight attendants and both pilots were waiting for him as he rounded the business class galley. They all respectfully bowed to him, precisely at the same angle.

“*Goriyou itadaki arigatou gozaimasu!*”

Mathis walked past them in a daze, dragging his wheeled carry-on bag. After the gate, there was a short walk. He scanned for potential assailants. He slowed to a stop before a set of security doors, catching the notice of a sharply dressed airport attendant. Mathis’ heart sank. Beyond the windowed wall, there were two men in suits and heavy overcoats—faces concealed by opaque goggles and scarves. Large men. Mathis paused shy of the doorway, involuntarily taking a step back.

“Okyaku-sama, ikaga nasaimashita ka?” the attendant inquired helpfully.

Mathis smiled, swallowed the hot spit in his mouth, and stepped through the security doors. The two men started to move towards him when a woman in black—speaking frantically and wearing a wide hat and a full-face mask—rushed towards him, accompanied by several men in security uniforms. She pointed in his direction, improbably jogging alongside the officers in her high-heeled boots with one hand on her hat to keep it in place. Mathis closed his eyes, ready to give up, and opened them after the officers ran past, shouting in Japanese. The woman was directly in front of him. Her articulating eInk patterns of her mask were arresting, and Mathis didn't know where to look for her eyes.

"We must go now, Mathis." Her breathless voice was heavily accented.

His head jerked away from her, and he took an involuntary step back. "Wait, how do you know my name?"

She shook her head, grabbed the suitcase from him by the short handle, and snapped closed the telescopic one. "Not now." She ran towards the exit.

There was a scuffle of commotion from behind Mathis, but he didn't hazard a glance back. Instead, he tried to keep up with the surprisingly fleet-footed woman as she sprinted through the public atrium, ignoring the startled or judgemental looks from the other people and slipping through the automated glass doors to the outside as they slid open.

By the time he caught up with her, she was already timing the traffic to get to an island designated for pickups on the other side of oncoming vehicles. There, a young woman dressed in an overlapping cacophony of colours stood beside an impossibly small orange *kei* car with a tall roof, tiny wheels, and an opened rear hatch. She smiled wide, waving enthusiastically with both hands. She might have even hopped, but Mathis couldn't trust his eyes. The temperature difference between Osaka and Toronto was probably more than a dozen degrees centigrade. There'd been snow when he left, and it was practically spring weather here. Everything felt surreal.

The young woman opened the door and leaned the front seat forward as they got closer. The woman from the airport threw his luggage in the back, slammed shut the hatch and gestured to the rear seat.

"Inside, please," she instructed with an economy of language.

Mathis slowed to a stop a few steps away. Even children knew not to get into cars with strangers. "Who are you?"

"*Nihongo hanasemasu ka?*"

"I don't understand, sorry."

The woman shot an anxious glance at the airport's entrance. "Bad men are coming, okay? Get inside now."

Not having time to vacillate, he awkwardly got into the back.

"Hajimemashite! Ichika desu!" the young driver chirped happily to Mathis, animatedly waving.

Instead of a speedy getaway, Ichika carefully drove the underpowered *kei* car with her hands at ten and two, signalled appropriately and merged into traffic conscientiously. She cautiously accelerated to precisely the posted speed limit and, once safely nestled into traffic, turned on music preset to a background volume of happy, hyperactive, all-girl J-pop. She bopped her head along with the melody, saving the rest of her attention for traffic. Two-thirds of the other cars on the road had no drivers.

"Who were the suits at arrivals?" When the woman didn't immediately respond, Mathis slowed down his speech and rephrased. "The men at the airport. Who were they?"

She removed her hat, retracted her mask into a neat band and put on an oversized pair of UkiyoAR sunglasses before shrugging. "They carried *chaka*... Guns. Not normal in Japan. You were last off the plane. They were waiting. For you, no?"

Mathis struggled to comprehend her words, given her thick Japanese accent. He angled his head, trying to catch her face in the rearview mirror. "Where are you taking me?"

The woman turned to face him, exposing the extensive swelling and bruising he hadn't noticed earlier. Her carefully applied foundation and artful use of makeup might conceal the damage from a distance but couldn't withstand closer scrutiny.

"Namba. There are foreigners there. Not many now, but some. By car, maybe twenty minutes."

The two women in the front seat exchanged words in shorthand and with small, intimate gestures. Whether friends or lovers, it struck Mathis as an odd pairing. Not knowing their intentions, he struggled for additional context or situational awareness, but there was little to grasp onto that didn't exacerbate his disorientation or confusion. The large display of the GPS showed they were heading south, but wasn't otherwise helpful, given the display was full of Kanji characters.

He was bewildered by the exceptionally dense city and aggressive Japanese signage. The number of augmented projections overlaying his Net contact's vision was disorienting. Invasive, high-energy advertising saturated his vision. Mathis tried to navigate the public access settings and found them confoundingly in Japanese. He tried to pattern the English interface from memory to minimize the advertising, agreeing to pay yen for each marketing message intercepted.

Although Toronto was a comparably large city by population, he never considered it as claustrophobic as what he was experiencing in Osaka. Strangers were walking practically shoulder to shoulder, vehicular traffic was tightly congested, and the sound of trains and the general noise was omnipresent. Everyone and everything was Japanese, too—which made sense on the surface, but coming from a city with more than half of the residents born in foreign countries, the uniformity was unnerving. It was one highly complex organism, and he was merely an unwanted foreign body. The average age of pedestrians appeared older, too.

"I have to get to Hikari International. In Umeda."

"Umeda!" Ichika chimed in recognition, pointing left towards a cohort of parallel rail lines leading towards a particularly dense section of office towers.

"First, we must talk."

Mathis' unease and nagging sense of lost agency grew. "Maybe you can let me off here? I'll give you my contact details, and we can meet later. Sounds good?"

"No, not good."

He waited for a rationale, but none was forthcoming. He considered protesting but understood he'd only get out of the orange *kei* car with the women's cooperation. He spent the next few minutes in unsettled silence.

"Shinsaibashi, " Ichika cheerily announced.

The area was an orgy of upscale shopping with an up-tempo energy, and the crowds on the street skewed younger. As they made their way through the district, he caught sight of about a hundred young Japanese gathered in an area, standing patiently. Small clusters were dressed in all-white, Minus One converts or posers, but mixing freely with the rest.

"What are they doing?"

"Waiting."

Again, Mathis's expectations of further context were disappointed, and he resigned to quietly endure the rest of the journey. After crossing an expressway overpass, the car headed back north for a couple hundred metres and slowed to a crawl before stopping at the side of the road with the hazards on.

"Tsuita de!"

The woman grasped Ichika's shoulder tenderly, squeezing it, and exited the car. She flipped up her seat before getting his luggage out of the back.

Mathis leaned forward, trying to get a better angle on Ichika. She looked considerably younger, though he suspected some of the disparity was the happy innocence she presented with.

"Thank you very much."

"Have fun, okay?" she responded sweetly in a thick accent.

He stepped out of the tiny orange car, immediately gaining the momentary attention of scores of nearby pedestrians. He was bathed in the competing lights from a chaos of neon signage stretching from ground level up to the height of the buildings. Even in the broad daylight, they were bright. There was an excess of vitality, movement and vibrancy—life with the saturation levels dialled up. He imagined the augmented reality advertising would've been chaotic if he hadn't paid the premium for Net-marketing silence. He closed the door gently, unsure if the vehicle could withstand force, and found the woman from the airport staring at him critically.

She pushed the wheeled carry-on bag towards him. "What do you drink?"

"Coffee?"

She shook her head disapprovingly. "Hungry?"

When he didn't answer immediately, she gestured to her mouth, but Mathis was too invested in consuming the competing sights and navigating the saturation of stimuli to notice. The woman walked away, leaving him to scramble after her, navigating his wheeled carry-on suitcase through the crowds of slower-moving pedestrians.

Not far, a gigantic, three-dimensional octopus flanked on either side by animated signage was affixed to the face of a building and hung precariously over the sidewalk.

"Takoyaki. Osaka junk food. Very popular with Westerners."

"Octopi are actually self aware, so I can't—"

She had already turned away from him and walked into the restaurant.

They were immediately greeted with a coordinated welcome of *irasshaimase!* by all the waitstaff and cooks. People filled the tightly packed tables, sitting practically back-to-back with each other, unaware of any inconvenience. There were no other Westerners in the place. The heavy scent of oil and an unfamiliar sauce filled his nostrils. It wasn't unpleasant, but it was the type of smell to demand and retain attention. The woman sat with her back to the wall at a two-seat table in the far corner. Mathis had to lift his suitcase to avoid knocking into people and chairs, but eventually made it to her.

A waitress came to them as soon as he sat down. She smiled at Mathis before giving attention to the woman across from him as she ordered for them. The waitress' smile wilted, and her eyes turned hard. She acknowledged the order and stepped curtly away from the table. Was he sitting down wrong, or had he already broken some cultural taboo? A self-audit came up empty.

"You don't think she thinks..." Mathis gestured discreetly to the bruising on the woman's face.

She pushed a small box towards him. "Translator, please."

He opened the box and copied her as she inserted one of the earpieces. Her whole countenance immediately relaxed, as though the device alleviated the tension and strain in her body from communicating in a foreign language.

"Tell me, Mathis, who were the men at the airport?"

It was a slightly disorienting sensation to hear her words spoken in Japanese and simultaneously into a high-grade synthesis of her voice in English. The reality patterned as though watching a badly dubbed version of a movie where the voice actors paid no heed to the mouth movements to time their dialogue. The concert of her voice, a language in each ear, also took considerable adjustment.

"I'm not trying to sound ungrateful, but you and your girlfriend pulled me out of an airport, and now I'm in a restaurant that serves octopus."

"She's a good friend," the woman said stiffly.

"Okay. Your good friend seems nice, and I'm thankful to you both, but I need to get to Hikari International in Umeda. Please, it's been a long flight. I'm tired, but I need to work. It's important. People are expecting me."

The waitress returned and dropped off two pints of beer without making eye contact.

"My name is Yoshida Rei. I'm an active investor in Hikari International and know of your wetware development. I was scheduled to meet the chief technical officer this week but had to postpone." Rei gestured at her face.

"What happened to you, Yoshida—"

"Just Rei is fine." She shook her head, lifted her pint and drained a third of it with the skill of a practised drinker. "I wore heels, the stairs were wet."

"And what is this?"

"This is a sincere plea to help me to understand. Why are you being hunted the moment you step foot on Japanese soil?"

He found himself overly invested in trying to unpack the implicit nuance of the English translator to what he was hearing in Rei's Japanese speech. It mirrored her sentiments but at an irregular cadence, making both languages slightly incongruent. Dark, oversized sunglasses obscured any insight from her eyes, but the intensity and sincerity of her words were arresting. She removed her sunglasses, exposing blackened eyes and lacerations. Stairs weren't responsible for Rei's condition.

He did a quick shoulder check to find disinterest from the other patrons. Their waitress was glowering at him, however. Unconsciously, he shook his head, trying to communicate his innocence, but her expression didn't change. When he brought his attention back to Rei, she had her glasses back on and was taking another drink from her pint. She set it down, two-thirds empty, and looked at him expectantly.

He took a sip of his beer, more as a prop than from thirst, buying time to decide to answer her question accurately. Despite the bizarre sequence of events, she didn't seem connected to Frost, and hadn't actually kidnapped him.

"I'm responsible for a disruptive technology that, if misused, would usher in a world where you had no true agency but were convinced you did. You could be made to perform actions you otherwise wouldn't and have your flesh memories manipulated to support false convictions. Played out, nation-states become meaningless, people become nothing more than agents, and truth becomes subjective when not actively coerced. Instead of unlocking the potential of humanity, we could be incalculably and forever diminished as a species."

Her face betrayed a struggle to place his words within an approachable context. "I don't understand."

"Wetware allows digital constructs to directly interface with your brain. I've been developing it for the last decade."

"No one would go through with the procedure."

"It wouldn't happen all at once but over the course of a generation. Remember how quickly the world went digital? The cycle of disruptive technologies is always the same. Early adopters are rewarded, mass migration is incentivized, industries align with the new technology, and holdouts are punished. Backdoors would be used sparingly but then with increasing regularity until there was no clear definition of self versus the will of a controlling external entity. This is the world those men waiting at the airport for me want me to create."

"Why would you create such a horrible thing?"

"If it's done right, humanity can be elevated. Like the evolution from our primate ancestors to who we are today. My colleagues have been imprisoned because they supported me. Next, they'll persecute my parents. I'll never be forgiven and don't deserve to be. No doubt, I'll get apprehended at some point and tortured into compliance, but not before I poison their ambitions. But I need time to make it so they can never unmake it. Someone is going to develop this technology, and it'd better be done in a way to safeguard our collective futures."

"You would sacrifice your parents. Truly?"

Mathis tried to suppress the grief and guilt swelling inside him. Finding his throat constricted, he cleared it twice. "I love my mom and dad. There are no better, more caring, or compassionate people walking the face of this earth. But there's an order of magnitude of difference between a handful of lives being ruined and the fate of humanity."

Rei's body shuddered, her eyes pinched.

"Hey, it's okay. I mean, it's not really okay, but this is the least worst way for it to play out."

"You've told me my family will die."

He took out the translator and inspected it for damage before reinserting it. "There may be something wrong with this thing. Can you say that again, please?"

Rei took off her sunglasses and delicately wiped her eyes with a handkerchief. "If you're willing to sacrifice your parents, how can my family survive? They're being held hostage and will be executed if you're not leveraged."

She faced her handheld towards him and navigated to images harvested from a bad video feed. The first showed a muscular, half-naked man covered in blood with bandages over his chest, shoulder, and forearm.

"My father. They put an explosive in his chest." The following image showed a woman with a shaved head, dressed all in white, with convex discs where her eyes should've been. She was being strangled. The deeply unsettling terror on her face defied inauthenticity. "My sister, Miyu. She got mixed up with Minus One when she was in Toronto. She was supposed to recruit you."

Mathis failed to reconcile the mental image of the strange young woman who he'd met at the small downtown park to the tortured image on Rei's handheld. His empathy for Rei only increased the burden he carried.

"Those people want something even worse. I'm sorry."

Mathis caught sight of the waitress coming to their table. Her lips curled in disgust, and she glowered at him throughout her approach. She appeared about to say something when Rei caught her attention with a small, sharp gesture. The waitress set down a plate of *takoyaki* and abruptly left.

The half dozen golf ball-sized objects were covered in brown sauce, glazed in a white sauce, and topped with finely diced spring onions and a generous helping of bonito flakes. The flakes curled and twisted under the heat of the *takoyaki*, as though writhing in pain, until they crumpled limp and, at last, were still.

19

Amrita

AMRITA'S MIND KEPT CIRCLING back to Maryam's perspective on Minus One, shared as they sipped gin together, waiting for Mia. *These people don't know anything about creation. Are they going to fix this neighbourhood? No, they'll make every other neighbourhood like it. They're destroyers.*

It took Mia more than two hours to arrive. By then, Amrita had been regaled with a litany of the old lady's stories. Maryam had somehow made her forget, however temporarily, how awful everything was.

On her way out of Bargain Traders, Amrita checked on the bodies lying in the inset doorway. The woman was breathing but not responsive. Amrita gave the hundred-and-twenty-five dollars Maryam let her keep to the girl with the mismatched shoes, huddling tight to the unconscious woman.

The skinny pre-teen accepted the money and, with a dead expression, whispered, "What kind of party do you want?"

Amrita didn't initially understand, and when it finally clicked, she wished it hadn't.

Mia cursed, and pulled her towards a waiting driverless sedan. Before entering, Amrita was scanned with a handheld device, given a blacked-out set of goggles to put on, and had her hood pulled forward.

"It's a public car, they record everything," Mia explained without ceremony.

It was difficult to know how long the ride was. It could've been twenty minutes or twice that. Time became elastic with no conversation or visual milestones to meter against. In the beginning, Amrita tried to count her breaths, but anxiety made her an unreliable timepiece. Shallow and rapid, her breathing flirted with hyperventilation. Amrita grew lightheaded. When she tried to sync to Mia's breathing, her mind wandered, trying in vain to unravel the Gordian knot of her situation.

Part of her wanted to be like Mia Locke, to possess some glimmer of the woman's spirit for life and adventure. Humiliating memories of her early teenage years came back—of printing photographs of actresses and models to pin on her bedroom walls, desperate in her private desire to be like them. Amrita had eventually torn them all down when she finally accepted she'd never be tall, beautiful, or glamorous. As unsatisfying as it was, she'd capitulated to the unsavoury truth of only ever being herself.

Eventually, the sedan stopped, and they entered a dimly lit industrial park. She followed Mia through alleys and fence holes, traversing multiple properties until coming to a nondescript industrial building with a parking lot full of vehicles—e-bikes, scooters, cars, vans, and commercial or city-marked special-purpose trucks. The whole time, there was no discussion between her and Mia. She tried to start a conversation a few times, but her offers weren't accepted. She was frantic with the realization that she might die here. She wasn't a field agent. She'd mess up. They'd find her out. Amrita checked over her shoulder, the path calling for her retreat, but she kept following Mia forward.

As they approached the industrial doorway, Mia instructed her to go with a giant of a man dressed all in black. *Hunter*, she called him. Amrita had been expecting some manner of critical reception and rehearsed a dozen prospective conversations in her mind, but they had all been meaningless in the face of a man well over two metres tall, more intimidating than anyone Amrita had ever encountered.

She back-pedalled, but he moved surprisingly fast for an enormous man and grabbed her by the shoulder. His massive hand gripped her firmly, and while painful, it wasn't meant to be excruciating. Just to pin her in place.

"It'll go bad if you fuss," he said.

His baritone voice sounded too low to come out of a human. Resonant. It filled her with terror and compliance. She allowed him to lead her around the back of the building to a shipping and receiving area. A piece of meat to be moved from one location to another. On one of the ramps, the plain white trailer of an eighteen-wheeler sat divorced from its truck. Hunter unlocked the rear door and gestured for her to go inside.

She couldn't stop herself from begging, "Please, no!"

He closed and locked the door, leaving her in complete darkness.

Hours passed. Amrita's eyes were cried out, her teeth chattered from the cold, and she was desperate to urinate. Her voice was hoarse from screaming for help, and her mind kept berating her mistakes. She wasn't a field agent. She had no training to know how to deal with being taken hostage, and none of her life experience could help her deal with her current reality. *If you want to make God laugh, tell him your plans.* Even the prospect of a CSIS black site and endless interrogations was more appealing. At least there'd be light, a legislated minimum of warmth, and a toilet.

When she couldn't endure the discomfort any longer, Amrita worked her way along the trailer to the back corner and relieved herself, burning with shame and humiliation. She fumbled her way to the opposite corner and curled up in a ball to conserve heat. It was too cold to think straight, and she savoured the unexpected reprieve of self-evisceration.

Amrita didn't realize she'd fallen asleep until the door to the trailer opened. It was night. She squinted against what little ambient light there was, desperately hoping it wouldn't be Hunter who had come to collect her. Her salvation came in an unfamiliar form. A girl dressed in all-white with a shaved head and strange convex discs where eyes should've been. Even compared to Amrita's small frame, the person was tiny, as though a strong wind could blow her over. Amrita unconsciously glanced back to the far corner, about to apologize, but her teeth were chattering too badly to speak.

"It's okay. Most of us did that the first time." The strange young woman's voice was thin. "It's easier in the spring or autumn."

Amrita was shivering from the bone-splintering cold. The woman offered her a hand. Amrita was shocked by how little there was to it when she grasped it. Skeletal. She held onto it as a guide, using her body and her other arm to straighten herself to a standing position.

"Wh–who are you? Where's Mia?"

"Mia's off doing Mia things." She shrugged. "I'm... not important."

"Could you tell me your name?" Amrita tried to smile disarmingly, but ended up baring her teeth psychotically. She forced her lips closed, aware of the oddness of her face. She'd never been this cold.

"Miyu," she eventually said, as though trying to remember it. "We should go inside now. Monsieur Rochon's expecting you, and we shouldn't keep him waiting. Most people don't get to meet him so quickly. Or ever, one on one."

The strange woman was drugged or broken. Maybe both. Beyond the eyes and emaciation, something struck Amrita as *off* about her. The stylish and impeccably white clothes increased the incongruence.

"What's going to happen to me?"

It was impossible to tell whether Miyu's expression held compassion, pity, or disinterest.

"It's warm in there."

It frustrated Amrita how consistently people didn't answer questions, especially when they mattered. "Please! What's going to happen now?"

She bit her lower lip, hesitating. "He's probably going to ask you to do things you won't like. It's important not to fail his expectations. I have. Failed, that is. There are always consequences."

Amrita glanced around, trying to catch sight of exits. Miyu waited patiently for Amrita to complete the rough mental catalogue of the area.

"I..." Amrita trailed off, cognizant she'd clumsily broadcast her options.

"They'd kill me. You wouldn't get far, either."

The unemotional resignation conveyed in Miyu's tone convinced Amrita of both forecasts. "I'm not going to run."

"Hungry?" She reached inside her jacket and offered Amrita a nutrient gel pack.

She was, but accepting the personal food cache from a malnourished individual felt unconscionable. Amrita shook her head.

"Let's go then." Miyu threw up her hood and started walking towards an unmarked door with no external handle. She tapped on it three evenly spaced times and entered after it opened.

From a distance, the heat and fast-rolling, melodic Quebecoise hip-hop tantalized Amrita inside. She caught the lively sound of animated voices, too. As her eyes adjusted to the bright lighting, she followed Miyu inside the first set of doors into a large stocking area heavily trafficked by young people dressed in white, rushing across each other's path lines, absorbed in their activities. They struck her as impossibly cool—fashion models set to task. There were scores of boxes and crates stacked in neat rows. She recognized the emblem of an arms manufacturer on several of them.

Still shivering from the cold, Amrita stayed close to Miyu as she led her straight through the assembly area to a long corridor. Amrita caught glances from the young people who passed her. It could've been because she was new or wore black clothes. Hunter wore black, too, but they weren't of a kind. No one paid Miyu any attention—not because she blended in with her hood drawn, but because there was something unknowable about her. She was right there but as elusive as recognizing absence.

Amrita was led past a double-door opening, exposing a massive open space packed with people who were clustering or moving around a ramshackle command centre. The music was loudest there but was barely registering above the din of sound. There were scores of people having animated conversations in as many languages. Vitality permeated the whole environment, with everyone seeming to belong and to matter. From her stifling background of government cubicles, enforced silence, and rigorous processes, the chaos and energy were intoxicating. She was in the global nerve centre of Minus One. Amrita slowed, drinking it in, until there was a tug on her sleeve.

"You shouldn't be seen looking." Miyu's quiet caution was somehow audible over the environment.

Amrita snapped her head away, nodded, and kept pace with Miyu up the stairs, trembling with the burden of knowledge she had no way to make useful. A GPS location and the right instincts from Mason Brand would see her rescued, her name cleared, and a return to her normal life.

At the top of the stairs was a landing and a plain grey steel door. Miyu rapped on it once, waited a few seconds, and opened the door, gesturing for her to enter. Amrita took a deep breath, exhaled, and stepped into the rear entrance of the spartan overseer's office. Benoit Rochon was standing at the glass, looking down upon his creation as though a proud father. Mia Locke was perched on top of the desk like a dramatic ornament. Legs crossed at an irregular angle, wild blue hair and an awkward posture Amrita couldn't conceive of relaxing in, let alone attempting. She wore a different set of impractical white clothing, transparent UkiyoAR glasses, and a bored expression.

Amrita was about to say something when Miyu got to her knees and folded her upper body over. Her forehead touched the ground. Amrita hesitantly started getting down to her knees when Benoit interrupted her.

"That's not for you." He turned to face Amrita, dressed impeccably in his white-on-white suit, and smiled charmingly. "Seventeen, why don't you explain what you're doing?"

"Contrition," she responded softly.

"Have you done something worthy of contrition, Amrita Chopra?"

"Probably," she answered too loudly, without any thinking or hesitation. It wasn't one of her rehearsed opening lines.

He walked close to Mia, brushing her cheek with the back of his hand. She leaned into it absently.

"Why have you come to us?"

"Mia suggested I might be useful here, and my old life is burnt." She winced as her pitch went completely sideways under his scrutiny. Her heart was pounding in her chest. She instinctively wiped her clammy hands on the sides of her legs.

"Having no other options can be a powerful motivator. What do you know of us?"

She focused on not sounding imbecilic. "There's an Indian expression, *the voice of the poor has no echo.* I think you're trying to change that."

Rochon smiled, looked at Mia and raised an eyebrow. "You didn't tell me she was poetic."

"She isn't," Mia replied, sounding bored.

Mia reached into Rochon's outside jacket pocket for a pack of cigarettes. She lit one, took a drag and handed it to him. He glanced affectionately at the red lipstick imprinted on the filter before taking a long pull.

"What exactly does the echo of the poor sound like?" He exhaled smoke as he spoke.

"Right now, like violence and death."

"Tssk, we're the ones dying."

"Sir? You know all about me. You have the data I was classified to access. Truthfully, I'm not sure what I can offer, but I'm earnest in being here."

Benoit turned to face Mia. "No foreplay, straight to the sex."

"No poetry," she commiserated. She took the cigarette from his hand, pulled and exhaled smoke. She offered it back to him, but he didn't accept it.

"People can surprise you with the value they can offer. Sometimes, it takes the right circumstances to bring it out. Isn't that right, Seventeen?"

"Yes, Monsieur Rochon," Miyu whispered.

Amrita didn't understand the need for Miyu's public humiliation. She accepted it was a lesson of consequence, but it had a chilling effect. "Mia told me you ran a Carnivore interrogation—"

"*Tabarnak!* Don't call it by that fucking name," Benoit glowered, eyes sparking in rage.

She flinched under his unexpected anger, unable to sustain his withering eye contact. "Your program said I'm earnest and eager for approval."

Mia recrossed her legs. "You missed unremarkable."

Rochon took Mia's cigarette and walked closer to Amrita. "Is what we're doing unremarkable?"

With the heightened perception of a prey animal, Amrita perceived him closer than he was.

"Quite the opposite, sir, but—" She stopped herself as her Goan accent thickened, before starting to spill words into each other. Amrita held her hand palm forward, and took a deep breath. "But a movement doesn't require everyone to be a leader. I'm good with systems and work hard. I know how things function. Complicated things. Even ones I don't know, I can learn and excel at." She was in survival mode, her breathing increasingly rapid. She didn't honestly know what she wanted other than not to die.

"Give me a good reason to let you leave this room."

Her mind scrambled through a dozen prospective options, but none were worth sparing her life. It was humbling to take inventory of the self and come up empty. Even in her position within CSIS, she'd had her potential relentlessly smothered and been relegated to being Mason's right hand—an extension of his will, saving him time and effort.

"The data!" she blurted out. "You have petabytes of raw data, but even with AI-assist, your people won't know how to interrogate it meaningfully. I can do that. I could practically write the data dictionary for half of it and know the rest well enough to extrapolate." She searched Benoit and Mia's faces for some indication her exaggeration resonated. "I could harvest the information you actually need."

Benoit again raised an eyebrow at Mia. "Not a bad pitch."

"She could poison the extracts. It'd take us weeks of audits to verify," Mia retorted.

Amrita pressed on recklessly. "It's true. But right now, you'd be set back weeks indexing and making sense of what you had. I could dive right in and take advantage of the time window before it closes. You could cross-audit my work easily enough with the right configuration. I don't know what you want, but if the data's there, I'll find it."

Benoit considered the offer. "Mia, get an offline setup for Amrita. Work with Teo to make it happen."

Mia rolled her eyes. "Teo?"

"Teo."

She made a disgusted sound, hopped off Benoit's desk and threw her jacket over one shoulder. She plucked the cigarette from Benoit's hand and took a final drag. "One gross move—" Mia crushed the cigarette out on the ground, exhaling smoke.

"They'll be nothing of the sort from him. Convey my expectations."

Frowning, Mia leaned up against him, kissed his neck and physically pushed off from him. Amrita found herself bewildered and enthralled, watching the dynamic unfold.

Benoit kept his admiring eyes trained on Mia until she exited the main stairwell. He took a white handkerchief to carefully remove the streaks of red lipstick on his skin. "It seems as though Amrita Chopra has won a stay of execution. Isn't that nice, Seventeen?"

"It's nice," she echoed softly.

"You'll get Amrita sorted. Clothes, a bite to eat, a place to sleep. No Net access, though."

"Of course, Monsieur Rochon." Miyu got back to her feet, eyes still focused on the floor.

Benoit walked behind his desk and poured himself a whiskey. "Say, does Mason Brand still walk with a limp?"

Her relief at surviving the encounter was so tangible it took Amrita a moment to recognize she was supposed to answer. "Yes, sir. Especially when the weather is changing."

"Did he ever tell you how he got it?"

"No, sir."

"Of course, he didn't." He shook his head, but the smile lingered on his lips. "I expect good things from you. Don't disappoint me."

"I won't, sir."

20

Miyu

SENSITIVE TO THE THRONGS of ardent Minus One converts who closely watched the comings and goings of Benoit's exclusive office, Miyu led Amrita out of the back exit of the overseer's office. She wanted to avoid seeing the deaths she was complicit in projected in the central area or hearing the gleeful reports of destruction chattering off everyone's lips.

Unlike others in the movement, Miyu had never truly begrudged privilege. She instead savoured her antagonism to those who'd broken covenants. The biohacker collective, Bearcat and T-Ray, and now, Benoit Rochon. She vacillated on whether Rodrigo deserved to be part of her list but appreciated actions under duress didn't deserve the same condemnation. The others were personal grievances of mutilation, rape, and betrayal. Those wounds would never heal, regardless of how much she could disassociate, subdue her emotions, or channel her rage into entropy. Each had taken something from her in a perversion of consent, leaving her irreplaceably less.

Miyu hadn't eaten in days. While not unusual, she was withering. *Just not fast enough*. The contrition Minus One demanded wasn't one she fulfilled out of self-preservation but from a deeply rooted self-loathing and a steadfast will to be reduced to nothing.

"Hey, Miyu, what are we doing?"

They were in front of her hiding closet. She had no idea how long they'd been standing before it. She was only half there, and the remaining portion was burning up in fever or whatever was mixed into the drugs Benoit had given her.

"They moved the wardrobe," she lied.

"Maybe we could get something to eat first? I mean, these clothes are fine for now, no?"

"To not wear white means something here." The explanation left Miyu's lips as though someone else was talking.

"Are you okay?"

Amrita waved her hand in front of Miyu's face. The rapid movement initiated a cascade of pixel fragments, cluttering her vision until they refreshed. Miyu smiled but shook her head. It was increasingly difficult to focus. Any introspection immediately robbed her of the ability to be present. Miyu returned to navigating hallways and doors until they arrived at an industrial storage room filled with racks and shelves of neatly stacked, high-end clothing and accessories.

"What size are you?"

"Size zero."

The pride in Amrita's voice sounded particularly weird to Miyu's ears.

"I don't know what that means."

Amrita was already glancing through the hanging racks, carefully checking labels. The premium white clothes were distinctive enough to defy fashion trends, and no two sets were alike. "There must be a fortune in clothes here."

"Yes."

"And I can pick anything?"

What you pick will be yours to protect. She caught herself lapsing back into feverish dissociation and made an effort to be present. "Choose something resilient that can layer well. It'll be your uniform."

Miyu could tell Amrita wasn't listening. The woman flittered between stacks of wardrobe, as though shopping for a wedding dress—seeing hope, advantage, and privilege in every set.

"I never thought I'd ever see a Shinsuke Mitsuoka off a runway!"

Part of her wanted to shake some sense into Amrita. People *earned* their uniforms in Minus One, and in the teething time of acceptance, they'd appreciate luxury items were a scourge of practicality and a fundamental inhibition. These clothes were designed to be a constant reminder of what they were fighting against—to be constricted by wealth, constrained by upkeep, and always one single touch away from being ruined. White represented the fragility of navigating a world not designed for the unblemished.

Amrita slipped into a particularly delicate overcoat and angled to see herself. "Is there a mirror?"

"Why are you being stupid?" Miyu regretted the snap of humiliation she delivered with her externalized thought.

Amrita recoiled, stung. "This is the first nice thing that's happened since everything went to shit."

"This is an ongoing penance." Miyu was amazed at how disconnected Amrita was from reality. She assembled a more utilitarian ensemble. An irregularly tapered leather overcoat, short boots, and a form-fitting three-quarter-length dress. "Put these on."

Amrita glanced around. "Is there a change room?"

Miyu stared at her in response until Amrita took the bundle and went behind one of the racks. After a while, she stepped back out, clothed in pristine whites.

"How do I look?"

Like a prisoner. "No one cares as long as your clothes remain white. Let's get you fed."

Amrita hesitated before taking a few steps closer to Miyu. "What did you do?"

"You're not supposed to ask those sorts of questions."

"But I don't know the rules."

"I just told you."

"I mean, I don't know how not to get punished here."

"Knowing rules won't help."

"Please! I'm tired of being punished for things I didn't do." Frustration painted Amrita's face. "I want to fit in."

It struck Miyu as a curious truth. "Really?"

Amrita closed her eyes for a handful of heat beats. "I just don't want to hurt."

Miyu had seen many people join Minus One, but none were such a square peg to the round hole of the movement. Amrita didn't strike Miyu as an idealist, and the internalization of privilege was part and parcel of the package she presented. It would be a matter of minutes in the wrong company before she was outed.

Amrita took a step closer. "Hey, are you okay?"

Again, time was lost to feverish disassociation. She'd allowed herself to become properly broken this time. "I might find some way to live through this, but you won't."

She laughed nervously, panic in her eyes. "I don't understand what you're saying."

Miyu spoke slowly and evenly, "You don't belong, you won't fit in, and you'll never be trusted. You're going to die here."

"Why are you telling me this?" she asked, horrified.

Amrita's face was wrapped in desperate incomprehension, as though Miyu had shattered the last safe refuge the woman had left in this world. Miyu's disclosure might have been to throw a wrench in Benoit's plans or for the simple idea this woman didn't deserve the fate she was unwittingly clamouring for. Part of Miyu wanted to be found out and properly punished. With her exposed and dead, they might lose interest in her father. Or he'd avenge her. She hardly knew herself anymore, and it was difficult to comprehend which truth she was acting upon.

"Snap out of it, please!" Again, with the waving.

Miyu tried to pull herself back to the present. "Everyone except for you and my father knows what it means to be here. They'll kill him anytime now. With you, it's just a matter of extracting value first."

Stunned, Amrita went to sit down.

"Don't, you'll get them dirty!"

Amrita snapped upright. Her face pinched as though expecting to be struck. "What if... What if we were to help each other?"

"Are you a surgeon?"

"No?"

"Then you can't help."

"But what if I could, though?"

"You can remove an explosive from my father's chest?"

"Are you serious?" Horror and disgust contorted Amrita's face. "They did that?"

The area around Miyu's eyes itched past the feverish pitch of her body. She rubbed them with moderate pressure and noted a disquieting amount of pus being expelled. She concentrated on the basic thought command for pulling up her vitals. It took several moments for her neural signal to spit more than digital garbage onto her optics. For the flickering moment she could maintain concentration, her vitals overlaid the top right of her vision, crystal clear beneath the smears of discharge, showing she was running a fever of forty degrees Celsius.

Something was waving in front of her vision, pulling her back to the present.

Amrita held out a cloth tissue with an outstretched hand and a face wrinkled in disgust. "Gross. I could hear that from here. Is there a doctor around?"

"He won't want to see me."

Miyu tried to wipe her implants and around her orbits, but the blood and pus smeared more consistently across her vision. Her mouth filled with hot saliva in a precursor to throwing up. Had she anything in her stomach, she'd be more worried. She turned the cloth over itself and tried rubbing the worst of the mess from the implants and dabbed around the ruptured skin. She bent over and started dry-retching.

"I don't think you have a choice, Miyu."

Miyu tried to find a clean corner of cloth and wiped the saliva from her mouth. The smell of discharge was sickening. She folded the fabric and walked it to the garbage. "I'll get you a new one."

Amrita reached to take her hand. Miyu recoiled, yanking it free.

"I'm fine."

"You're burning up."

Hearing an acknowledgement of her condition robbed half of what little strength she had left. "Maybe Rodrigo will spare a few antibiotics if I promise to stay out of his face."

Miyu shuffled past Amrita and started walking towards the clinic. Amrita started blathering, nothing meriting a response. It was the anxious talk of someone uncomfortable under scrutiny but less comfortable without it. Miyu turned to face Amrita and silenced her with one finger before her closed lips.

As they passed Minus One members walking briskly through the hallways, the sound of music and chatter increased until they reached an open set of security doors to the central nerve centre of the movement. The area was swarming with activity. Miyu shook her head at Amrita, gesturing for her to keep her eyes down, amazed at how little self-preservation the woman had. She led Amrita along the side walls, hoping to avoid the maelstrom of activity in the centre as they headed for the clinic entrance. The crowd of members awaiting medical attention were mostly dispersed. Red-streaked stains from a few haphazard swipes of an already soiled mop remained.

As they got close, Amrita skipped ahead to hold one of the metal doors open but didn't get entirely out of the way, arrested at the scores of wounded stacked on beds or cots and the frantic administration of teal-clad medical professionals weaving between the clusters of wounded who sat with their backs to the walls. Considering how many were injured and dying, there was surprisingly less noise than Miyu had anticipated. The dull buzz of dozens of people suffering with the occasional outburst, calling for attention.

In the centre of the disorder, Rodrigo, flanked by an assistant, examined a patient. His left cheek was swollen and covered with a small, translucent bandage. His eyes darted up at the sound of the door and held Miyu's gaze. Rodrigo frowned and spoke to his assistant before walking towards her. Miyu stood paralyzed on the threshold. A confusion of rage and regret amplified by fever and further disorganized by narcotics.

"Doctor? She's in a bad condition. Her eyes keep leaking blood and pus," Amrita explained with morbid enthusiasm.

"Who's the new girl?" Rodrigo asked Miyu in Japanese.

"No one. About your face..."

"Did your dad teach you to throw a hook like that?"

Miyu shrugged, finding it impossible to hold her justifiable anger over Rodrigo and his disarming smile.

Amrita, excluded in both verbal and body language, postured closer. "Uhm... Excuse me?"

"You can sit over there." Rodrigo pointed at the far wall.

"Okay, but if you need something, Miyu, just ask, okay?" Her interest and earnestness weren't acknowledged. Dejected, she bit her lip, turned and walked away with her head slumped low.

"A little dramatic, isn't she?"

He smiled and took a quick temperature reading with a short-range sensor. His mouth returned to a frown. *A most natural state on him*. Miyu remained locked in place, but the urge to escape grew irrationally stronger. She took a step back, pivoting towards the door.

"Now, come inside and let me take a good look at those eyes."

"I'm not sorry," she whispered.

"I know."

"What you did to my father was terrible."

"I know that also."

She hesitated but followed behind him as he weaved through the cramped layout of cots and gurneys. Patients called for his attention, occasionally reaching out, but he brushed past without slowing. Some of them grasped at Miyu. One patient clutched her with force, stopping her dead in her tracks. Turning to him, horror transformed his face as he let go, repeating, *I'm sorry.* She wondered whether it was her weeping infection, biohacked eyes, or skeletal appearance. Miyu had no words to excuse him or herself. She caught up to Rodrigo as he was ejecting another patient from a gurney amid a torrent of protests which abruptly stopped as Miyu neared.

She must have let things get pretty bad this time.

Rodrigo tapped the relatively clean linens. "Up you go."

He said something in Spanish to one of the nearby assistants. Miyu hadn't often heard him speak in his native tongue. He sounded majestic to her ears. Rodrigo communicated with the compassion she always wanted to surround herself with but believed she had lost the privilege of.

"I suppose that answers my question about difficulty focusing."

Time was slipping through her fingers. She was lying down now, and Rodrigo was sitting beside her, with his doctor's UkiyoAR glasses lowered.

"Why haven't you been eating?

"I don't know."

"You know the drill. Real answers with me."

"Time, maybe. When I have some, I don't feel like eating anymore. Most days, I just want to be *less*."

He was effortlessly melting her distance—as he always had. She wished she could close her eyes. Miyu turned to the side, her gaze following a tube running from her veins to a large intravenous bag hanging on a portable rack.

"Antibiotics. When you're done, we'll get some drip nourishment into you." He pulled back his UkiyoARs, fully exposing his compassionate brown eyes. "I thought we had an understanding about the truth. Why did you tell me you had no family?"

"Shame." She left it open for him to assign, scanning the gurneys and people filling the triage environment.

"Are you looking for your father or the girl who brought you here?"

"Either. Both."

"She's at the far wall, drifting her way closer. Your father's recovering in my office. Interesting fellow, your dad. He has some good stories."

"So..." She crossed her arms in front of her, skeletal fingers clutching at sharp elbows. "So he's okay?"

"Not okay, but definitely resilient."

"Can I see him?" She didn't know where the glimmer of hope came from or what it could mean if she was given permission.

"You ask too much sometimes."

"I know," she quietly acknowledged.

Rodrigo's demeanour eventually softened. "It could be I'll become occupied with my duties and unable to keep track of all my patients. Once your IV has run its course, though."

"Thank you."

"But you have to promise to return. I need to get some electrolytes and fluids into you."

She nodded.

"This isn't an option. Between the bacterial infection and the abject cruelty with which you've been treating your body, you'll need them. Promise me in words, Miyu."

It was the first time he'd called her by name. She found it arresting but not unwelcome.

"Okay. I promise."

21

Tatsuo

TATSUO WOKE ABRUPTLY AS the office door opened. It struck him how he could sleep through the sounds of injury and general commotion in the adjacent room but startle alert at the gentle creak of old door hinges in Rodrigo's office. He pushed himself upright on the couch, ignoring the pulling strain and discomfort from the fresh stitches on his chest, arm, and shoulder. His eyes adjusted to the wash of light coming from outside as his daughter pushed a wheeled IV drip into the room. She was clinging onto it like a fragile elderly person would a cane. Her ghastly eyes and emaciated body compounded the illusion.

"Hey, kiddo." He hoped his heartbreak didn't come across in his voice.

"Hey, Dad." She closed the door behind her, removing all but the ambient light from the barred window. She shuffled towards the light switch and hesitated. "Is it okay if we stay like this?"

"Yeah, sure. Why don't you come here? Plenty of room on the couch."

She ambled forward a few steps and stopped. "I'm sorry I got you mixed up in all this." Her voice was choked up.

"I'm okay. We'll always be okay, right?"

"Not this time, Dad."

He patted the couch, smiling disarmingly. "Come here."

She reluctantly closed the distance between them with her head down. He reached over and scooped her onto the couch beside him with one arm, careful to pull the wheeled IV drip along with her. She offered no resistance and had the same weight as when she was a child. He slung one arm around her shoulder, pulling her tight against his chest. She yielded to his manipulation and, when he was done, pulled her knees tightly to her chest and tucked her face into them. He waited for her to relax, but her whole body was tense and hot to the touch. He stroked her shaved head—fingers dancing lightly over the subtle ridges of scar tissue. All he had were questions, but few of them truly mattered.

"Have you and Rei kept in touch?"

"Only when she wants something."

"Shame. The two of you used to be close. You know, she was the one who told me about your first steps. She was proud of you, too. Your mom was... occupied in those days." He shook his head, surprised at how his ex-wife's rapid decline into addiction remained a bitter memory. "Promise me you'll reconnect, okay?"

She trembled against him. Her whole body shifted with him as he took a deep breath.

"I wish I knew how to be a better father. I never realized how you... I wish I could've given you whatever you needed when you needed it."

"It's not about you," she whispered.

"Then help me understand."

She shook her head.

"Please."

When she didn't respond, he angled to try to face her, but she nestled into him, trembling in his arms.

"Miyu?"

"You wouldn't get it, Dad."

"Try me."

Her finger threaded the IV line. He waited, each moment growing longer as she slowly twisted the slack out of the line.

"I'm just so tired. Tired of trying. Trying to fit in, trying to score another fix, trying to stay alive. Trying not to hate myself or be crushed by how pointless and pathetic it all is." She crimped the IV line, pinching it tight between thumb and forefinger. "Everything's so hard. I don't have it in me to keep trying anymore. It's exhausting. I'm exhausted. I wish I could die already, but I can't even manage to do that. I'm too much of a coward to kill myself and too weak not to accept help."

He gently grasped her hand. It went slack at his touch, allowing the IV to flow again. His daughter's consuming despair was impenetrable, infectious. Tatsuo didn't know where the conversation was heading and opted for silence.

"You were never supposed to see me like this. Just my ashes when they got sent back home. And now I've killed you," she said, ethereally thin.

"I'm still here. It'll take a lot more than a bomb to kill me."

She laughed but then went quiet for a handful of heartbeats. "It's that. I never had your optimism. The doctors told me I wasn't supposed to live past twenty—"

"Fuck those guys."

"You don't get it. I've never been able to have plans or dreams. For a while, being alive and useful to someone was enough, but it's not. I've been waiting for it, but death won't come quick enough."

"You're not sick anymore, Miyu. Fucking idiot doctors, scaring a kid like that."

"There's no way back for me now."

"There's always a way." He took her by the shoulders and carefully made space to stare into her eyes. He hoped his sincerity could pierce those weird metallic disks, but all he saw in them was his desperate reflection. "Let's do it together, okay? We can go home. Get you sorted out."

"We can't even get out of this room together without Hunter coming."

"Doc said he likes you."

She shook her head. "He kills people, Dad."

"The guy doesn't look all that tough." He flashed her a grin. Tatsuo gave her IV bag a final squeeze before straightening out Miyu's arm and yanking out the needle. "Let's go."

"I promised Rodrigo I'd finish it. Now, you'll have to fight him, too."

"Too bad. We got on pretty well, all things considered."

Tatsuo lifted her easily to her feet as he stood. He didn't know what to do except get his daughter out of this accursed place. He took Rodrigo's white overcoat off the hook and draped it over Miyu, channelling his powerlessness and anguish into action.

"Ready?"

She shook her head vigorously, both palms out in front of her. "No, not at all ready. This is suicidal, Dad."

"I thought you wanted to die." He winked.

His dark humour caught her off guard long enough for him to open the door to the infirmary and pull his daughter through the door along with him. She was leaning on the rolling IV stand for support and offered no resistance.

From across the room, Rodrigo's eyes widened at the sight of the two. He wove through the makeshift beds, rushing to close the distance between them. Tatsuo rolled his shoulders and neck, trying to smooth the motion of his shopworn body. As Rodrigo got close, Tatsuo punched him in the face, knocking him sprawling into an occupied bed before he crashed to the floor, stunned in disbelief. Patients started shouting and screaming. One of the nurses bolted out of the room, and the other two cowered.

"Dad, what are you doing!?"

Tatsuo reached down, grabbed Rodrigo with both hands and yanked him up. "Sorry about this, Doc, but I have to sell it." He pitched Rodrigo into another makeshift bed, knocking it and the occupant to the floor. "Stay down!"

Rodrigo, already bleeding from the nose, awkwardly scrambled and clawed back to an upright position. "You're going to get her killed, idiot!"

"She's going to die here anyway. Stay down after this one, okay?"

The doctor wiped his bloody nose with his forearm before lunging at him with a sloppy overhand right. Tatsuo easily slipped the punch before dropping Rodrigo with a lead left counter. Given the way his legs crumpled under him, the doctor was properly stunned by the time he hit the floor.

Tatsuo grinned at his horrified daughter. "Good guy, that Doc."

Full of vitality, he gestured to Miyu to follow him as he passed a host of wounded Minus One recruits cowering at his approach. One a little further up stood and tried to block his path, but Tatsuo grabbed him by the face and pitched him sideways. He did a quick shoulder check for Miyu and found her engaged with a young, animated woman.

"Get away from my daughter!"

The girl flinched at his command, saying something in rapid and incomprehensible English.

"It's okay, Dad. Amrita's harmless."

"Tell her not to get in the way."

As he stalked forward, potential adversaries stepped back and away from his path. They encountered no direct resistance until they made it through the infirmary doors to the main assembly area.

A dozen young Minus One adherents were formed in a semi-circle a few meters back from the door, with a nurse standing behind them, pointing at Tatsuo, agitatedly saying something. Tatsuo scanned the opponents, noting most seemed petrified. Only two looked as though they'd been in a real fight before. Behind him, Amrita stood in front of Miyu, preposterously protective.

He gently shoved her aside and grabbed the wheeled IV from his daughter's grasp. "Sorry, kiddo. I'm going to wreck this on your friends."

"Those aren't my friends, Dad." A glimmer of a smile broke through. "But thanks for the warning."

Tatsuo gave her a quick kiss on the top of her head. "Get ready to run." He took several steps forward, brandishing the rolling IV post like a club. "Which one of you fuckers is first, huh?"

As a group, they took a wary step back. A man off-centre started shouting something and the others joined in. Tatsuo dashed forward, swung the IV rack and savagely knee-capped him. He went down howling in pain, and the others skittered back further. Movement on his right. He angled back, swinging, and crashed the IV stand directly into a man's temple. Even before the body hit the ground, there was an explosion of movement towards him. Three or four people.

Tatsuo swung the IV stand in dangerous, wild arcs above his head. "Get out of here!"

He didn't have a chance to check if Miyu had obeyed his command. He clubbed one man, skipping the rollered base off his shoulder and into the back of his head before angling the backswing to sweep out another man's legs. Someone on his left tried to tackle him, but Tatsuo's body instinctively angled to absorb the impact and stayed upright. He let go of the IV, tightly grabbed the person's head in a Thai clinch, threw two quick knees to their face and let go when the body went limp. He soccer-kicked the other attacker's face as he tried to get to his feet, sending the man rolling limply aside.

The last of the immediate opponents was a lanky young teenager. He was shooting his mouth off, trying to buy time for others to gather their courage and assist him. Tatsuo snapped his head back with a step-in jab and straight right. The quick succession of impacts set him reeling, falling backwards, clutching at his face.

More had come. Minus One associates had abandoned their duties and started crowding in. He was about to get swarmed and sought leverage. He swept behind an unconscious opponent, lifted him to a seated position and grabbed him firmly by the chin and top of the head.

"One step closer, and I'll break his fucking neck!"

While he recognized few spoke Japanese, the implicit physical threat gave the group pause. People shouted or screamed their hatred until a sudden hush came over the assembled group. The crowd parted in the center for the hulking man Miyu had called Hunter.

Hunter said something in a low, baritone growl everyone strained to hear.

Tatsuo held up one finger, and when Hunter acknowledged it, he dragged an unconscious member out of the way. He didn't want to lose his footing against such a monster. Hunter snapped his fingers, and several Minus One members did the same for the other three. Another gesture from the man got the crowd to shuffle back to give them more space.

Tatsuo gave his shoulders a final roll. "Alright. Let's see what you've got."

He put his hands up and skipped into a loose fighting stance—a hybrid of boxing and Muay Thai, keeping him light and mobile. Hunter took an orthodox boxing stance, high guard, with his chin tucked and eyes focused. He shuffled forward a few steps and shot a surprisingly fast jab Tatsuo barely slapped off-target with an open-handed parry. The follow-up straight was narrowly slipped.

Hunter grinned and said something for Tatsuo's ears alone.

"I don't speak your fucking language," Tatsuo lied. They were conversing in violence, and in that, he was fluent.

Tatsuo feigned with a jab, closing Hunter's guard, and lunged forward with a left body hook before breaking away with a switch-leg calf kick. His punch's impact was solid, but nothing registered on Hunter's face. The calf kick was defended with a check-shin. The two stepped back to reset and circled each other in wary appreciation.

The assembled crowd of Minus One followers were chanting, *Hunter! Hunter!* It was all pleasantly nostalgic for Tatsuo. Despite the recent surgical trauma, his body was warm and loose. A thin layer of perspiration covered his skin. Everything was slightly electric and exhilarating. Hunter charged forward, crouching low and weaving to evade Tatsuo's jab, and threw a series of strikes. A lead body hook Tatsuo managed to get his elbow between, another hook to the opposite side to drop Tatsuo's other guard and finally, a lead-hand uppercut landing not quite flush, but with enough force to send Tatsuo stumbling back. Hunter lunged forward into a deep underhook, reached for a knee tap with his free hand, and propelled them to the ground with crushing force. Hunter was already posturing up to rain down blows as soon as they landed. Tatsuo instinctively tried to wrap up the man's body with his legs and pull him into a closed guard.

The crowd exploded into a frenzy as Hunter started bludgeoning fists and elbows on Tatsuo, attempting to smash through his desperate guard and hitting with enough force to fracture Tatsuo's forearms. Hunter's weight on him was crushing, and the relentlessness of his powerful attacks was equally shocking. Even trained fighters needed to pace themselves.

Tatsuo lunged up, wrapping up one of Hunter's arms from the shoulder, and tried to sweep the man with a scissoring of his legs. Hunter was too enormous and stable in top position to fall for the technique, but Tatsuo had a limb and was creating an opening for himself. As Hunter used his free hand to try to push Tatsuo's face down, grinding him into the concrete floor, Tatsuo managed to get his hips free. Like the thousands of times he'd drilled, he swung his leg around Hunter's neck, adjusting his grip and posture, threatening an armbar. Hunter tried to brute-force out of it, but the split second of extra space it afforded allowed Tatsuo to synch in the joint lock. He twisted his position and arched his back, extending the leverage on Hunter's elbow until it audibly snapped. A total rupture of flexor tendons and UCL. In a monumental effort, Hunter lifted Tatsuo's body entirely off the ground and slammed him into the concrete.

Tatsuo frantically rolled clear, scrambled into a three-point stance, and got to his feet. He wiped the wetness from his face, his fingers registered the forming hematomas. Blood covered his hand. He knew a couple of shots got through his guard, but the savage damage of partially blocked strikes was shocking. His stitches had all sheared open, and blood was leaking from the reopened wounds. Glancing around, he was relieved to see Miyu had gone. He knew he had to buy her more time, though.

Tatsuo smiled broadly, revealing bloody teeth. "You hit pretty hard, huh?"

Hunter cracked a brief grin and said something in his rumbling baritone. His boxing stance shifted from orthodox to a Philly Shell, with the shoulder of his injured arm high and the good hand guarding his chin on the opposite side. The stance was long. Hunter's lead leg would be an easy target for a takedown or getting battered with kicks, provided Tatsuo could manage the distance and stay on the outside. The crowd of Minus One members were yelling and cheering feverishly at Tatsuo's blood and Hunter's phenomenal aggression, not recognizing Tatsuo had the upper hand. Both the combatants understood the gravity of the current dynamic and how it would inevitably play out.

Tatsuo whipped a roundhouse kick into Hunter's knee, momentarily buckling it, and easily evaded the counter. He started picking Hunter apart with ranging jabs and leg kicks, constantly circling to the outside, forcing Hunter's rear-hand counterstrikes to fall short. Hunter switched his stance with his good hand forward, but all it did was allow Tatsuo to hit with rapid two and three-strike combinations, sacrificing the first to a parry but ensuring the follow-up strikes landed flush. It would be an execution in stages. There was a grim recognition on Hunter's face as the man reverted his stance. A hush fell over the crowd as the frenetic cheers were replaced by incomprehension and intermittent shouts of encouragement. Twice, Hunter rushed for a takedown after being lit up, but Tatsuo masterfully pushed off and regained range. Soon, there was only the sound of sliding feet and dull thuds of impact.

Though Tatsuo was bleeding freely, he was vital. His movements were flowing, and his accuracy was on point. Battered and surrounded by hostiles, he was reborn. An anointed protector, a champion crowned in blood. In these precious seconds, he was euphoric. He circled some space from Hunter and took the time to fully absorb the moment. The fear and horror of those witnessing the spectacle, the grim defeat in Hunter's eyes and even the disbelieving expression on Rodrigo's face as he watched through his doctor's UkiyoARs from the infirmary doorway. Tatsuo was bathed in the memory of the deafening cheers from when he was a crowd favourite in the Osaka Dome.

Yoshida! Yoshida!

An older man dressed in a crisp white-on-white suit parted the crowd. At his command, Hunter bowed to Tatsuo before limping beside and behind the new arrival. The man spoke with a gravity which might have affected the dynamic if Tatsuo understood a single word of what was said. Tatsuo let the man prattle on, basking in the glory he'd stolen and eventually turned to face Rodrigo.

"Hey, Doc! Tell this worthless piece of shit he's lost. My little girl's gone, and this whole fucking operation is going down."

"I can't do that!" Rodrigo protested, face painted with dread.

"Let me have this."

As Rodrigo conveyed what he hoped was his full sentiment, Tatsuo nodded in recognition to Hunter. The gesture was acknowledged and sombrely reciprocated. The older man in the suit scowled, muttered something and snapped his fingers. An exotically dressed, blue-haired woman stepped forward to place a device in his hands. She clung to his shoulder, but he shook her off in frustration. He spoke in the tenor of threat, harsh-sounding words metered with drama, and brandished the handheld like a weapon.

It was all absurd to Tatsuo. He laughed aloud.

"Stand down, or he'll detonate the explosive," Rodrigo frantically conveyed. "Benoit doesn't bluff. He'll kill you where you stand."

"Yeah, he looks the type." Tatsuo regretted he'd never have a chance to see his girls again, but they were probably better off without him. Rei, especially. At least they wouldn't see him like this. "If you can track down my girls, tell them I love them both and that it's not their fault."

Rodrigo gravely nodded his response.

"Okay, Doc. You can tell him to get fucked now."

Tatsuo lifted one hand in victory as Rodrigo hesitantly translated his words. Benoit's eyes widened in rage as he pressed at the handheld, and the small, shaped charge in Tatsuo's chest exploded. Tatsuo dropped to his knees, held upright for a moment and folded over himself before spilling lifelessly onto the cold concrete floor.

22
Mathis

MATHIS HAD GONE THE last few hours without seeing another non-Japanese as he walked from the *takoyaki* shop and crowded streets of Shinsaibashi to Umeda's bewildering, towering landscape. He apparently didn't know how to walk right or had broken some other taboo—other than taking off his winter coat in winter. He'd suffered the sideways sneers of the locals and freely given instructions of the more stern-looking elderly women.

His language parser required a Net connection, and he'd elected not to risk one after Rei had instilled a deep fear of discovery into him. His heart lurched as his mind leaped to all the wrong conclusions whenever he saw a cluster of youth dressed in white or corporate types dressed in black. With no mapping overlays for his Net-enhanced vision, he was effectively lost, too. Confoundingly, streets in Osaka weren't laid out in a grid system and on more than one occasion, he'd doubled back on himself or veered further off his intended course.

As Mathis walked, he scanned for the universal symbols for one of the 24-hour Net cafes Rei had advised him of. They were cheaper than capsule hotels and accommodated the fringes of society with anonymous tech stacks. He had Rei's Net handle, but outside of that, there was little Mathis knew of her. A resourceful and intelligent battered woman with a maybe-girlfriend who had saved him from illegal apprehension at Itami airport and forced him to eat octopus while burdening him with her family's imminent execution. She had even given him some paper yen and a suite of tactics to remain off-grid in Japan. It was too weird of a long play to extort money, and nothing about her lined up with his admittedly limited expectations.

After fifteen minutes of desperate scanning, he found a series of symbols leading him to an overnight Net cafe in a tired-looking, four-storey building. He entered an unmarked door and navigated several flights of stairs. The dark stairwell was partially exposed and under-serviced, the adjacent building's height robbed the light, and half of the ceiling bulbs had burned out. The sharp odour of stale urine on the blind corners of the first two flights cut through the damp concrete scent and the blanket dullness of accumulated pollution. On the fourth-floor landing, he found the unassuming entrance to what he imagined was the Net cafe. A steel door painted in muddy green and plastered with irregularly placed stickers. He tugged it open.

The inside smelled of instant noodles, cigarette smoke, and unwashed clothes. On his left, a balding, middle-aged man dressed in a rolled-up buttoned shirt and tie slung over his shoulder was methodically handwashing a few dishes over a small sink amid a countertop filled with various kitchen devices. He looked at Mathis with dead eyes and offered an insincere smile before returning his attention to the dishes. A younger man dressed in layers of dark cotton clothes sat at a large table by himself, noisily slurping noodles. Behind him was a wall of shelves with colourful book spines and vending machines. The door closed loudly behind Mathis.

"Are you lost?" the noodle-eater asked in serviceable, thickly accented English.

Hearing English, Mathis exhaled in relief. "Maybe?"

There was a single long hallway on his right with shoes and an eclectic mix of suitcases neatly placed in front of densely spaced doors on either side. The rooms had two-meter-high walls and no ceilings. Everything was painted black, including the ceiling, exposed metal joists, and HVAC piping. Even the industrial fans churning the stale air were black. Old fluorescent lights with naked tubes hung suspended low on precariously thin cables.

"I'm hoping to rent a room with a Net connection."

"First time?"

Mathis nodded, less certain by the moment.

"Ah. Okay then." He took another slurp of noodles and stood up. "I'm Yuki—means snow in English. Three and a half years, room four. That's Tanaka-*san*. Well, maybe. He doesn't talk about himself, but he looks like a Tanaka, doesn't he?"

Tanaka glanced over his shoulder, face betraying no expression. Mathis waved, but Tanaka didn't reciprocate.

"He's room two, and the *senpai*. No one knows how long he's lived here. I'm second longest, though." Yuki gestured around. "There's the kitchen, behind me is food and the rooms are over there. The far right is free. Room eight. No one likes it since it has a direct overhead light and is beside the washroom. You can hear people when they go." He took another slurp of noodles, talking as he chewed. "Everything works on tokens. The machine is beside the cup noodles. It's old school here, cash only. Do you have yen?"

Mathis resisted the urge to prove it. "Yes. Your English is very good, by the way."

Yuki grinned. "I learned through movies and sitcoms. Do you speak any Japanese?"

He shook his head. "No, I arrived this afternoon."

"How did you go so wrong so quick?"

Tanaka made an admonishing noise and spoke in a harsh, low tone without turning to face Yuki.

"*Sonnan iuna.*"

Yuki laughed. "Tanaka-*san* understands English!? Amazing!"

"Uhm, I might try to get sorted." Mathis walked over to the token machine and was confronted with a worn touch-screen covered in Kanji. "Hey, Yuki, what button is for room eight?"

"There's a language toggle in the top right. Press on the flag."

The interface layout was unlike anything Mathis had used. It was coherent once understood but operated on an entirely different set of cultural understandings. He navigated it like a child despite everything being written in English. He selected room eight, stacked four consecutive checkouts of six hours each and fed most of the paper yen Rei had given him into the machine. A key attached to a brightly coloured USB dongle spilled out in a previously concealed dispensing tray. Mr. Tanaka and Yuki were staring at him, as invested as zoo onlookers are at a monkey attempting to solve a simple mechanical puzzle. Yuki nodded as he ate his noodles.

Mathis forced a smile and displayed the key like a prize. "Got it, thanks. Are there any rules I should be aware of?"

He shrugged. "Keep quiet, clean up after yourself, and be tidy. No drugs or guests. Don't knock on people's doors, and only talk to them if they want to be talked to in the common area."

"*Ibiki kakuna,*" Tanaka gruffly added. He gestured at Yuki with a sharp nod of his head.

"Tanaka-*san* asked you not to snore." Yuki lifted the colourful polystyrene bowl and drank the instant noodle broth. "So, what do we call you, room eight?"

"Mathis." He remembered to bow. "Thanks for all your help."

Tanaka had already finished washing up but kept his back turned, occupying himself with a drying towel. Yuki waved and put on his UkiyoARs, immediately ignoring Mathis.

Mathis carefully navigated between the neatly aligned shoes and other suitcases, lining up his shoes and kit similarly. The door unlocked at his fob's proximity—toothed key unrequired. The room was slightly longer than he was tall and a little wider than he was broad. The thin black mats covered in plastic on the floor didn't squeak under pressure, and a couple of red cushions finished in the same material lay in a neat stack in the corner. A thin, low table was tucked against the room divider, raised high enough to point his feet up underneath. On it, an older generation handheld and oversized UkiyoAR goggles with integrated hearing perched on a plastic stand beside a fresh box of tissues and clean ashtray. The room had no ceiling, and the fluorescent light directly above shone brightly overhead. He put on the goggles and activated the handheld. The guest mode initialized, and within a few minutes, Mathis confirmed the VPN and cloaking routines were both competently configured and no data trails were being leaked or captured.

The guest account had no profile data. He temporarily removed the goggles and initialized a scan of his face. A camera bee detached from the handheld and completed several radial circles around his head. A moment later, the three-dimensional composite formed in his Net vision. The program auto-corrected against blemishes or imperfections and added configurable layers of style. He opted for *neutral, actual,* and *business casual*. After his avatar manifested in a sport coat and tie, he dialled down to *casual,* cycled through a few dozen options, and eventually accepted a muted set of clothing he could conceive of wearing.

He tried to isolate all the things he needed to do—gain privileged access at corporate headquarters to safeguard humanity's future, develop a scheme to liberate his colleagues back home, compel his parents to flee impending incarceration, and evade capture by two separate organizations functionally operating in a nation he didn't understand the first thing about. He didn't know where to place Rei's family within his list of impossible burdens and slotted them in as a discreet addendum. Daunted, but committed, he implemented an additional layer of data obfuscation on the handheld and navigated to his corporate account. One message auto-executed as soon as he logged in.

"Mr. Grenier, my name is Fumiko Inoue. I am the executive assistant to Kazuo Ogawa, the global CTO of Hikari International."

Her crisply delivered English matched her lip movement too perfectly to be an emulator. Her appearance was borderline unnerving. An animated stock image of a Japanese career woman with her neatly parted shoulder-length hair, the faintest makeup application, and impeccable posture. Even her professional attire, a white button shirt done up to the top under a navy-blue suit jacket, was immaculately ironed and rested crisp on her slender frame.

"Mr. Ogawa has generously offered to clear time in his schedule to meet you. He'd like to understand why you have sabotaged fifty billion yen and three years' worth of investment across international locations dedicated exclusively to realizing the program you've been implementing. Mr. Ogawa is certain there is a legitimate reason you've jeopardized the fundamental value of Hikari International and eagerly awaits approving your proposed remediation plan."

She hadn't moved her head or changed her expression as she talked, and Mathis hadn't perceived her blinking, either. He reluctantly initiated a conference request with Fumiko, which was accepted a few seconds later.

"Mr. Grenier, thank you for reporting in. I didn't expect you to reach out from a personal account."

Mathis could see her consternation at his avatar entering corporate records. "It's definitely me, Ms. Inoue."

"Inoue," she corrected.

Mathis could've sworn he'd said it exactly the same. He faked a smile. "I'm nearby and would welcome the chance to explain the situation to Mr. Ogawa."

"Given the time of your flight's arrival, Mr. Ogawa expected you to be at the office already, executing remediation."

Her lack of blinking was subconsciously making Mathis blink twice as often. "Yes, I understand his expectations. And they're entirely reasonable. But I've attracted the attention of some bad actors who want to corrupt the wetware program."

"I apologize for my poor English, but I'm not certain what you're trying to express."

He swallowed the lie and decided to play it straight. "I'm not safe."

"This is Japan, Mr. Grenier. Japan is safe."

"I almost got abducted at the airport!"

"I trust you're not referencing the gentlemen tasked with escorting you to the corporate headquarters."

"They had guns."

She cocked her head slightly, adding to the uncanny valley-like experience. "Did you personally see the firearms, Mr. Grenier?"

"No, but—"

"And did you allow the gentlemen to identify themselves?"

He clenched his teeth. "No."

She smiled unnervingly with only the corners of her mouth. "International travel can be taxing and disorienting. Mr. Ogawa appreciates this and generously expects you to arrive well-rested promptly at eight tomorrow morning."

"Ms. Inoue," he started, half-expecting to be corrected. When he wasn't interrupted, he continued. "I had to flee Toronto. Minus One broke into my home, physically assaulted me, and has been trying to intimidate me into compromising the program. Frost has illegally incarcerated my colleagues, threatened my parents, and promised to do worse to me if I don't create a backdoor for him."

"Minus One is a Western problem. In Japan, they are merely a social nuisance. As for Mr. Frost, he is a corporate partner to Hikari International, representing a near-unlimited wealth of investment and deployment opportunities. He was also essential in exposing the coordinated sabotage your colleagues participated in, which you'll no doubt be able to justify convincingly to Mr. Ogawa tomorrow.

Provided your explanation is as robust as your remediation, they'll be returned to liberty."

She offered Mathis another unnerving smile.

"Maybe I wasn't clear. Frost *threatened my parents*," he frustratedly protested.

"I'm certain it was a misunderstanding. Mr. Frost will be onsite tomorrow afternoon and has requested a meeting to level set." Her eyes flicked up without changing the orientation of her face. "Yes, I believe those were the words he chose. Level set."

He swallowed and processed a moment. "He's coming to Japan?"

"He should arrive before noon and is staying at your hotel, which, according to their records, you haven't checked into yet."

Mathis grappled with the concept of a four-hour onsite window to convince the corporation to fundamentally go against its own benefit. "Not yet, no."

"Mr. Ogawa wishes to be assured we've come to an understanding. Have we, Mr. Grenier?"

He couldn't see a way out of it. "Yes, Ms. Inoue."

"I look forward to seeing you at eight tomorrow morning."

She terminated the connection before he'd had a chance to reply. The entire exchange left a bitter taste in his mouth. Fumiko was as effective at controlling a situation as Evy Carter but lacked any of Evy's humanity, charisma, or style. She was the anti-Evy.

He scanned his corporate account, finding scores of unread messages. Conspicuously absent were any from Evy, Logan, or Tariq. They had been removed from his upcoming calendar entries, and as far as he looked, any meeting, conference, or reference to his colleagues had been purged from corporate records. He tried to message them but immediately received errors. *No such account exists.*

Mathis scanned their social profiles, hoping to find activity since the time he'd left Toronto. Instead, the profiles had all been deleted. No trace was left of their digital legacy. Even the rare instances within his own personal and professional profiles that tagged his colleagues had been contested and suppressed from public consumption.

With increasing dread, Mathis toggled to his personal account and initiated a conference request to his parents. It was accepted after a curiously short alert time and he was met with his mother's worried face captured by the camera on her refrigerator console.

"Mom, is everything okay?" Mathis couldn't conceive of her being awake this early.

"Oh, I'm fine, bunny." Ingrid cast a sharp glance to the left.

"Is Dad around?"

"He went out to run a quick errand but hasn't returned yet." She forced a smile, but her eyes betrayed anxiety. "So, how's Japan?"

"Confusing? When will Dad be back?"

"Oh, don't worry about us. He probably ran into the Cruickshanks. The ones a few doors down the street with the little sausage dog? You know how your father likes to talk. How long will you be gone for?"

His stomach sank. His mother was the socializer, and his father had always suffered along with it. Mathis had never known the Cruickshanks to keep a dog, either.

"I... I don't know yet."

Her forced smile faded. "Stay there a good while, okay?"

"What aren't you saying, Mom?"

"Your father and I believe you need to do what's right, Mathis. Always and no matter what."

"Mom?"

"We love you so much, bunny. We're so proud—"

A finger flickered into view, terminating the connection. No matter which way his denial tried to frame it, his mother was too far away from the screen to have touched it without leaning forward. He didn't know how to process the emotions drowning him. He heard himself whimper and covered his mouth with both hands, desperate to choke back the sobbing overwhelming him. He removed the goggles and closed his eyes, curling up in the fetal position on the uncomfortably thin mats.

There was a quiet tap on his door. Mathis took a tissue and wiped his eyes and nose before scrambling into a presentable sitting position. Cautiously, he opened the door to find Yuki crouched at his head height and Tanaka in his suit jacket standing behind him, frowning.

Mathis waited for them to say something. The weirdly tense silence felt alien and constricting. He was compelled to break it. "Yes?"

"Uhm, Tanaka-*san* would like to remind you everyone's life is hard, and crying will only resurface other people's miseries."

Mathis didn't know how to respond.

Tanaka gave Yuki a little nudge. *"Nakunara benjo ittekoi."*

"If you must cry, the shower is best for it. But obviously, not when anyone else is in there."

Mathis nodded on autopilot. "I understand. I'm sorry."

Tanaka held up a fist dramatically. *"Minna ganbarankai."*

Yuki also raised a fist, although less convincingly and lower. He nodded to Mathis and smiled sardonically. "We're all trying our best."

Yuki bowed his head and gently closed the flimsy door, leaving Mathis disoriented and bewildered under the stark light of the naked fluorescent lamp.

23

Rei

Rei's social accounts started getting messages. A handful initially, but they started coming in by the tens and soon amounted to hundreds, with more arriving every few moments. The display of her UkiyoARs was constantly refreshing, and new messages pushed older ones from her field of vision. Her eyes skimmed the previews, but her mind couldn't fit them into her reality. There were condolences and requests for interviews or statements from the family.

Her father was dead.

Rei would've fallen had she not already been sitting at her desk. Not wanting to engage any particular message for fear of a read-receipt, she executed a quick Net search and found a stream of her father's execution circulating like wildfire on Japanese social networks. There had been millions of views and tens of thousands of shares in the last few hours.

#tatsuoyoshida, #minusone, #execution, #japan, #trending.

Her fingers were shaking uncontrollably. She balled her hands into fists, squeezed her eyes shut, and forced herself to breathe. Her mind conjured a torment of imagery—unsettling, visceral. Too brutal to linger within her imagination, Rei snapped her eyes open, and hesitated before committing to the playback.

The Netstream started abruptly with a rear-view of her father surrounded by dozens of people dressed all in white. Four of them littered the floor before him. As Tatsuo angled to take in the crowd, he was unlike anything Rei had ever seen—calculating, brutal, incapable of mercy. When a colossal opponent conspicuously not dressed in white entered the area, her heart raced. The giant of a man was the same one who'd come for her sister. The man said something barely audible. She ran back the footage and used filters to isolate his voice from the rest of the ambient sound. Eventually, she could piece it together through audio manipulation and some lip-reading.

I used to watch your fights.

It struck Rei as an odd admission, given the context. A raw, visceral dread gripped her. She wiped away her tears and was transfixed as they engaged each other. When her father was getting crushed on the ground, smashed by a relentless series of punches and elbows, she hastily ripped off her glasses, saturated and overwhelmed, and paced away from the desk. Rei forced herself to stop moving and squeezed her eyes shut, but her father's merciless beating played out in her mind's eye, the terrible echoes of the cheering crowd lingered.

She blamed herself for forcing him overseas. In Japan, she could've done something to keep him safe—sequestered him in a countryside rental or another prefecture. The Mori clan might have found him, given her father's inability to lay low, but at least he would've had a fighting chance. His brief time overseas had proven disastrous beyond comprehension. Met by a junkie daughter, abducted by terrorists, implanted with explosives, and beaten to death in front of an audience before suffering a posthumous humiliation in Japan. Her knuckles were white from clenching, and her nails dug painfully into her palms, leaving marks when she opened her hands. Her sister was supposed to have kept their father safe. Rei's seething resentment for Miyu was all-consuming.

Trembling, she willed herself to the bathroom to splash water on her face. Rei looked at herself in the mirror. Beaten, broken, emotionally spent. She tried to summon up a reserve of determination. As awful as it was to witness her father's last fight as her first time watching him in combat, she vowed to see it through to the end. With a daughter's grim duty and great trepidation, she returned to her desk, put on her UkiyoARs and resumed the horrifying playback.

Rei didn't understand what her father was doing as he squirmed and locked his limbs around the giant's arm and neck. Anguish distorted the monster's face as his arm snapped at an unnatural angle. He savagely slammed Tatsuo to the concrete and backpedaled a few steps. When her father got back to his feet, the man's face had regained a stoic composure. The giant said something. It was more challenging to pick out this time amongst the cheering and enthusiastic screeches of the assembled crowd, even with her filters and audio isolation maxed out. Eventually, she got it.

You're still amazing.

Rei was awed by her father's incomprehensible dismantling of his opponent. Fast kicks, swift dodges, and well-timed combinations. He was unstoppable. His face was covered in blood, already swollen with large lumps, but he seemed... ebullient. She couldn't fathom it. Rei and Miyu had always believed their father was a bit of a loser, coming home badly beaten after every match, but she started to grasp from the Netstream the depth of his skill and determination that had won him widespread popularity with fight fans back in the day. His desire to succeed went far beyond the fear of pain or apprehension of death.

An older man dressed in a formal white suit arrived, commanding the giant opponent to his side. Rei didn't need to isolate his audio since everyone went silent, hanging on his every word. She paused the playback, zoomed in on his face and extrapolated the angle to yield a clean frontal view for a Net search. The results matched him as Benoit Rochon, a noted Canadian anarchist and central figure of the global Minus One movement. Rei struggled with the Quebecois accent and was thankful the auto-generated subtitles could function on the clear audio.

Are you proud of yourself? Of this hopeless situation and the miseries your actions will inflict on your daughter? Every wound you've given my members will be borne by Miyu. Broken bone for broken bone. She'll be crippled for life because of your cheap heroics. If you don't stand down now, I'll drag it out and have her mutilated in the process.

Her father made men in positions of power want to inflict their punishment on his daughters—this Rochon asshole, the Mori clan, and even her yakuza boss and allegedly her father's best friend, Ichirou Shinoda. They sensed Tatsuo's capacity for suffering far exceeded their ability to coerce obedience.

Her father turned to 'Doc,' the one whose Netstream she was viewing, and asked him to translate. Her father's expression of love and absolution devastated her. His death immediately following was impossibly serene, as though he'd taken all the victory there was to achieve with him.

The Netstream held on his body for a moment before cutting to a still frame from one of her father's legendary fights in the Osaka Dome with his hand held high in victory. His face was battered, inexpertly wiped of blood, but joyful and proud. The man who'd translated for her father spoke overtop the image with the thick accent and weirdly inflicted cadence competent foreigners had when speaking Japanese.

Miyu and Rei, I don't know if this Netstream will find you, but I hope someone who sees it will share it with you. And if they can't, that they share it with someone else who will. I didn't know your father well, but as someone who treats the sick and wounded, I know death. Tatsuo Yoshida didn't die today. Your father became immortal. Please see it as such and be proud of him.

The Netstream ended.

Rei was overcome with emotion. Grief, pride, horror, respect, loss, and love. She knew in her heart there was no place in this modern world for her father. He wouldn't have wanted to go out another way, too—provided Miyu made good on his sacrifice. Her sister should carry this burden. Rei couldn't stomach risking another encounter with Miyu's insufferable avatar, so forwarded the Netstream to her without any preamble or additional context.

The message notifications kept coming in.

Rei removed her glasses, closed her eyes and tried to focus on breathing. Although she was emotionally saturated, she found there wasn't anything in particular to hold onto. Rei walked to the small kitchenette, opened a bottle of whiskey and poured two healthy measures neat into plain shotoku glasses, honouring her father's peculiar habit of using the small beer glass for hard spirits. She slid down the face of her refrigerator, lit an emergency candle and set it between the drinks on the floor.

"Here's to—"

Her voice cracked, words dying abruptly. She lifted one glass, touched it gently against the other and took a sip. And another. Rei swallowed all the words she'd never be able to say to him. She put the glass down to refill it. Well into her third, her unit's helper AI interrupted in a crisp Tokyo accent.

"A police officer is approaching your door."

Rei cursed herself for overlooking the priority access available to law enforcement in her otherwise tightly regulated building. "Who is it?"

"I'm not licensed to identify members of the constabulary. Would you like to upgrade your service?"

"No."

A gentle knock sounded on her door.

Rei pulled herself to her feet, careful not to disturb her father's glass, and checked herself in the hallway mirror. There was nothing to do about her face—the cool lights of the interior would highlight every bruise and abrasion since she'd washed off her makeup. With a gesture, the mirror's display swapped to a security videocast of the hallway immediately outside her unit. A policeman in uniform stood there, head bowed and hat angled to conceal a direct view. He held two large, matte black bags in one hand, and the other was held open at his side.

She swapped slippers as she stepped onto the cold tiles of the lowered entryway. Rei's heart raced. She didn't know which of her many schemes and corresponding lives were about to be exposed and didn't know which persona to adopt. She straightened her posture, steeled herself, and opened the door to find Officer Ken Matsumoto's sombre face.

He stepped back, took off his hat and bowed low. "I sincerely apologize for the intrusion on your evening, Miss Yoshida."

"Matsumoto-*san*," she acknowledged relieved, returning his bow. She tried to sound normal and spoke indirectly, hoping to mask the scent of whiskey on her breath. "What can I do for you?"

"I'm sorry to ask, but would it be okay if I were to step into your *genkan* for a moment?"

Rei took a few steps back and a half-step up to synthetic wood flooring, swapping back into her home slippers as she did. Officer Matsumoto stepped into the lowered entryway and carefully closed the door behind him.

He bowed deeply again. "Miss Yoshida, I've come into possession of some terrible news I felt needed to be delivered in person."

"That my father's dead?" Rei didn't mean it to sound as it did to her ears. "I'm sorry, Matsumoto-*san*, but I've been bombarded with messages from strangers." She took a deep breath. "I might not be handling it well."

"Of course."

"I probably should have expected you, though. Whenever Dad got in trouble, you were always around. I considered you as a kind of uncle growing up." Rei glanced at the two matt black bags, recognizing the silver logo of an upscale kimono maker in Kyoto. "Are those for your wife?"

"Ah, yes." He shifted nervously on his feet. "I apologize for being presumptuous, but I thought you might want to avoid the public eye for the time being."

He carefully offered the two bags to Rei. They were surprisingly heavy.

"You see, my wife's sister was also ill. Passed from stage four cancer several months ago, unfortunately. Before Aiko's condition worsened, she purchased a kimono for mourning. She never had a chance to wear it since it was delivered after she went into hospice care. You and she are of similar build, and this might be one less thing for you to concern yourself with."

"I don't know what to say." She bowed and set the bags down gently, not knowing how to internalize the Matsumoto's compassion amidst the chaos of emotions she was struggling to contain.

"It's nothing, truly. I'm sorry for burdening you."

"How is your wife, Matsumoto-*san*?"

"She delighted in the floral arrangement you'd sent. It's so rare for her to smile these days. It was very considerate of you."

Rei failed at smiling, and gestured the air without meaning, saturated. She exhaled slowly, forced her hands to her side, and collected herself.

"I was having a drink with the spirit of my father. Would you care to join, provided I'm not detaining you from being with her? I'm afraid I don't have an extra set of house slippers."

"Truthfully, Aiko rarely notices I'm there anymore. I'm sure she wouldn't begrudge us this time, even if she had her wits about her. Also, I never particularly cared for house slippers." Matsumoto unlaced his well-polished shoes and carefully faced them towards the door after entering the apartment.

Rei's modest home comprised of a small kitchenette, a Western bathroom and a long room with a bed, desk and a large wardrobe to flesh out the finite closet space. A modest stack of shelves neatly displayed favoured jewellery, accessories and wigs supporting her personas. The unit was highly efficient for a tidy, single person but not meant for entertaining. There was no art on the walls, little colour and even the accessories on shelves or lined up on her desk were neatly arranged.

There was a modest amount of surplus space where she might've tucked a small dining table or a comfortable recliner, but Rei preferred it empty.

She gestured to the chair at her desk. "You know, you're the first person outside of building maintenance to visit. Please, have a seat."

Rei went to the kitchen to pour a glass of whiskey for him, topped up her own in the process and grabbed the one she'd set aside for her father from the floor. She brought the three drinks to the desk, set two down, and clinked her glass against her father's. She wanted to say something, but the words didn't form in her mind. Her throat constricted, and her eyes watered.

"To the most unique, fearless, and big-hearted man I'll ever know." He gestured his glass toward the one reserved for Tatsuo.

Rei cleared her throat and tried to wipe her eyes inconspicuously while taking a drink of whiskey. She was light-headed from consuming alcohol on an empty stomach and from the burden of trying to hold herself together in the presence of unexpected company. She sat curled over her knees, close enough to the bed to lean on it if needed.

Matsumoto made a show of appraising the whiskey. "It's nice. What is it?"

Rei hoped he could detect her gratitude. "The Yamazaki twelve. A taste for it is one the few things I shared with my father."

"I hope you'll forgive me for saying this, but I see his best qualities in you."

She gestured to the bruises and abrasions on her face. "I see you've picked up on the growing resemblance. You've been good not to ask."

"May I?"

She shook her head. "Thank you for coming in person." Rei danced her finger along the rim of the glass, hesitating. "Have you seen the Netstream?"

"Yes."

She waited for more, but he seemed reluctant to comment first. "Think they'll be caught?"

"Canada has a well-respected judicial system. Once the people involved are identified, they'll eventually be incarcerated."

"It's Benoit Rochon. It took less than a minute to figure it out!" She exhaled. "Sorry, my frustration isn't directed at you."

Matsumoto nodded gravely. "I'm no expert in foreign judicial matters, but from what little research I've done, it seems there are challenges in executing justice swiftly in Canada. It's a slow process of legal phases. A non-insubstantial percentage of cases can stretch years before there's a resolution. It's not like Japan. Perhaps with how high-profile this case has become internationally, there will be more emphasis on resolving it expediently, but considering the chaos happening overseas, I wouldn't count on it."

"What do you know about Minus One? I see people dressed like them around Osaka, but they don't seem to cause trouble."

"Not for you. Here, the protests are more tactical. Assaults on private property or capital have been deliberately orchestrated to avoid disturbing society. I can assure you, however, there are a lot of victims and far more active cases now than we can prosecute."

"I'm sorry for pulling you away from your duties."

"This is the most important one I have." Matsumoto shifted and leaned forward. "Would you let me know if you needed help?"

Rei nodded, finishing what was left of her whiskey. "I'm okay." *We'll always be okay*, she heard her father's echo.

Matsumoto frowned.

"I met someone who might need help, though. A Westerner who just arrived in Japan. Minus One used my father as a hostage to coerce my family into recruiting him."

"You used a few words to say a lot. Could you offer more context?"

Rei shrugged. "It's not important anymore. Dad's dead, the guy's here."

"Are they pursuing him now?"

"Someone is. I rescued him from the airport before some guys could grab him. The Westerner seems pretty harmless. Some programmer-type who's in over his head. And—what are you smiling at?"

"Your father also had a hard time ignoring people who didn't know they needed help." He clinked his glass on Tatsuo's and took a drink.

His genuine appreciation struck her as inappropriate. It was undeserved and unwittingly shamed her. She was far short of whatever imaginary benchmark Matsumoto was holding up. "That's not what this is."

"Of course."

"He's connected to my father's murder and seems so... defenceless."

"I'm afraid the police services are overwhelmed now and may not prove helpful. You might want to consider instructing him to arrange private security. If he arrived from overseas, he must be of economic means or important enough to people with them. There might not be a lot of private security professionals available these days, though. The wealthier segment of society appears to have secured virtually everyone on the market. Some of your father's old friends might be able to offer insights on protection. Of course, this is merely the idle speculation of someone who knows little about such things."

Rei knew not to comment but nodded her comprehension.

"In case it comes up, what's this stranger's name?"

"Mathis Grenier. Late-thirties, Canadian. He works for Hikari International. I'll send you a clean source to pattern-match against once I can stomach the thought of putting on my Net glasses again."

"You've given me more than enough." Officer Matsumoto finished his glass, carefully set it down and stood up. "I'm sorry for being a burden in your time of grief, Miss Yoshida. Please let me know if I can do anything for you."

Rei was humbled by the quiet policeman. "Thank you for your concern and generosity." Rei cleared her throat, got to her feet and bowed low. "Please pass along my best wishes to your wife."

With an economy of effort, Matsumoto walked to the *genkan*, laced up his shoes and put on his hat. He bowed to her in silence and closed the door gently behind him.

Matsumoto's visit had been a comfort of sorts, a rare and unexpected human experience, but it left her exposed and somehow inheriting expectations she didn't wish to fill. After a time, she reverently took the items from the large bags Matsumoto brought and delicately unpacked them. She recognized the many individual pieces making up a kimono but hadn't worn one since her heartbreaking *seijin-shiki* ceremony when she'd come of age. She remembered renting kimonos with her girlfriend and how shamelessly her first love had flirted with the young men at the *izakaya*. Rei still felt the pangs of bitterness from being unexpectedly cut off in the following days. There was no room for the purity of teenage love in the serious world of adults and ambition.

This gift from Matsumoto was no rental. Handmade, embossed paper wrappings covered the layers of the exquisite *mofuku* kimono ensemble. The plain, black kimono showed no sign of imperfection despite being handcrafted of layered chirimen. The black-on-black *obi* was delicately accented with a muted snowflake pattern. The gently-textured *obiage* and intricately woven, flat *obijime* starkly contrasted the white inner layers of the *nagajuban* and *tabi*. The second bag held the accessories—black *zori* with a matching handbag, a black, lacquer enamelled fan, plus a handful of minor items she'd have to watch a Netstream to figure out how to use.

It was a precious gift from a worthwhile man to a dutiful daughter to honour her dead father. Excuses and context aside, the weight pressed hard against her long-held, juvenile reservations.

She neatly stacked the items on her desk before taking out the last thing in the second bag. The *kouden*, an elegant and sombre money envelope, contained enough condolence money to position Matsumoto as a relative. Rei drank some of her father's whiskey.

"How many times has I-*chan* reached out?"

"Ichika Fujita has made six requests as recently as seven minutes ago. She is exhibiting agitation. Shall I initiate a conference?" the helper AI offered.

"Tell I-*chan* I already know, that I'm okay and will be in touch soon. Avoid answering questions and distill a manifest of anything important for me to follow up on."

Rei understood their relationship hadn't been the same since she'd turned up bloodied and broken. Her carefully managed distance had thinned, flickers of truth had emerged in word and action. Rei caught herself seeking excuses to be in Ichika's company. To see her smile, feel her warmth, and enjoy a brief illusion the world wasn't collapsing all around her. She hated herself for growing soft.

Rei ran her finger along the lip of the whiskey glass and idly wondered whether all the years of lies and sneaking around had been worth it. Her father had given her an abundance of freedom and had never wished her ill, yet she'd done everything never to be subject to his judgment. He may have loved her as unfathomably, inadequately, and completely as he always had if she'd been more honest. Death had robbed her of his acceptance. She closed her eyes, trying to find her bearings, but found only his absence.

"I wish you weren't gone."

She allowed herself to fully experience her grief and regret before forcing her mind back to the present. Her father's death had set the stage for catastrophic betrayal, and there were a lot of moving pieces she had to account for if she wanted to survive it.

24

Amrita

THE ROOFTOP OF THE Minus One headquarters was surprisingly stark and free of obstacles. The winter wind cut through Amrita's designer fabrics, which were never intended to endure the elements, robbing her of the little warmth she'd recovered from her brief time inside the building. It was teeth-chattering cold. Again. No hint of sunlight pierced the overcast sky as the starless night transitioned to the bleak dawn of day.

Crouching low to keep out of view, Amrita scowled at the narrow perimeter surrounding the building. An unassailable expanse. Why had they climbed the metal rungs of the safety ladder and hadn't made a run for it instead? At least, she could've. Huddled into a ball and drowning in an oversized white overcoat, Miyu could barely function anymore.

Minus One teams physically walked the surveillance-saturated perimeter, searching for them. They'd seen several drones operating on preset search patterns go further afield until they'd disappeared from view. They'd managed to evade detection thus far. At least, Amrita assumed they had since no one had apprehended them as yet.

She had acquired nothing of value to offer Mason, and now, there didn't seem to be a path towards clearing her name. She was almost entirely out of options, and her one remaining gambit required cooperation from an increasingly despondent companion.

Miyu had severed her Net connection early in their escape and ditched her handheld. The only technology not connected to Minus One they had access to was the generations-old, substandard tech stack Miyu had barbarically grafted into her. It had taken Amrita the better part of three frustrating hours to coach Miyu through a handful of system configurations, allowing her to connect to the low-bandwidth public network blanketing the city that provided a minimum of Net access to the poor. With no external screen, Amrita had to painstakingly mentally navigate Miyu through command-line instructions, installation of packages, and targeted reboots.

If you want to eat an elephant, you have to do it one bite at a time, the voice of her Auntie reminded her.

Miyu's thought interface was wildly unpredictable and forced dozens of attempts to execute a single command correctly—all of which increased the signals of pain playing out on Miyu's skeletal face. She looked like the haunted dead, a parable of unimaginable torment.

Amrita wasn't close to Miyu, the girl was a lifeline out of her predicament, but she empathized with her. She hoped Miyu was simply struggling with fever or had become exhausted again from the strain of mental processing. She could work with those easier than despondency and hopelessness. The last set of instructions Amrita had given was fifteen minutes ago. More than enough time for Miyu to execute the task several times over, even accounting for the technical gaffs the thought interface would inflict.

"Where are you on the update?"

Miyu was squeezing her head with both hands, rocking back and forth, muttering a stream of repetitive nonsense in Japanese.

"Miyu?" Amrita grabbed her shoulders and harshly whispered, "Snap out of it!"

Miyu craned her face to Amrita, trembling. "The Net connection works."

"What's wrong with you?"

"My sister, she—" Miyu swallowed. "My dad."

Amrita pretended not to understand. "We can rescue him later, but now we need to contact my boss, Mason Brand. He promised to send help."

She shook her head, curling up into an even tighter ball. "He's dead."

"Miyu, *our* lives depend on you getting your shit together. Okay?" She tried to sound encouraging, but it came out flat and hard. She cursed the cold dementing her expression, angling herself to be directly in front of Miyu. "Please. Can you Netcast?"

She nodded reluctantly. "Not for long. Not well, either. It's painful."

"My boss normally wouldn't connect with a stranger but flag it from Amrita Chopra. Mason Brand of CSIS."

She blind-coached Miyu through the best channel to conference her boss. Eventually, Miyu nodded.

Amrita straightened the line of her coat, corrected her posture, and ran her fingers through her hair a few times in a clumsy half-styling. "Where am I supposed to look?"

"He'll see what I see. I'll have to tell you what he says, though. The gear's audio is bone conductive."

"Okay. Tell me when he's connected."

A short while later, Miyu gave Amrita a signal.

"Mason, we're connected through an intermediary. Miyu—"

"Yoshida," she added reluctantly. "He wants to know what's wrong with the connection. He thinks it's fake."

"We're using Miyu's internal gear. She's a biohacker. No time to explain, though. We're at the Minus One headquarters. Can you get a fix on the GPS coordinates?"

"He says yes. He's asking so many questions. Numbers, Rochon, capabilities. He's talking too fast, I can't... I can't keep this up." Miyu started squeezing her temples with both hands. Her face distorted as she winced in pain.

"Rochon is here. There's probably more than a hundred members, and they have arms."

"He's saying something about a strike team. Taking time to arrange. No... No, I can't filter it!"

"Shhh!" Amrita shot an anxious look around the perimeter at Miyu's outburst. "Mason, when can you rescue us?"

"He wants to know why I'm showing him a dead guy. No, I can't control it." She bared her teeth, snarling. The expression made her impossibly more skeletal. "Fuck you, he was my dad!"

"Mason?"

Miyu shook her head. She rubbed her eyes, reflexively checked her hands for discharge, and dabbed at the swollen pustules at the edges of her implants with a tissue.

"Your boss is a piece of shit."

Amrita faced away from the woman who just tanked their one hope of rescue with a waking fever dream. She felt foolish and powerless, dreading her family would forever be tarnished with the shame of producing the greatest traitor in the country's history.

"Well, there's a fifty-fifty chance Mason will just treat us as collateral damage for the strike team and personally take credit for liquidating Minus One's leadership. No explanations required, guaranteed praise, and career advancement."

"Or?"

"Or he could face endless tribunals to clear my name and get professionally sanctioned for overseeing this fiasco." She laughed sardonically, shaking her head. She was desperate for something her family could hold as proof of her innocence, or at very least, a shield against the relentless condemnation her actions would thrust upon them. "Miyu, could you do one more thing for me?"

"No more. Please, it hurts."

"I'll be quick. Thirty seconds, I promise."

Miyu covered her face with the upturned overcoat collar, curling up even tighter. "I can't control anything. I push garbage into the stream when I can't focus. Connecting is painful. Like my brain's on fire."

"Can you send a file?"

Miyu nodded mechanically.

"Then harvest the conversation with Mason from your scratch memory and send it to Maryam Carter of Bargain Traders. Title it, *Amrita Chopra, final check-in*."

"I don't understand."

"You don't have to, but it may just prove to be our ticket out."

Miyu trembled in an irregular staccato rhythm. Amrita anxiously paced in the silence.

"The address didn't bounce, but there wasn't a digital handshake either."

Amrita imagined what Maryam would do with the file, provided she opened it. It was a wild hope—desperate, unhinged, and tenuous.

"So, what now?"

Miyu shrugged. "Wait until we're found."

Amrita laughed nervously, and got closer. "No, seriously. There's got to be something we can do."

"The first drones should be running out of power. They'll spot us on the way back."

"How can you say that? Like you're bored with it?"

Miyu focused on the expanse of industrial buildings. Her weird eyes, shaved head, and skeletal face made Amrita feel she was talking to an emissary of death.

Amrita's mind raced to find some angle to play. "Do you have any friends in there?"

There was a long pause before Miyu finally spoke. "Sometimes it doesn't get better."

Her frustration was boiling over. "Why won't you help me?"

Miyu turned to face her, paralyzing Amrita with her disconcerting focus. "I've been suffering for hours for you already."

"I—" Amrita choked back her misplaced anger. She'd made the mistake of placing her salvation in Miyu's hands and had unknowingly signed a death pact in the process. "I want to live, Miyu. Don't you?"

"You're wasting words now." Miyu turned away.

Amrita sat down, defeated. She resisted the urge to push for more, knowing she'd taken all there was from the husk of a person Miyu had dwindled to. She started running a list of all her regrets in life, unconsciously interspersing banal social encounters with opportunities lost and a litany of shame endured. Her life was a series of missteps, and the closest she'd ever come to living was when she was throwing it all away. Now, the monstrous man in black would come for them. She didn't know if her teeth were chattering in fear or from cold.

She became aware of Miyu speaking softly in Japanese, with all the pauses and irregular patterns of a conversation. Miyu's face contorted in pain, but all the while, her thin words kept pace until they stopped. She clutched her lowered head in agony. Eventually, Miyu curled herself tight in the oversized overcoat.

"Last goodbyes?"

"A promise." Miyu's focus was on the southern skyline. "Drone's coming."

Amrita scrambled to find somewhere to hide, but there was nothing but a flat rooftop painted bright with their thermographic signatures. The rooftop of the adjacent building was too vast a chasm to attempt. The metal rungs of the safety ladder were within the drone's trajectory, and jumping down on the far side would guarantee injury. She tried to convince herself they weren't high up, about seven meters, but glancing over the edge, it might as well have been seventy.

Fear made her restless and desperate. "Why are you okay with this?"

"I'm tired."

The drone was now visible to Amrita's naked eye. Having piloted many, she knew there was no avoiding discovery at the height and distance. The drone lazily circled once overhead before disappearing below their point of view.

There was no last-ditch escape idea and nothing to put her hope into. "Why did you lead us to get trapped up here!?"

"It was never my intention to leave."

"You're killing me, too."

Miyu shrugged.

There was the sound of movement below. Amrita crouched down and scampered closer as Hunter approached, flanked by a half dozen Minus One adherents. He directed them to various positions around the building. His one arm was in a sling, his face was a swollen mess full of abrasions, and he was limping.

"New girl!" Hunter's cavernous voice sounded as severe as his countenance.

"What?" Amrita could barely hear herself from the terror constricting her voice and tried again. "What!?"

"Down in ten, or you'll catch a bullet."

Amrita didn't want to believe they would shoot her. She quickly convinced herself she was too crucial for Minus One, considering she could legitimately cross-map petabytes of sensitive stolen data. She stood up tall and shook her head. She choked back her fear and tried to sound authoritative.

"I don't think you appreciate how—"

Hunter snapped with the fingers on his good arm. Her ears hadn't even registered the crack of the long rifle before a bullet tore through her calf, ripping flesh and splinters of bone out the other side. She collapsed in a howl of pain, desperately clutching at the wound. Blood pumped through her fingers, staining the white canvas of her elite clothing. The pain was excruciating. The colour drained from her face and she started trembling violently in shock, hyperventilating.

"Eight. Seven."

She'd lost numbers in Hunter's countdown. She fixated on the sniper dressed in all white on an adjacent rooftop, still aiming at her.

"Four. Three."

"Wait! Wait, damn it! I'm coming, okay!?"

She clawed and scuttled to the edge but froze at the sight of Hunter's face devoid of humanity, an unkillable storybook villain to scare children and elders alike.

She clamoured awkwardly down the rungs, hopping on her good leg and bleeding freely with the other. Her shaky hands lost their grip on the slick metal rungs. She desperately regained her grip as she slipped, smearing her blood across the white fabric of her clothes.

She dropped to her knees on the asphalt, and held both hands before her face. "Please, no."

Hunter's lips curled in disappointment. He took a combat tourniquet from a shoulder pouch and threw it to Amrita. "Wear it."

He waited impatiently as Amrita fumbled dumbly with the contents before he limped over, yanked it from her grip and applied the tourniquet himself, oblivious to her cries of pain as he pulled tight the strap and twisted the rod until he was satisfied.

Hunter reset his attention to the rooftop. "Your turn, Seventeen."

Miyu ambled right to the rooftop's edge at the top of the ladder rungs. She stared down, scanning each of them silently before fixing her gaze on Hunter. With a slight movement of her shoulders, Miyu shrugged out of her overcoat. The wind pulled what little fabric she wore tight across her withered form. Walking in narrow steps along the edge, she shuffled a few arm's lengths from the ladder, hesitating before completing the last step. She stepped back with her lead foot and pivoted to face them again.

Hunter paced in agitation. "Quit screwing around."

Agonizingly slow, Miyu craned her neck back, face to the sky. When she brought it back down, there was no trace of emotion on her features. She gestured to Hunter with a lazy, skeletal finger. Hunter and the Minus One security team stopped moving, straining to listen. Amrita, too, was captivated by Miyu's actions and unconsciously controlled her breathing. The pounding of her heartbeat defied the sensation of time standing still.

"Dad had you beat." Miyu's thin voice carried in the anxious silence.

Hunter's face took on a sombre expression. "Yeah." He frowned. "Yeah, he did."

"It wasn't right you did nothing."

His jaw flexed as he clenched and unclenched his teeth. "No, it wasn't."

A weird smile crept across her emaciated face.

You owe me, she mouthed.

Hunter cursed as he dashed towards Miyu while she calmly fell forward.

Her body crashed into Hunter's outstretched arms and chest, sending him staggering back with the impact and shouting in pain as his bad arm twisted violently to an unnatural angle. He tossed her to the ground and, stone-faced, wrenched his elbow and shoulder into position. As though pulled up by marionette strings, Miyu picked herself up from the heap she lay in and stared at him with those haunting, unknowable discs.

Bleeding, warped in pain and terror, Amrita was utterly bewildered by the surreal exchange. She couldn't parse what had transpired, no matter what angle she interrogated it. A pair of Minus One members unexpectedly yanked her to her feet. One on each arm, they dragged her towards the main building.

"What happens now? Where are you taking us!?"

“Shut up, new girl.” Hunter’s strong, limping strides overtook her. He effortlessly cradled Miyu like an infant against his chest with his good arm, and she nestled into him.

Hunter and Miyu exchanged guarded words, but it was impossible to imagine what they were saying. Miyu’s mouth moved little as she spoke, and Hunter’s face revealed nothing. They were close—almost intimate in how he held her.

Amrita tried to block out her agony and fear, desperate to find anything to grasp onto for hope. Neither of the men dragging her acknowledged her suffering or awful struggle to shuffle-skip along with them. She went to wipe the tears from her eyes, but the man holding her arm effortlessly resisted the movement. Soon, Amrita was pulled through the doorway into the energetic interior hallway. Minus One associates darted past her, faces grave or scared. Some held clutches of assault rifles or boxes of ammunition, whilst others were clearly rushing to tasks out of sight. Everyone made way for Hunter, and the rest of their group followed in his wake.

The main chamber was crowded with people and full of activity, but the tenor had changed. Before, it had been euphoric, whereas now, it was intense and urgent. People spoke in shorter sentences, their movements clipped. There was no idle wonder or discussion, and no soundtrack underscoring their actions.

She recognized some of the same faces from before. Their exhaustion was palpable. More armed members hustled in groups of twos or threes. From the overseer’s office, Benoit Rochon and Mia Locke were staring out the window. Mia was speaking, but grave-faced Benoit didn’t give her his attention. The gaze of Minus One members followed them as they passed on the way to the overseer’s staircase with the temporary attention of passing motorists witnessing a flaming car wreck from the other side of a highway.

Amrita’s leg banged on the first stair going up, and she yelped in pain. The men holding her didn’t pay any attention. She tried frantically to hop on her good leg, holding the other back and slightly raised to avoid repeating the same mistake, focusing on the basic mechanics of movement until she found herself at the top of the stairs, staring through the window into Benoit's stern eyes.

Irrationally, she grasped onto the railing, refusing to be dragged into the office and violently struggling against the strength of her captors in a losing conflict. Mia's piercing laughter penetrated the single pane of glass. When Amrita had her grip wrenched free, she was thrown into the room behind Hunter. Miyu casually climbed down his body to assume a supplicant position, face down and body over knees, in front of Benoit.

"Her clothes are filthy," Mia complained, gesturing absently to Amrita. The tall drink in her unsteady hand sloshed clear liquid on the unfinished concrete.

Benoit shook his head in shared criticism. "And after only—"

"Three and a half hours," she said, slurring.

"She promised to be useful, indispensable, but she's shown us who she is."

"Ungrateful." Mia hopped up on the desk, taking three tries to sit, and lifted one leg to cross the other with her hands.

"Unworthy," Benoit continued.

Amrita pointed at Hunter accusingly. "It's not my fault! He shot me!" she cried in horror.

"Hunter?"

He shrugged. "She wasted time."

"Please," Amrita begged. "I need a doctor."

"Thanks to this one, we don't know where ours is. Tell us, Seventeen, how did you manipulate Rodrigo into betraying the cause?"

Benoit gave Miyu a rough shove with his foot, pushing her off balance. She immediately struggled back into her supplicant kneeling position.

Miyu didn't raise her gaze from the floor. "I can't seem to get anyone to do anything."

"She's got a point," Mia added snidely, sipping her drink.

"You failed to secure Grenier. You broke your vows. You brought your father here." Benoit kicked Miyu over, his face momentarily twisting into a sneer. "I *know* the scope of your betrayal."

Miyu regained her kneeling posture. "Yes, Monsieur Rochon."

"Get up."

Miyu struggled to her feet, angled to one side, with her elbow pressed tight against her ribs. Benoit grabbed her roughly by the chin, lifted her straight, and cocked back his fist. Mia shifted forward, delighted. In a confusing burst of movement, Hunter intercepted Benoit's hand before it struck. Benoit tried to pull it free, but it was held firmly in Hunter's monstrous grip.

Benoit's eyes widened in shock before quickly narrowing in outrage. "What are you doing!?"

"You'll get blood on your clothes," Hunter evenly explained.

While the two men stared at each other, neither giving space for compromise, Miyu's skeletal hand drifted to Hunter's curved knife and delicately grasped the handle. Hunter released his grip on Benoit, inconspicuously flicking open the catch on the knife's sheath as he stepped back without breaking eye contact. Miyu pulled free the karambit blade from its curved sheath as he did so.

Expressionless, Miyu pushed the knife into Benoit's stomach to the handle.

The room became an expression of chaos.

Hunter struck the side of Miyu's face hard enough to send her skidding along the floor, senseless and limp. Mia screeched like a wounded animal as Benoit staggered back—his face frozen in disbelief, his hands clutching the handle of the weapon deep inside him. Blood saturated his three-piece suit and pumped through his fingers.

"Don't pull it out!" Amrita shouted instinctively and immediately regretted doing so.

Mia rushed to Benoit's side, pointed to Miyu and screamed, "Kill her!"

"*Trouvez-moi un médecin.*" Benoit's cadence was disjointed. He trembled visibly as Mia guided him to a seated position and set herself behind him as a brace.

Hunter turned to the stunned security team who'd assisted in Amrita and Miyu's capture. "Find Rodrigo."

The team scrambled out of the overseer's office. Four through the front, two through the rear.

"Are you waiting for a fucking invitation, Hunter!? Kill the traitor!" Mia shrieked.

"I'll have her confined until she comes to."

"She dies now!"

Hunter dragged Miyu's unconscious body by the ankle directly in front of Benoit, unholstered a black semiautomatic pistol, and offered it grip-forward to him. Heart pounding, Amrita opened her mouth to say something but was remained paralyzed as a spectator. Benoit, ashen-faced, took the weapon in his bloody hand and levelled it at Miyu. Mia's greedy hands caressed his face, and she was whispering something Amrita couldn't make out in his ear. Hunter stepped outside the firing arc, frowning. It felt indescribably pathetic and ignoble to execute a helpless person. The injustice and horror choked Amrita, constricting her throat and smothering her protests.

Benoit hesitated. The pistol's barrel dipped. Mia's emphatic words gained passion and intensity, but stopped entirely as Benoit lowered the pistol until the gun rested on the unfinished concrete.

"I'll lock her in the trailer. We'll deal with her later." Hunter extended his hand for the gun's return.

Benoit nodded.

Incredulous, Mia wrenched the gun from Benoit's loose grasp, scrambling to stand over Miyu's unconscious body. Mia pulled the trigger three times. The sound of gunfire was deafening in the enclosed room. The sound waves reverberated in Amrita's chest. Her ears rang. The scent of cordite filled the air as the gunshot wounds lazily coalesced blood on the stark white clothes covering Miyu's still chest.

Amrita found herself staring down the barrel of Mia's bloodlust and threw her hands in front of her face in sudden terror. "I didn't do it!"

"*Ça suffit*," Benoit weakly called. "Enough, Mia. We need her."

Hunter grasped Mia's gun hand, enveloping the barrel and jamming the slide and hammer. She desperately pulled at the trigger to no avail. With disgust, she let it go and returned to Benoit's side, entangling him with her limbs, oblivious of his discomfort, seeming to seek an impossible solace.

Hunter towered over Amrita, and she withered under his gaze. He appeared stricken as he holstered the pistol.

"Deserve it, new girl."

25

Mathis

MATHIS WAS SPIRALLING, LOST in the dense tangle of storefronts in the non-linear backstreets of Osaka, desperately trying to find *Aki no Sora*, the *izakaya* he was meeting Rei at. He checked his detailed, hand-written instructions again, scanning in yet another circle for some clue. A rivulet of sweat dripped from his temple. His whole body was moist from perspiration, having fast-walked at increasing speeds in his search for the past thirty minutes. His survival instincts took over, and he scanned the evening crowds for yet another pleasant-looking, elderly woman to help him.

Mathis smiled, bowed, and pointed. *"Aki no Sora wa acchi no hou desu ka?"* He hoped he remembered the phrase correctly.

The elderly woman smiled in return, acknowledging his clumsy effort, and unleashed an expressive torrent of Japanese, bewildering Mathis. There were repeated gestures for him to zip up his coat, but outside that, he had no idea what the lady was saying. She seemed to be reminiscing more than speaking to him directly. He nodded, smiled, and patiently waited for the lady to stop talking.

"Aki no Sora wa acchi no hou desu ka?" he repeated, pointing to a different location.

"Issho ni ittaru wa."

She interlocked her arm with Mathis' as though they were courting from another era and took him on a strangely enjoyable stroll through some of the same backstreets Mathis had previously searched. The lack of sidewalks forced them to carefully navigate the abundance of signage, vehicles, and pedestrians to maintain their linked walking style. She made eye contact or the occasional funny face to other older ladies they passed. These intermittent exchanges punctuated what he assumed was an elaborate story the woman was unfolding for her entertainment alone. He picked up the rhythm of interaction, making sounds when she paused to let her know he was listening, which seemed to please her. Eventually, they stopped before a black lacquered wooden door with muted, unilluminated signage written in Kanji. Mathis wouldn't have found the place even with the aid of technology.

"*Hai, tsuita de.*" Grinning, the lady reached into her conspicuously large purse and warmly handed him a wrapped candy.

He gratefully accepted it and bowed as low as he could. "I'm sorry I don't know how to thank you properly in Japanese. But I truly appreciate what you did for me." He squinted his eyes, placed his hands over his heart, and bowed again, hoping she could grasp his meaning.

"Kamahen, kamahen." She gave him a slight bow and waved enthusiastically before heading off into the bustling evening streets of the city.

Mathis stepped through the auto-retracting, lacquered front door. The deceptively small frontage of *Aki no Sora* belied the size of the interior, which was laid out in a deep L-pattern and could accommodate thirty seats. More, if there hadn't been a modest, raised stage tucked in beside the bar. Thickly milled and darkly stained wood made up the furniture and countertops. Every seat was occupied, with many people standing.

A mature lady dressed in a bright red kimono elegantly embroidered with cranes and flowers, accented by a broad gold and white patterned *obi*, held court over a boisterous group of middle-aged businessmen along with the adjacent tables of customers. Mathis was awed by the lady's chemistry and charisma. She had all the assembled patrons fully engaged with her uncommonly expressive cadence and unnecessarily elaborate gestures or expressions. He stood dumbstruck at the entrance, watching her lean forward and whisper something while playfully pinching the cheek of a giggling senior salaryman, eliciting a host of cheers. Afterward, she bowed theatrically to the tables paying her tribute, elegantly glided up to Mathis, and effortlessly took him by the elbow to lead him to the bar. The assembled patrons whistled and cheered. One of the men at the bar vacated his seat at their approach.

"You look like you need a drink, handsome," she suggested with dramatic gravity.

"You speak English?"

"One of the few benefits of having taken international lovers." She winked.

If pressed, Mathis would've placed her at approximately the same age as his mother. A sudden pang of guilt for own parents' temporarily derailed the the lady's charismatic spell. He fell in line with her strolling gait, and allowed himself to be guided to a seat directly before a stern-looking, middle-aged man in a casual blue chef uniform with the hint of an exposed white undershirt. Dead-faced, the man reached under the counter and put a small edamame dish in front of Mathis. The lady swept behind the counter and shooed him away.

"Don't mind Taro-*kun*. He's like that with strangers. Now, let me guess." She sized him up theatrically. "You're someone who drinks wine... infrequently and as little as you can get away with socially."

"That's incredible!" Mathis was genuinely awestruck. "How could you know?"

"It's a good thing we aren't drinking wine."

She reached behind her to the racks of neatly displayed alcohol and placed a bottle between them. Magically and without breaking eye contact, her other hand brought forth two plain glasses. "Kokuto shochu. Lovingly made on the

Amami Islands off the south coast of Kagoshima prefecture. Clean, easy to drink, and refreshing. Perfect for the reluctant drinker to develop a habit." She smiled, pouring for both of them. *"Kanpai."*

"Kanpai," he echoed, drinking the distilled liquor neat. It wasn't awful, which was about as generous as he could frame it. Her charisma made him mindful of his manners. "I'm Mathis Grenier. It's a pleasure to meet you."

"Oh, you've gone and ruined the mystery." She frowned. "Are you Rei-*chan*'s foreign friend?"

Mathis had no doubt he was pegged the moment he'd stepped in but played along. "I'm supposed to meet her here shortly."

She drank her shochu in a single raise, set it down, and evaluated him critically. "It's unlike her to bring boys by. Tell me why you're special."

"I'm not, sincerely. We're practically strangers. Rei just took an interest in helping me."

"She's helping you?" The lady cocked a critical eyebrow. "And what exactly are you providing her?"

"Complications?"

"Tssk. The foolish girl's got the dynamic reversed." She playfully shook her head. "You know, I practically raised her in this bar. She's as close to a daughter as I've ever had. Given Tatsuo isn't here to put the fear of god into you—"

"Tatsuo?"

She gestured lovingly to a small, framed portrait of a fighter in a boxing ring of a packed arena, surrounded by coaches and commentators, with his arm raised in victory. It occupied a prominent shelf on the otherwise cluttered and exposed cabinetry, incongruent with the atmosphere of *Aki no Sora*. Lit candles surrounded the portrait, and a pair of thin, fingerless combat gloves lay stacked in front, creating a makeshift shrine. The woman filled her glass, faced the patrons, and dramatically lifted the shochu high in the air. The guests all fell silent, drinks held aloft, anticipating instruction.

"Tatsuo!" she called out.

"Tatsuo!" they echoed loudly and drank.

Even the stern-faced Taro took a break from drying the inside of cleaned glasses with a white towel to join in. Notes of sombreness undercut the assembled patron's enthusiasm, but one table of half a dozen men cheered louder than the rest. They were larger with hard faces and ears misshapen to resemble cauliflowers. They wore their suits as though it were a special occasion—competently assembled, but as though their muscular bodies were actively fighting against tailored restraint.

"Rei-*chan*'s father, loved by anyone with a warm heart and the ability to see past mistakes. He was murdered overseas this very day, and all the regulars are here to remember him. Empty your glass in his name so I can refill it."

"For Tatsuo." He awkwardly forced himself to consume the remainder of the shochu, failing to conceal his grimace. His tribute felt insincere, shaming him for his indirect role in the murder of Rei's father.

The lady poured him another drink and topped up her own afterward. "So, Mathis, tell me of your *complications*."

"I honestly wouldn't know where to begin, Miss—"

"Aki." She smiled like a spider might at the sensation of movement on the threads of her web.

She locked his eyes, clinked his glass, and drained her own in a single raise. Mathis recognized Taro and all of the patrons were watching him. He was unnaturally compelled to follow suit. A dribble of shochu spilled out of the corner of his mouth as he forced down the alcohol. Before he could wipe it, Aki caressed his chin with a lace handkerchief. Her gaze penetrated him, her lingering touch disconcertingly sensual. Mathis had to remind himself she was probably the same age as his mother as he anxiously looked aside.

"Aki, I—"

"Aki-*san,*" Taro abruptly corrected.

"Kibishii na!" She playfully scowled at Taro and refilled their drinks. "Unburden yourself, Mathis."

He was paralyzed and unable to fulfill the spoken demand. Grief, shame, and pathos played out across his face.

"I… I don't know how," he finally admitted in a muted agony.

"It's always the way with young men." Her tone conveyed equal measures of whimsy, fondness, and disappointment. "How long before you leave Osaka?"

"I'm not sure. A week or two?"

"Play your cards right, and I might teach you." She clinked his glass. "Now, apologize for monopolizing my time. Do it reluctantly."

"I'm sorry for monopolizing your time, Miss Aki-*san*."

Effortlessly, she drank the distilled alcohol as though it were water. Everyone was staring at Mathis. He resented becoming the centre of attention until he recognized only Aki's spotlight illuminated him. He dutifully consumed his generous measure of shochu. The taste was becoming surprisingly less unpalatable. Aki gracefully stepped out from behind the bar and glided to Mathis' side. She put one hand on his shoulder and faced the regular patrons. They fell into a hush.

"Ano ko wa…" She strung out her judgement, building collective anticipation. *"Daijoubu ya!"*

The crowd of patrons cheered, especially the table of hard-looking men. Mathis' face flushed—whether from embarrassment or alcohol, he wasn't certain. Aki leaned forward until her cheek was beside his, bringing with her a faint and delicate scent of exotic citrus.

"Behave, and you're welcome to return." She winked coyly before gliding off to the excited company of her other admirers.

Taro, stone-faced, picked up the bottle of shochu and started to pour him another round.

Mathis shook his head in protest. "No, please. I've already had too many."

"Eigo hanaserehen," he replied flat and hard, completing the pour and returning the bottle to the alcohol shelves behind him.

Mathis was amazed at how quickly he'd run up what would undoubtedly be a steep bar bill. As he awaited Rei's arrival, he unconsciously fell into the same pattern as everyone else—transfixed by Aki's performative and impossibly inclusive conversation.

Aki was able to gift each person with brief moments of her attention before shifting her focus to another patron with preternatural grace. Occasionally, someone passing Mathis on their way to the restroom would pat him on the back, saying something enthusiastically in Japanese, to which he smiled and thanked them. He knew he didn't belong, but their acceptance resonated. He nursed his drink enough to avoid Taro's judgement, increasingly inebriated. Mathis couldn't remember the last time he'd been drunk. Sometime early in university.

After a time, the patrons started calling for Aki to do something she theatrically tried to eschew until she finally consented amid an eruption of cheers and applause. With dramatic flair, she stepped onto the small stage, took the shamisen and a large, wedge-shaped pick from the wall, and stood motionless with her eyes closed until all the sound evaporated from the crowded environment.

Her pick hand fluttered into motion, stabbing at the strings as the fingers of her other hand danced with relentless precision across the length of the fretless neck of the instrument. Her body was otherwise entirely still—poised, refined, and resembling a portrait painted to idealize a distant past. When Aki started to sing, the melody was unlike anything Mathis had been exposed to. Single syllables danced across octaves and fluctuated irregularly. He had no idea what the song was about, but the wealth of emotions she infused translated into something haunting and forlorn. A tragic love or handwritten suicide note. It tugged at his pathos, pulling him incrementally deeper within himself.

There was movement beside him as the patron occupying the adjacent bar seat left. At the same time, Taro expertly wiped down the countertop, stepped back a pace and bowed.

"*Kokoro kara okuyami moushiagemasu.*"

"*Arigatou, Taro-san.*"

Mathis turned to face Rei, awkwardly fumbling off his seat, and tried to bow. He was most certainly drunk. "I'm truly sorry to hear about your father."

She removed her oversized sunglasses, revealing her blackened eyes. Her modern clothes were black, as was her broad hat and the atmosphere she brought with her. She guided Mathis back to his bar seat.

"No falling, or you must leave." She opened the box housing the pair of translator earpieces and set it on the counter. She adeptly wore one and patiently waited for him to do likewise.

"How many have you had?"

Mathis followed her gesture to the half-filled glass of shochu. "Um, three? Maybe four?"

"Aki-*san*'s pace?"

He nodded. She shook her head. Taro put a glass with two fingers of neat whiskey in front of her. She reached into her purse and set a handheld on the table.

"This is a clean device, preconfigured to maintain anonymity."

Mathis had to close his eyes to focus on the translator's voice layering over Rei's. Challenging in his inebriated state. He initialized the device, paired his Net contacts, and skimmed the configuration. Next, he audited transactions through a raw console.

"This is amazing! It's subordinating insecure Net-enabled devices before having them slave subsequent devices at the edge of their range. And it's recursive! The protocol's leveraging virtually everything into a mutating, distributed network, from toasters to billboards, to buffer data packets into a coherent Net stream."

"I don't understand a single thing you're saying, Mathis."

Mathis' legs were bouncing with excitement. He was basking in the first moment of relief since stepping foot in Japan. "The handheld's making itself everywhere and nowhere. I can't thank you enough, Rei. How much can I transfer to you for this and all the money you gave me earlier?"

"We'll sort it out after meeting Shinoda-*sama*. You don't look like you can protect yourself. And you can't be heard slurring words. He may be able to provide you with security, but you need to let me do the talking."

"Who is he?"

"He's—" She pursed her lips. "He's a man who knew my father well. A dangerous man."

"Like yakuza?"

Taro glowered at Mathis, sucking his teeth.

"This isn't the West. There are things we don't say out loud."

Mathis had no idea what she meant but nodded anyway. "Is there anything I should do when we meet him?"

"Follow my lead, and bow when I do. Otherwise, stay quiet, sit straight, and try not to move."

He started to appreciate the liability he'd be in the encounter. "Why am I here, Rei?"

"Maybe I wanted to know if you'd pass Aki's test." She sipped her whiskey, eyes fixed on Aki's performance. "This *izakaya* is sacred ground. No one would dare risk violence or an escalation. All the clans know and accept this. The repercussions of improper behaviour are severe."

Applause and cheers saturated the environment as Aki finished her song and took a theatrical bow. The crowd of patrons shouted, and Aki demurred, feigning protest. The patrons grew silent again, in rapt attention as Aki produced a slow, sombre melody on her shamisen. Her singing and pitch were different, too. Whereas the last song scored depths of emotion in a contrived manner, Aki's voice took on a profoundly heartfelt tone. A tangible weight blanketed the entire environment, fostering sensations of loss and grief.

"She's amazing."

"This song was practically a lullaby for me as a child."

Mathis tried to imagine the grizzled fighter from the picture with kid versions of Rei and her sister sleeping on the hardwood of the bench seating. There was something at once tragic and beautiful about it. Now, their father was dead because he refused to be recruited. Perhaps he'd be mourning his own parents next. Instinctively, he reached for his glass, but Rei's quick, prohibitive gesture stopped him.

"I can't have you falling over when we meet Shinoda-*sama*."

"And when's that?"

"After this."

Rei closed her eyes, swaying delicately with the emotional swells of Aki's singing. Her face hinted at her concealed anguish through subtle tells. A slight wince, the clenching of her jaw, the near-imperceptible movement of her lips staving off a frown to maintain a neutral expression. In his inebriated state, Mathis had lost track of her suffering and was ashamed to have become an additional burden.

As the song's final notes reverberated in near silence, one patron shouted praise, unlocking a torrent of cheers and applause from the rest of the bar. Aki performatively bowed low, put away her shamisen and pick, and deferred the encouragement for an encore to sweep gracefully towards Rei and Mathis. Though she was smiling brilliantly to the patrons as she passed them, her eyes were full of gravity and concern. Solemn, Rei stood to face her.

"*Tsurai na,*" Aki commiserated with a depth of affection.

Rei's eyes watered. She seemed to be trying to kill the expression on her face, but tears streamed down her cheeks. While it wasn't appropriate to lurk on the conversation, Mathis toggled the translator to intake omnidirectional input so as to capture the unfolding Japanese conversation.

Rei took her time responding. "It cuts deep."

Aki wiped Rei's eyes and cheeks with a mother's affection. "You know my view on tears."

"A woman should never compete with her pain for attention," Rei repeated obediently, visibly trying to steel herself.

"Maybe today we can bend the rules a little," Aki conceded, wrapping her arms around Rei and pulling her into a tight embrace. The long sleeves of her young woman's kimono draped down Rei's back, exposing Rei's quivering. "Tell me, who did that to you?"

"It was a *misunderstanding."*

"Whose misunderstanding?"

Rei stepped out of the embrace, wiped her blackened eyes, and shook her head.

"Rei-*chan*," Aki admonished.

She looked down and away.

"You and I will have words on this another time." Aki gestured towards Mathis. "About this one, as well."

"Another time," Rei echoed. She opened her mouth to speak but caught herself, biting her lower lip. "Miyu passes her best."

"Is she safe?"

Rei shook her head again. "I can't reach her anymore."

Aki sighed heavily. "Shame. She was always a good but troubled girl. Be careful you don't complete a tragedy today. Shinoda-*sama* is waiting for you when you're ready." She gestured to an area partitioned from the main area with screened walls. Aki turned her attention towards Mathis, effortlessly discarding the matronly atmosphere in favour of her outgoing, performative nature. "Tell me you'll be especially good to Rei-*chan* now."

"I'll try my best."

She leaned forward, pressing her hands to his chest and nestled her face beside his. "That's not what I asked."

He focused on not slurring. "I will be especially good to her."

Aki playfully tapped his cheek with an open hand, stepped back, and smiled before allowing herself to be enveloped by the insatiable attention of the waiting patrons.

"You can stop staring at her now," Rei chided.

Mathis reset his attention on her, nodding gravely. Aki was the same age as his mother, he again reminded himself.

"Remember, you must act like you're not there with Shinoda-*sama*." She frowned, evaluating him critically. "Try not to make eye contact, either."

Mathis fell in behind Rei as she slipped through the crowd of patrons. Each step heightened his blind anxiety. The group of hard-looking men paid her special attention, nodding stiffly as she passed them to enter a room partitioned off with paper-screened walls. Inside, a grave man with a shaved head sat cross-legged on a thin cushion at a low table wearing a dark gray suit, crisp white shirt and a plain black tie. Rei bowed, and Mathis clumsily tried to do the same. She removed her ankle boots as she entered, sat directly opposite Shinoda and gestured for Mathis to sit at the far end when he was done fumbling with his shoes.

"Thank you for making time, Shinoda-*sama*."

Mathis was struck by the different texture of Rei's voice. Reserved, crisp, and formal. Whatever vulnerability and humanity she'd exhibited moments earlier had been enveloped by this persona she'd adopted. Shinoda poured Rei a whiskey and topped up his glass in the process. There was no third glass for Mathis, and no second thought was given to one.

"Your father finally pissed off the wrong person."

Rei didn't respond and held Shinoda's gaze unflinchingly.

"His death doesn't cancel the debts to the Mori clan." Shinoda circled his glass in agitation, dangerously close to spilling. "A hundred million yen."

"I don't have it."

Shinoda slammed his palm on the low table, rattling the glasses. "You should've pulled ten times that from Hikari already!"

"I'm realigning the opportunity, Shinoda-*sama*."

"I'm not an idiot like your father to trick with clever phrases. If you can't make it happen within a week, I'll have no use for you."

"I understand."

"You've at least bought us a few days by bringing me this one. Mori-*san* has agreed to delay settling the debt and even surrender the disputed sections of Namba in exchange for him."

"That's not what we agreed upon, Shinoda-*sama*."

"No, but it's what I've decided."

Mathis couldn't rationalize the situation. He wondered if the translator he wore was misinterpreting the conversation. "Rei, what's going on? Am I some sort of bounty?"

Shinoda glowered at Mathis before addressing Rei. "Why is the *gaijin* speaking?"

"He shouldn't have spoken. You have my apologies for his misbehaviour."

Shinoda gulped his whiskey, setting it down on the table harder than appropriate. "Explain what he said."

"It's not worth repeating. I'm curious why the Mori clan would trade for him."

"That's not your concern."

"It is my concern when you change our agreement because of it."

Shinoda leaned forward, appraising her critically, but she remained unflinching under his gaze. The intensity of their locked stare infected Mathis. He started to fidget, unable to look away. Eventually, Shinoda frowned and sighed loudly.

"Word went out to all the clans. Both Minus One and some Westerner named Frost are looking for this one. Given the amount Minus One is willing to pay for his capture, I'm half amazed you've managed to hold onto him." He leaned forward conspiratorially. "Tell me, why is he important?"

"He apparently controls a technology."

"How could we benefit from it?"

"I don't know."

Shinoda glared at Mathis. "Answer."

Mathis couldn't maintain eye contact with Shinoda, so focused on Rei instead. "They want to control the future. If either group got me and the source code, they would within a generation. Unless your boss has some social agenda to implement and a means of production, he'd be selling off the codebase. If he can find it. It's hidden, and I don't have it on me. This is about humanity's collective future, though. If all he cares about is money, I can access—"

Rei discreetly sliced the air with two fingers, cutting Mathis off. "There's only the bounty."

Confused, Mathis opened his mouth to contradict her, but Shinoda beat him to it.

"He said a lot more than that."

"Westerners don't understand the economy of language."

"Fine. Deliver the *gaijin* to Hiroshi. He should be waiting outside now and will complete the handoff to the Mori clan."

Rei picked up her glass and raised it to her mouth but didn't drink. She set it down and traced her fingertip along the edge. "No, I don't think I will."

"I must have misheard you."

"Minus One killed my father, and you're willing to profit from them."

"Tatsuo was a dead man either way."

"Still."

Shinoda narrowed his eyes, mouth forming a scowl. "Have you forgotten the lesson from your last *misunderstanding*?"

"I'm especially sensitive to it, Shinoda-*sama*. Thank you for providing the light to reflect on it correctly."

Rei stood up. Hastily, Mathis fell in beside her, sharing her precarious threshold. He tried to force out his inebriation but became dizzier. His body was sluggish and dull.

Shinoda rose to his feet, grabbing the whiskey bottle by the neck as he did. "Turn your back to me, and it'll be the last thing you do."

Rei turned sharply and started walking to the partitioned room's entryway. Shinoda's eyes narrowed before he leaped towards her, swinging the bottle like a club. Rei didn't show any hints of self-preservation, and in sheer desperation, Mathis threw himself between her and Shinoda's attack. The bottle slammed into the arm he'd curled around his head and bludgeoned him wildly off balance. Mathis crashed through the paper-walled partitions and onto the well-worn floorboards of the main bar area. His arm throbbed painfully, and his face was wet. Instinctively, he probed and found his hand covered in blood. There was a scramble of sound. Chairs shifting, the fast movement of bodies, and then stillness. Shinoda glowered with the whiskey bottle in hand, frozen in place. Rei stood perfectly still, facing away from him, expressionless.

Strong hands grabbed Mathis' shoulders and yanked him to his feet. He found Aki flanked on either side by the half dozen muscular men with cauliflower ears—one of whom had effortlessly lifted him off the ground.

Aki's voice projected. "Shinoda-*sama*, you've violated the covenant of *Aki no Sora*, and your betters will be informed of your transgression."

Shinoda dropped the bottle and fell to his knees. "Aki-*san*, it was a misunderstanding. There's no need to have this go any further."

"Is this true, Rei-*chan*?"

"There was no *misunderstanding* this time."

Panic started to set into Shinoda's expression. "Tell me what I need to do to make this right."

Aki took a step towards Rei, holding her gaze. "Can he address this?"

"He cannot."

Shinoda roughly shoved Rei aside, trying to scramble for a gap to escape. Two muscular men deftly blocked his path, and another pair formed behind them. Shinoda hesitated, sizing up the situation. Finally, he picked up the whiskey from the floor, returned to his seat, and refilled his glass with what was left inside the bottle. Unsatisfied, he grabbed Rei's drink and poured it into his own. The whole time, he was glowering daggers into Rei's back.

"I'm complying," he grumbled.

Mathis was reflexively blinking the blood from his left eye, panic flaring. He frantically wiped the blood from his face, trying to probe the damage, before a strong hand stayed him.

"Scalp wounds bleed a lot, but yours doesn't look bad. Two stitches at most."

One of the large men handed Mathis a cheap, folded handkerchief that had seen more wash cycles than was designed to sustain. Mathis accepted it awkwardly, holding it uncomprehendingly in front of him. The man shook his head and guided Mathis' hand to cover the wound with the cloth.

"Thank you," Mathis stammered, taking a moment to remember the Japanese. *"Arigatou."*

The man clapped him on the back in a friendly manner, but Mathis registered the impact throughout his chest.

Aki guided Rei out of the room and towards the bar by her elbow. "You've created quite the mess, Rei-*chan*."

"It seems I'm becoming more of my father's daughter. I'm sorry for the inconvenience."

The two women walked out of the translator's effective omnidirectional range. The shape of the conversation was there, but it lacked definition. Mathis quickly slipped on his shoes, laces undone, and started to walk after them, but wobbled, awash in dizziness. The man who'd given him the handkerchief guided Mathis past Aki and Rei to his former seat at the bar.

"You'll be okay." The man patted him firmly once more on the square of his back before leaving.

Taro set a warm rolled towel on the bar counter for him. "For your face." He turned away, busying himself at the bar.

Mathis wiped a prodigious amount of blood away. He didn't know what to do with the stained cloth. He neatly rerolled it to how it was provided and set it back on the counter. Despite the attention Aki commanded as she resumed working for the crowd, people were staring at him but would dart their eyes away when he glanced around.

Taro set a cloth filled with crushed ice and a fresh glass of shochu in front of him.

"Drink," he instructed. "Shinoda's paying."

His head was throbbing with pain and booze. Mathis rolled up his sleeve, revealing a large portion of his left forearm swollen and deep red with pools of blood formed under his skin. It throbbed and was tender. He was transfixed with his injuries and didn't notice Rei's arrival until she started speaking.

"I appreciate what you did, Mathis."

"Were you trying to get clobbered?"

"I was prepared to accept it, but thankful I didn't have to."

Taro set a whiskey glass in front of her. They nodded to each other with an implicit nuance born of years of familiarity.

Mathis' head was pounding. Irritated, he glanced back at the big men in suits. "Couldn't you have gone into the meeting with Aki's muscle instead of me?"

"Those men are my father's training partners from his MMA club. They have nothing to do with this world but agreed to perform this one favour in his memory."

"Wait, you planned all this?"

"With Aki's cooperation. She and my father enjoyed a long and unique relationship."

He replayed the sequence of events, participants, and variables in his mind, trying to unravel the setup. He could see the set pieces but didn't comprehend why Rei would've deliberately put herself in jeopardy to close the trap.

"What did all that accomplish?"

She let out her breath, shoulders lowered and face calm. Mathis was struck how the subtle transformation made her almost appear as a different person.

"Everything. I'm free now."

26

Rei

Rei slowly rolled the bottom edge of her whiskey glass on the bar counter, increasingly anxious at the time Taro had been gone sourcing a coffee for Mathis at a neighbouring cafe. Far too long for the task at this hour. Aki was shamelessly sitting on the lap of one of the fighters from Tatsuo's MMA club and baiting the others with stories, effortlessly enticing them to feel remarkable for engaging her.

Squinty-eyed, Mathis wobbled back to the bar after his third washroom visit and sat heavily beside Rei.

"How long do we have to stay here?"

His slurring was growing more pronounced, and he was hunched forward on his elbows.

"You need to sober up. Drink." She gestured to yet another glass of water.

The front door opened, and Taro hustled in, glancing anxiously over his shoulder. He carried a large disposable cup and a fresh welt on his face. He shot Aki a glance, shook his head in response to her shifting expression, and returned to his position behind the bar.

"Expensive coffee." Rei tried to mask how unnerved she was. Someone assaulting a member of *Aki no Sora*'s staff was akin to assaulting Aki herself, regardless of whether it had occurred within the *izakaya*.

"Several clans are parked outside, a pair of dangerous men I didn't recognize, and a bunch of those Minus One assholes."

"I see. Were they the ones?"

"I slipped away when some Mori enforcers got involved." Taro gestured to Mathis. "Is he worth it?"

"Enough people think he is. How did they know he was here?"

"The cafe staff said he'd been seen wandering the neighbourhood. Went for a lengthy stroll with some *obaachan*. With so few Westerners in Osaka these days, word got out."

Rei shook her head at Mathis' idiocy. She had explicitly instructed him to be discreet, and everyone knew how voraciously elderly ladies gossiped...

She snapped her fingers in front of Mathis' closed eyes. "Coffee. Drink it."

"I'll fix him up some *ochazuke*," Taro grumbled.

Mathis fumbled with the lid until Rei took the cup from him and irritatedly opened it. She tried to catch Aki's gaze and waited patiently for her to extricate herself from the group of fighters and join Taro behind the counter. Aki took in the situation and sent Taro away with a barely perceptible gesture.

Rei bit her lower lip, anxious. "I'm hoping you'll allow me to cause a bit of a spectacle."

"Moh! You've caused quite enough trouble already, Rei-*chan*."

Mathis perked up, grinning like a schoolboy. "Hi, Aki-*san*. I'm terribly sorry for breaking your place."

Aki smiled at Mathis, delicately traced her fingers across his cheek, and tugged the translator from his ear, masking the action in a caress Mathis dangerously leaned into. She guided his head onto his folded forearms and stroked his hair absently a few times.

"For this one?"

"It's not right of me to ask," Rei acknowledged.

"Men are supposed to throw themselves into danger for us. That's the natural order of things." She shook her head. "Are you willing to risk further tarnishing my reputation for a foreigner? I admit, he could be seen as handsome to some, but I'm surprised the first man you'd fall for would be a weak one."

"It's not that." Rei couldn't conceive of a world in which she'd be attracted to Mathis, irrespective of her sexuality. It felt more akin to unexpectedly safeguarding an infant discovered wandering in traffic.

Aki poured herself a drink and clinked Rei's whiskey glass.

"Your father was closer than a brother to me. A troublesome, wonderful man… I treasured our time together but knew he was always destined for such an end. And your sister, sweet little Miyu, always more troubled than troublesome. What of her?"

"She promised to take responsibility for Dad. I—" She bit her lip. "I haven't heard from her since."

Aki effortlessly waved off the calls for her attention by the spoiled patrons. "You were always smarter, sharper, more self-possessed than most. Like me, but a few years younger and arguably only a shade less attractive." Her expression turned grave. "Now, you darken my doors with your black eyes and mortal plots on the day of your father's death, willing yourself into a danger that doesn't belong to you." Aki took Rei's gaze hostage. "You don't have to be like him. There's been tragedy enough for one day."

"I value your concerns and thank you for them."

"But?"

"But what good is the freedom you helped me secure if it's temporary?" She gestured to Mathis. "He believes he's trying to protect humanity from some calamity."

Aki scoffed. "He's drunk and had a head injury. Besides, it's the nature of men to exaggerate their importance."

"Before reducing him to this state, you talked to him. Judged him. Did you detect even a hint of guile or savvy?" Rei waited for objection. "How can someone so unremarkable have so many people pursuing him otherwise?"

Aki finished her drink and set it down delicately on the wooden countertop. "So, you're taking up his fight?"

Rei frowned, somber and reflective. Mathis was the trigger that seen her father murdered, and very likely, her sister, too. Rationally, she recognized it wasn't his fault, but he was still the one pursuing a prospectively apocalyptic technology, and only idiots believe they can change the world without the new order being architected on victims.

She shook her head. "I just want to get him out of here."

"Your father was a sucker for lost causes, too."

Rei didn't respond to either the sentiment or fondness in Aki's tone.

"So, what was the spectacle you asked of?"

"Call in a favour from a family friend, Officer Matsumoto, and ask him to pick us up."

"Impossible. I can't have it understood police would dare accost a patron. I may be able to get this one into a car service, though. But not like that. Get him sobered up."

"Taro's bringing *ochazuke,* and I've been funnelling water into him."

Aki stoked Mathis' head on one side, careful to avoid the matted blood. Instinctively, he smiled and angled towards her touch. With a surgeon's precision and a prestidigitator's grace, she slipped back the translator with her other hand. Aki rubbed his shoulders and tapped him lightly on the cheek.

"It's not proper for a grown man to lay his head on the counter."

Mathis pried his eyes open and struggled up to a slumped posture. "So sorry, Aki-*san*."

"I know you would never intentionally disappoint me. You must be suffering from your earlier heroics."

"To be honest—" He shook his head, his face painted in shame. "I'm actually kinda—"

"Shhh. Can you do something for me, handsome?"

He managed to sit straight. "Anything!"

"I want you to do everything Rei-*chan* tells you to the best of your abilities."

Mathis nodded heavily as he tried to adopt a serious expression. "Understood, Aki-*san*."

Rei couldn't pick out Aki's whisper to Mathis, but his cheeks grew flushed as she spoke. When he started to say something, Aki put her finger across his lips.

"Ssh, not another word."

Rei shook her head, marvelling. "You're incorrigible."

"Those strapping young fighters will escort you to the car service in twenty minutes. They just don't know it yet."

As Aki threaded the packed tables of guests clamouring for her attention, making a fun-spirited game of who would win the privilege of her company, Taro set down a bowl of *ochazuke, a* set of chopsticks, and a large wooden spoon in front of Mathis.

"We leave in fifteen minutes. Eat," Rei instructed in English.

Rei had to block out the mess of Mathis mechanically consuming. She wasn't sure whether it was his ignorance of table manners or his inebriation, but she found herself disgusted and disappointed. Shamed, too, given how Taro appraised her critically before turning his back to attend to prep work. She idly weighed the option of looking the other way and letting Mathis stagger out the door to face whatever consequences awaited him.

"This is really good," Mathis enthused. "I like this place, and Aki-*san* is incredible."

She couldn't bring herself to respond, and looked away in annoyance.

Mathis was drinking the last of the broth from the bowl when Aki led the group of fighters to the bar. He set down the bowl, wiped his mouth, and sat up as straight as he could, eager for her approval.

Aki smiled sweetly. "Your ride awaits you, my prince. And these mighty gentlemen have generously volunteered to escort you safely to your carriage."

Mathis got to his feet, bowed dangerously low, swaying as he did. "You're magical, Aki-*san*."

Aki smiled, lightly danced a finger along his cheek, and transfixed him with her gaze. "Rei-*chan*, make sure this one rides safely off into the sunset."

Rei stood up and bowed to Aki and Taro. "About tonight—"

Aki silenced her with a pointed finger. "You owe me a long conversation."

Rei nodded and led the group outside. Several clusters of men were lurking in the shadows or staring out the tinted windows of idling sedans. A gathering of Minus One associates loitered on both sides of the next intersection. More than a dozen in plain view. She put on her razor gloves and engaged her mask as Hiroshi Kono, her father's old partner, stepped out of the shadows and approached Rei's group.

"What did you do to Shinoda-*sama*?"

As he approached them, the first men were getting out of cars. At least three clans' worth. Rei instantly recognized Akira Mori and the pair of older enforcers who had played witness to her beating. A quick Net scan for facial recognition showed two other groups belonging to the Sugimoto and Takeuchi clans. Someone whistled, and the gang of Minus One started closing the distance. Many were holding lengths of pipe or bats. Some had long knives. Men she didn't recognize were approaching from the right, too. They wore black tactical gear and moved like soldiers. All avenues of escape were blocked. The economical hatchback from the automated car service was idling tantalizingly close—a few meters beyond the closing perimeter of hostiles.

One of the six fighters from the bar stepped between Rei and Hiroshi, "Back off, asshole."

Hiroshi pulled a long blade from his coat. The fighters started to fan out, a few releasing sounds of exasperation. Body rigid in fear, Rei fought against her overwhelming flight impulse.

"Put it away, Kono. We're here to take possession of the *gaijin*." Akira gestured for the Mori enforcers to join him.

The sound of pipes scraping on the asphalt signalled the arrival of Minus One, half of which had squared off against the soldiers of the other two clans. The fighters nervously glanced at each other, shifting their weight.

"Fuck this, I'm out!" One of the fighters from the *izakaya* put up his hands, backed up to the storefronts, and began shifting sideways to exit the area.

"I didn't sign up for this either."

Two more fighters followed their companion's lead. The three remaining, increasingly nervous fighters spread out to stand in front of Rei and Mathis.

One shot Rei an anxious glance. "What the hell is going on?"

Rei couldn't respond. She hadn't mentally prepared for any of this. With teeth clenched, she glanced at Mathis—the imminent danger seemed to have sobered him into alertness. All around, shops and apartments were closing their shutters or blinds. Minus One followers tried to intimidate the soldier-like men with rough language.

Hiroshi pointed with his blade at Rei. "Answer me, Yoshida!"

All her options were escalations. She wrenched her focus from the weapon to Hiroshi's equally dangerous gaze. "We're clanless now, Kono-*san*."

Akira Mori cackled. "Step aside, *katagi*," he taunted.

Hiroshi reacted as though he'd been slapped by being called a *normal person* in yakuza slang. His eyes narrowed venomously on Rei. A deafening gunshot reverberated in the narrow alley, bouncing off the walls of the tall buildings. One of the Minus One crew lay on the ground, unmoving. Another shot from the soldiers rang out, and the cluster of men swarmed into a desperate melee. Rei caught sight of Hiroshi lunging towards her, his blade poised to pierce her chest. The professional fighter beside her cut a quick angle and caught Hiroshi flush on the chin with a short straight, sending him to the ground. One of the other fighters kicked away Hiroshi's knife before he got back to his feet.

Bloody fights erupted all around. The air was filled with screams, the sound of impacts, and occasional gunshots. Bodies were littering the street, unmoving or writhing in agony. Rei was roughly jostled as Hiroshi tackled the fighter on her left and was thrown to the ground as one of the Mori clan enforcers roughly shoved her aside to get to Mathis. Another fighter locked him up in a clinch, dragging him to the side.

"Run, you idiot!" Rei shouted to Mathis in English.

Instead of doing what he'd been told, Mathis offered Rei his hand to help her up. He was rewarded with a hard kick in the chest by the other Mori enforcer, who was immediately assaulted by the last professional fighter without an opponent.

Police sirens wailed in the far distance.

Akira nimbly wove between the clusters of combat towards Mathis with a long tanto blade held like an ice pick, delighting in the chaos. His eyes burned bright, exuding vitality. Behind him, a few Minus One members holding pipes or knives were closing in, bloodied but functional. Rei scrambled to her feet, engaging the razors on her gloves. Mathis was struggling to get up, whether from drink or the powerful kick, she couldn't tell.

"Stay down, *gaijin*," Akira taunted before focusing on Rei. "This won't be like last time."

Terror ran through her. Akira closed the distance as she backpedalled and mentally prepared for death. The three Minus One recruits rushed for Mathis. Two picked him off the ground, and the third punched him hard in the chest.

Frustrated, Akira spun around and sank the long tanto blade deep through the shoulder and into the lungs of one of the men holding Mathis. "The *gaijin* is mine!"

He yanked out the blade, spraying blood in an arc and narrowly sidestepped a swing from one of the Minus One assailants. Mathis dropped to his hands and knees, retching violently. The density of the police sirens was increasing. It sounded as though they were coming from all directions.

Akira warded off the two Minus One attackers angling to blindside him with his tanto—an addict on the verge of a long-delayed fix. In desperation, Rei rushed him from behind, digging her razored fingers into his face, frantically clawing for his eyes. As he whipped around, face covered in a legion of shallow lacerations and blood, a Minus One convert cracked him across the back of his head with a length of pipe.

Akira fell forward and lay on the ground, twitching in sporadic convulsions. Gunfire. A bullet whizzed past her.

Beyond the immediate melee, a half dozen combatants were fighting each other, seemingly at random. Now, a cluster of Minus One were harassing a pair of bloodied-up yakuza, and other yakuza were wrestling a handgun from one soldier while the other lay still on the ground. Hiroshi was on his back, desperately trying to block strikes from a professional fighter, and the other two fighters from the bar were locked in savage grappling and clinch strikes with the more durable Mori enforcers. The two nearby Minus One members split up. One yanked Mathis up to his feet and the other turned towards Rei. An angry teenager, in over his head. His white clothes were spackled red, his acne-covered face too young to have consistently known a razor.

The teenager held the length of pipe high above his head and stepped toward Rei, forcing her to back up again. Mathis was struggling against his kidnapper, but another Minus One recruit had come, and between the two, they were alternating between beating and subduing Mathis.

The one grappling Mathis called out to the teenager, "Finish her off and give us a hand!"

Rei held up her bloody hands in front of her face, cowering. There was movement behind the teenager and the crisp sound of wood striking bone. The kid fell forward, unconscious or dead, revealing a baton-wielding yakuza with blood on the left side of his face. He was the Mori enforcer who'd helped her to her feet after being thrown from Akira's car.

The old enforcer appraised Akira's mutilated face and Rei's bloody gloves.

"Hmmn," he grunted before stowing his baton, throwing Akira's unconscious body over his shoulder, and walking back towards the clan's S-class sedan.

The sound of police sirens was loud and close. The fighting all around peaked in a frenzy. Combatants tripped over bodies or slipped on blood. There was no pretence of technique or organization in the melee. Flailing assaults, grappling or gouging, and excessive strikes. Mathis was curled up on the ground as different yakuza clans fought the Minus One members around him. He was getting trampled.

The door to *Aki no Sora* swung open, and Aki, dressed in her young woman's kimono, stepped out, immediately followed by Taro, holding a chef's knife. A stream of dozens of *izakaya* patrons emerged—a motley crew of salarymen and retail workers whose anxious expressions betrayed this moment was as close to conflict as they'd ever been in all their lives.

"Enough!" Aki's commanding voice pierced the night air.

Taro stayed by Aki's side, but the rest of the group rushed to Rei and Mathis, forcing the remaining upright yakuza and Minus One associates to stagger back. The sheer numeric discrepancy made the situation absurd to Rei, and her sudden relief was only partially accessible. As the patrons hustled her and Mathis to the car service's hatchback, the three fighters were either helped or carried back into *Aki no Sora*.

The Minus One and yakuza capable of walking tried to help their surviving members escape, leaving the alleyway littered with the dead, grievously injured, and unconscious. The *izakaya* patrons stuffed Mathis into the driverless hatchback unceremoniously, pushed Rei inside, and blocked access to the doors once they closed.

"Destination, please?" the automated assistant requested.

"Umeda Sky Building." Rei's instruction got the car service moving. The reflection of police lights illuminated the windows of the alley's tall buildings. "And tint the windows."

As the hatchback pulled away from the protective circle of patrons, Aki and Taro urgently directed people back inside the *izakaya*. The first police car passed them, then a second. When the hatchback turned at the traffic lights, the scene behind them was already being closed off by responding officers, the night air full of the sound of sirens.

Mathis had been spared catastrophic injury, but was superficially beaten. His lip was puffy and split, and his face was marked up and swollen from dozens of lesser strikes. His clothes were covered in street dirt, and he wore traces of blood from when he'd stepped between her and Shinoda. She'd seen his body get hit hard in the melee and suspected non-visible trauma.

"Are you okay?"

He shook his head vigorously, eyes wide. "Not at all okay, no. That was terrifying."

"But are you hurt?"

He leaned forward and whispered emphatically, "Everything hurts!"

The smell of alcohol on his breath was overwhelming in the hatchback's enclosed cabin.

Rei cracked open the windows for some fresh air. "Send me the location of the Net cafe."

"Shouldn't we go to the police? We almost died back there." His eyes widened in drunken realization. "A bunch of people probably died back there."

Rei had to change the topic. Car services recorded everything. "There are already enough police at the scene. The cafe location, please."

Mathis pulled out his pirate handheld and sent the address to Rei's UkiyoAR mask with a gesture.

"Change in destination." She offered a location a few blocks away from the cafe.

"Route updated," came the automated response.

"I'd feel better if we went to the police."

"No, and stop talking."

Mathis slumped back in the seat, drunk or petulant, as Rei considered the implications of the battle. She'd orchestrated a clean exit from the world of the yakuza and threw it all away for him. She tried to recall how many times she'd raked Akira across the face and figured it must have been at least four or five. With eight fingers slashing in irregular patterns with all her desperate strength, she'd effectively mutilated the son of one of the most influential crime bosses in Osaka and almost certainly blinded him.

Adding to her troubles, Hiroshi Kono's rage at Rei for destroying their clan and, by extension, his place in this world. Her debt to Aki was another thing too daunting to consider fully. Being a surrogate daughter wouldn't cover the catastrophic damage to Aki's reputation and the reparations the proprietress would be saddled with. And for what? Rei found herself sneering at Mathis under her mask.

Her father couldn't help but find trouble, and now she had unwittingly taken up the unsustainable mantle.

"Arriving at destination," the car service announced.

Rei paid the fare from a crypto account and unceremoniously exited into the back alley dense with narrow storefronts and foot traffic weaving around the hatchback. Mathis struggled out a moment later, bewildered by their surroundings, irrationally trying to avoid the augmented reality advertisements.

"None of this is familiar."

"Mute your AR settings." She walked off towards the Net cafe, conscious of all the attention they were receiving from passersby.

"Oh, that's better." Mathis caught up with her, trying to walk abreast, but the lane was too narrow with traffic and oncoming pedestrians. He fell close in step behind her. "What now?"

Rei clenched her teeth in frustration. The ignorant foreigner was fully putting his precarious safety into her wildly unprepared hands. She wanted to scream but choked back her resentment.

"I get you to your Net cafe, and we're done."

"Done?" He appeared bewildered at the concept of being cut off, like the people who assumed a steady stream of unconditional favours from others.

"Yes, done. You'll settle your account with me and, by extension, Aki-*san*."

He drifted a bit behind her, slowing his pace. She assumed he was grappling with the enormity of being alone and unprepared in a hostile world for the first time. Eventually, he came to a complete halt. Frustrated, she spun around to face him and was surprised to find him smiling at her with unblemished gratitude.

Mathis bowed low to her, wobbled and braced against a storefront wall. "I owe you my life, Rei. I can't thank you enough."

"Stop making a scene." She steeled herself against his disarming sincerity.

"If I ever have a daughter, she'll have your name," he vowed ardently.

"You're drunk and talking nonsense now."

Rei hastened her walking speed, and he tried to keep up. She peeled off her razor gloves and discreetly deposited them in a recycling container attached to a stall of the ubiquitous vending machines littering alley intersections. Whatever anonymity her mask offered was countered by the beaten-up, drunk Westerner loping behind her. Rei resented the attention and was thankful when they made it to the concrete staircase of the Net cafe. Eager to be out of sight, she rapidly ascended the stairs, waiting in the relative darkness of the first platform for Mathis to catch up. He was struggling badly, gripping the handrail with one hand while the other clenched his ribs.

"Three more flights, Mathis."

Hunched over and gripping the rail with white knuckles, he smiled at her, thankful. She tried to empathize with his situation momentarily, but it was too pathetic and desperate to entertain. If the world truly needed saving, fate had selected the single most unprepared person to be its saviour. She turned away, raced up the stairs, and waited for him at the next landing, repeating the process until they finally arrived at the unassuming steel door of the Net cafe. She retracted her mask before they entered.

Rei hadn't been in such an environment since she was a kid and her family had again been run out of their apartment in the middle of the night. She experienced a fond nostalgia for the endless rows of manga novels, a steady diet of instant noodles, and the claustrophobic rooms with no ceilings, which had always given the illusion of safety and connection. They were oddly happy memories that stabbed poignant reminders of her father's death and her sister's unlikely survival.

From the table in the common area, a young man looked up from his handheld, immediately transfixed at Rei's blackened eyes, broken nose, facial bruising, and torn clothing.

Mathis wobbled uncomfortably forward from behind Rei. "Hey, Yuki!"

Yuki made a face. "First day in Japan? You don't waste any time making the worst of it, huh?"

A middle-aged man dressed in a shirt and tie who'd been wiping up a section of the floor with a dishcloth stood up and scowled at Yuki. "There's no medicine for idiots." He slightly bowed to Rei. "They call me Tanaka."

"Pleased to meet you, Tanaka-*san*. I'm Rei."

Tanaka gestured to Mathis. "I was going to suggest the *gaijin* brings trouble, but it looks like it already found you."

She smiled at the middle-aged man's blunt phrasing. "I appreciate your concern. I should mention the *gaijin* has a language parser active now."

Mathis nodded guiltily.

"Maybe he could explain why the men came here, searching for him. Two different groups already. They made a terrible mess of the place *someone* isn't bothering to help clean up correctly."

"Hey, I had the manga and the noodles. You had the broken dishes," Yuki protested.

"The volumes aren't ordered right, and you mixed up the manufacturers." Tanaka gestured angrily at the instant noodles.

"We'll just have to redo it when the next batch comes and busts everything up again. You have to ignore Tanaka-*san*, Rei. He's—"

"Show some respect," Tanaka angrily insisted.

"It's not like she said her family name!"

"Yoshida," Mathis slurred helpfully.

Rei closed her eyes and clenched her teeth.

"No way! Do you know who she is, Tanaka-*san*?"

"No, and I don't want to know, either. And neither should you."

"Her father took down—"

"I'm not my father," Rei interjected firmly, maintaining polite grammar. "I'd be interested to hear of the men, though. When were they last here?"

Tanaka sucked his teeth. "As recently as a half hour ago. They're probably hitting up every love hotel, Net cafe, and capsule for that one."

"Mathis. My name's Mathis. Rei, can you apologize to them for me? I didn't mean to cause any trouble. But it's also important to know if they gave me up. I mean, I'd understand if they did since they don't know me. But it's super important to know if anyone went through my stuff. And most importantly, whether they took anything."

Even with the translator and her limited native English ability, Rei had difficulty discerning his drunken words from his slurring. "He's sorry for the inconvenience and wonders whether his belongings were searched."

"There's something valuable in his suitcase," Yuki added for Tanaka, ignoring Rei's glare.

Tanaka went to the cutlery drawer, lifted the tray, and grabbed something from underneath it. "Next time he has anything worth hiding, he shouldn't leave his suitcase tags in place." He tossed the identification with Mathis' neatly written name and address visible onto the common table. "Knowing others is a burden."

"So, my stuff's okay?"

Tanaka folded his arms across his chest, scowling. "People shouldn't steal from those who've already lost everything."

Yuki grinned. "We got your back, room eight."

27

Amrita

Mia stood dangerously close to Amrita, drunk, unfocused, and with pistol in hand, looming like an executioner.

"Why the fuck do you keep staring at her? Get back to work."

Amrita couldn't keep her eyes off Miyu's corpse—mouth agape, emaciated, with the ruins of her eyes blankly focused on her. She wondered if Miyu's gear was still recording. No doctor had come for Benoit, and Hunter hadn't returned since the gunfire started. The noise was relentless. The screams, shouts, and shots of automatic weapons from all around in exchanges lasting long minutes at a time. It was an escalated siege. There was only death and the threat thereof inside the overseers' office.

"I'm going as fast as I can!" She piped views of her interface directly to Benoit and Mia's UkiyoARs for oversight.

Mia whispered constantly into Benoit's ear as he was slowly bleeding out from his untended wound. Her eyes remained fixed on Amrita, as did the barrel of the Glock 20 she'd retrieved from Benoit's desk drawer earlier. The hammer was back, the slide was retracted, and a 10mm bullet was in the chamber.

Amrita's clothes reeked from the stale odour of fear-based sweat, but she was too exhausted to internalize it. Sleep deprivation, the staccato of gunfire, and the constant threat of execution had dulled her fight-or-flight instincts into a banal acceptance. It was all she could do not to steal looks at Miyu's horrific form and focus on the task at hand. Amrita executed another winnowing select in her algorithm's complex suite of SQL queries to extract the most toxic poison from the tens of millions of data records of Canadians and any who'd passed through the country's borders.

"You scrubbed most of the results," accused Mia.

"I'm excluding anyone with a median net worth less than the top five percent, with the exception of governmental caseworkers and supervisors who've authorized overrides for those within range. I know you're against the wealthy, but the data I'm curating is being vetted for corruption and abuse."

"Mia, enough." Benoit coughed weakly. "She's good. Better than anyone here besides me. And we have so little time."

The cacophony of gunfire and human noise below hit a crescendo to underscore the point.

"Everyone is corrupt, my love. Society is a cancer. Everyone needs to pay."

Amrita considered the prospective damage to her family if their modest skeletons were laid bare for prosecution. "It'd facilitate a purge. Immigrants, radicals, the inconvenient. The courts would be tied up for years executing easy convictions, but the wealthy wouldn't suffer. They'd scoop up assets, stonewall with lawyers, and draw out the process until they bought whoever they needed to escape punishment."

A slow smile spread across Benoit's lips. "Our last convert, Mia."

"Fuck her. She'd betray us if she didn't have a gun to her head."

"Oh, but she already has," Benoit countered lovingly.

With a gesture, he sent a Netstream to Mia and Amrita's displays, auto-playing the conversation with Mason Brand on the rooftop—courtesy of the social account of Maryam Carter, Bargain Traders LLC.

Maryam had explicitly tagged Amrita by her full name and account profile.

What little was left of her operational reality fell apart. Amrita opened her mouth to protest, but vomit came out instead of words. She retched to her immediate side, partially soiling herself. A moment later, her head was wrenched back hard enough for Amrita to fall backwards along with her seat and crash to the unfinished concrete floor. Mia, eyes filled with vengeance, jammed the pistol into her mouth, chipping Amrita's front teeth in the process.

Benoit weakly gestured with his hand, palm out. "No, Mia."

"But she's killed us!"

"We're already dead. Seventeen recognized it and elected to go out on her terms, as much as it inconvenienced me." Benoit coughed. "Shh, Mia. It's already done, and there's much to accomplish. We need her."

Mia roughly covered Amrita's nose and jammed the barrel deeper, choking off her air. Amrita started involuntarily convulsing. Mia ripped the barrel out of Amrita's mouth, chipping more teeth in the process, and spat in her face. The saliva was acrid, reeking of alcohol and cigarettes. Amrita scrambled to wipe her face and scooted to put distance between them. Mia towered over her, trembling in anger.

"Let me explain! I didn't—"

Amrita howled in pain as Mia kicked her wounded leg.

"Back to work, traitor."

Amrita got to her feet, righted the chair and sat. Her fingers shook too severely to operate the interface, and her vision was too blurry with tears to see the screen. It was a consummate act of will merely to maintain her posture and what was left of her composure, her breathing shallow and laboured. Her tongue found the chipped enamel segments and worked them out of her mouth mechanically. The ends of her front teeth were ragged and sharp.

Benoit gestured for Mia to come closer. "You don't seem to appreciate this is Ms. Chopra's baptism."

"Don't get all churchy. You know I hate it when you do that."

"Saul was a Pharisee leader charged with hunting the Christians to enforce Jewish traditions. Once he accepted the truth, he became the most important figure of Christianity after Jesus. Look past your disgust and see her for what she is."

"A fucking Judas who's sold us out for a bag of silver?" Mia shifted self-consciously under Benoit's admiring gaze. "What? I went to a Catholic school as a kid. Why do you think I'm so fucked up?"

Benoit lovingly stroked Mia's cheek, leaving a streak of his blood on her fair skin. "She's the apostle upon whom the church of our ambitions will be built. Aren't you, Ms. Chopra?"

Amrita wasn't raised Christian and didn't understand the context. She was many things that no longer resonated—an indentured prisoner, a national shame, a semi-dutiful daughter, a powerless victim, a competent worker, a desperately lonely person struggling with a life of no measurable purpose. The scant definition of each was dwarfed by her sense of insignificance.

"I'm nothing." Amrita was freed as the two words escaped her lips.

"Poetry," Benoit said appreciatively, lowering the barrel of Mia's firearm.

"Pathos," Mia countered.

"Regardless, her unravelling is fascinating. Besides, I'm dying and want to spark the ember to consume the world before I go. Carry on, Ms. Chopra."

Amrita forced herself to restart working the petabytes of data, winnowing to abstract values she'd never conceived existed. Case notes advocating for prosecution but overridden by a cabal of supervisors and directors. She did a quick lookup on Mason Brand's unique user identifier, expecting it to yield a damning litany of exceptions and overrides, but found it surprisingly clean of corruption. She scoured his banking records, finding nothing deviating from the expected parameters.

She looked up Aiden Frost's records, finding a long history of aliases and protective overrides to usurp security processes, but they were from Mason's superiors or predecessors. The data proved there was good in the system, but corrupt stakeholders undercut the proper execution of the law. The travesty was illuminating. No words could radicalize her the way the data could.

Hunter burst into the room, cradling an assault rifle in his sling-arm, startling Amrita. His eyes lingered a moment on Miyu's corpse, then to the vomit on the floor.

Mia closed in on Hunter. "Where's the fucking doctor?"

He shook his head. "We're holding, but an armoured vehicle just arrived. From the shape, it's got to be a drone carrier."

"Tabarnak! I need more time," he spat.

"There's no stopping a swarm. We run or die."

Benoit laughed weakly.

"We need another option. You always figure shit out, Hunter," pleaded Mia.

"There's nothing to figure. If you're going, it's got to be now."

Benoit waved him off. "Then I thank you for your service."

Mia shook her head. "I'm not leaving him."

Hunter gestured to Amrita. "New girl?"

"She stays."

Hunter opened a pouch on his tactical jacket and pulled out a translucent sheet. With a practiced movement, he snapped it open and wore it like a poncho. "It's been memorable."

When no one responded to the sentiment, Hunter pivoted on his heel and exited the room without further ceremony, surprisingly quiet for a man his size. His slight footfalls were easily lost amongst the sound of gunfire and the cacophony of desperate voices below.

"Broadcast what you have," Benoit instructed.

"Not yet. People won't know how to parse it." Amrita was structuring a truncated database of the worst offenders. "I'm close. Another ten minutes."

Benoit shook his head.

Amrita couldn't let it go. "Five?"

"If Hunter left, things are about to go bad fast."

Amrita frantically invested detail and clarity into the data schema, focusing on personal information, wealth, and patterns of abuse or corruption—imperative dissociating fear. A unique user identifier would offer the thread to pull the sweater of an individual's life apart. She started secondary linkages of assets, tax records, and known associates.

"Elegant work, Ms. Chopra. You have an eye for the essential."

She stifled a smile at Benoit's unexpected acknowledgment, unsure why it mattered, and hurriedly wrote the recursive scripts to populate the data schema. She sought his approval before initialization.

Screeches of panic and distinctive, loud pops sounded as the data populated. Mia ran to the glass window, looking down on the common area.

"Drones!" she breathlessly whispered, backpedalling from the glass in shaky steps. "There are so many..." Mia turned to face Benoit, eyes desperate. "They're killing everyone. Even the runners."

A smile spread across Benoit's ashen face. "This is how much they fear us."

Mia ran to Benoit's side, pistol in hand. "I want to go out on our terms. Fuck their victory."

Benoit ran his fingers delicately along her cheek. "We've already won."

Mia pressed her back against Benoit's chest. His arms weakly embraced her. She set the Glock 20's barrel directly over her heart.

"Let's go together," she begged.

"Soon, I promise."

The script was executing. Data tables were actively populating with corruption and privilege. "Less than two minutes," Amrita reported.

"I can't... I can't be brave so long." Mia's hand trembled. Tears ran down her cheeks, streaking her thickly applied mascara. "Please, Benoit. While I still can."

The large glass window panel of the office exploded into fragments, and the spent, smouldering husk of a tiny, quad-copter suicide drone lay inert amongst the fragments. A dozen more drones flew through the opening in a tight V pattern. Mia levelled her pistol towards them and squeezed off as many shots as she could before one of them slammed into her temple, detonating a small, shaped charge.

Pop.

Benoit's grip on Mia stiffened reflexively. A fraction of a second later, another drone crashed into the side of his head.

Pop.

Benoit and Mia fell together to the cold, unfinished concrete floor. Even in death, Benoit's arm remained slung around Mia's corpse.

Amrita was frozen in terror as the drones hovered before her. With a monumental effort, she raised her hands.

"Amrita Chopra! I work for CSIS. Please, my name is Amrita Chopra!"

The drones continued to hover.

"Director Brand knows everything! I'm the reason you're here!"

There was a smattering of gunfire and a few pops in the background. She'd already been identity-matched, and suspected people were debating the consequence of keeping her alive.

"Please! My name is Amrita Chopra. I work for CSIS..." Her voice trailed off in an exhaustion of hope.

After an unnerving length of anxious moments, the lead drone angled and led the remaining ones out of the shattered window of the overseer's office in a tight formation. The metaphoric cord holding Amrita upright had been cut, and she collapsed on the desk.

Her display showed the data transformation process was complete.

All around her was death—Miyu, Benoit, Mia, and the countless adherents of Minus One below who'd been purged by the drone swarm or hails of bullets. Police and special service teams who'd been assaulting the building, too. Too many had died in these short Days of Anger. Tens of thousands as part of the global protest, and countless millions more would become victims from the systematic violence inflicted on the poor. All the while, the people on her curated list would remain protected in privilege.

The gross perversion demanded justice.

Amrita glanced at the death embrace of Benoit and Mia, oddly envious. She'd never lived any portion of her thirty-one years the way either had lived their every day. They had been monstrous to her, but somehow, Amrita couldn't poison her envy. They had lived with courage and conviction, aiming to shape the world. While they fell short, Amrita swore not to.

Amid occasional murderous pops and the odd rounds of gunfire, Amrita wrote a routine neatly exporting each linked data record into a comprehensive incrimination report, ensuring Aiden Frost was first in the index. She serialized their distribution across a dozen well-trafficked data havens on the DarkNet.

She sent a list of registered media contacts access to the read-only data havens, and offered context as to what they would find. Since Amrita had logged into the Minus One system via Mia Locke's credentials, the messages were from her dead captor's profile, but she'd signed them off as Benoit Rochon. Someone may eventually note both were dead at the time of delivery, but Amrita wasn't dissuaded. This moment represented a brief flicker of time in which change was possible.

Organized calls of command and response came from below. The tactical teams were starting to sweep the site, and she had a few minutes before they would find her.

Inside the governmental data dump was the modified Carnivore framework. She sorted the raw data for active governmental positions, inside and outside Canada, and wrote a script to compartmentalize the Carnivore executable into fixed instances seeded with each politician's data. Amrita targeted execute-only DarkNet data havens for the boxed instances. Her script would take time to process, but the Minus One headquarters would remain an active crime scene for a while. A hidden process running on a single terminal would take time to investigate. She loaded the media contacts into an anonymous message service and scheduled the disclosure delivery in six months.

Politicians had much to answer for, and their Carnivore instances wouldn't lie, evade, or protect themselves.

Heavy footfalls approached from the stairwell. Amrita took off her Net gear and raised her hands above her head in preparation. Two tactical officers pointed automatic weapons through the shattered window while another opened the door and closed the distance to her with his weapon trained on her chest. Her Minus One uniform was covered in dirt, blood, and vomit. He glanced at the carnage of bodies in the room and back to her.

"My name is Amrita Chopra, and I work for CSIS. I'm the reason you're here," she said with a resolve and conviction she'd never heard in herself before.

28

Mathis

THE FIRST THING THAT struck Mathis as he woke was how everything hurt. He tried to open his eyes to the dimly lit interior, unsure whether his squinting was making his surroundings completely foreign or if he actually was in a place he had no recollection of going. He was in a full-sized bed, silently agonizing under a pleasingly floral scented, thick white duvet.

"*Ohayou gozaimasu, Matisu-san! Kouhii aru yo*!" The crisply delivered syllables of Ichika's chipper voice acted like ice picks to Mathis' consciousness.

"*I-chan, shizuka ni shabare,*" came Rei's familiar voice in a mercifully hushed tone. "There's coffee, Mathis."

He struggled into a sitting position, gasping from pain. Rei and Ichika were facing each other on the small studio apartment floor, sitting intimately close with coffee cups to the side. The desk beside them had an empty whiskey bottle complimenting a half-full one and a pair of glasses. Rei wore different clothes, an elegant, dark grey pantsuit with a crisp white shirt with the top few buttons open, and her hair was damp. Ichika wore an oversized cardigan over a striped sweater and colourful leggings.

There was no art on the walls, no personal items on the thin nightstands flanking the headboard, and an overall deficit of colour. The room was a monochrome composite of whites, grays, and black, intermittently punctured by glass and steel. A modest section of shelves with neatly displayed wigs and organized accessories betrayed the environment as Rei's living quarters. Otherwise, he could've imagined it as an upscale hotel suite.

"What time is it?" His mouth was thick, as though talking through dirty cotton. He made a face, swallowed reflexively, and immediately regretted it. His mouth tasted like something had died in there. He recognized the telltale signs of hangover, but it'd been more than a decade since he'd endured the discomfort.

"Near seven. Soon, you must fight!" Ichika held up a fist, thumb tucked beneath fingers.

Both women looked exhausted, like they'd been up all night. As Mathis angled, the duvet fell off his naked upper body. His torso and arms were covered in bruises. He concealed himself and glanced underneath to confirm he was at least wearing underwear. He had no recollection of anything past the chaotic top lines of the previous evening. Getting struck by Shinoda, a lasting imprint of irrational fondness for Aki, a terrifyingly chaotic fight and flight, and bits and pieces from the Net cafe. Everything after was sketchy or absent. Trying to remember was like holding onto a dream hours after waking.

"How did we get here?"

Rei shook her head. "Shower now. You smell of drink and fear. After, we'll talk."

A fresh change of Mathis' clothes was folded neatly on the desk chair beyond Rei and Ichika.

"Uhm..."

"Mazu ha migaitara." Ichika smiled sweetly, gesturing in the universal toothbrushing action.

Rei said something to Ichika, and they both giggled. Mathis had previously encountered Rei in her formal, tightly-held persona, but the two women's interactions were genuine, in sync, and affectionate. He recognized he knew next to nothing about her.

He awkwardly stepped out of the bed, failing to cover himself up, and glanced around in a panic. Both women pointed to where he should go. He mumbled his thanks and hustled towards the bathroom, closing the door behind him. It shut firmly but didn't mute the shared mirth from the main room. It took Mathis a moment to clue into his reflection in the mirror. His face was severely swollen, bruised, and covered in shallow scuffs and lacerations. Dark brown dried blood was crusted on his scalp and across portions of his face and neck. His upper body looked like a soccer team had done kicking drills on it. He'd gone his whole life without getting beaten up, but he'd made up for it with interest over the past few days.

The shower was uncomfortably hot, and a surprising amount of dirt, grime, and dried blood came off his body as he gingerly washed. He started piecing together fragments of memories. Tanaka refusing any more drama at the Net cafe, a flicker of struggling to fit his suitcase into a locker at some train station, and enthusiastically bopping along to J-pop in Ichika's little car. Mathis had no recollection of whether he'd taken the microdrive and panicked that it was either lost or forgotten in a train station storage locker he couldn't conceive of finding again.

His sensitive skin was acclimatizing to the scalding shower heat, and his aching body released some of its tension. His life had unravelled to the point of being homeless, savaged, and unwittingly adopted by Japanese lesbians. His parents were incarcerated, his colleagues were being actively punished, and his life's work was on the verge of perversion. In a little more than an hour, he'd be forced to capitulate, and shortly after, Aiden Frost would make him suffer for his ineffectual show of resistance. It was a uniquely consuming brand of pathos, leaving no room for anything else.

Ichika's words haunted him. *Soon you must fight!* Mathis barely had the will to continue standing.

He tried not to look at himself in the heated mirror as he towelled off. He opened a fresh toothbrush and liberally applied what he assumed to be toothpaste. His teeth hurt to the touch, and a few had been knocked loose. There was some blood when he spat out the paste. Mathis wrapped the towel high on his waist and stepped out into the living room, spying his clothes neatly folded on the chair beside Rei and Ichika. He apologized ferociously as he reached over to grab them, unintentionally making contact with Ichika.

"*Konna chikaku de hadaka no gaijin mitan hajimete,*" Ichika giggled.

Rei burst into laughter, and Ichika joined in. Mathis was blushing furiously. He made for the relative safety of the bathroom to put on a mercifully fresh change of clothes, trying to block out their shared amusement. One of the women must've had the presence of mind to remove a set of business casual clothes before stowing his suitcase. His old clothes were nowhere in sight. Fully dressed, Mathis rejoined the women, awkwardly sitting cross-legged with his back against the foot of the bed. Rei thankfully tossed him the translator to wear, and he was all too eager to use it.

Ichika put on rose-tinted UkiyoAR glasses with thick frames and over-ear pink retro headphones decorated with cat ears. "Okay," she chimed in English before continuing in Japanese. "How do you take your coffee?"

"Black, please." He was hunting for the lingering tail of the joke made at his expense, but the moment had passed.

"For me as well, I-*chan*."

Ichika disappeared into the small kitchenette.

"Seems you were up late." Mathis gestured at the whiskey bottles on the desk. Rei looked looser and more relaxed but otherwise unaffected. He wondered if all the women in Japan could drink like sailors.

Ichika entered the room and set an elegant black enamel cup and saucer on the floor beside him, placing another in front of Rei before sitting beside her.

Rei set the coffee to the side. "What's your plan?"

Mathis stalled by drinking coffee—strongly brewed with high-end grinds, leaving a silken residue on the surface of the cup. He savoured the taste of it, unconsciously closing his eyes in ardent appreciation. When he opened them, the women were staring at him expectantly.

"Uhm, I'm going to try to convince a multinational corporation to break a binding, profitable, and highly functional partnership with the most dangerous type of intergovernmental agency?" It sounded ludicrous to his ears as he said it.

"Good! But how?" Ichika asked, cocking her head slightly.

Mathis smiled nervously, drinking his coffee to stall for time.

Rei let out a sigh. "He doesn't have a plan."

"Why doesn't he have a plan? Didn't he tell you his parents are being tortured, and the fate of the world is at stake?"

"I'm still working out the specifics, but I have a good rapport with Mr. Ogawa."

Rei turned serious. "I've tried to find a weakness in that man for months. Despite his posturing, he's not a visionary, he's a chameleon. Whenever I peel back a layer, it exposes another skin. If you even get to meet him in person, you won't find a common language with the man. He's a predator who will guide the knife to your throat and make you believe it was your idea all along to slice it."

Mathis tried to reconstruct the few conversations he'd had with Ogawa, and while part of him wanted to deny Rei's succinct take, it all patterned appropriately. "Oh."

Ichika turned to face Mathis, her expression ardent. "Why are you risking so much with so little preparation?"

Mathis finished his coffee, trying to parse the question into an answerable sum. Professionally, he'd always figured things out when it mattered. He had built a history of career brinkmanship and inspired last-minute solutions. Part of him believed this would be no different, that he'd perform under pressure as always. Of course, that hadn't been working out particularly well recently. He did some quick mental math on the ruin his fumbling reactions had generated, and found the sum to be incalculable.

"Maybe a touch of hubris?"

Ichika frowned expressively. The pink glasses and cat ears made her sentiment somehow more acute. She reached over to grab Rei's hand. "That's shameful."

The two words disciplined Mathis harder than any other time he could recall.

"I'll arrange a car service for you. When you exit the building, walk two blocks to your left and wait at the corner." Rei's instruction had the resignation of offloading a failed investment.

He struggled to find anything to say. "I'll wire you whatever you tell me."

Rei shook her head, disgust etched across her face. "I believed in you, and it's cost me everything."

He stood up, withering under her judgemental gaze, forced to internalize the consequences of his inadequacy, and all the she'd lost or risked trying to aid him.

Before he could say anything, she pointed to the door. "Just get out."

Mathis removed the translator, set it carefully on the bed, and brought his empty cup to the kitchenette. He put on his shoes and overcoat at the door, waiting for either Rei or Ichika to make eye contact, but they didn't, and it became obvious they wouldn't. After confirming the microdrive was in the inside pocket, he zipped up his overcoat, more for a false sense of protection than a need to withstand the elements. He left, opening the door just wide enough to slip through sideways.

The elevator ride to the first floor and walk to the designated pickup spot were the loneliest imaginable.

Mathis struggled out of the driverless sedan a few minutes before eight o'clock. He was aching everywhere, and his head still throbbed from the lingering effects of a hangover. He smiled awkwardly at the sidelong stares of salarymen and career women as they hustled past on the busy Umeda sidewalks. Several slowed or gasped at his appearance.

The Hikari International head office was an impressive structure—a narrow base, branching out in innovative outcroppings and covered in a lattice of patterns to catch, intensify, and disperse light. The brightness coupled with Mathis' hangover, made him physically wince. Below the structure, a courtyard of raked sand and moss-covered stones was bathed in light. A broad path of hand-worked stone slabs filled with chips of reflective granite created the impression of walking through the past to an impossibly bright future.

He painfully trod the steps, passed by scores of his Japanese colleagues. Immediately inside the door, a series of biometric scanners and security turnstiles monitored by a suite of corporate security officers posed an immediate barrier to the expansive foyer behind. There was no background music and no conversation. The noise in the grand foyer was the sound of crisp, efficient movement toward task. He approached a sharply dressed young man in a corporate uniform working what he assumed to be a guest check-in. The attendant didn't acknowledge him. Mathis cleared his throat, and the attendant pretended to occupy himself with a task hidden below the counter.

Mathis had already configured his handheld to interpret audio input and project English translations to his Net contacts in the car service. It wasn't as effective as the translator earpiece, but it was serviceable. Unprepared for a non-confrontation, he logged into his Hikari corporate calendar and sent his invite to the attendant's UkiyoARs, eliciting a scowl.

"I have an appointment with Fumiko Inoue."

"Inoue," the attendant corrected, and continued in Japanese. "Wait against the far wall, please."

Mathis followed the direction of the attendant's gesture to an alcove out of sight from the passing Hikari workers. People were staring at him. The slowed influx of workers caused a slight queue to develop. Resigned, he walked across the grand foyer to take a seat tucked out of the common view. He still didn't have a plan. Rei and Ichika's condemnation clung onto him like a bad smell he couldn't acclimatize to, growing incrementally more foul. The impending confrontation with Frost and his parent's incarceration tormented Mathis.

By the time he'd assured himself the situation couldn't get any worse, the crisp click of perfectly metered steps signalled the approach of Fumiko Inoue. She presented virtually no different in person than over video conference. An impeccable business pantsuit, the crisp collar on her white button shirt, and her hair retaining a harrowingly immaculate form despite movement. Once he overcame the uncanny valley sensation, Mathis got to his feet to endure her visual inspection. She curiously skipped over his extensive injuries and stood unnervingly close.

"We have a dress code at head office, Mr. Grenier. I'd advise you to please respect it the next time you are onsite."

"Good morning, Ms. Inoue." He tried to smile, but the gesture hurt his lips. He was already wearing the most professional outfit he'd packed.

She stared through him, unblinking. "Mr. Ogawa eagerly awaits you. As stated, Mr. Ogawa has very generously cleared his morning appointments to accept your full cooperation and the immediate remediation of the unprecedented challenges you've inflicted upon Hikari International."

Whether from the ongoing pain he was enduring or the night of actual terror he'd experienced, Mathis was inoculated from Fumiko's passive-aggressive tactics and the imperative to meet expectations. Instead of saying anything, Mathis stared into her unblinking eyes, shifting impatiently on his feet. She engaged unflinchingly in the stare-down, lingering unnervingly long in tight proximity. When some opaque mechanism signalled the interaction was satisfied, she pivoted crisply on one heel and strode towards the far bank of elevators. Additional security officers guarded it. Mathis found it challenging to follow her rapid pace, given how acutely everything ached. She waited at the secondary security kiosk, cutting through him with her hostile gaze.

Mathis could've sworn she finally blinked.

The security staff at the executive elevators were more competent and imposing. They had the hard faces of inquisitors and the upright muscular posture of career soldiers. The security team picked him apart—every bruise, laceration, and hidden injury affecting his movement. Unlike Fumiko, they managed to contain whatever disdain they might've had from showing in their neutral expressions.

The symbolic barrier to the executive elevators retracted. Fumiko turned sharply towards the biometric interface of the far elevator, and the stainless steel doors opened to reveal an all-glass enclosure. She stood directly in the centre, forcing Mathis to navigate carefully around her. He might've been caught off guard if he hadn't seen Evy Carter use these sorts of power tactics. He idly considered the two locked in professional combat.

"Is there something about this situation amusing to you?" Fumiko sharply questioned.

"Have you ever worked with Evy Carter out of the Toronto office?"

"I work exclusively to realize Mr. Ogawa's ambition." Her face was painted in mutating rays of brilliance as the elevator raced through external sections of the Hikari International superstructure.

Mathis toyed with seeding a tantalizingly apocalyptic conflict between the two women but shame quickly stifled the prospect. He liked Evy, and she would continue to suffer exquisitely until he could find a way to right the wrong. And liberate his parents. And save the future. And maybe even himself. Moments away from a face-to-face with Ogawa, Mathis still had nothing.

As they reached the top floor, the elevator locked neatly in place into the division of an external manicured landscape resembling a temple's grounds and an expansive internal office. Virtually everything was glass, but the expected amplified sunlight was diffused as it passed through the transparent structure. Some subtle mechanism or additive in the manufacturing was used to achieve the dampening effect. Instead of acting like a functional greenhouse, the interior was pleasingly cool with noticeably fine-tuned humidity.

A handful of furniture pieces were drowned by the vast internal area. A pair of black leather couches stood facing each other with a long, narrow black wood coffee table between them and an elegant coffee service off to the side. There was a nearby attendant wearing clothing and a full-faced UkiyoAR mask reflecting the exterior blended into the environment. It was a fluke that Mathis' eyes picked the attendant out from the slightly imperfect way the light refracted around the figure.

Upon a raised dais, Kazuo Ogawa sat behind an impressively sized desk of solid black wood anchored into the seamless white stone floors on a single side. Dressed in a conservative black suit and white shirt with the top two buttons undone, Ogawa stood up and walked unhurriedly toward Mathis. His clear UkiyoAR glasses captured a gesture, and the attendant in reactive clothing silently rushed to pour a coffee for him.

"Good morning, Mathis. I can call you Mathis, correct?" Ogawa's English was clearly pronounced with a mild Japanese accent.

Fumiko shifted closer to Mathis. "Insist it's your privilege."

"Mr. Ogawa," Mathis acknowledged, opting to ignore her advice.

Ogawa slowed his stride, smiling as he appraised Mathis.

"Apologies for his ignorance, Mr. Ogawa," Fumiko bowed in assumed responsibility.

"Does Ms. Inoue have to be here?"

Ogawa laughed. It sounded genuine. Fumiko's jaw clenched, but her face otherwise betrayed no expression.

"I'm sure Ms. *Inoue*'s attention won't be required." Ogawa leaned into her family name, pronouncing it exactly as Mathis had.

"I await your instruction." Fumiko bowed sharply and went through a series of near-invisible glass doors to stand at attention in the garden outside them.

Ogawa gestured at the attendant. "Don't mind him. His sight and vision are muted when he's not required. Would you like a coffee?"

Mathis wasn't sure whether it was his hangover or the lavish absurdity of wealth on display, but he had difficulty processing it all. Historically, Ogawa had always presented himself in a modest corporate environment, but the man in front of him existed in an opulence Mathis could never even conceive of.

"Black, please," he managed to say.

Another gesture from Ogawa set the attendant back into motion, pouring and serving Mathis' coffee before stepping back a respectful distance and fully blending into the environment. Ogawa sat in the middle of one couch, motioning Mathis opposite him, keenly scrutinizing Mathis' every movement as he complied.

"It seems your limited time in Osaka has been eventful."

Mathis appreciated the acknowledgement. It was weirdly insulting how his injuries were willfully overlooked by others. "I tried to explain I was being hunted to Ms. Inoue."

"She's excellent at dismissing concerns conflicting with her responsibilities, and her job is to make my life easier." He smiled appreciatively. "So, tell me, how did you come by this conflict?"

Mathis sipped his coffee, intending to use the time to weigh the question, but was sidetracked by how unusually superb the taste was. It had unexpected notes of peach and toffee. "This is incredible! It might be the best coffee I've ever had."

"Yirgacheffe Organic out of Ethiopia. Hand-roasted in small batches. Please enjoy as much as you'd like." He smiled magnanimously, leaning back in the middle of the deep leather couch. "If you were to join me here at the head office, you'd find the coffee is just one of the lesser perks."

Mathis found himself unconsciously shedding his meager defences, but Rei's warnings about the man jolted him alert. "I can appreciate you must be pressed for time—"

"Nonsense. Ms. Inoue is unusually sensitive to such things and tries to inflict the tyranny of schedules on everyone she encounters. While I appreciate and rely on her productivity, I also allow for vision. And here we are, two visionaries set to change the world together. Why should we rush? Tell me the tale of your hunters. Who were they?"

Mathis stalled, drinking coffee, contemplating how much he should disclose. "Several groups of yakuza, a pack of Minus One, and Aiden Frost's agents."

Ogawa's face lit with amusement. "You took them all on yourself? You must be some fighter!"

"No, mostly, they fought amongst themselves for the right to kidnap me. I had help, though." Mathis noted Ogawa's raised eyebrow. "A couple of lesbians, the proprietress of an *izakaya* and some of her patrons. Also, a pair of Net cafe long-timers."

Ogawa clapped his hands in delight. "Exquisite! What a unique first night in Osaka! You must share all the details." He gestured, and the attendant topped up Mathis' coffee.

"I'm not sure I could. My role in the whole affair was limited to getting beaten up. Also, I'd been drinking, and my memory is a bit sketchy," he admitted.

"And yet, here you are finally. Safe and with the wetware source code, I trust?"

"Yes. But I'd like to have a conversation about that."

"I expected nothing less. Is this a sitting or walking conversation?"

Mathis angled his head.

"You see, sometimes when I'm carrying the weight of the world, I stroll through the garden, walking the winding path towards the centre, and allow myself to be gently influenced by the natural world's order. Come, join me in the Sky Garden, and see if it doesn't lend you its clarifying influence."

Ogawa slapped his thighs, sprang to his feet, and started walking towards the glass partition between worlds with the enthusiasm of a far younger man. Mathis took a large gulp of coffee and chased after him as quickly as his aching body allowed. The near-invisible, proximity-triggered doors retracted silently. Fumiko stood motionless outside, poised like a fearsome gargoyle several meters to the right.

They walked safely out of Fumiko's earshot. Ogawa turned to face Mathis, stepped in, and set his hand on Mathis' shoulder. Ogawa gave a quick squeeze, travelled his hand to Mathis' bicep, and squeezed again. Mathis ineffectually flexed reflexively, paradoxically feeling both comforted and violated.

"What's troubling you, Mathis?" he asked with the concern of an adoptive father.

Mathis stared at Ogawa's hand, angled, and stepped back to release the gentle grip. "Hikari's relationship with Aiden Frost. He's abducted my parents and my colleagues back in Toronto, trying to pressure me into creating a backdoor for him."

Ogawa shook his head, but the disapproval wasn't apparent in his expression. "Shame. I'd explicitly instructed him to leave your parents out of it."

Mathis was incredulous. "You knew!?"

"Of course. Changing the world is a messy business. It's my gift and solemn responsibility to navigate insurmountable problems, allowing people such as yourself to focus on providing the scaffolding for Hikari's mission to be realized."

"He'd enslave humanity."

Ogawa slowed his pace. "The world is complicated, Mathis. It's full of regulations, incumbents, and adversaries. To govern it, you need generals, bureaucrats, and the occasional disruptive artist." He winked at Mathis. "Frost is merely the general of a conquering army, and conquerors never make good occupiers. Once his use is fulfilled, he'll be put to pasture. At least, he would've been. He's somehow been freshly compromised by a data leak out of your hometown. Now, he's too toxic to get into bed with, so we'll wait for whoever the new Frost is."

Mathis struggled to process everything Ogawa had disclosed. "I'm sorry, are you suggesting you want to rule the world?"

"Isn't that every man's ambition? Look around, Mathis." Ogawa swept his arm theatrically. "In the past, people shared the same heart, but now everyone acts of their own accord. The world needs order and purpose. It lacks harmony. You see, Hikari means light. With wetware, I can bring light to every connected person on the face of the earth and influence the generations yet to come. No more senseless wars, no more class struggles. A universal effort against existential problems guided by magnanimity and purpose. What issue could be beyond remediation?"

Mathis stopped walking. He glanced over his shoulder, noting Fumiko was hovering behind them like an opportunistic highwayman. "Free will."

Ogawa regarded Mathis as though he were a child. "Free will is an illusion which guarantees suffering. It's burning the world in misguided anger and rage."

"Your vision won't alleviate injustice. It'll just suppress it."

"For now. Humanity requires a panacea."

"Maybe all it needs is hope."

Ogawa laughed. It wasn't malicious or condescending, it was the laughter of surprise. He resumed walking the winding path at a stroll, and Mathis instinctively kept pace.

"Once a year, the Yoshino trees bloom spectacularly. The Sky Garden falls under a magical canopy of cherry blossoms. When I was a child, *ohanami* came at the beginning of May. It's barely March before it starts now, and the delicate blossoms rarely last." Ogawa caught Mathis' eyes and spoke emphatically. "Instead of a few weeks of spectacular glory, fierce winds and torrential rains violently strip the blossoms from their branches."

"Wetware won't turn back climate change," Mathis countered.

"I'll stop the hemorrhaging. Japan's elderly bake in the summer, incapable of finding solace from the oppressive heat and humidity. We pull them out of their homes when the smell alerts the neighbours. The young are leaving. Did you not notice the lack of children in Osaka? Not having children around is real poverty. Few want to sacrifice new lives to the banal terrors of this inhospitable world. My country is dying."

"So, now you're a patriot?"

"How could I not be in my position? I have the unique opportunity to provide the world with a future, and Japan will assume a prominent place within it. Your *free will* has ensured crop failure, populations decimated by famine, and reclaimed lands swallowed by hostile seas."

Mathis weighed the words. Ogawa had angles on every line of reasoning and played them out as a rigged game.

"I reject it—all your aspirations of conquest and godhood."

Ogawa dropped his facade of congeniality. His eyes narrowed, brow furrowed, and lips tightened in a scowl. He straightened his back, shoulders down and out. "You lack vision."

Mathis shook his head in genuine disappointment. "You're not that smart. You're just a man people stopped saying no to. Isn't it enough to be rich and recognized as revolutionizing humanity? Do you have to enslave the world to consider yourself successful?"

Ogawa slowed his walk. Mathis matched his pace, continuing when he was confident Ogawa was listening.

"Cities are burning because of the gross disparities of wealth and opportunity. All the while, you live disconnected in your glass tower, dreaming of being a god emperor." The more Mathis spoke from his heart, the more conviction he felt. "Why can't you give people hope? You can provide the world with knowledge, equity, and the means to do what you can't."

Ogawa scoffed. "I can—"

"You're one man! A smart one, to be sure, but still a single man of limited intellect with a habit of subordinating everyone you interact with. You're not enough." Mathis stepped closer, speaking ardently, "You'll never be enough."

Ogawa started walking the winding path again. After a dozen paces, he stopped, and held motionless a long moment, facing away. "What are you proposing?"

"Make wetware open source."

"Impossible," he scoffed, glowering over his shoulder at Mathis. "The shareholders would revolt even if the board of directors didn't oust me for suggesting it."

"Then make the transaction model open source. Implement a GPL agreement wherein Hikari retains rights to patents if you have to, but fortify it under the pressure of the world's scrutiny. Invest in a double-checksum model and have a user's neural key authenticate every transaction to the blockchain for audits and memory rollbacks. Commit to owning the patches and safeguarding the future of the species. You can commodify or licence wetware in a hundred ways, and we can work together to make Hikari unrivalled in distribution. Your shareholders will make their money, and you'll be synonymous with the greatest achievement the world has ever known. You'd be the man to both usher in a transhuman future and make it unassailable."

Ogawa's face was neutral. He continued walking the winding path silently until he reached the garden's centre. There was a single stone boulder, a throne without sharp edges. Ogawa sat on it, legs wide, body angled forward.

"You'd have me murder my country by omission."

"Your vision would produce livestock instead of countrymen. Put in the work, invest the wealth you'll generate into the future you want." Mathis shuffled closer. "You claimed to be able to navigate insurmountable problems. Don't make it an empty catchline."

"You demand everything yet offer nothing. Hikari's share price is predicated on wetware getting to market, and your proposal would inject catastrophe."

"I'll provide Hikari a gateway technology, then." The words escaped Mathis' lips before he'd had a chance to parse them for consequence. "I've been developing thought-connected Net contacts in my off-hours. I need a little more time and focus to get them into a consumer-ready state. Hikari could pivot in the short term, safely deploy and refine the thought-control models, and prime consumers for wetware adoption."

Ogawa scowled. "And how is this not already part of Hikari's pipeline?"

Mathis shrugged. "My contract allows for external IP. But I'm willing to give it freely."

"It's not enough."

"Then I'll give you my life, my fidelity, and my purpose. I'll be your fiduciary and most ardent ally."

"I doubt you understand what that even means."

"It means you'll finally have someone to argue with." Mathis braved a smile. "Benoit Rochon compared me to Prometheus, and I'm strangely okay with it. This isn't the time for cowardice."

"Do you know what Ms. Inoue would advocate?"

"That you throw me off the balcony and collect the microdrive from my dead body."

"It'd be simpler," Ogawa casually said.

"It would, but you'd still be creating a world of livestock." Mathis weighed the silence. "You don't need blunt leverage, generals, or to become a god emperor. Find the courage to make good decisions, and let others shape the broad strokes of your vision. And free my parents and colleagues."

"Things could go far worse for them still."

Mathis gambled that he was addressing the banality of evil and not a more villainous manifestation of it. His hands were clammy, his heart pounding. "You're not that guy."

Ogawa took stock of Mathis' defiance, weighing it carefully. "There's a saying here. *It's better to bend than to break.*"

Mathis shook his head, willfully ignoring Ogawa's request for compromise. "There can be no bending with the fate of our species in play. I'm all in, and you need to be, too."

Ogawa closed his eyes, deliberating. Mathis considered saying more but recognized he'd already said everything essential. Fumiko hovered at the edge of the garden's centre, glowering at Mathis as though he was a fundamental threat to the natural order.

"It was the coffee, wasn't it?"

"It was the coffee," Mathis replied, sealing their unspoken agreement.

Epilogue

Rei

Aki was busy entertaining a group of salarymen when Rei arrived at the *izakaya*. Taro had a glass of whiskey waiting for her by the time she got to the bar without a word. She didn't know what Aki shared with him, but access to the unlocked funds of the racketeering operations she ran for the Shinoda clan had settled the considerable debts of duty and reputation that terrible night had incurred. Apparently, with room to spare since Taro had been refusing Rei's money and alluded to credit she was working down. Sum unknown. The other person she'd paid out was her father's old partner, Hiroshi Kono. It wasn't enough to replace the loss of a career in the Shinoda clan, but it proved sufficient to have him stop stalking her.

While Mathis was effectively dead to her, Rei had finally agreed to meet him at *Aki no Sora* after Ichika's persistent logic had eventually won her over. He was alive, the world wasn't any different, so perhaps he'd been successful. But everything was different for Rei. After weeks of looking over her shoulders, she finally caught word Akira Mori had never regained consciousness and was being maintained on life support with extensive brain damage he'd received during the melee. The old Mori enforcer hadn't given her up for blinding and mutilating Akira. One more debt to her father posthumously repaid.

Rei had been inundated with messages, anonymous gifts, and the unexpected return of millions of yen worth of small loans. Some were accompanied by lengthy written messages or short, near-oblique notes. Apparently, Tatsuo had been secretly helping people for years—as far back as when she and Miyu were kids, and the family had struggled to purchase groceries or school supplies. She'd always assumed people gave her father a pass because he used to be local-famous, had an easy manner about him, and out of wary respect for the fighter he once was. If she were truthful, she also imagined people pitied him for being punch-drunk. She never considered how many deposits he'd made into the metaphoric favour bank over the decades and how little he'd withdrawn.

She briefly tried to imagine what needless sufferings and humiliations could've been avoided had her father not been so generous at her family's expense, but abandoned the what-ifs for the unfulfilling, immolating torment they were.

Aki had been a reluctant lore mistress for Rei's untraceable correspondences of scant context and unknown names or initials. More often than not, Aki could shed light on a tragic backstory. Tatsuo had helped countless lives, mostly against Aki's caution since he'd frequently asked and ignored her counsel. Aki had never explained her and Tatsuo's deep and lasting connection, no matter how many glasses of shochu Rei had seen her consume. The two had shared a profound and unconventional history. Aki prided herself as a woman of secrets, and some of them were too sensitive to remember.

It was fitting Tatsuo's ashes had been added to his small shrine at *Aki no Sora*, along with her sister's. Aki had framed a photograph of Miyu on the eve of her sister's flight to Toronto. In the image, Miyu appeared reluctant and uncertain. As though she were committing to an action she could never take back. Rei acknowledged she was probably projecting into the picture. She hadn't understood her sister since a flawed prognosis had demented Miyu's future.

A strange woman from Toronto named Amrita Chopra had unexpectedly connected with Rei once. She explained how Miyu had knowingly sacrificed herself to avenge their father. Little of what the Canadian communicated made sense to Rei. It'd been a swarm of words, undercut with an imperfect and too-personal account. The conversation had netted out to a commitment, however. Amrita would assist in identifying the bodies of Rei's family and provide Rei's information to the authorities overseas for their safe return.

Rei was surprised at the speed at which the corpses had been shipped to Osaka and subsequently released to the funeral director Aki had put her in contact with. A handful of people had been at the *otsuya*, a ritual traditionally strictly reserved for immediate family. Since Rei was the last of her bloodline, she'd asked Ichika, Aki, Taro, and Officer Matsumoto to attend, as well as two of the three professional fighters who'd recovered sufficiently to be discharged from the hospital. Aki had helped her dress into the exquisite *mofuku* kimono ensemble Matsumoto's wife had purchased. She'd felt like an imposter, uncomfortable in her skin, but the sensation diminished as she gave herself over to the Buddhist rituals Aki gracefully coached her through.

Her father and sister had been surrounded by an eruption of perfectly selected flowers arranged on a half dozen tiers spanning the room's width and surrounding the framed photographs of her deceased family. The delicate scent and vibrancy of the blooms had made the ceremony more surreal. After the monk's lengthy chanting and prescribed rituals, the group had eaten sushi and drank beer or green tea in the same room as the caskets. A final meal with the departed. Aki had been instrumental in elevating the mood and encouraging people to share fond stories. Rei had spoken few words and found it impossible to concentrate on what the others had said. Consuming anything had also proven difficult. It all tasted like loss and regret.

The second day of the funeral, the *soshiki*, had started in a tatami-floored waiting room at the funeral home, making origami figures and sipping green tea at a low table. The origami had been Ichika's idea, and she'd proved to be the most prolific creator. Rei had absently completed the handful of folds for the pieces her girlfriend had prepped for her. The same group had attended to partake in more rituals, listen to chanting from the monk, and observe the one-week death anniversary at the same time. Then came the moment that had broken Rei—the casket lids had been removed, and the funeral staff presented the origami the group had fashioned on an elegant tray for the mourners to place on the bodies. Ichika had held her hand tightly and whispered loving words, lending Rei the strength to risk confronting her family's death.

She didn't know how they did it, but the morticians had removed those accursed discs from Miyu's eyes, pumped fluids into her emaciated face, and rebuilt her to appear resting peacefully. Miyu had resembled the image of the young woman who was destined to go overseas for the first time, chasing an elusive meaning until it had proven fatal.

Her father, on the other hand, had required far less work to reconstitute into a presentable form, but he'd looked like a stranger without his animated, expressive personality sewing warmth and emotion into his rugged features. He had been greatly diminished in death, and it struck Rei how profoundly terrible it was she'd never know his curious, often infuriating brand of affection again.

The staff had reverently cut the flowers, a cluster at a time, and dutifully presented them on ceremonial trays for the group to place around the bodies. An endless procession of delicate bouquets had been curated until all the flowers were cut and blanketed her father's and sister's bodies, leaving room only for their faces. The four men from her group and two of the funeral home attendants had carried the coffins to awaiting hearses. They had proceeded to the crematorium as a group for more ceremonies before the bodies were solemnly loaded into the incineration chambers.

The macabre ritual of picking out carefully curated bone segments from the cremated remains with long, uneven sticks, the tops painted black or white, had been difficult to endure. The group had lined up in front of the remains, and a staff member from the crematorium fully narrated what she was doing. She'd detailed the significance of each bone segment, starting from the toes and working her way up the body, expertly snapping larger pieces in a controlled manner. One at a time, the group of mourners had performed their duty of lifting the curated bone segments and delicately depositing them into a small receptacle with the uneven sticks. Performing the ritual once had been hard enough. Enduring it twice, with the same script delivered in the same intonation by the same staff member with the same line of people standing in the same positions had made Rei want to scream.

She had endured, however, and received two silken-wrapped packages of bones as a reward for her suffering duty.

Rei had tried to follow up with Amrita the day after the *soshiki* but found the account deleted. A Net search had revealed a wealth of news reports detailing a CSIS operative who'd infiltrated the Minus One network and helped dismantle the global operations. Alternately, a CSIS agent had sold out her country as a Minus One operative and ruined tens of thousands of lives in the process. Amrita was no longer employed at CSIS, and every social profile had either been recently deleted or belonged to a similarly named but unconnected person. It was as though the woman had burnt every portion of her former life as the shadow of criminal prosecution loomed but hadn't yet amounted to incarceration.

The closest thread Rei had managed to track her was a relative who'd posted extensively on Amrita, defending the woman from speculations of treason and relentlessly celebrating her as a hero. A young man named Ajay. Rei had exchanged a few messages with him, but he'd been uncommonly suspicious of her and refused to disclose any contact information. Rei understood burnt lives and had nothing to gain from forcing more out of the woman. Rei had been provided a service—a favour withdrawn from the metaphoric bank her family had no doubt deposited into extensively. She considered it a debt repaid.

It'd taken a lot of awkward convincing, but Aki had finally added the dogeared photograph of Rei's mother to her family's makeshift shrine. To hear Aki speak the name *Kaiyo*, Rei understood there was a river of bad blood in the past, and she accepted Aki's reluctance to navigate her decades-old prohibition. *That woman was never supposed to show her face here and never will.* There was no backstory on offer. Aki's condition was that the portrait of her mother would be face-down or not at all. Rei figured it was enough to know her family, as imperfect as it had always been, was finally reunited in death.

Miyu's death had proven impossible to reconcile. There was no closure between them, and they'd spent the last years in avoidance, deceit, or suspicion. Rei still blamed Miyu for their father's murder, and the visceral sense of injustice endured despite the window into her sister's suffering existence and her self-sacrificial attempt at redemption. They'd been so close as children. So many of Rei's formative and naively happy memories were intertwined with Miyu. Now, she was a little box of bones, equal in size to her father's.

Rei was the last of her line. The concept made her irrationally insecure. The fact her family had never truly known her and never would made Rei borderline inconsolable. It shouldn't matter, she told herself, but somehow it was all that did.

The sound of Taro sucking his teeth and the sight of him frowning meant Mathis had arrived. A moment later, he joined Rei at the bar, upbeat and enthusiastic.

"Thanks for agreeing to meet me, Rei." He reigned in some of his exuberance and spoke in Japanese. "I regret my actions, Taro-*san*."

Mathis' accent was awkward, and he inflected too many syllables—even for people from Osaka. He wasn't entirely incomprehensible, and the effort didn't go unnoticed.

"Ask him what he wants," Taro grumbled.

"Soda water, please." Mathis' Japanese was slightly less atrocious. A practiced line.

Taro directed his dissatisfied response to Rei. "This is a bar. People drink alcohol at bars."

"Please charge him for a proper drink and pull it off my credit," Rei pleasantly responded.

Rei took a translator set from her case, wore one, and perfunctorily slid the case to Mathis.

"No need. I've spent the past few weeks figuring out how to function in Osaka. I've got a real-time translation engine hooked into a small sub-dermal implant I'm experimenting with. It even coaches me how to speak Japanese."

"Don't. It hurts to listen to you." Her posture was stiff, her tone icy. Although she'd managed to contain the blowback of their last encounter, Rei retained an unreasonable hostility towards Mathis. While not a direct line, her sister and father were dead because of him. She couldn't believe she'd jeopardized her life and those she loved for such a person. "You can thank Ichika I'm here at all."

He slid a thick envelope across the bar counter to her. "It's not enough to justify all you risked for me, but I'm hoping it helps prove my sincere thanks for everything you and your girlfriend did to protect me."

"She's not—" Rei caught her reflexive denial. "She's more than that." Rei resisted peeking inside the envelope. If it were filled with ten-thousand-yen notes, it'd amount to about three million.

"I can get you more, but this is a two-week advance on my salary, and it'll take time to settle my affairs in Toronto."

"Seems your conversation with Ogawa-*sama* went well."

"It did!" Mathis' excitement burst past her thick cynicism. "The guy who imprisoned my parents is disgraced and on the run, and Ogawa agreed to use the exposure to sever corporate ties."

"You should add an honorific when speaking about your employer," she commented irritably. He was amongst the highest-paid professionals in Japan and oblivious to the fact or what it meant. The injustice was galling.

"Understood, and thanks. Ogawa-*sama* freed my parents and my colleagues back in Toronto. They're desperate to speak with you. My parents, that is. My colleague, Tariq, kept asking for an introduction after I assured him we weren't dating nor had any plans to."

"How does your colleague even know who I am?"

"You're practically a legend at Hikari. Everyone knows what you risked to save me. That said, Tariq likely doesn't like being lead dev and having to deal with Logan. He's probably angling to work out of the head office with me. And objectively, you're pretty beautiful."

Rei clenched her teeth and exhaled slowly—Mathis still had no idea of the true cost of saving him. She locked his gaze. "What makes you believe I want to be objectified or used for a visa."

"Umn, nothing? Please forget I even brought it up. Could you spare a few minutes for my parents, though?"

"It's not necessary."

"Please? It'd mean the world to them."

"It's six in the morning in Toronto."

"They're early risers." Mathis pulled out a new high-end handheld, and its integrated camera bee silently took flight. "Just two minutes."

Taro tried to swat the camera bee out of the air, but defensive movement algorithms kept it free from assault.

"What's this idiot doing? There's no recording in here!"

"Two minutes, Taro-*san*. Please. My mother and father," he pleaded in clunky Japanese.

Taro glanced at Aki, but she was immersed in entertaining. "Two minutes."

Rei had recently endured a *family conversation* with Ichika's parents, disclosing their relationship. Though it had gone surprisingly well, the congenial thirty-minute discussion had aged her five years. "Wait, I didn't agree to—"

"Thank you, Taro-*san!*" Mathis gestured to share the incoming video feed to Rei's UkiyoAR glasses. "They've been asking to speak with you all week."

The conference was accepted on the third alert. Ingrid's pleasant face filled the screen—sleepy but immediately perking up with excitement. "Oh, good morning, bunny!"

"Hi, Mom."

Ingrid fussed to straighten her powder blue buttoned pyjamas with navy piping, ran her fingers through her hair several times, and smiled overly sweetly. "Casper, come to the refrigerator. It's Mathis, and he's got a girl with him!"

Rei glowered at Mathis as Casper, out of frame, said something the audio didn't quite pick out.

Ingrid shook her head, facing her husband. "No, no. It might be the girl who helped him. You know, the one with the dead father?"

Mathis winced, avoiding eye contact with Rei.

Dressed in matching pyjamas, Casper fumbled with his glasses and crowded the screen. He had stitches on his right cheek and a fresh scar on the bridge of his nose. "You should've let us know you would introduce a girl. We would've put on proper clothes."

"It's not like that, Dad."

Ingrid dramatically slowed her speech and raised her voice. "I'm Ingrid. That's Casper. We're Mathis' parents."

"I think she got that, Mom. And you don't need to say it so loud or pantomime. She can speak English."

Rei swallowed the humiliation, bowing as she introduced herself. "Yoshida Rei."

Ingrid cocked her head, confused. "Did she say it backwards, Casper?"

"Shh. I'm... Grenier Casper, and this is my wife, Grenier Ingrid." He bowed awkwardly to the refrigerator console. "We're very pleased to meet you. Mathis told us how you and your friend saved his life."

Rei deeply regretted not preventing the encounter. "It was nothing."

"That's not how Mathis explained it, Yoshy..."

"Yoshidy Ray," Casper finished, pleased with himself.

Mathis cleared his throat. "Uhm, I have a time limit here, and—"

"Don't they have unlimited data in Japan?" Casper stroked his beard, head slightly askew.

"I thought they were more technologically advanced over there. I've seen some feature segments of the most wonderful things! Robots that look like people, trains as fast as airplanes, and cute little AI homework assistants for the kids who act as family pets. Why wouldn't they have unlimited data, Casper?"

"I don't know." He shrugged. "Maybe it's a roaming thing?"

"Bunny, do you need us to wire you some money to upgrade your roaming package?"

"I'm okay for money and roaming, Mom. Rei's just short on time."

"Well, I feel foolish for wasting it talking about robots and roaming! We're delighted our little boy has already made a dear friend. You know, as a mother—"

"Not now, love," Casper admonished gently.

"As a mother," Ingrid insisted, "it was difficult enough when Mathis left home to go to the big city. Now, he's all the way across the world, in a completely alien culture."

Casper shook his head. "No offence. Ingrid means it's alien to us. Because we're Canadians, and—"

"And we're so happy to know our boy has been fortunate enough to make a good friend there. Friends can be surrogate families, which makes us all family now, doesn't it, Casper?"

"It does, my love. If you ever find yourself in Canada, you have a home with us."

Ingrid practically beamed. "You also have our heartfelt gratitude, Miss Yoshy Ray."

Rei forced her expression to be neutral. "Thank you. I accept and appreciate your words."

Mathis already had his hand hovering by the handheld, cringing behind a fake smile. "I'll be in touch soon. Okay?"

"Love you, bunny!"

Casper cocked an eyebrow. "Hey, buddy. Spies, right?" Finger guns.

Ingrid playfully swatted her husband. "Casper! Not in front of Yoshy!" She dramatically mouthed the words, *tell us after!*

Mathis waved stiffly. "Goodbye now. Love you both."

Both his parents waved, overly animated, as Mathis terminated the conference.

Rei drank the rest of her whiskey in a single raise and tapped on the counter for Taro to refill it. She had assumed Mathis had a saccharine upbringing from how naive and unprepared he was for life, but it was another thing to experience it firsthand. They reminded her of Ichika's parents. A little too invested and far too emotionally expressive. Her own father had been uncomfortably physically affectionate, but at least he'd never tried to be her friend. Or maybe he had, and she'd spent years pushing him away. Her father had always showered her with praise, but he'd been a simple man even before becoming noticeably punch-drunk. It'd been easy to lose his kindnesses amongst all the shame he generated for the family.

"Are you okay? I know they can be a bit much, but they're thankful beyond words. They would've gushed for an hour if I didn't cut them off."

"I'm fine, thank you."

The encounter with Mathis' parents reinforced the impression something was broken inside her. People could operate on a pure, emotional basis, and the same stimuli offered her revulsion and anxiety. The single exception was with Ichika—after a few drinks.

"You know, they meant what they said. You're like family to them now. I'll coach them on how to say your name for next time."

Before Mathis could say more, she changed the topic. "So, did you end up saving humanity? We didn't see any difference."

"I suppose that's the way it goes. The big stuff doesn't have a lot of drama to it. Just an awkward conversation on a rooftop, and then, well... My whole life's different, I suppose."

Rei gestured at the money. "You've made out pretty well if that's two weeks."

"Yeah, I haven't had a free moment to process it. Ogawa-*sama* has me working around the clock, helping him pivot the technological pipeline and workshopping corporate messaging for pitch decks. I don't really do anything I'm good at anymore, but the coffee is consistently excellent. He's also hired a bunch of ninjas to trail me these days. It's weird. Like, I'm never alone. I don't know their names, and they never interact with me. They're constantly lurking, waiting for things to go wrong."

"You're still being hunted?"

"Maybe? I know you don't appreciate what I do, but it's actually important. Technology will fundamentally change people, and I've always wanted it to be for the better. I get why Minus One, governments, or anyone with a vested interest wants to own the process and manipulate human behaviour, but that's not how I was raised. *I believe in people.* Technology should have the potential to elevate the poorest person in the most desperate region of the world born into the worst circumstances into a titan. The trick is to make sure they are who they think they are at the end of the process."

"You're saying words I assume are supposed to mean something."

Mathis took a deep breath and spoke in a controlled cadence. "I'm creating a mass-market system to synthesize memories indistinguishable from lived experience." He waited a beat before continuing, "Imagine the potential for a moment. Now imagine how easy it would be to poison it."

An intense and uncomfortable anxiety filled her as she allowed her mind to consider the concept. "I can finally see why people were after you. You should've explained it as such earlier."

"Inoue-*san* has forced me to work with marketers. I'm finally learning how to speak to normal people."

"Marketers aren't normal people, and you're saying the family name wrong. It's Inoue."

"Inoue?"

"Less bad."

"She'll despise me however I say it. But what about you? What's your life like post-yakuza?"

"Eventful."

"All you're going to offer is one word?"

While she owed him nothing, he'd finally proven not to be a waste of her belief, risk, and efforts. She sighed audibly.

"I've spent most of the last couple of weeks wondering when I'll be killed, only to recently discover I've been granted a stay of execution. I've been too honest with I-*chan* about things I swore never to speak of, and somehow, she's still with me. Otherwise, I'm unemployed, drinking too much, and recently cremated my family." She agitatedly drummed her fingers on the countertop, heart rate elevating. "And these producers keep trying to pitch me on a movie or book deal. Fucking vultures want to pimp me and my family's story across all the media outlets and won't take no for an answer. And I still don't have a clue why my father and sister elected to be murdered by some shithead anarchists halfway across the world."

Rei stopped herself, amazed at how little it took to set her off. She was a raw nerve, and no amount of time or solace could make sense of how her life had been devastated by actions she had no insight into. It was a slap in the face each time she encountered small pockets of youths dressed in all white across Osaka, oblivious to the trauma the organization had inflicted upon her family.

Minus One retained broad appeal to the disaffected, but its leadership had been decapitated, and tens of thousands of wealthy individuals were destined to accompany a host of corrupt governmental agents for a well-orchestrated lynching to appease an outraged public. Governments of other countries, Japan included, had pledged to rigorously investigate corruption and follow the same pattern of prosecutorial appeasement as Canada. There was still a wealth of unspent societal rage, but it'd been blunted with the promise of blood and systemic change. Minus One's seductive counter-culture cache saw its influence spread even as the purpose of the movement had been diminished and diluted.

Mathis' face was painted with deep empathy. "I'm sorry, Rei."

"You didn't do it."

"No, that's not what I mean. You always seem so buttoned down and in control. I didn't register your truth. I'm sorry for being so insensitive."

The notion of *her truth* stuck Rei as intrinsically abhorrent. "I don't expect anyone's sensitivity."

"It doesn't mean you don't deserve it."

"That's enough, Mathis." She lingered on his deceptively genuine sincerity.

"If you're looking for honest work, I could always put in a word at Hikari..."

She laughed. "In no world would I ever wish to report to you."

"So, what will you do?"

Rei had enough money to lick her wounds and figure it out. Rebuilding her life without the people who'd provided her formative axis would be a painful, bewildering transition—one requiring support she was reluctant to accept. Since childhood, she'd spent her life constantly reacting to problems, whether directly or in anticipation of them. Sometimes with the illusion of agency, but mostly not.

For the first time, she had a clean slate and the opportunity to draft herself into a world of choice.

Rei acknowledged she was damaged and had deeply internalized pain with no way to gauge or excise it. She was starting from less than nothing, but her father's example had provided a path forward. People could accept and value even the most flawed individuals if they lived their truth compassionately.

"I don't know what I'll do, but I'm okay," she said. "I'll always be okay."

Thank you

I'M GRATEFUL YOU'VE READ *Minus One* and hope you found value in it. Please consider sharing the novel and leaving an honest review online. Your feedback and support would be truly appreciated.

For more information, please visit https://kolody.com

Printed in Dunstable, United Kingdom

71927694R00188